NEW LEGENDS

Caster • Castle • Creature

A Fantasy Anthology

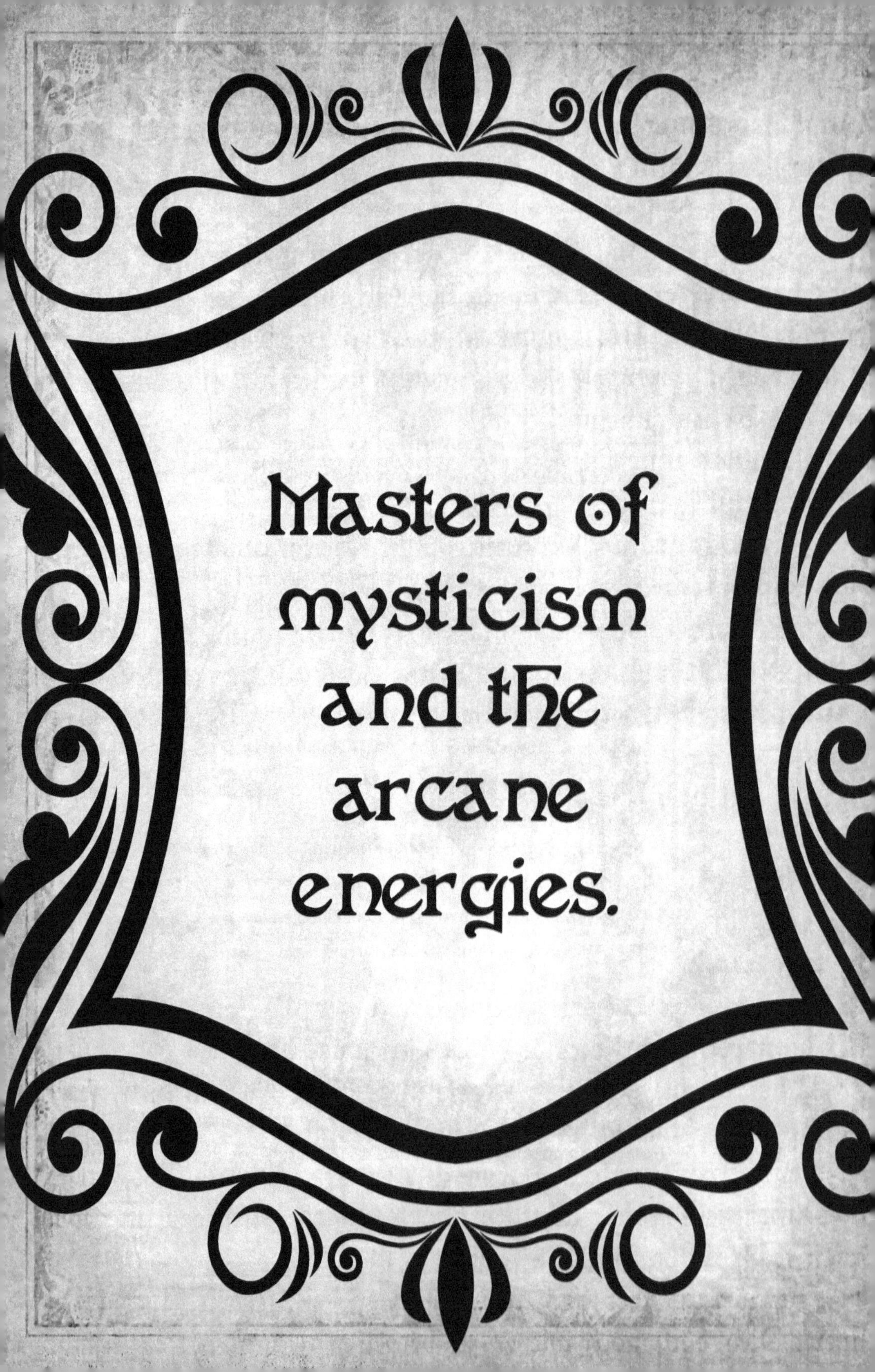

Masters of
mysticism
and the
arcane
energies.

Caster

Homes of
the kings
and queens
who rule
the realms.

Castle

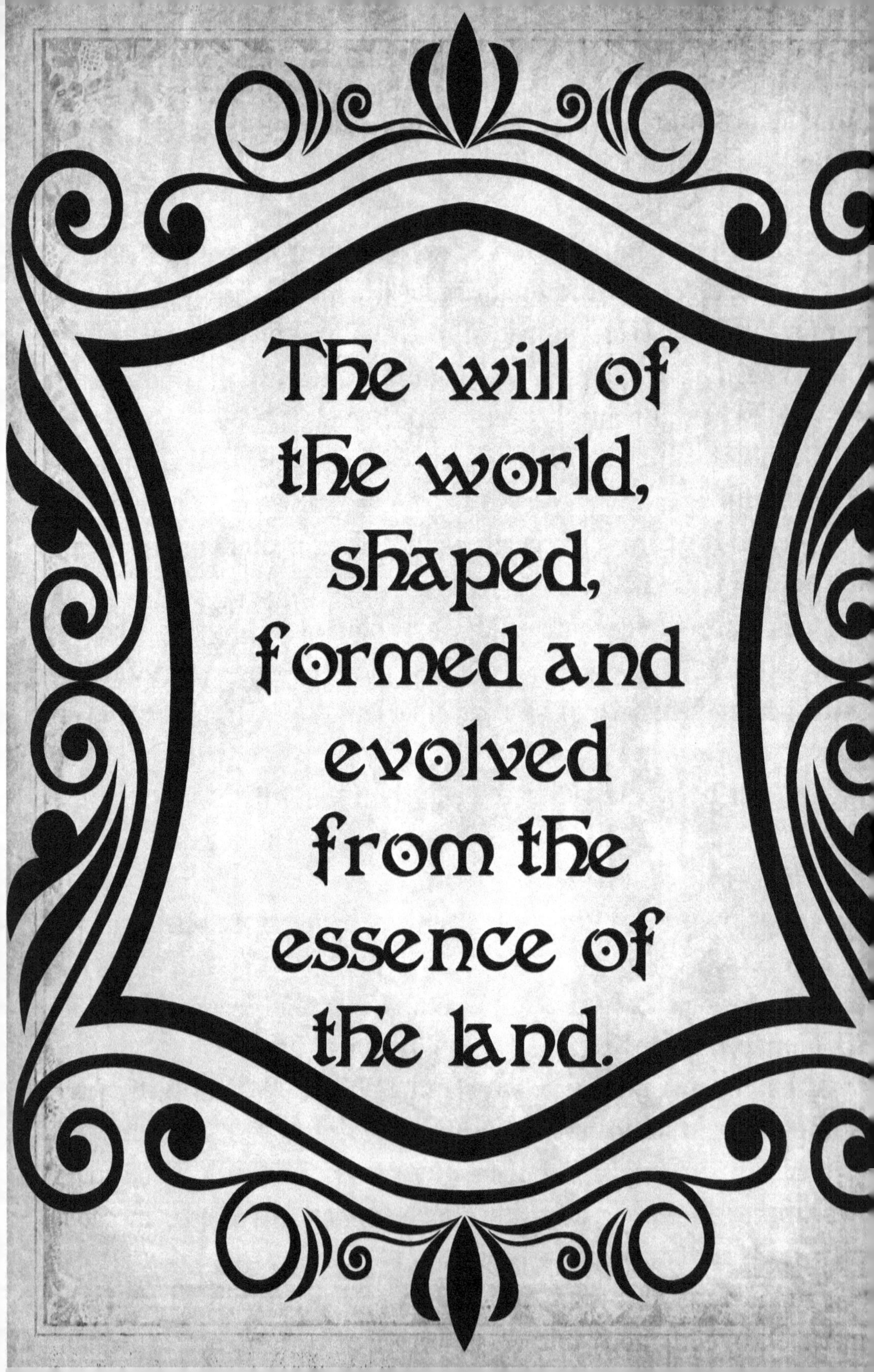

The will of
the world,
shaped,
formed and
evolved
from the
essence of
the land.

Creature

NEW LEGENDS
Caster • Castle • Creature

A Fantasy Anthology

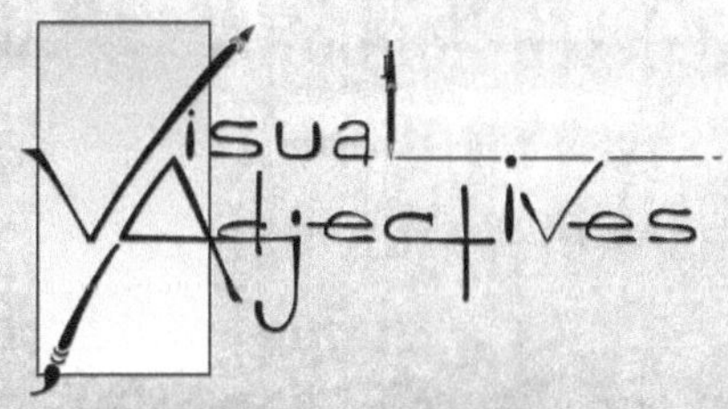

CONTENTS

To Walk Again the Night

Kenneth Caroli

Darkness, hot, smothering, airless and sightless, it enveloped like a heavy shroud, overwhelming all the senses. Had there ever been anything other than this blackness? A faded memory staggered through the mazes of the half conscious mind.

"Light?... Yes, I remember the word," came the answer to the unvoiced question. A faint patch of iron gray hovered on the edge of the thought. It was dark, yet not as utterly black as its surroundings. Slowly it brightened. "That must be the light!" The concept flashed, clear in an instant. There had been other things too – air, cool and crisp, as well as dark masses, tall and green. "Trees! Trees and bushes, and a hard surface on which to walk... to walk, to be free again!" How long had it been? The memories came in a rush.

He'd been ill, weak as water. With each passing day, more of his strength had faded, almost as if it had been drained, somehow siphoned off. His wife had tended him loyally, rarely leaving his side, save to get him something. Images reeled through his brain. His village, his home and family, all these and more became clearer as he understood. He'd overheard the village doctor talking to his wife, when they thought him asleep.

"He's dying." The old man had pronounced his sentence. "It's the wasting sickness, I fear; there's nothing I can do."

His wife had sobbed slightly, then dried her tears when she realized he was awakening. The wasting sickness. Everybody in the village knew what that meant: death, and afterwards... well, he'd not wanted to think on that.

A shred of consciousness remained when they came to take him. The old fool of a doctor had pronounced him dead, much to his young wife's grief. How he'd tried to tell them that he still lived, but no words would come, not even a groan. "Don't do it! Please don't put me in there!" His mind screamed. No sounds escaped his lips. There must be a way to let them know, there had to be! Otherwise they would bury him alive! Already they were placing the lid on the coffin; soon he would be trapped!

With panic surging through his veins and despair in his heart, he realized they had succeeded. He must be inside the tomb by now.

"Oh Lord!" He cried, "I've got to get free, got to get out." He raised his arms. All he could do was push at the lid; the space was too confined for much else. Idly, he wondered how so much of his strength had returned, because the lid moved, if only a little.

Hunger gnawed at the pit of his stomach, and thirst rasped in his dry throat and parched mouth. Despair crushed him. The lid would give no further. He scratched at it, wishing he had the claws of a beast. In truth his nails were long, but they broke and his fingers grew bloody as he sought to escape. It was no use. He let his aching arms drop to his sides again. There was no way out. Was he to spend eternity here? Was this hell? He called for help, crying desperately through lips dry and cracked. No answer came.

What he wouldn't give for a drink! His thirst overcame his fear and hunger, and became all-consuming. Almost unthinking he brought his hand to his mouth. Something warm and wet moistened his lips. Blood! His own blood! It must be. At first he balked at drinking his own blood, but the thirst was too strong. Anything was drinkable when nothing else was available. To his surprise it tasted good: rich, warm, and faintly salty. Before long he'd licked his fingers clean. He must have more! He must get out and get more!

Then he heard footsteps on the stone! They sounded hollow in the quiet of the crypt. There were whispering voices too, but what they said was unintelligible. Rescuers! Someone had realized he still lived when entombed and was coming back to free him! Freedom! To walk again the night! That would be glorious! His thirst would be assuaged!

The voices and their accompanying steps came closer. He could hear them now: "'E's in this 'un, o'er here. Ye got the tool?" Wheezed one of the voices with a raspy timbre.

"Are ya sure?" Retorted the other. "The Doc weren't all that clear on it. He only said they was supposed to be fresh. How d'ya know this one be?"

Grave robbers! Well, any release was better than staying where he was.

"He be fresh alright, can't ye see the flowers? Died three day ago, 'e did, or I ain't an honest man."

It was hard to believe, but they'd know better than he would in this case. He smiled to himself. Soon he'd be free.

They set to work with what seemed to him to be agonizing slowness. Still they were prying the nails up, one by one; all things as they were, he would wait. He had no choice. The sounds of their voices and the creaks of the wood resounded in his ears. He had nearly forgotten how much he'd missed sound.

At last the nails had all been drawn and the coffin's lid began to move. Joy and anticipation peaked within him. The lid creaked open with a painful screech of the hinges. Light poured in, blinding him at first, glaring even through his closed eyelids as he squinted. Fresh cool air embraced him, softly caressing his pale flesh. When he opened his eyes he saw that it was night; the light that blinded him was the full moon, which shone brilliantly silver beyond the crypt's open door.

"Looks like this 'un's fresher 'n we thought! These country doctors don't know a live 'un from a dead 'un."

He recognized the voice as the first one he'd heard. In the shadows of the crypt he couldn't make out the men's features, but he knew they meant him no good. Body-snatchers sold the dead, not the living, to their clients in the medical profession. Those not already dead were helped on their way by such as these. He was not about to be "helped along" in that fashion.

If it had been any others he would have rewarded them for his freedom. These two deserved what came next. With blurring speed his arms shot out and grasped their throats in a stranglehold. The fools had leaned over him too closely in their greed, not expecting such life in one supposedly dead. He throttled them without emotion, as if they'd been insects to be crushed. This was strange, for before he'd never been a callous man even to those who deserved it.

When they lost consciousness he let them drop to the ground beside his casket. Then with a sinuous, almost animal grace for one so long entombed, he stepped forth from the box. He bent over each in turn and left them cold. Moonlight caused a glint of sharpest ivory and deepest liquid crimson. Once his thirst was slaked, he strode from the crypt without a backward glance. He cool darkness beckoned. He was free at last, to walk again the night.

Trace the Soul Snatcher

Nicole Kurtz

The Falling season had come early and the trees of the Western Forest had shed their leaves prematurely, leaving the forest naked. The only trees retaining their vegetation were the Bandons and a few everblues and evergreens. Frosty puffs escaped Trace's lips as he took the blue sphere from his pocket. It was no larger than a grapefruit.

The ball seemed to be the bluest Aryl had ever seen.

"Tomorrow the humans may come for us." Trace didn't worry about it.

Aryl frowned, crinkling his SMOOTH, dark skin in serious concentration. "Of course."

Trace sniffed the chilly air and discovered the faint scent amongst the earthiness of ice and danker dung. His cheeks puffed in and out as his breathing escalated.

Even in the leaving light, Aryl could see him snarling like a coyote, his full lips pulled back, his teeth a dim white. Pointed incisors stood out against his velvety dark skin.

"Dinji will not be pleased if we fail." Aryl's voice rose above a whisper.

Trace's woolly black hair stuck out in stubby dreadlocks. He pulled his hood over his pointed ears. Across his chest, a square silver clasp held his robe tight against the icy wind.

"No. He won't. The ceremony is tonight."

Aryl's eyes widened. They seemed to glow as they caught the last few rays of sunlight. "We will not fail."

"No. See there? Amongst the thicket of Bandon trees?"

Aryl's eyes followed Trace's pointed finger to a clump of interlocking trees where a campfire burned.

"Three humans." Trace wet his lips in anticipation. He gripped the ball and descended the cliff. As he reached the edges of the woods he crept in with a quick glance back at Aryl.

Aryl followed closely behind him. His job was to provide back-up for Trace. Despite his scrawny frame, Aryl's strength could rip through any human; bone, muscle and all. The energy required to sustain such power came from the amount of food Aryl ate. Between soul snatchings, he ate leftover human flesh, stored in the dungeons on ice. He was almost always eating and not nuts, berries or leaves, but meat—the more rare, the more delicious, for the blood enraged Aryl and endowed him with sheer, raw power.

He watched as Trace was swallowed up by the dark night. Trace's boot crunched on the layers of snow. He whipped in and out between the trees. They carried no lantern or light. His midnight robe blended into the gloomy patches that huddled in crevices.

Ahead in a tiny camp of two handmade tents were three girls. From this distance, Aryl could see one was older, perhaps in her eighteenth rotation while the others were in the grips of early youth. The younger ones' souls would be pure and full of unchecked emotions. Of yes, Dinji would be thrilled.

Aryl's stomach rumbled. Tender meat awaited and he could smell it. He watched as they played while the eldest picked up wood.

A scattered bunch of human colonists camped throughout the Western woods. This camp appeared unprotected. Perhaps they were new to Veloris 3…

The eldest girl spun around, her heavy blonde braid thudding around her waist. "Shush!"

Aryl could see the eldest scanning the cheerless, unlit forest. In her arms she hugged more kindling to her chest. Close to the fire the two girls fell silent, their game momentarily forgotten.

When nothing moved and nothing happened, the two giggled, but it was a nervous, shrill giggle.

"Be quiet!" The eldest cried.

The two smaller girls huddled close together, hearing the fear in the eldest's voice. They cast terrified glances out into the woods that circled around them.

Aryl heard the panic behind the words. It curdled in the air.

He smiled.

Not far from him, Trace stopped abruptly just at the edge of the camp. The sphere pulsated and glowed in his black-gloved hand. The shadows hid him from the girls' view.

"Who's there?" The eldest asked, for it seemed the woods stirred restlessly. "My husband is asleep! Do not make me wake him!"

But from her voice, Aryl could discern that she did not speak the truth.

The girls jumped up and ran to her. Their tiny hands eagerly clutched and grabbed the bottom of the eldest's dress. She in turn reached down and pulled them into her, hugging them close.

"Show yourself! You're frightening the children."

"As you wish." Trace approached the camp. The forest seemingly parted to be away from him.

The eldest girl gasped. Her eyes widened as she screamed, "Goddess of Algora…elves! Elves! Run, run for your mother's sake!"

She tried to force the girls to run, but they stood, rooted to the spot. Frozen, they only gaped and burrowed further into her dress.

She stepped in front of them as if to protect them. "Please, please, take what you will…"

Trace snarled. "Stupid humans."

Trace threw the sphere. It stopped just before them, hovering in the frigid air. It cracked in the middle and a flash of searing blue light erupted from it. The illumination filled the forest. Aryl could hear the girls screaming, high and wretched into the night before falling quiet. The sphere closed up and returned to Trace's gloved hand.

Aryl emerged from the forest and into the clearing. Anxiously, he scurried to the spot where mere moments before three girls stood. In their place sat stolen piles of bodies. Where the eyes once were, were now only blackened empty sockets.

Immediately, Aryl dropped to the pile and began to shove squishy flesh into his mouth. Carefully, he avoided the bones; he didn't want to choke.

"Be quick, Aryl!" Trace came further into the camp's clearing. He rummaged through the tents, but found no silver or anything of value. The raid was still a success. They'd gotten what they came for.

Trace spied in the distance the glow of lanterns. They seemed to float in the gloomy dark. He heard the sound of shouts and the fall of footsteps.

"Come! We have guests."

Aryl nodded, his cheeks stuffed. Blood stained the corners of his curvy mouth like croonberry jelly, sticky and red. His head cocked to the left, as he listened to the voices as they grew louder. He stood and tore the fingers from one of the girls' right hand. He shoved them into his robe's pocket. "Ready?"

Trace smiled. The campfire cast shadows across his face. The edges of his mouth stretched wider, but the smile seemed sinister, not joyful. His gray eyes appeared to brighten as he gazed into the throbbing orb. "Absolutely."

Trace immediately dashed into the forest. Effortlessly he ran through the trees; for all living things feared the elves.

For the elves brought death.

King Dinji's thirst for entertainment knew no limit. He sat on his throne, his face twisted in irritation. Tonight was supposed to be the semi-annual feast of souls. His pointed ears stuck out as if shut off from his head by his emerald-crusted crown. Black, like his mood, long, twisty dreadlocks hung down his back.

The castle's floor, splattered with blood from a previous fight to the death, lay as testament to the day's activities. Still, Dinji yawned and called, "Next, entertainer!"

"There is no more, Sire. All have retired." The guard hesitated before moving back a step.

"Then wake them up!" Dinji barked. "I am the..."

Dinji's words broke off as Trace and Aryl entered the Great Hall. At the sight of the blood, Aryl's stomach growled. He took out one of the fingers and shoved it into his mouth.

Dinji's velvet cobalt robe brushed the tops of his boots; its hem embroidered with miniscule coyotes. "Trace!"

Trace bowed at the waist. "Dinji."

He nodded at Aryl who bowed in turn, wiping his mouth on his robe's sleeve.

"The orb?" Dinji asked, his voice betraying his impatience.

Trace bravely met his eyes and removed the ball from his pocket. At once it glowed casting an azure shadow across the hall.

Dinji held out his hand for it and Trace climbed the three stone steps up to the throne. He carefully placed it into Dinji's hands and returned to the area by Aryl. Already Trace longed to be outside the boisterous hall and in the quiet of his cottage.

"It's so warm." He gazed into it for a few moments before announcing, "The ceremony is on!"

Aryl shouted in joy and Trace merely smiled that same grin that never quite reached his eyes.

"Think, Trace, think of it! How long have we snatched human souls? Centuries, and still they lie like fat, lazy kowlatas, unsuspecting..." Three souls swirled about in unrest.

"The human camps to the northern part of the Western woods were prepared. Last night we tried them, but they had formed some sort of army. Not more than twenty or so, but still, they were ready for us."

Dinji snorted, his eyes bright. "So what if some of them show signs of intelligence."

"Sire, remember the oracle's words. The time of soul snatching is drawing to an end."

"That is one understanding." Dinji shifted his attention to the lanky guard at his right. "Get Tara in here now!"

The guard closest to his throne disappeared behind the smooth, kowlata curtains. Kowlatas, animals known for their fur, once were abundant over the woods, were now only a handful due to soul snatchings before the humans came.

The guard returned with a young maiden. She struggled against him, but the guard paid no mind.

Dinji took his eyes away from the glass orb long enough to meet hers. "Tara, we need some redecorating. We need to have a feast!"

Tara's eyes were so pale they were nearly opaque. Her thick raven hair had been braided into thin, individual plaits and beaded with tiny pearls. It hung to just below her waist.

Her face was crumpled into an angry scowl. "Fine!"

"Remove her bracelets," Dinji commanded. He lifted the key from the chain around his neck and gave it to the guard. The guard unlocked the bracelets, but kept his eyes on her.

She lifted her hands and whispered a chanting spell as old as the foundation on the floor of the Great Hall. At her words, the bloody floor vanished and was immediately replaced by hand-woven carpets, tables and colorful curtains. Magically, musicians appeared and began to play a lively song of battles won and the ceremony was on.

"Happy?" She spat. Her eyes were nothing more than pits of fury. "Am I dismissed?"

"Lock up her bracelets." Dinji's tone was bored, but perhaps not so much as downright apathetic. So infatuated with the orb he'd become that he waved her off without a second look. "Return her to her room."

Tara's skin, unblemished and as dark as Trace's, seemed to shimmer amongst the candlelit hall. Trace, however did not wave her off. He'd never seen an elf speak to Dinji that way without losing her head that very moment. It wasn't just her iron will and bravery that caught Trace's eye. In fact, he could not take his eyes from her. Stunning, he had never seen such a beauty before. His stomach tightened at the thought of possessing her.

But it was not to be. He was a soul snatcher.

"Let's celebrate!" Dinji ordered.

The noise thundered through the castle, infusing the air with happiness and joy. The elves of Veloris 3 crowded into the Great Hall and rejoiced with songs and bottomless mugs of ale. They had another successful snatching.

Trace watched from the main entranceway. A space had been cleared and many danced in the candlelit hall to the musicians' tales of myth and legend. He did not dance, for dancing was for those of the court, noble high-ranking elves.

Sure, his father had been king, but that had been years ago.

A lifetime ago.

Dinji danced with three pretty cocoa-skinned elves. Their long raven hair spun around their waists in a blur as they twirled. Their gray eyes sparkled with joy and perhaps some magic spell as well.

Aryl did not leave his feast table. He ate and drank continuously, the bloody rare meat of kowlatas, also known for their gamey taste, and humans. He saw Trace by the door and raised his mug in greeting.

"Do you not dance?" Asked a silky voice from behind him. A hint of amusement rose to the top of it.

Trace jumped and whirled around, his hand on his dagger that lay strapped to his thigh. When he saw that it was Tara, he relaxed, but his stomach fluttered.

"No, I do not dance, Mistress Tara."

She smiled, but it was quickly replaced by a frown. "You do not partake of the food and the ale? It is a celebration. You successfully returned with souls."

"No." His eyes drank in her lovely complexion. Her lips, full and thick as his, were the color of dried blood. Her ears...were not pointed!

As if sensing his alarm, she turned to him. "Surprised?"

Trace's hand went back to his thigh and gripped the handle of his dagger tightly. "Human. What are you doing here? In his court?"

She tossed back her braids. "It is not by choice that I am here. I'm a prisoner. Dinji stole me from my colony some ten rotations prior."

At that she pulled back the heavy sleeves of her turquoise robe and showed him the thick silver bracelets on her wrists that he had seen earlier. Stamped onto the front of each cuff was a picture of a coyote, howling at the moons. Dinji's animal.

"They prevent me from leaving the castle grounds. I am his and he uses my powers to his benefit."

He felt his heart slowly move up to his throat. A human amongst elves? What did Dinji think he was playing with? Humans were dangerous, somewhat lethal animals. They were not pets.

With a sweeping growl, he tore his eyes away from hers and hurriedly left the main entranceway into the soothing arms of night.

Outside the castle, the bitterly cold air rushed against his face, freezing the sweat on his brow. Swiftly, he walked through the town's square toward his two-room cottage.

The walled elfin city of Graimere resided on top of a large plateau. Dinji's guards patrolled the wall at all times with crossbows, spears, and arrows, ready to pick off any humans that might threaten its population or retaliate from Trace's soul snatching.

The castle took up most of the space at the northern end of the city. It sat pushed back against an undersized slope and protected as well by guards.

As Trace entered his cottage at the eastern end of town, he thought back to his day. Captured human souls would provide the oracle with enough energy for another few months, but then he'd be called upon again to go hunt for souls.

And so the cycle has been for centuries. His father was king, but his uncle was a soul snatcher. All soul snatchers served the king, to provide souls to replenish the oracle's energy and thus that of the town. It citizens depended on the oracle's predictions. Still, during his uncle's tenure as soul snatcher, the oracle had prophesied snatchings demise.

At least that is what one priestess predicted. Others, however, believed the prophecy to mean that the return of G'hatora, a goddess of Veloris 3 would return to rule Graimere.

A smile tugged at Trace's lips as he thought about his uncle, Terron. Rumored throughout Graimere, Terron was the best snatcher, sweeping huge amounts of human souls in one night.

As he thought about humans, his mind drifted to Tara.

If Dinji had Tara for ten rotations, why had he not seen her before? Why did he not notice earlier that she was not an elf?

And why did he care?

Long after the feast had ended, Dinji sat naked at the foot of his bed. Nestled in his palm, the orb glowed, illuminating his inner chamber. He peered inside and the three, watery souls cried and whirled about. It was time and he knew it.

Trace and Aryl thought he used souls to power the city's oracle, but that wasn't true. The oracle needed the souls, yes, but Dinji needed it more.

He moved over to his fireplace where a fire licked the bottom of a round, black cauldron. He peered inside the cauldron and noted the boiling white substance. He dropped the orb into the cauldron. It stopped mere inches from the piping liquid. Suspended in the air, it waited.

"Born into the air, sea and trees, that which humans have stolen from thee, their very essence is the key."

The orb broke open and the souls, silky gray wisps, flew into the cauldron. The liquid instantly cooled and Dinji picked up a ladle and scooped it greedily to his lips.

He drank it, feeling its chalkiness on his tongue.

He collapsed to the floor. His eyes rolled back into his head. The coyotes howled and some heard Dinji laugh amongst them.

A vengeful mob of colonists' reached Graimere by noon and attacked the town. The sun's strong shine failed to warm the chilly air, but the raging fire of hatred burned in their hearts. They were spotted immediately and the guards rained down arrows and bows that lodged into the colonists' chests, necks and backs. The colonists tried to throw their spears and pitchforks, but from their lower position, they were dead within a few hours.

Aryl watched from Trace's window. "They are so determined. Look, even as one dies beside them, they still fight."

Trace, already fully dressed in his robe and pants, sat on his favorite chair, constructed of strong wood from the Western Forest. "Does not the kowlata still attack, even though its kin are dead? They are animals, nothing more."

Aryl could hardly contain himself. "Fresh meat. It's over. Come let us get some before it's gone!"

Trace grinned. It died before it reached his eyes. "All right."

They left the cottage and already, Trace could see the three meat wagons were already surrounded by elves bidding for the prime cuts.

Aryl scurried ahead, and disappeared into the mob. Trace could hear bids of twenty silver coins and higher for cuts. The butchers, one for each wagon, cut and sliced as folks pointed. Trace watched with disinterested eyes. As a soul snatcher, he could not eat meat, for the blood tampered with his ability to call the orb. He only ate garden greens, nuts, berries and the like.

He watched as Aryl returned with the hairy, broad arm of a man. It was extremely pale and missing its hand. Aryl's voice had grown heavy with disappointment. "This is all they had left for three silver pieces, adults. Most of the other cuts are too expensive for me."

Trace laughed. "Did you not get your fill last night?"

Aryl scoffed, "Fill? Of course not."

Just then, up ahead, Trace saw the back of a turquoise robe and raven braids disappear into the crowded street. He left Aryl and shoved his way through the mob until he reached the robe. He snatched the sleeve, "Stop!"

She turned around with a confused expression. "Excuse me?"

The elf's older face was irritated as she held an armful of human hands. "They make great stew."

His heart thundering in his chest. What was he doing? "I thought you were another."

She nodded and went about her way.

Aryl screamed after him, "Trace! Trace! Dinji wants your presence at the hall."

Swearing softly, Trace hurried to the castle with Aryl on his heels. When Dinji called, one did not ignore him.

The main entranceway opened as Trace approached.

Dinji stood in front of his throne. "Trace, you brought me the absolute best souls last night."

"I am glad you're pleased, Sire." If the souls were the best, then why had Dinji summoned him here the very next day?

"Why? Because I want more. More!"

Trace's head lifted. He can hear my thoughts?

"Oh, yes, Trace, I can read your thoughts and those of everyone in the castle." Dinji sat gingerly down on his throne. "The souls provide the final ingredient in a potion that allows me to do this wondrous thing."

"No! You drink the souls of others?" He immediately emptied his mind of any thought. Dinji was not one he wanted inside his head.

"Now, the reason you're here is because I want more souls. This business of collecting them twice a year is, well, not enough. Yes, I know your complaints about the oracle's prophesy, ceremony…"

Trace's eyes widened. "Dinji, as I have warned you before, there aren't enough human souls. Some of the humans have banded together. The hunting of humans is drawing to a close. The oracle-"

"Silence! I know what the oracle says, but I am king! My priestesses say that the oracle's prediction can only mean that the great goddess is to return. When she returns is a matter of conjecture." He shrugged. "Finding more souls is your problem."

Trace's lips pulled back into a snarl, his temper inched steadily toward exploding. "Dinji…"

"Have you forgotten who is ruler of Graimere?"

Trace did not answer. The usually crowded hall seemed to close in on him. Hot and trying to stem his temper, he gritted his teeth.

Dinji went on, "The throne once belonged to your family line, did it not? They were overthrown several rotations prior by my grandfather, because they were weak!"

"Yes, Sire." Trace said slowly, his voice smooth and devoid of the terrible rage that boiled inside him. His eyes spied the turquoise sleeve just before it vanished behind the curtains that lined the wall behind Dinji. "Forgive me, Sire. I will leave at once."

Pleased by Trace's devotion and not able to pick up anything that might contradict his words, Dinji smiled again.

"At your ready. I will see you tonight."

Trace left the Great Hall. He knew that Tara could not leave the grounds, so he hurried around the back to the outdoors courtyard in the rear of the castle. He seemed to know that this was where she would be.

As he stepped up the broken stone steps into the courtyard, he immediately spotted Tara sitting under an archway. The packed patches of dirt muffled his footprints for no vegetation grew here. Instead it was decorated with stones and colored glass.

She smiled when she saw him. "I knew you would come. There's little time."

How she knew, Trace could only speculate that her ability to do magic also gave her the gift of foresight. He sat down beneath the archway and the world faded away. A smoky cloud snaked around the archway, hiding it from outside view. "

"What dark magic is this?"

She chuckled, the way young elfin girls often do. "This's no dark magic, but my own. Here, Dinji cannot read your mind."

He heard the amusement in her voice. "What is it you want of me, human?"

At the word human she winced. "Dinji's family stole the seat from your line. I have read the royal tapestry that hangs in Dinji's bedroom. You're the last. Would you like the throne returned to its rightful owners?"

Trace slipped his blade from his thigh with such fluidity and speed that he held it to her neck before she could swallow. "Evil witch! Speak not of my family! Or your own blood will stain this very courtyard!"

She tensed under his blade and her eyes moved over to his. "Do what you must, but the fate of this planet and others depends on you, soul snatcher."

The blade bit into her neck, producing a single drop of blood. The ruby droplet slid down her neck and pooled in the collar of her robe. "Will you lick my blood? Eat my flesh like your brethren?"

He shoved her backward and replaced his dagger. "I do not eat meat. I must be clean and untainted to handle the spheres, as I am sure you are already aware. Witch!"

Tara placed her hand on his knee—forcing him to flinch and knock it off.

"The key to the future of this planet and others depend on your ability to join with the humans."

Trace abruptly stood. "I am a soul snatcher! I kill humans!"

"That's the reason you must replace Dinji and make peace between humans and elves. If Dinji has his way, he will murder all of the humans on this planet!"

His eyes clicked with hers and he growled. "If it is their fate... they are only humans."

"Yes, but once this planet is rid of humans, who will Dinji turn to for souls? His potion is all he craves. Think, damn you! If not my own, think of your people."

She placed her hands onto his chest and gazed up into his eyes. Her lips tilted upward and she leaned in until they were inches from his.

He stared into her eyes. They reminded him of a storm-coming sky. He wondered if her beauty was some sort of enchantment, like the archway and the celebration feast. He felt the tug of lust rise hard and fast in his heart, but she was a human.

Disgusting.

With a short shove he pushed her back from him. "I do not trust you. Nor do I care for your kind."

She sighed heavily. Fear crept into her voice. "You don't trust me because I am human. But you do not trust Dinji either, and he is elfin. He stole the throne from your family—your kin."

"You are a witch and have resided here with Dinji for ten rotations," he snarled, "Let the humans' lots fall where they may, for it is fate that determines it."

She bit her lip in thought. "Soul snatcher, your fate is with me, whether you know it or not. I have dreamed of us...I have been to the oracle."

At the thought of a human at the oracle, violating its sacredness, he growled and stomped out of the archway. He would hear none of it.

Trace descended the Algora plateau, with Aryl at his side and headed for the Western Forest. The sun was still high, but he could see the emergence of the two moons. Dusk would be upon them by the time he reached the forest, and then he would do what he was born to do: snatch souls.

Behind him, Trace could hear Aryl's labored breathing. Ahead of him lay another human campsite, ripe with children and adults. It appeared to lack any defense. From this distance he could hear their chatter and smell their innocence. It sickened him to go out again, tonight, but his duties were clear.

"Are you not the last? Would you like the throne returned to you?" Tara had asked.

Trace shuddered and shook off her words. It mattered not whom the throne rightfully belonged. Indeed he was the last, for he had not married, nor could he. He was a soul snatcher and that meant purity in both body and mind. Someone in his extended family—his kin—would have to become a soul snatcher if Trace became king.

But Trace was not king, nor did he desire it.

Even as he thought this, he knew it to be untrue. He did desire to be king, but why waste his desire on something that was unobtainable?

Still, Tara's words circled around in his mind, taunting and teasing him, silkily seducing him. He could not stand for such intrusions. He had work to do.

He stood abruptly at the edge of the Western Forest. The sun's slow descent was underway and it hugged the horizon.

Aryl stopped too. "You're thinking too hard."

Trace nodded. "Indeed."

Aryl took this to mean that he was right. "If it is Dinji that plagues you, know that there is nothing we can do about his demand for more souls. He may even pay us more this time."

Trace nodded again and pulled his hood up. He tied it quickly with nimble fingers. The night was almost upon them. The moons' duel faces shimmered just behind the sun's setting rays.

Aryl ceased talking. He wasn't one for a lot of conversation and who was he anyway to lecture Trace? He had served Trace's house for centuries.

"At your ready."

Trace smiled his usual grin and this time it, too, failed to reach his eyes. It waned like his interest in food.

Without warning, he zipped into the forest, moving faster than any human eye could track. Aryl was right behind with a large, carnivorous grin, for he too could smell the human children and knew that the eating would be good tonight.

Hours later, Dinji stretched as he turned from his window that overlooked the decrepit courtyard and out over the Eastern Forest. The sun's rays dipped under the horizon and night blanketed the world.

Tara sat on the floor near the fireplace. The outside chilliness would soon seep into the castle, turning the floor to ice.

"I know you were with him today." Dinji's voice had become absent of accusation, but filled with certainty. "I forbid further contact between you and the soul snatcher!"

She ignored him. Her fingers traced invisible circles on the floor, her mouth moved, but no sound could be heard.

He snatched her up by her robe. He lifted her to her feet and leaned in so close to her face that his nose gently bumped hers. "No spells here! You know the rules. Break them, Tara and so help me you'll be back in the dungeon, on a heap of ice!"

She laughed so hard that tears spilled and slid down her smooth, dark face.

Unsure and unable to read her mind for she was not an elf, he dropped her to the floor. "Do not mock me, human. Or you'll find yourself served up for evening meals."

At this she stopped laughing. He needed her to sustain the balance of power in Graimere. The Solance gave him the ability to read minds, but it did not make him strong nor did it make the people love him…Tara's spells did that.

"You are a thief and a tyrant." Her eyes clicked with his, but she wouldn't look away. "Your days are numbered for the soul snatcher is on to you."

He raised his hand and slapped her across the face, sending her sprawling to the floor. "The soul snatcher is no concern of yours!"

Her eyes met his, and she spit a bloody splat onto the floor. She rose up.

"Do that again, Dinji and it will be your last act of violence. I am no elf, and I have grown tired of this game. I demand my freedom as promised."

His lips curled into a grin. "The bracelets stay on those tiny wrists, forever."

"Your word, you promised! The throne, Tara and Graimere, for your freedom. You promised!"

"You have violated our agreement, Tara. You have betrayed me with the soul snatcher!"

"I have not. I have been faithful and obedient!" Tara shouted back at him.

Three hard knocks against the door temporarily interrupted their dispute.

"Come!" Dinji called, his chest heaving in anger.

A guard came into the room. "Sire, the soul snatcher has returned."

The guard's face was sapped and slightly aghast, yet Dinji took no notice. Glee filled Dinji's face and his anger at Tara was forgotten as he hurried into the Great Hall with her right behind him.

As soon as he entered the hall, his smile slipped from his face, for Trace was covered in splats of blood. His midnight robe glistened under the lanterns and small droplets of blood dripped down from his shoulders. His face was stained with splashes of wet, dark liquid. His gray eyes stared out at Dinji, and his lips were pressed together tightly.

Aryl stood beside him, greedily holding on to several human arms and legs in one hand, and a ripped torso in the other. He too had been bathed in blood. His slim face and ears were covered in the reddish liquid. His boots, his hands and his robe were no longer brown, but a deep reddish color. At his feet were chunks of unidentifiable human parts.

Trace stuck out his gloved hand and the orb glowed through the smears of blood. "Here, Dinji. Enjoy, for this may be the last of the human souls you ever ingest. I warned you of the dangers of daily intake. We should have waited until time had passed, like always. We scanned the camps tonight…"

Dinji sat down carefully. "Explain the meaning of this!"

"Can you not read my mind?" Trace asked, his fury seeping through his usual calm demeanor.

"Still your tongue, or I will separate you from it!" Dinji ordered. But his eyes were wide with fear. He turned to Aryl and barked, "Explain!"

"Sire," Aryl began. "The humans decided to camp together and post guards. A trap was set and once we arrived at what we thought was an unprotected camp, they attacked. They were ready for us… our element of surprise had been, well, trumped. I, I have never felt better." He picked up a section of arm and tore into it, his teeth slicing effortlessly through the skin, breaking it and driving into the actual meat of it.

He chewed.

Trace glanced at Aryl before saying, "As a result of your greed, there are now only a handful of defenseless humans remaining in the forest. No more than twenty. Those souls are the last, for Aryl butchered dozens tonight to protect me and the orb as is his sworn duty. It is only a matter of time before those humans join with the others…"

Dinji's eyes were frozen in disbelief. "You lie!"

"Drink! Drink your potion and tell me that I am lying," Trace spat, indignantly. "Twice a year, on a rotating schedule so that they always remained off balanced and the colonists were not ready, but daily and you have sentenced us to die. Without the oracle, Graimere is a tomb!"

"Silence!" Dinji thundered and leapt to his feet. "If I cannot have human souls, I will have elfin souls! The souls of kowlatas! It is no matter! It is only the Solance that is important, soul snatcher!"

"Do you insist on our demise? Kowlatas are our supplemental food between snatchings. Once they are gone you would turn to our brethren?" Trace swore heatedly. He nearly dropped the sphere as his eyes met Tara's. She had been right. "You are mad! The souls of your own kin? I will not engage in such blasphemy!"

"Then you will die!" With wild eyes, Dinji waved his hands in the air as if to catch the souls himself. "Guards, restrain him!"

"Better I die, than reap the souls of my people. I am the last soul snatcher."

Dinji grinned. "You are the last of your line, 'tis true. But you are not the only soul snatcher. Aryl is capable of such. His line has produced those who can call the orb."

Aryl frowned at Dinji and placed a small human hand into his mouth. He chewed noisily—his interest already wavering.

Trace laughed for Aryl did not have the discipline for soul snatching. The guards took the orb from his hand, and it immediately went dark. They removed his dagger and dragged him down to the dungeon, where no light shined and no one escaped.

As he was led away, he heard Dinji say, "Aryl, take that hand out of your mouth at once!"

The darkness did not bother him. Yet, Trace knew that when the sun's rays kissed the frozen land tomorrow, he would be put to death. No one defied the king. Yet Dinji's plan to reap the souls of elves was hideous. It was lunacy. It sounded like a half-cocked plan of a human, but Dinji was no human.

Tara was human and her presence tonight at his side, only added to Trace's level of distrust. It did not matter, for he would be dead by noon.

He was the last in his line of kings and soul snatchers. For once the Kings of Graimere had the ability to snatch souls. There had been humans on Veloris 3 for a hundred or so rotations. Still, the balance had been maintained. The humans were surprised when he snatched souls because there was no set time between snatchings. Twice a year, but never on the same days and never in the same season. Sometimes snatchings occurred months and other times days. There was no rule on how many days rested between snatchings, only that it should not occur more than twice a year. Daily, the humans were ready. They weren't stupid.

He sat on the floor of his cell, hearing the dripping of water from some underground lake and the celebration in the Great Hall. He had, after all, returned with souls. That meant feast of souls.

After a few hours in the gloomy cell, Trace's eyes grew heavy and he dozed.

It seemed as soon as he closed his eyes, he heard, "Wake, soul snatcher! Your time has come!" Whispered a silky voice.

Trace bolted up and back away from the cell's bars. Despite the murky darkness, he could see her outline. The hood of her robe was pulled over her black hair, but he could still see the smile that tugged at her lips. He had no idea how long he'd been asleep.

"Be gone. Allow me to die with honor! Your presence here…"

"That is not your fate, this day."

She removed her hood and dug into her robe's pocket. In her hand she held a key and unlocked his cell door.

"Come."

"Tara, I will not be betrayed by you. Go back to your master."

She grimaced. "These cuffs are the same as this prison which you now stand in. Would you throw away your life so easily without a fight?"

He was silent.

"Will you throw away the lives of your people? He is already preparing Aryl for the purification ceremony."

Trace's head snapped up. Sighing, he came out of the cell, and followed Tara through the dungeon, up the stairs and out into the courtyard. There weren't any guards posted for none were needed. Dinji believed in the power Tara's spells had over the people, including the guards. No elf had ever escaped the dungeon.

She fled through the archway and he followed. Once there, she sat down on the bench.

"Tonight, you must tell the people of Graimere of Dinji's plan."

"But they will not listen to me. They are devoted to him. As are you…"

Tara shook her head. "They are under my spell. If you agree to tell them, I will cancel it."

Shocked, he stood. "What do you mean?"

"I mean," she said impatiently, "that the only reason the people of Graimere follow Dinji is because of a spell I placed on the city. Until now, no one has challenged him nor did they have reason to, but this madness of killing elves and humans for their souls, every day-"

He stared at her. Now? Now she was willing to cancel the spell over the Graimere people. Why suddenly the change of heart? Ten rotations had gone by...

"Do not look at me that way, Trace. For five years I wasted away in that bottomless pit of hell, he calls a dungeon. He made me promise to help him win the people—for he already had the throne—and I would gain my freedom once I proved faithful."

"Why did you not wave your magic and open the bars?" He asked his hands clenched into fists, his heart still disbelieving.

"Because of these." She lifted her wrists. "Dinji places them on me after I have done whatever magic he wants. These do not allow me to leave the castle or to cast spells. But over the years I have practiced and learned of other spells that Dinji knew nothing of."

Disgusted, he turned away from here. Five years? That is why he had never seen her before. Dinji had her hidden, tucked away like his favorite robe in the dungeon.

"These last five years, I have served him with the hope that he would free me. He has not and only recently did he tell me that he has no plans to do so," she went on, her voice filled with sadness. "Listen, please, I know I have not behaved honorably, but, if you kill him, the spell would be canceled."

"Are you mad? Murdering a king?" Trace's voice rose. "I will be hanged."

"You're already condemned to die, soul snatcher. We must do this, together. Human and elf." She took his hand in hers. "For Veloris 3."

"Allow me to die with honor." Trace snatched his hand from hers as if she was diseased.

"With honor? You disobeyed the king. You don't have any honor left."

He looked away, avoiding the honesty in her face. Tara was right for she knew Dinji better than most. Dinji would make sure he did not have an honorable death.

"How am I to kill him?"

"With this." Tara removed a dagger from her cloak as if she knew he'd agree. "It's one I took from the guard, along with the key to the dungeon. When he's shocked at your appearance in court, throw it at him, aim for his throat."

"At your ready."

This time it lit up his face.

He followed her around the courtyard and through the doors to the Great Hall. Trace stepped inside with Tara, shoving their way through the thong of people, most of the town was clambering in to witness Trace's execution. Immediately the musicians vanished and the quietness surprised the packed hall.

Dinji stood up, his mouth slacked with surprise. "Guards!"

The guards hurried toward them, but Tara was ready. "Eternal Sleep!"

The guards collapsed to the floor, dead.

Aryl stood a short distance from the doors, dressed in a white, gauzy robe.

No one moved. Dinji's eyes were round and furious.

"You dare use magic! With him?"

"I do. The bracelets do not block woodland magic."

She turned to Trace. "That's all I can give you."

Dinji frowned. "The...the...woodland? No, no!"

Trace took the dagger and hurdled it at Dinji, but Dinji ducked the oncoming blade and drew his sword. With speed, he raced down the stone steps toward Trace. "You dare ruin what is mine? Die!"

Aryl suddenly leapt into the air and pounced on Dinji. Dinji swung his sword, but it was too late. Aryl was on him. Using his scrawny arms, he tore Dinji's arm from his body. Dinji's howling screams of agony and searing pain could be heard across the plateau and on to the Eastern Forest where the coyotes joined him.

Aryl was not done. Blood flew and splattered as he demolished Dinji's body. The crowd seemed to step back and away from the carnage, for body parts were strewn about in a haphazard manner. No one offered to save the king. Not allowed to eat for several hours because of the purification ceremony had left Aryl hungry.

Someone had physically threatened his master to whom he had sworn to protect.

As Dinji's last cry faded, Tara screamed. All eyes went to the main entranceway, where she stood, with her arms lifted, free of her cuffs.

"I'm free! Free!"

As if awakened from a daze, the elfin people of Graimere blinked and whispered as the spell wore off.

"What happened?"

"A human!" Someone screamed and the crowd grew anxious.

Trace stepped up to the throne. He glanced down at the crowd, for almost all of Graimere's elders were here.

"It's the soul snatcher! Silence!" They cried to one another until they settled down to listen.

"I am Trace, soul snatcher and heir to King Tran. Listen, people of Graimere for much has happened."

Murmurs and outright shouts swelled up against the castle's ceiling.

"Listen! Listen to me!" Trace shouted over the rumblings. "It is a human that has saved us from destruction."

At first, the mob of elves violently resisted this notion. Yet, soul snatchers were pure. They were honest and they dealt in death. There was no room for error or lies.

As they looked to him, he continued.

"I am Trace, heir of King Tran and a soul snatcher. The oracle's prophesy has come to past. The time of soul snatching is over. Together, we will find a way to live together…in peace."

An elder member of the court spoke through the uneasy silence. "Your line has been returned to the throne, which is proper. If a human has done that, then we are grateful."

With slow applause, the elves clapped and Trace bowed in Tara's direction. She nodded, unable to speak, for she was crying.

The End.

The Grande Performance

James Davis

The song still played as the buildings fell. It skirled and rang as the fires raged. Dancers' shadows were thrown across the ruined city. Through it all the song played. A mournful song of chaos and death and loss.

~~

"Troupe Master! Troupe Master!" The youthful voice called out as a young man raced into the large, flamboyantly decorated and coloured tent of Troupe Master Zaun. A piece of parchment was clutched in one hand, and a grin was on his face.

Zaun only took a few moments to remember the boy: Varreg Ho – a boy from the southern badlands who was already a promising Actor. A smile split the forever-youthful features of Zaun as he extended a long-fingered hand the colour of fresh snow. "Now what, pray tell, is this you have for me, dear boy?" He asked in that feather soft, parchment thin voice.

The folded paper was placed into the proffered hand. Though, he quickly recited the basics of the note. "We're tasked with a performance at Daerenhaeg. The entire troupe is requested."

Zaun's eyebrows rose as he read the note's extremely wordy and unnecessary contents. "The writer of this would give some of our poets a run for their purple quills..." He refolded the parchment and set it on a desk littered with so many different pieces of art it seemed to be a madman's nightmare of culture. He lightly pinched the bridge of his nose, eyes closing as he let loose a small sigh. "The entire troupe? By the Great Muse that'll be a task in and of itself." Dark green eyes opening, he offered a resigned smile. "I suppose there's no helping it."

Rising from his seat, Zaun stretched out – he towered above most men and could have been mistaken for an ogre had he not been so skeletally thin. He glanced to Varreg, nodding his head. "Go on and rouse the lot of them. I'll prepare to address a band of drunk and exhausted artists." The rest of his sentence had barely finished before the young man was out the front of his tent.

It was not long until a chorus of angry shouts and jeers were calling for Zaun to answer for the rude awakening. The Troupe Master, as was his wont, flung the flaps of his tents outward as he emerged in the near-entirety of his ensemble. Garishly coloured robes that made the eyes hurt if looked at too long, stitched in reflective and sequenced silks, laced with silvers and golds. He was a walking eye sore, but only hoots and cheers left the gathered crowd at the majesty of their leader. "My friends! My fellow artists! No doubt you all wish to go back to your drunken stupours, but alas I cannot allow this! For we have been called upon for a Grande Performance!" He paused and there were gasps of excitement. "Gather your things! Ready yourselves! For such a thing has been too long in the waiting!"

The congregation scattered to the clutter of their camp to prepare themselves. Zaun smiled, turning to one of his chorus. "Fetch my marching robes. This occasion calls for as much pomp and ceremony as we can muster!" The young girl rushed off, the kindly gaze of the Troupe Master turning to sweep the rest of his chorus. "As for the rest, a song! A song to lift our spirits and ready us for the Grande Performance!" He cleared his voice as the singers began, his words booming to the corners of the camp. "Musicians an accompaniment! Dancers, begin your dance and distract us from the poets blathering!"

Laughs and jeers echoed through the camp as minstrels began to play and the dancers spun – leaving it for the stagehands to pack for the now occupied performers. Zaun laughed and clapped his hands. The vitality in the camp was never as it was before a performance.

~~

The rain slashed against the troupe – but the music, song and dance was undimmed through the treacherous weather. Zaun, sodden and smiling added his own deep voice to the song from time to time which sent the dancers into new flights of frenzy. Each night they would rest and then the following day the song would continue. This had gone on for more than a week before they had arrived at their destination.

Daerenhaeg – the site of their Grande Performance. Zaun reined his horse as a short, pugnacious man in fine military brocade marched toward their troupe. Soldiers in faceless steel armour flanked the small man, each one shifting near-imperceptibly as they came to a halt. "You are Troupe Master Zaun?" The voice was short and clipped, thick with the accent of the Midlands.

Zaun bowed in his seat, smiling wide at the small man. "I am indeed! I am to presume I'm addressing the esteemed High Lord Aldrech von Dorren, Field Marshal of His Divine Majest's Crusaders?"

The short man flinched back as the Troupe Master bent low. He steadied himself, squaring his shoulders and giving a firm nod of his head. The motion sending thick jowls wobbling and the bristling black of his muttonchops to waving. "I am indeed. We expected you two days ago." Aldrech replied tersely, the High Lord finding some nerve again as he stuck out his gut then his chest – the polished silver buttons of his red and gold uniform first to bursting around his belly.

"I should say that for one to expect a troupe of artists to arrive on time is the height of insanity." Zaun slid from his saddle, smoothing the rainbow-hued robes down. He watched as the rest of the group dropped from saddles or fell down from exhaustion – a camp haphazardly being set up behind him. "Besides, we are here now so that is one less reason to complain. After a night of rest we'll be ready for our performance."

"Rest? Daerenhaeg was supposed to fall by today! I'll be damned if I let you and your no good-." He froze as the full weight of Zaun's eyes fell upon the short man. The emerald of his eyes seeming to burn as he fixed the Field Marshal in his gaze. "R-Rest... yes. Yes. You know your followers better than I." Aldrech gave a nervous titter as Zaun's expression softened.

"Prepare your men for tomorrow, dear Lord! And try not to be so nervous, after all we are here for your entertainment." Zaun turned, robes sweeping out behind him as he retreated into the mess of his camp.

The Field Marshal swallowed as he turned and marched away, the posture of the knights visibly relaxed now that they had left the presence of the troupe.

Though that night none of the soldiers received any rest as the troupe carried on in song and laughter well into the dawn. The Field Marshal even cursing vehemently about the lies of a need for rest.

~~

Dawn broke and the soldiers of the Imperia lined up, bleary

eyed and irritable. The Field Marshal was horribly disheveled, his eyes were thick with black rings and he looked slightly sick from lack of sleep. At odds was Zaun's rabble who continued to carouse and laugh as if they hadn't spent the entirety of the night being a nuisance. The Troupe Master himself walked over to warmly greet the sleep-deprived commander. "A wondrous morning, my Lord! Simply wonderful for our performance!"

"Yes." Aldrech snapped, lips a thin line. "Would you get on with it already?"

Zaun clucked his tongue. "Tut tut, my Lord. One can never rush art." He turned away before Aldrech could reply, arms flinging outward as he cried out. "Musicians! Began your harmony! Dancers, to the walls!" Strings drew back, a soft melody, before they sounded in a quick succession followed by a flight of flutes as arrows whistled through the air. The volley of notched projectiles creating a sound all their own in harmony as the archers drew and fired again and again – every arrow a shrilling note that pierced the defenders.

Under the flight of symphonic death the dancers spun and twirled. The men could only watch as these men and women rushed to the walls. Thorgorak blades strapped to wrists, fingers, ankles and toes gouged the walls as the War Dancers writhed across the stone sides – scaling the walls in moments to leap and spin amongst the archers. Arcs and trails of blood following their wild and writhing motions as they cut their way through the lightly armoured archers.

Zaun smiled as the screams added the perfect pitch to the song loosed by the arrows and harp-bows. He turned from the Field Marshal, stalking toward his tent. "Now if you'll excuse me, my Lord. I must dress for my own performance." As the Troupe Master disappeared into his pavilion, Aldrech could only turn and stare at the bloodied crenelations and the corpses dangling from them.

The War Dancers continued their swaying, bloody dance even as no more defenders tried to ascend the walls. They were slaves to the music of the Harpers and could do nothing more than cavort to the orchestral death. Then the Harpers were joined in a low thrum of song. The choral elements of the troupe began a low and sonorous note. This note they held until they were joined by their master. Striding to the stage Zaun wore his war regalia. Muted blacks and whites, steel lined robes that hung about him like a funereal shroud. His arms spread out as Zaun lead his chorus in their song.

It was the powerful chanting of monks, a dirge that throbbed in the very bones of the earth. Rock shuddered and cracked as the Dirge sang their mournful song. The walls began to vibrate beneath the feet of the War Dancers who only laughed as they were driven to new heights of gamboling. Power sparked in the air. Glistening lines of light linking each singer to Zaun. The song reached its crescendo and the spell was unleashed. Air was hardened and released, smashing into the gates of Daerenhaeg and cracking the wood – yet they held firm.

A grin split Zaun's face as the song fell into the second verse. The skeins of power between the sorcerer and his assistants becoming all the brighter as once again the spell was unleashed in a cracking of air and wood. The gate buckled and groaned, frightened screams from within at the supernatural assault giving strength to the Dirge. They had to go to the final verse. This truly was a Grande Performance. The song reached a new height, words which had been unsung for too long. The lines of power were too bright to look upon. The spell throbbed behind the eyes of everyone gathered. A constant and dull headache as if the charge before a storm. Zaun's arms rose as he held the penultimate note before releasing the spell. The gates shattered, hurling backwards into the city they had sought to protect. Wood speared defenders and lanced through stone. The granite around the gates cracked and groaned ominously – a single note shouted as one forcing them to hold.

Daerenhaeg was wide open. Zaun need give no command as the Blood Poets set to their work. The men wore breastplates and greaves of steel. Outrageously feathered hats decorated their heads and accompanied the flamboyant clothing beneath their armour. With a war cry shouted in a hundred tongues the Poets charged. In one hand they carried their signature weapon: the hollow sword. In the other it varied, shields or daggers, axes or maces – uniformity was only required in their main weapon.

This was butcher's work refined to an art form. This was gore condensed into verse. Block and slash and parry parsed down to brief spurts of inevitably anticlimactic duels. The hollow swords drank greedily of their kills. The thorgorak blades filled to overflowing with the blood of the slain – and in those moments the Poets paused and let their fellows continue on. Scrawling elements of their brief combat writ upon wall and ground in the lifeblood of their opponents.

With the Poets now engrossed and taking the attentions of the more heavily armoured defenders, the War Dancers retreated from the battlements and into the killing ground below. Dancing behind the Poets the Dancers finished off those forgotten to the ennui of their fellow artists.

Zaun's chorus slowly dispersed behind him, filing away toward the city to unleash their own songs of destruction even as the symphony continued above their heads. Zaun turned his eyes toward the pale-faced Marshal standing behind the horrified lines of imperial soldiers. "My Lord – your men are free to follow any time they wish. I'm sure my Poets, Dancers and Singers will leave some for them."

"That..." Aldrech cleared his throat as his voice cracked. "That won't be necessary, Troupe Master Zaun. The uh... the matter of your payment is still up for debate?"

Zaun's thin eyebrows rose nearly to the top of his bald head. "Debate? My Lord, there is no debate. For a Grande Performance we are afforded the regular sum of five-hundred thousand divines." His fingers steepled beneath his chin. "If we take the city and shatter the resistance that price doubles for the cost of materials, manpower and training for those who must replace those who perish." His mouth became a pale slit. "You wouldn't be seeking to try and disvalue myself and mine own for all the work they've done would you, my Lord?"

Though Zaun's tone was amiable enough the look in his eyes was one of dire threat. The ever present feeling of the imperial knights vanished from Aldrech's back as even the staunch warriors retreated in the face of the sorcerous Troupe Master. Spluttering and mopping a grossly sodden brow Aldrech offered a nervous smile of acquiescence. "It is m-my fault, Troupe Master. I... I was so overwhelmed by your soldiers that I... I misspoke." He licked his lips quickly, waiting to see what the effect of his words was.

Zaun's expression shifted into one of bonhomie near instantaneously. "Artists, my Lord! We are not soldiers, we are artists!" He folded his hands into his sleeves and bowed low. "No affront is taken either, my Lord. I can quite understand the awe our Grande Performance can have on those unused to our presentations. I myself am oft taken aback when I stroll through the streets and read what my wonderful Poets have written of their battles. Now! I must be off to see how the scenes progress. I trust to see you at the victory supper tonight."

Without waiting for a response Zaun was off – marching toward Daerenhaeg and beneath the wall still held by his magic. The sounds of battle had mostly died away. It was not the oppressive silence of death that hung above the city. But the broken and battered silence of oppression once more restored.

All done in the name of art.

BORED WITCH

ANNA CATES

In the middle of a hill, surrounded by midnight lightning, stood a castle where there lived a bored, yet terrible, witch. Because bright light tired her eyes, the witch cast a spell about the castle so clouds would always block the sun, and the grass grew sparse and yellow all over the hillside. Only the witch's weed patch of bitter herbs thrived by magic.

The witch stared at the world with lash-less eyes of icy blue. Her raven hair with glints of silver flowed down to her waist without a single curl. Purplish veins crisscrossed her sunless skin, and necromancy had stained her fingers grayish yellow. With nails so discolored, her hands always appeared dirty, even after she indulged in chamomile or lavender bubble baths.

The bored witch dressed in tight leather pants and black boots that clicked along the stone floor as she swaggered about the castle, the scent of brimstone heavy about her, a colorful variety of see-through blouses showcasing her nipples. She enjoyed the occasional blood cocktail and slept in a coffin like a vampire. In fact, she was part vampire, though her teeth appeared quite normal, if only a bit yellow.

The bored witch kept one slave, Lizander, a creature bred from a human and a red dragon. Don't even ask how she managed such a feat; that's a terrible tale that should never be told, except perhaps to a wizard.

Lizander was mostly human, with only a dash of dragon blood running through his veins—just enough to tint his skin a coppery hue and give him leathery wings, allowing for flight. His mother beat, mocked, and ridiculed him every day from the time he was a small child—poor wretch. She considered him a boring thing indeed and never neglected to tell him so.

But each week he'd sweep down the hillside to the nearby village and fetch his "Mom-ster"—as he called her—lambs, sheep, or piglets for the dinner table. He'd carry each animal by a single hoof back to the castle, his wings flapping like a vulture's. The villagers fled at the sight of him, crying, "It's the demon from Lightning Hill!" They considered the castle "the demon's" lair and knew neither about the witch nor that Lizander wasn't a demon, though he did look like one, especially from a distance. He grew into a man, kind of, while the witch never aged at all but only grew more bored each day.

One morning the witch declared, "I'm so bored! I've nothing here to entertain me, just stupid Lizander! How I wish I had a beautiful young virgin to help me cast more terrible spells!" Seated at the table, she stared at the distant wall, cluttered with roach-laden cobwebs, tapping her stained fingernails on the arm rest of her chair.

Lizander zipped to her feet, shame-faced and groveling. "Shall I fetch one for you from the village, Mom-ster?"

The witch's lips curled into an evil grin. "Certainly, if you could bring me a virgin, you'd never be as boring to me again."

With hope beating in his heart, eager to please his disapproving mother, Lizander swept off the castle window sill and whooshed through the air, down the meadow slopes, and over the towering pines. He knew a pasture just outside the village where a shepherdess tended her flock; in fact, he'd stolen from her pasture before, so in that direction he descended.

Danae was walking along the border of the forest, staff in hand, when a shadow passed over her. Before she could even lift her head, two arms locked around her, her feet left the ground, and she soared into the air. She screamed, but no one was there to hear but bleating lambs, sorry to see their mistress go. She ascended high above the tallest evergreens, gliding toward the castle on Lightning Hill. Higher and higher she rose, daring not to struggle, lest she should fall unto her death. Her mind passed into a dreamy blackness, and her head toppled forward onto her chest.

She woke hours later, lying on her back on a slab of cold stone. "Where am I?" She wondered, looking around the room that seemed like a broom closet, and way above her head, up out of reach, a window loomed. I must be in that dreadful castle, Danae thought, shuddering.

"Hello," a voice spoke from the corner.

Danae looked over, and terror filled her eyes. "You're a demon from Lightning Hill!" She said, placing her fist against her chest and sliding backward upon the slab of stone until her back pressed against the wall.

"Mom-ster calls me 'Lizander.' You'll probably hate me, as she does, because I'm so boring, but she's never called me a demon before. I don't think that's what I am. I've been bruised and bloodied many times by her beatings, but demons are spirits without flesh that cannot be harmed, so that must not be what I am."

Danae didn't know what to think. "Then I'm sorry I called you that," she said at last. "I'm Danae, a shepherdess." She stared at the man creature, naked from the waist up, ragged burlap pants covering his lower extremities. Wavy black hair framed his face, and he peered at her with intelligent eyes. He looked like any other man, except for the reptilian wings with their crooked joint claws. Strangely, he was almost even handsome.

"No, you mustn't be a demon if you get bruised and bleed," Danae said. "Anyway, I hope that's not what you are."

Lizander laughed, something he rarely did except for the occasional fit of insanity. "I'm worse than anything; I'm so boring."

"You shouldn't say that," Danae said. "Those aren't nice words."

Lizander tilted his head, surveying Danae quizzically. One of his talons had accidentally shredded the top of her bodice. Her braid had come undone in the wind, and her auburn hair flowed over her shoulders in waves. How different she seemed than his mother — such kindness in her face, as if she didn't want to hurt him or anyone. He gazed into her sea green eyes, and immediately, he wanted nothing else in life but to possess her heart.

"I hear talking in there!" The witch's husky voice sounded from behind the closed door.

"That's Mom-ster," Lizander spoke with urgency. "She told me to tell her when you awoke. I must go and do so." He hastened out the door, his wings following after.

Seconds later, the door opened, and the witch entered the room.

"Well now, what have we here?" The witch swaggered over to Danae, still bewildered, resting on the slab of stone. "Are you a whore?" The witch asked, glaring down at the girl with eyes colder than ice.

Danae flinched at the shocking question. "No, Ma'am!" She said. "That would make Father cross. I must be getting home to him at once."

Eying the open door, Danae scooted forward on the stone.

The witch grabbed Danae beneath her chin, wrenching up her heart-shaped face. "You'd better not be lying to me," she said through shriveled lips, her eyes slitting with inquisition.

"Sometimes I tell lies, but I'd never lie about that!" Danae said, choking within the witch's hold, trying to pry away her iron grip.

The witch studied the girl, her eyes narrowing further. "What I want to know is, could you pet a unicorn?"

"I can and have, but only once when I met one at the brook." Danae choked and sputtered.

"Good. Good!" The witch grinned, releasing Danae from her grasp and placing her hands upon her hips. "That better be true, Toots, for if you're lying to me, I'll chain you up by your toes in the dungeon and let the rats gnaw off that pretty face!"

Danae gasped in horror then began to cry. "You must be a wicked woman to say such things. I want to go home now!" She scrambled toward the door, but the witch, well-nourished by black magic, knocked her back against the wall with the strength of a lumberjack. Danae crashed against the quarried rock, hitting her head and knocking the breath from her body. She collapsed onto the stone slab, her eyes hazing over then closing, her head falling to the side until her cheek rested against the cold stone.

"You ain't going nowhere, Toots!" The witch said. Then her head rocked back with laughter.

Several hours later Danae awoke, head throbbing, body stiff. She groaned and opened her eyes. As she stirred, Lizander moved forward from the shadows, where he'd sat in wait of her revival. From a wooden table, he retrieved a sponge from a bowl of cool water, wrung it out then swabbed Danae's temples.

"Mom-ster is mad at you, so you won't get any supper tonight," Lizander said as if he cared. "You tried to run away from the castle, and she hates that. She wants to keep you here, forever, to help her with her witchcraft. So many advanced spells require the blood or hair of a virgin. I hope you won't get bald too quickly," he laughed weakly. "Mom-ster gets terribly greedy about necromancy. She's already snipped off one piece of your hair already. Whatever you do, try not to bore her."

Danae clutched the sides of her head. "I'm not going to help her do anything!" She said, keeping her voice low, rising to a seated position.

"Mom-ster must make sure you're not lying about being a virgin. It's dangerous to cast spells with ingredients that are supposed to be from a virgin but really aren't. I think she plans to start with one of the simpler of the advanced incantations, just as a test trial."

Danae gazed into Lizander's dark eyes, wondering if she should try to befriend him. Though the witch was mean, she was his mother, so that would be a difficult task, Danae supposed. She couldn't imagine doing anything to betray her Father, her only family. "Will you be my friend?" She asked, daring to be brave. "Help me escape from out that window, and I'll tell you the secret of where to find a hidden peach grove that bears the most delicious fruit!" Her eyes pleaded with him wildly.

Lizander's eyes gleamed for a moment, but then a look of sadness filled them. "I must keep you from escaping. Mom-ster would destroy me."

"What's going on in there?" The witch said, throwing open the wooden door with a crash. "Awake from your little nap, Toots?"

The witch had changed into a blouse of see-through lavender, her dark hair streaming down her back. She sauntered forward, her black boots clicking along the floor. She grinned at Danae's frightened face. "Bring her into the great hall. She can sit in the corner while we feast." The witch turned to Danae. "Try to run away again, Toots, and I'll blast a fire ball right through that belly." She poked her fingernail rather painfully into Danae's abdomen, causing her to wince.

The great hall was not as grand as Danae had expected. A chandelier of crude metal, looking more like a torture device than a light fixture, fitted with many candles, hung down from the ceiling. Several unlit torches protruded from the walls, on one of which hung a very large mirror. The table had been set with two cracked plates, drinking goblets, and silverware, and a platter of mutton and bitter herbs steamed atop a placemat beside a wine bottle. Outside, evening was shifting into night, and had there been any crickets near the castle, they would have just begun to sing.

The witch poured herself a glass of wine then sat at the head of the table.

"Fetch my plate, Lizander."

Lizander hastened to the platter and cut off several slivers of rare mutton. He added a forkful of seasoned greens before hurrying back to the witch with her portions.

Sitting on the dusty floor, back against the wall, Danae eyed the doorway of the castle with longing as the witch slurped up her food, slobbered down her wine, and belched loudly. She wanted to flee for her life, but fear kept her motionless.

"Can I give Danae a cup of water, Mom-ster?"

"Who?" The witch looked up from her plate, wiping her greasy mouth with her hand.

"Danae." Lizander motioned toward her. "We mustn't let her juices get depleted."

"Oh, Toots. Very well," the witch said, licking a stained finger.

After the witch and Lizander had finished supper and the kitchen utensils were cleared away, the witch slammed down a fat and antiquated spell book onto the table. With the tip of a fingernail, she peeled back the pages to the end of the book. "Aha!" She said. "Chapter Thirty: Spells to be Used with Virgins!"

The witch ran her fingernail down the columns of each yellowing page, turning one after another. "No," she'd mutter, "not that one," considering then rejecting each spell. "Aha!" She said at last. "Doctored Disguises. Perfect!" She rubbed her hands together then placed the thin strip of Danae's hair in the crevice of the book like a marker. "I've had black hair long enough, and now it's gotten boring. Maybe I should try... orange! Orange with golden sparkles!" The witch's crazed eyes fluttered about the room as she imagined the grandeur of the change.

Lizander, who'd learned enough about necromancy to know what came next, fetched a bowl from the cupboards. He retrieved from the herb and potion racks several dusty bottles full of foul elixirs. Meanwhile, the witch took up her measuring spoon, pouring into the bowl the proper portions. "Fetch me some thistle," the witch asked Lizander, and he complied. "A pinch of wormwood!" She commanded, and he hastened to the task.

The witch shredded a bit of Danae's hair into the bowl with a pair of scissors, completing her sludgy porridge. Danae gazed, wide-eyed, as the witch picked up the bowl and peered down into it with savor. Eerily luminescent, the brew ignited the hollows of her visage, giving it a skull-like appearance so that she looked like death itself. Pink steam hissed off the surface of the pending spell, waiting for the witch to drink. Finally, she did. Danae watched her Adam's apple bob as she guzzled, two streams of brown liquid trickling down either side of her mouth. The witch swallowed hard as if the taste were difficult even for her practiced tongue.

The concoction entered her bloodstream, energy seized her, and her eyes rolled back. She ran around and around the kitchen table, shrieking. "Doctored Disguise!" She screamed the spell's name, "Give me orange hair with sparkles of fire!"

BORED WITCH

The witch buckled over, her body shaking and smoking. An explosion rocked the castle. Soot stung Danae's eyes. She coughed into her sleeve, choking.

When Danae looked up, the witch was swatting at the air to dissipate the putrid cloud. Then, "Doom-da-la-boom!" She declared with a wave of her arm. The rest of the lingering smoke disappeared out the window with a rush of air, rustling the cobwebs.

The witch stood before the mirror, hanging along the wall. "I'm beautiful!" She clasped her hands together, gasping at the glass as if she would never forgive herself for looking so good. "I won't be bored for a very long time! And curls!" She spoke with astonishment and glee, running her stained fingers through the ringlets. "I didn't even ask for curls. This spell works better than I'd imagined. Why didn't I get a virgin sooner?"

That night the witch locked Danae in a room on the second story, vacant but for a bed of stale hay. The only window was barred and the lock impossible, Danae discovered, fighting with the latch until her fingers bled. The thought of her poor father searching the woods and fields for her kept the tears coursing down her cheeks as she paced her cell, alone in the dark, clouds outside the castle blotting out every star as silent lightening scratched the night sky, ripping across the blackness. Finally, exhausted and hopeless, she sunk onto the straw and fell asleep.

The next day the witch kept Danae busy in the kitchen, stirring a bubbling cauldron and mixing potions to keep the shelves stocked for magical needs. Not as angry as the day before, the witch allowed Danae bread crusts with her water. "Cheer up, Toots," she'd tell her. "Keep that chin up," she'd say, grabbing Danae beneath her heart-shaped face and placing her own visage so close that the poor girl thought the witch wanted to kiss her. "You'd better not bore me, or else!" She'd warn, lifting high her palm to speed a fire ball out the window. Danae tried not to cry at such horrors.

Later that day Lizander returned from the village with a squealing piglet, which he prepared for supper, as industrious with his cuisine as his mother was with her spell craft. Yet that night, just as before, as he and the witch supped at the table, Danae sat on the floor against the wall, her peasant's dress getting dirty and ragged. She nibbled bread and sipped water from a cracked cup, not daring to refuse what little nourishment the witch offered, for she'd warned her about ingratitude, saying, "You'd better appreciate my scraps, Toots, or else!"

After the witch had eaten and Lizander had cleared the table, the witch stood before the mirror, studying her reflection. "What shall I change next?" She scrutinized her image. "My hair is perfect. What now?" She pondered then snapped her fingers. "My eyes!" She blinked at her lash-less image. "For hundreds of years my eyes have been the same color, and now I hate my boring, blue eyes!" She stomped her foot, wrinkled her nose, and clenched her fists with loathing. "I want dark, exotic eyes with long, luscious lashes!" She declared, head knocked back and arms held high as if she intended to puck them down from the ceiling.

Off of the shelf and onto the table came her fat book of spells with a thump. Bottles clinked together, forming a congregation. "Jezebel Root, Hoo Doo Elixir, Mojo Beans, Tincture of Devil's Shoestring," the witch read from the spell book, sending Lizander scurrying back and forth, to and fro from the spell racks to the table. "Maguey Bundle, Vervain, Vandal Root," the witch went on, measuring herbs and tonics.

The witch stirred the thickening concoction. Ready for the final ingredient, she picked up the scissors and snipped away at the end of Danae's lock of hair. After stirring, she lifted the bowl to her face. She breathed the pink mist smoking from the surface, her eyes closing. She drank, Adam's apple bobbing, drips oozing down her chin.

The witch ran around and around the table, strawberry blond ringlets spiraling out as she turned corners. "Doctored Disguise!" She screamed the spell's name, "Give me big, dark, beautiful, doe's eyes!"

The witch buckled over, her body shook, and the room smoked. Danae covered her nose as the explosion shook the castle. Soot stung her eyes, and the witch cackled with glee. "Doom-da-la-boom!" She cried, whipping the smoke with a kitchen towel as the air rushed through the castle, removing the smolder and upsetting the cobwebs.

The witch approached the looking glass, and her mouth fell open. "I'm beautiful! Beautiful!" She batted her long lashes, turning from side to side to admire the view. She undid an extra button of her blouse, pushing up her cleavage. "Woo Hoo!" She cried, leaning back again and laughing. "I'm so sexy!" She sauntered toward Danae. "Look at me now, Toots! I'm gorgeous with my perfect hair and beautiful eyes. And you thought you were so pretty. Hah!" The witch chuckled then strutted back toward the mirror.

That night Danae cried into the dingy straw of her tiny cell on the second story. "I'll never get out of this castle! I'll never see Father again!"

A knock sounded on the door. "Who is it?"

"Lizander. May I come in?"

"Yes." Danae wiped her eyes.

Lizander opened the door. "I brought you soap and a bucket of water to sponge bathe. And would you like some leftovers from supper?"

"That's very kind." Danae reached for his offering, which he pushed through the doorway. "Help me escape!"

"You know I can't do that." Lizander ducked his head. "Momster would destroy me—and you too, probably."

"Please help me!" Danae clutched his hand.

"I must go now! I hear her coming! She'd be bored to see us talking!" The door locked shut.

A week passed. The witch spent her time walking about her luxurious coffin-chamber, admiring her image in her many mirrors. There on the upper level, among the colorful tapestries, she dressed in gowns that hadn't left her closet for centuries. Even naked, she pranced about in high heeled slippers, their pink pom-poms jiggling in time with her breasts, flouncing her strawberry blond curls and batting her luscious lashes.

Then one morning she awoke feeling bored. Very bored. More bored than she'd ever felt before. More bored than the time she locked herself in a coffin for 120 years and didn't care to see daylight again. The charm of the spells was waning, and now she hated herself.

She tore at her hair, screaming, as if it were fire burning her. She wanted to scratch out those beautiful eyes, and would have if eyesight hadn't been so important. Choking on her sobs, tears streaming down her reddened cheeks, she rushed for a razor and hacked off her curls until she was just a bald woman, staring in the mirror. "At least now I only have beautiful eyes and not also beautiful hair. But I'm still bored!" She growled, her vampire blood churning. She stamped her foot. "How could I have been so stupid as to only think of beauty? I've made a fool of myself." She ripped at her red silk gown and threw her pink pumps out the window.

Bald, naked, and beautiful-eyed, the witch sat in a chair, gazing out the window at the yellow grass on the hillside, the towering pines in the distance. She tapped her discolored nails upon the sill. Then her lips curled into a wicked grin. "Evil," she whispered to herself philosophically. "The answer is evil. That is the solution to my problem."

It occurred to the witch that the most exciting times in her life had also been the most evil, from harvesting babies for blood cocktails to breeding her son from the dragon. "I know what I'll do," she said. "I'll cast a spell so diabolical, the mere memory of it will entertain my thoughts forever. I'll feel excitement every time I reminisce about it." She chortled, raking the air with her nails in anticipatory ecstasy. "Yes!" She hissed. "Why didn't I think of evil sooner? I've been a very silly witch," she giggled, raising two fingers to her lips as if timid about a belch. Then she hurled herself down the stairs for the spell book.

That night at supper, as she sat on the floor against the wall, Danae noted the witch's baldness but, of course, said nothing. Yet toward the end of the meal, Lizander inquired. "Mom-ster, whatever happened to your beautiful hair? Did the spell wear away?"

"No, idiot! I shaved my head. My beautiful hair got boring."

"You still have beautiful eyes, Mom-ster."

"I hate my eyes, stupid!" She slammed her fist onto the table, jittering the dinnerware.

Lizander flinched. "I'll never mention it again."

The witch grew calm. "Thankfully, I've thought of a spell that will amuse me forever, so I'll never feel bored again. I'll need a cup of virgin's blood, which I'll get from Danae. The other ingredients I have here in the castle, except for Devil's Breath, a rare weed that grows in the forest and which I'll hunt for this evening. Tomorrow night you'll help me cast the spell."

"Are you going to tint your lips violet, Mom-ster?"

The witch's eyes shriveled into useless holes as she moved beyond anger. "No, fool! I'll rain down fire and brimstone on the village and destroy all the people!"

Lizander's mouth fell open. "Surely, Mom-ster, you wouldn't enact a deed so heinous."

"Surely, I would!" The witch said. "And that's just what I am going to do."

"Please," Danae said, rushing forward from the shadows, cobwebs in her hair, to beg at the witch's feet. "Don't do that! Father is down in the valley, and my sheep, and in the village, kittens and puppies and pet monkeys, and all the people I love: Patar the bard, and Drad the farmer, and Miss Prissa the school mistress, and Mr. Alvesso the blacksmith, and Mr. Verna the baker, and Mrs. Moyd the seamstress, and Jackimo the juggler. Oh, please!"

"Now, I wouldn't hurt poor Jackimo, would I?" The witch said, grinning. "You better stop trying my patience, Toots, or else! She turned to Lizander. "Take her upstairs, and lock her up. I'm sick of her whimpering."

Lizander left his plate unfinished. "Come along now, Danae." He helped her off the floor. "We mustn't displeasure Mom-ster." He walked behind her up the stairs as the witch affixed a kerchief to her head and began fishing through the closet for her walking stick.

Lizander and Danae arrived at the door of her cell. "Please help me escape!" She whispered. "I must warn the villagers!"

"Hush." Lizander placed a finger to his mouth. "We mustn't speak in the hallway. If Mom-ster hears us, that will bore her. Let's step inside and shut the door." And so they did.

Danae clutched his arm. "I can't bear to have Father and all the townspeople destroyed. We mustn't let her cast that spell. We have to stop her!"

"You must love your father and the village very much. But I can do nothing to hinder Mom-ster. Her powers are too incredible."

"Why can't you?" Danae asked, her hands balling up with rage. She struck his chest. "This is your fault!" She pelted him, one punch after another. "If you hadn't brought me to this awful place, none of this would be happening! You're the one to blame! I hate you!"

Lizander crumpled to the floor in a heap. He quivered, wretched sobs escaping him.

Danae knelt beside him. "I'm sorry," she said. "I didn't mean to hurt you." She touched his back between his shriveled wings.

Lizander rose to his knees. His head rolled back, tears coursing down his cheeks, his expression tortured. "You're right. It's my fault. I'm horrible, boring, and I don't blame you for hating me. I hate myself!" He clenched his teeth. I'll never possess her heart, he thought.

"I don't hate you," Danae said, "I just desperately need your help."

Lizander stopped crying. "There is something we could do that might thwart Mom-ster's plans, but I doubt you'd be willing to do it." He averted his gaze.

"Tell me what it is?"

And so Lizander did, leaning over and whispering his plan into her ear.

The witch walked down Lightning Hill, passing into the forest, searching. She crept on all fours like a wolf, sniffing the ground, hunting, her vampire blood pumping. Beneath a dead oak, she found a clump of Devil's Breath. Choking with glee, she hurried back to the castle.

The following evening after supper, the witch grabbed Danae from her place along the floor, spilling her cup of water and sending her bread crusts flying. "Come, Toots! It's time for your blood-letting."

"Leave me alone!" She said. "Let the villagers be!"

The witch ignored her protest. "Leave that carving knife and wine goblet on the table," she told Lizander as he was clearing the table. "And fetch my spell book."

"Yes, Mom-ster," Lizander replied, and even bowed a little, which was more than his usual custom.

The witch grabbed Danae by one arm, holding her wrist over the empty wine goblet. She took up the rusty knife and cut Danae's flesh, causing her to wince. Blood welled up around the wound, forming a crimson band of liquid that dripped down into the goblet. Slowly, the chalice filled to the rim. The witch wrapped the wound with a strip of clean linen.

"Anise Star!" She said to Lizander, already rushing to the table with the spell bowl. "Colt's foot! Dog's grass! Master of the Woods," she listed each ingredient as Lizander sped back to the spell racks for sacks of dried herbs and bottles of potion.

In no time the witch had finished mixing the foul concoction, complete with Danae's blood. She lifted the brew to her nose, sniffing the purplish vapor. "Ah," she breathed in the putrid fumes. "Won't this be delicious?"

Danae, uncertain what would happen next, heart pumping wildly, backed up against the wall. Lizander drew near her until he stood just an arm's distance away.

In mad, gluttonous gulps the witch slobbered down her stew. "Ah!" She exclaimed, setting the empty bowl back on the table. "Dire Destruction!" She said, head tilted upward, arms lifted. "Destroy the village with fire!"

The witch didn't laugh. Her smile failed. A worried gleam flooded her eyes. She coughed, lurched over to vomit, but nothing came from her throat. Bewildered dismay crossed her face, one hand at her throat, the other cupping her belly. Her eyes rose to Danae and Lizander as they stood against the wall like two school children, waiting in line for class.

"You!" The witch rasped, pointing at Lizander, her face drying and wrinkling. "What have you done? You wicked creature! I know what you've done! I know what you've done! When did you do it? You knew it would kill me! And you!" She looked at Danae. "You whore! You whore! You filthy little whore!"

Danae covered her mouth and giggled. Lizander laughed too, not a sick laugh as in a fit of insanity, but a healthy laugh that signals freedom and victory.

"Sorry, Mother. You were growing dull." He put his arm around Danae.

"You were just too boring!" Danae stuck her neck out.

The witch continued crumbling, disintegrating into dust. Soon she was nothing but a puddle of ashes.

A cool breeze rushed through the castle and carried the cinders away. The clouds outside lifted, letting in moon and starlight, and crickets began to sing. Danae fell, sobbing with relief, into Lizander's embrace. "Your father and the villagers are safe," he said, holding her and stroking her auburn hair.

The next spring, Danae gave birth to a beautiful baby girl. Her hair was black and wavy like her father's, but she didn't have the wings of a dragon. Only two pink stubs protruded from her back near the collarbones. She had her mother's heart-shaped face, and her mother's heart as well, Lizander came to think.

Daisies, foxgloves, bluebonnets, yarrow! Passing travelers marveled at the beauty of the wildflowers growing on Lightning Hill, which no longer thundered with lightning, except for the occasional rain shower. Lizander gave Danae the whole castle and all the treasure his mother had stolen from the dragon. He kept for himself the only thing he'd ever wanted: Danae's heart.

The Morrigan Sisters

Amber Davis

They came when we were not expecting it, when the night was full and heavy with fog.

I awake to the screams, chaos and confusion reigning in the village, and I burst from my blankets to grab up my sword. My sister Brendolyn is at my side as I reach the door, her own weapon in hand.

I throw open the barrier and we are met with smoke, fire and the resounding clash of swords against swords. The fog is tainted orange from the inferno that consumes the main hall and sleeping houses. People scream as tall men, painted blue for battle, surge through the mist, cutting down anyone in their path. Men and women are slain, children scooped up and carried off, their cries echoing in the dark.

"Aife, watch out!" Bren cries, and I duck the blow of a sword just in time. The warrior comes at me again, and this time, I match his swing with my own. Brendolyn jumps in, and together we overwhelm the brute, strike him down as one.

We have always fought best when we are together.

"What're they doin' here?" She gasps the moment our enemy falls. "Who are they?"

"I don' know," I pant. I see another warrior of our own get slain, and the blood in my veins boil. "But they made a mistake comin' 'ere."

We charge across the square of grass, past fallen bodies and into the smoke and fog, choking for air. Bren pulls to a stop and as I bump into her, she spins. Her sword flashing in the dim light, and she blocks a blow from behind that had been destined for my skull. I turn out from beneath her, swinging my own sword. We are surrounded by four warriors, and they are closing in. We stand back to back as they come at us; she swings up as I swing down, blocking, slashing and jabbing.

Bren lets out a harsh laugh, but then it's cut off as something heavy knocks us both to the ground. My sword slips from my hand, the world spinning from the impact as my skull cracks against the hard ground beneath me, the gritty soil muffling my cry. Suddenly the weight lifts off my body, and as if from a great distance, a ringing scream reaches my ears.

Through the fog invading my mind, I recognize Brendolyn's voice.

"Let me go! Aife!" Against the force spinning my head, I try to sit up. A wide figure drags a smaller one away into the midst of the tumult.

"Bren. No…" I heave myself to my knees. He has my sister! I am about to stand when a sharp kick to my ribs bowls me over and pain explodes though my side, making me gasp and gape breathlessly. I feel something cold touch my knuckles – my sword. I grab it and swing – striking my attacker in the leg. He falls with a grunt.

I roll away, holding my side as if keeping pieces of myself together. A chorus of screams and shouts rises up. Dozens of people are running across the square in a blind panic – right through me. I cry out, but they trample me, and the world goes dark…

I wake slowly, the throbbing in my head nearly unbearable as light pierces my eyes and I groan. A cot creaks beneath me, and I wonder how I got there. The last thing I remember is Bren being carried off… "Bren," I cry.

"Easy," says a low voice as cool water sprinkles my face and trickles past my cracked lips. "You gave yer father a right good scare. Was 'bout ready to gut someone fer ya."

Gulping, I try opening my eyes once again. The glaring of the light fades, and I can see the face looming over me. Long, plaited grey hair tickles high cheeks, and clear green eyes peer down at me over a crooked nose pierced with a boar's tooth. "Iwan?"

A corner of his mouth pulls up, widening the wrinkles around his eyes. "Figured ya wanted to see a friendly face when ya woke."

"Don' flatter yerself," I mutter, and he laughs. I sit up, and he puts a hand on my arm. Flashes of the night before fly from my mind. "What happened? Bren-"

"Aife, I'm sorry about yer sister," he interrupts, not meeting my eyes.

"Iwan. What happened ta her?"

His head hangs from his shoulders. "T'was the Cruithni. They attacked us, middle o' the night, tha cowards. Killed many, took many. Yer sister among 'em."

A pit opens up in my chest. The Cruithni are ruthless, battle-hungry and never satisfied with their spoils. Fierce and murderous, they are. There is no doubt that Bren, and the others who were taken, are better off dead than with the Cruithni.

"They take anythin' else, 'sides our people?"

Iwan shakes his head. "Nay. They were fought off 'fore they could find tha main hall."

"So our people're slaughtered, but our treasure is secure," I say, a bitter taste on my tongue. I would trade all the gold in the world to have my sister by my side again. Iwan grunts, and we fall into silence. I wonder if he could have predicted this, Iwan. He is the druid of our village and works closely with our leader and the most seasoned warrior in the clan, my father. I am Iwan's apprentice, learning to become a druidess – but I had not envisioned this either. I mull over the possibility of any way this could have been avoided.

"There's no changin' what's happened, Aife," Iwan says, standing up to pace. We are in a small building, one of the structures on the outskirts of the village; the walls are hung with hundreds of bundles of herbs and leaves, and dry oak branches dangle from the ceiling. Sunlight pours in from the open doorway. This is Iwan's home, and it had somehow escaped the fires from last night. It is familiar to me; all the days I can remember were spent here. If any house deserves to stand, it is this one.

I begin to rise, but a low ache in my side makes me grimace. Iwan hovers, but I wave him off. "I'm fine."

Someone comes to the door. "Is she awake?"

Rogan. My heart swell at the sight of him, and when his dark eyes meet mine, some of the weight that has been squeezing the air from my lungs is lifted. A fresh wound cuts down the side of his otherwise handsome face, but a greyish salve has been pressed into it, dulling the crimson blood that graces his cheek.

"Aife," he breathes, and in two strides is holding me against him. "Yer alive, thank Lugus."

"Rogan," Iwan greets him, and Rogan releases his hold on me to grasp hands with the druid. They are uncle and nephew. "Is e'rone else cared fer?"

"Aye, treated Padraig not a moment ago. 'E insisted on bein' the last one."

Panic sweeps in. "Is Da hurt?"

"Mere scratches," Rogan reassures me. "After fightin' as many battles as he, one comes near untouchable."

I sigh with relief, thankful that I have one less person of my family to worry over. Reaching up, my fingertips touch the wound on Rogan's face. His eyes close and his lips graze my palm.

"I worried fer ya," he whispers.

"Ain't I still 'ere?"

"If ya two're goin' ta get talkin' like that, ye can 'least take it outside," Iwan grumbles, shaking his head and fussing over a salve in the mixing bowl.

Rogan laughs. "Poor ol' fool. Ain't ne'er been in love b'fore in his life."

I can't help the smile that creeps onto my face before burying it in Rogan's tunic.

At sunhigh, my father calls a gathering of his advisors into the great hall. Smoke tingles my nostrils when I walk into the blackened building. The fire had been put out before too much damage was inflicted. I am the last one to arrive, but the gathering has already begun.

"We need to retaliate!" Ferguson paces before the chair where my father sits, anger lacing his every move. He strikes out and knocks a goblet off the grand oak table, sending it and its contents spilling across the floor. "They struck cos we were complacent! We must avenge our loss, take back what is ours!"

His words ring off the walls of the main hall, and my jaw clenches as I take my seat. The ache in my head returns.

"I don' disagree with ya," my father replies slowly, fingers running through his streaked beard. "But we don' have the strength. They reduced us to 'alf our numbers in a single plight. How're we goin' te fight an entire clan when we are so badly wounded an' outnumbered?"

Ferguson scoffs, his rage boiling over again as he flings another goblet across the room.

"Trust me, brother," hisses Da as he stands, towering in his great height and menacing with the sword marks and scars across his arms. "I want revenge just as much as ya do, but I must think of ta safety o' our people first. We ain't goin' ta survive if we fight again so soon."

Iwan speaks up, his voice low, "Padraig, I cannot forsee anythin' fer our victory. The gods have forsaken us ta this slaughter. I ain't heard from dem in days."

I frown. I had not predicted any of this, but surely a fight so devastating to the lives of our people would have come in a dream or vision to Iwan? Yet there had been nothing. I've been training to consult smaller spirits, while Iwan consults the greater ones. He never told me they were not speaking back. "Forsaken us?"

"Aye," he replies, pushing off the wall across from me, twirling an oak twig between his fingers. He does not meet my eyes, but looks to my father. "They don' answer my prayers, and I ain't had any dreams since te full moon. I believe they have abandoned us."

"Then we ought to beseech them," I return. "There has te be one – just one, who'll be willin' te help us."

"Bah!" Ferguson scoffs, his face twisted with disgust. In that moment, despite being my father's brother, he looks nothing like the man, his features coarse and ugly unlike my Da's gentle brow and clear eyes. "Ya speak of the gods as if they give a fig about us. Well, I tell ya, they 'bandoned us a long time ago. No use tryina seek 'em now."

"What other choice do we 'ave?" I ask. "B'sides sittin' 'ere and let the Cruithni carry off our people, or get ourselves killed te get them back. I hear the Great Queens ain't above a bargain er two-"

"Absolutely not."

I look at my father. "Da…"

"No." He rises from his chair, jaw set and fists clenched. "I know what yer thinkin', Aife, an' I won' let ya do it."

"Da, ya don' know-"

"Ya ain't seekin' the Morrigan!"

I expel a forceful breath to calm myself. "Da, if ya would just listen, ya would see reason."

"Reason?" He says softly. His eyes are sad, and I know he is seeing me as the small child he had raised after Ma died, and I knew he is seeing my sister being dragged away by the Cruithni. "Ye'd be chasin' a ghost, Aife. No one's seen the Morrigan sisters an' lived, and I wouldn't want ya ta be the one ter find 'em. They bring nothin' but trouble, the hags. And… and I ain't losin' me other daughter."

"I have te do somethin'," I practically beg. That hole is opening up in my chest again. I know he doesn't want to lose me, much like I don't want to lose him. But if we do nothing, Brendolyn will be gone for good. "Tis my fault Bren was taken. I owe it te her te try. Please, Da."

He gulps, then looks at Iwan. "You know more 'bout ta gods than I. What's yer say in this?"

Iwan says nothing, but clamps a hand on my shoulder and pierces me with his stare. He has given me the look before – when I cast a spell wrong, or forget an ingredient to a salve. He wants an explanation.

"Bren an' near half our people're gone or dead. If I can get the Morrigan ta help us, ta be on our side, then we'd be near unstoppable." I look at my father, at Ferguson seething on the edge of the room, and finally back at the man who'd taught me everything I know. "Tha Morrigan're haggish, but they ain't pitiless."

"That might be so," Iwan says slowly, "but they ain't generous, either. They'll want somethin' of ya. Least of all, yer life. There ain't ne'er reasonin' with 'em."

I stamp my foot, feeling like a scolded child. "If it means helpin' with this fight an' gettin' our people back, then I'm willin' ta give it."

Everyone is silent after that. Finally Da sets his hand on my other shoulder, a sad smile across his face. "Never was in yer spirit te give up, I know. Yer sister's the same way. As was yer ma." I nod, and he continues. "All I can ask is that ye come back in one piece."

I nod again. "I will, Da. Ye have my word."

He embraces me swiftly. "You ought ta get ready, then. I'll leave ya to it."

And with that, he walks away, gnarled fingers combing his beard and eyes on the floor. Iwan squeezes my shoulder and offers a wan grin. We leave the main hall.

Rogan is outside waiting, and comes up to us once we are past the doors. "What happened? Are we goin' ta fight or what?"

"I'll let ya two discuss it, then," Iwan says, heading off through the burned ruins of the village toward his home. "Aife, when yer done, I'll help ya prepare."

Rogan looks at me. "Prepare fer what?"

I am almost ashamed for leaving. But I have to do this, I need to. I owe it to my people, to my sister. So I straighten my shoulders and say, "We cannot fight the Cruithni on our own, so I'm goin' ta find tha Morrigan sisters and ask fer their help."

"The Morrigan?" His voice drops and his dark brows pull together. "Are ya serious?"

"Do ya think I would be lyin' about this?" I shake my head, tugging on my tunic, but Rogan grasps my hands. I meet his gaze, but he is not angry, perhaps worried. "I'll be back on the morrow. The Paps're less den a day's ride. If I leave now, I can make b'fore sundown."

His eyes roam my face as he says, "Be careful, me love."

"Everyone says that," I tease. "I don' know why."

He gives my cheek a kiss. "Cos we know ya, Aife. Ya only think after all the fightin's over."

I squeeze his hands before leaving him next to the main hall.

"An'... that should be all." Iwan pats the straps of leather tethering my supplies to the horse, a black mare. He gives me a once over as I swing on the black hooded cloak. "Yer sure ya don' want me to come with ya?"

"Aye." I climb onto the beast, patting her mane. "Padraig needs ya here. B'sides, we cannot spare a person. I can do this meself."

Iwan nods. "Then good luck to ya. And may tha Morrigan be merciful."

I take off on the mare, heading north to the Paps of Morrighan, where the goddesses are often told to be found. It is my best chance of finding them. If I cannot meet them with my eyes, I will pray and summon them using a spell. That's what Iwan had packed for me.

It takes the better part of the day to reach the bottom of the crest of hills, flying over moorland and grass fields and through sparse wood, and by then, the sun is near ready to set. I tie up my horse beside a stream and look around; the trees are closer together here than they were while I rode. I will have to search on foot, so I untie the satchel from the horse and quickly follow the stream up into the hills.

The farther I walk, the more I wonder how I will ever find them, or if they even want to be found. What if Da was right, and I'm only chasing a ghost? A phantom, an imagination? Then all this is for naught, and I am wasting my time.

I pull to a stop, doubt and despair gurgling inside of me like poison. Flashes of memory come at me then, vivid and clear as the water in the stream. The fires of the attack, the men carrying off my sister like a bag of meat, being trampled under the feet of terrified people. My resolve is made up. I am going to find the Morrigan if it's the last thing I do.

All night long, I trek all across those hills; I cry out to them, pray to them, but there is no sign. Neither raven feather, nor footprint. The sisters are nowhere to be seen. I search well on into the night, when the sliver of a moon is rising and barely piercing the veil of tree cover. I pull a candle and flint from my satchel and, once I have light enough to see, painstakingly make my way through the woods. It is time for a spell.

I have saved this as a last resort. Spell casting is dangerous, and without proper training or the added Magick of a cingulum cord, the energy drain from a summoning spell can easily kill a person, druid or not.

It is difficult with the little light that I have, but I eventually find a thicket of young oak trees with a small clearing in the center. It is so small, that if I stretch my arms out, I can touch the saplings on either side of me. But it will have to do. Using a fallen oak branch, I cast my circle, calling to the North, the East, the South and the West. My white candle sits in the middle of the drawn circle, and I pull out the dried sage, my cingulum cord, and a small, stone blade from my satchel.

With the cord draped over my neck, I prick my finger with the blade, the drops of blood falling around the candle. A slight hum vibrates the air. I take in a breath and say to the night, "With deepest love an' respect, I invite inta this circle o' the four ancient elements, the illuminatin' radiance o' tha Morrigan. O great ancient ones, I call upon thy presence, mysterious an' divine, ta be wit me now in this space an' time, ta witness, protect, and guide tis witch's rite of Magick. So mote it be."

I hold my breath, and...

Silence.

Nothing stirs in the woods around me except the softest breeze in the leaves overhead. I shake my head once, nearly all of my energy drained by the spell. And yet, I must have done something wrong, said something wrong – they are not here! The heavy weariness falls on me completely then, and I head back to my horse. I must try again in the morning. I will try until it works. I have no other choice. When I drag myself back, the mare has settled down, and I sit beside her; sleep comes over me quickly, trumping my defeated thoughts.

It takes me several heartbeats to realize there is something wrong when I awake. Where there had been heavy breathing from the animal beside me, there is now silence. Not even birdsong reaches my ears. And I feel someone watching me.

Scrambling, I grab my sword from its hilt and stand.

And that is when I see the raven, perched atop the body of my horse, now dead. My chest rises and falls alarmingly fast, and I scramble back from the scene. The raven watches me curiously, tilting its head to one side, and then the other. One of its eyes is cloudy, like it is blind. It seems to be gloating, as if laughing at my distress.

I stare. No, it can't be...

"A-are you tha Morrigan?" I gasp, then bite my tongue for sounding so foolish. But the bird simply leans forward, as if to speak. I step in – and shriek when it erupts in a cawing fury of black feathers, flying a breath away from my face. I throw up my hands, but the bird does not touch me save for the caress of feathers on my palms. And then all is still. I look around, but the bird is gone.

"For a druidess, you are not very bright."

I start at the coarse voice, whirling to find a woman standing before me. Her hair is a flaming red, and her eyes so pale that they are nearly white. She wears robes and leathers so black, they seem to meld together; the raven is perched on her shoulder, beady eyes still watching me.

"You..."

"Yes," she interrupts, walking towards me. She rolls her eyes. "We are what ya mortals call the Morrigan, tha Queen o' Phantoms, Fate an' Death, an' whatever rubbish ya lot can come up with."

She sounds unimpressed, but I am still standing frozen in place, struck by the situation. My spell worked?

Her eyebrows rise as she looks at me. "Well spit it out. Ya got somethin' ta say, or ya jus' goin' ta stand there with yer mouth agape?"

My jaw snaps shut and I swallow, my hands beginning to quiver. "I came ta beseech you."

She sprawls against a fallen tree, the raven hopping off her shoulder to balance on an oak limb, both of them waiting.

"My village is a tribe o' da Dáirine clan, only a day's ride from 'ere," I explain, gaining confidence with each word. "We were attacked in our sleep, 'alf of our people taken prisoner or by death."

"And ya think I had somethin' ta do with'at?" She crows, offended. She stands, her eyes alight with fury. "You come 'ere lookin' to avenge yer dead an' gone? You thought that I'd-"

"No! No, I came seekin' yer aid."

She stops, perplexed.

"We are 'alf what we were two days ago. But we cannot get our people back without help," I explain. The raven bobs its head at me, as if to go on. "And no person born knows life and death like ya do. Please. We need yer help."

"And what does my help enlist?" She asks. Relief that she hasn't outright refused courses through me like blood.

"Just yer blessin' on our warriors, and victory on me people. We just want what is ours."

"And what of you?" The sister comes towards me once more, peering at me much like the raven had. A lock of fiery hair falls across her face. "Seldom does a born mortal care so little o' themselves as ta not ask me fer somethin' on them."

"Me sister was taken," I reply. "T'was my fault. That is why I need her back."

She nods, circling me slowly. I realize that I still have the sword in my hand, and sheathe it quickly. I need her to side with me, not find a reason to refuse me. She comes up behind me, clasping my arms tightly and whispering in my ear, "And what would ya give in return?"

"Anything... Does this mean yer goin' ta help me?"

She releases me, and I spin to face her. She only smiles and pulls on the hood of her robe; the seam is pointed like a raven's beak, casting a shadow across her face.

"Oh, I will do more'n that, my dear," she replies, her teeth glinting beneath the robe. Her hand snatches up mine and she turns it over. The wind begins to pick up, swirling the leaves beneath our feet, and the raven caws. "I am more'n simply the commander o' fate and lady over death. I am also the giver of live and o' Magick.

"I can give ya power beyond yer dreams, little druidess. You could be tha keeper o' souls, my right wing. I can make ya immortal. Ne'er be sick, ne'er be struck in battle. Yer enemies would lay slain on the field, and ya would be tha one t'escort 'em to the afterlife. Imagine savin' yer people without a scratch laid on ya."

I blink. I could save Bren? And no one of my village would have to be killed because I could take on the Cruithni. I could bring more than the Morrigan's blessing. I could do it.

"O' course," she continues, and I break out of my thoughts, "that sort of power does come with a wee price."

"I told ya," I say. "I'll pay anythin'."

Again, that brow goes up. "I haven' even told ya-"

"Anythin'. I ain't sayin' it again."

She purses her lips, but then they curl into a smile. She looks at the raven. "Babd, my dear…"

A flutter of wings sounds, and then human footsteps. An old woman stands where the raven had been not a heartbeat ago. One of her eyes is clouded and blind, but she stares at me all the same.

"Not tha smartest beastie I've seen," the hag croaks.

"But she is determined," the other replies. They are sisters made, not born. Both the Morrigan. Babd is the Raven, so the younger woman must be Nemain, Fury. They lay their hands on me as the wind swirls faster, howling and ripping at the trees until the air is thick with branches and dirt and alive in a sudden flurry around us. Where their hands touch me, a coldness sinks into my bones, and I gasp. It is a painful, agonizing cold, the kind where you just wish for the numbness to begin so you cannot feel it anymore. My body will not move. I cannot breathe…

But just as the edges of my vision begin turning black, a raging heat sparks in my chest and burns through me all the way to my fingertips and toes. My head falls back as a scream rips from my throat, and then – it is all gone. The ground greets me like an old friend.

A soft hand on my forehead rouses me from unconsciousness. I've had the strangest dream. I ought to tell Iwan…

"Do ya think it worked?" An old, dry voice asks.

Another replies, "I know it did. Otherwise, she would be dead. Er, more dead than she is."

More dead? My eyes open, and two faces peer down at me, one

old and haggard, and the other finely lined but still with youth in the eyes and lips. The Morrigan sisters. A gasp escapes me, and they smile. Babd has no teeth.

I force myself to sit up. The world seems to have gone wrong – orbs flit around in the air and colors are much brighter than they ought to be. Soft, ringing sounds like whispered songs reach my ears. A fiery heat seems to pulse under my skin, alive and breathing. "What's goin' on? What have ya done ta me?"

"Well if some person had not been so rushed as ta hurry this along, I might 'ave explained it to ya!" Nemain thumps me on the head, and I back away, rubbing my forehead. Then she grins. "How do ya feel?"

Despite the burning fire within, and the cold that had consumed my body hardly moments ago, I feel just fine. Grand, in fact. Like I can take on armies. "Good. Almost… powerful."

Babd cackles, a strangled noise that is all at once too harsh and too soft, like the rattle of dry bones. "Aye, tis workin' then."

"What is workin'?" I look at Nemain.

"Our price," she explains, pulling down her hood and letting her bright hair fall down past her waist. "T'was ta make ya like us. Our sister."

"Sister?" I stare at the two of them. "What can ya mean?"

"Immortal," Babd cackles again, sticking her good eye at me. "Powerful. You would complete us."

"The Hag," Nemain nods at Babd, who snorts, and then puts a hand on her own chest. "The Mother."

"An' tha Maiden." Babd strokes my arm with her twisted, bony finger, and a chill runs across my skin. "We were not complete b'fore. Powerful, aye, but not as powerful as could be."

I frown at the leaf-strewn ground beneath me. The leaves seem to flicker, like a dying source of light. "Ya mean ta say, that – that I'm…"

"A goddess-"

"Of War."

"War?" My head is reeling. This is not possible. All I wanted was to save my village and my people. I didn't ask for this. But… I had promised them anything.

Babd lets out another wicked giggle. "Oh, seems she ain't likin' what we done fer 'er. Tis too late now. Only way out is ta die at yer own hand."

My jaw clenches. I meet the old woman's gaze, and the laugh dies in her throat. "I ain't a coward. I ain't backin' out o' this."

Babd nudged Nemain. "Maybe she will be good fer it. She got a hot temperament, there."

I bite back a retort. She is right, and it reminds me of Rogan's words, Ya only think after all the fightin's over. Rogan. "Can… Can I still go back? Ta my life, I mean. Ta my family?"

They look at one another, but I already know the answer. I can't. I can save them, and I will. Over and over and over again, I will save them. But in the end, my place won't be with them. An overwhelming sense of loss floods over me, and it is like losing my sister again, but worse, so much worse. Like I am losing pieces of myself, and I can't bring them together to fit back in their places.

"Ya have ta know," Nemain says, her voice soft, "ya can be with 'em, but ya can never stay. It only gets harder the more ya cling ta yer old life."

Babd nods. "Mortals're weak, fragile. They drop like gnats, they do."

A tiny spark of hope flutters near my heart. So I can still be with Rogan, if I choose to. Things might be different, but we will find a way to make it work. I know we can – I believe it. I can still stay in the village with my father and sister, and I can teach Iwan what I learned. Oh, won't he be in for a surprise. I know the sisters were right; if I am immortal, then I will outlive everyone I love. But I will deal with the pain when it comes to me. For now, at the least, I can still be happy.

But I have to go back and right the wrongs done to my people.

"Ya said I would be able ta fight?" I ask, my fingers tracing the sword at my side. I suddenly itch to use it.

Nemain notices, a sly look crossing her face. "Aye. B'fore we go, formalities are yet ta be made. As ya know, she is Babd. I am Nemain. What is yer name, sister?"

"Aife."

"Aife is no more," Babd comes up from behind me. She and Nemain join hands, and they take either of mine. "Yer new name is Macha – you are Battle. An' together, we three're the Morrigan."

When I stride through the village, the sun is just setting, and yet everyone is still out. Many are rolling freshly cut logs towards burnt buildings and halls. Others are at the whetstone sharpening blades and swords. Others still run here and there, trundling their loads to different projects. I am not at first noticed, but then, the village is busy with rebuilding itself.

I stop at the edge of the square and look at the ravens perched on my shoulders. Babd on my right, Nemain on my left. I can tell them apart by the clouded eye on Babd and Nemain's shinier feathers, a sign of her relative youth. Nemain settles herself, her wickedly curved beak nipping at my ear, and Babd coos. I straighten and walk to the main hall, where I know my father will be.

Whispers and muted exclamations rise up as I walk, people sighting me and the birds on my shoulders. Perhaps news of my journey has spread. The heavy wooden door pulls open, easier than ever before. They said I will be strong; and in a shorter time than it had taken to ride, I had run from the Paps all the way home, the ravens flying overhead. I don't doubt the sisters. My sisters.

Padraig, Ferguson, Iwan and a few others – all seasoned warriors – are arranged around a table at the head of the room, talking to one another. They all look up when I enter.

"Aife," Da says, his voice echoing across the room. My heart swells as he stands from his chair and crosses the floor. He pulls up short when he sees the ravens. "Are those-?"

Babd and Nemain take off, flying up to roost in the rafters. Da looks back at me, eyes studying my face. He frowns. "Aife, you… there's somethin' different about ya."

But I ignore what he said and hug him, my face pressing into the coarse material of his tunic. To my relief, his arms wrap around me as well. Someone clears their throat, and we release each other. Ferguson has his arms crossed, casting glares at the black birds in the rafters.

"Aife, ya care ta explain what's goin' on 'ere an' why ya brought these animals inside?"

Fierce caws sound from both birds.

"They are not animals," I correct, feeling fiercely defensive myself. "They are Babd and Nemain."

"What can ya mean?" Padraig asks, and yet the confused look can't take away the love in his eyes. It hurts to see that now, because it means he will be hurt by my new choices of family.

"They are my sisters." The birds fly down and settle on my shoulders once again. I take a deep breath and add, "An' we are the Morrigan."

"You?" I look at Ferguson as he scoffs at me. "Ya ain't nothing but a wee child! An' we ain't seen ya but two days ago! I don' know what kin'a trick ya pullin', but I ain't fallin' fer it!"

The flutter of flapping wings whispers next to my ears, and the weight of the ravens becomes tight-gripped hands on my shoulders.

"If ya think this is a trick, boy, ya got somethin' comin' to ya," Babd cackles, her hand shaking with her laughter. Ferguson, and nearly every other man in the room, tumbles backwards in shock.

I look at my father, but he is once again staring at the women beside me.

"Da."

He looks at me, surprise written all over his face. "Aife, what did ya do?"

"What she had to," Nemain replies, and offers me a small grin. I try smiling back, but I am finding it hard to do so.

"I can secure our victory in this battle," I address the room of frightened men. "I ask that ya trust me in this. We will not fail."

Iwan speaks up for the first time since I entered the main hall. "I trust ya, Aife." I meet his eyes. He is proud. It radiates from him, and I can almost see it, a sheer red light just barely there to outline him. I nod, grateful that he isn't afraid of me or my choice. Babd squeezes my shoulder.

"You still're me daughter," Padraig says gruffly, although he does not meet my eyes. "I will follow ya."

Follow, not trust. But it is something. I haven't completely lost him. "Thank ya, Da."

Ferguson is staring at the three of us sisters like we are a wild fiend, ready to rip into him. And so I am most surprised to hear him say next, "I believe ya. Aife. I believe ya."

Eventually all the men nod or mumble their willingness to follow me. I reply solemnly, "We ride tomorrow."

And with one last look to my father as he stares at the floor, I leave the main hall with my sisters. When we walk out, people are no longer trying to be quiet about their surprise. A small child cries out, and many openly gasp or questioned us. I suppose the fact that I walked into the hall with two birds, and walked out with two strange women is something to fear. We ignore them, and instead go right for Iwan's building. Once inside, there is only to wait.

None of us sit. I no longer feel the need to, and they seem perfectly content to stare and sniff at the herbs and berries pinned to the walls.

Babd sniffs and turns to me. "Where does 'e keep his mistletoe? I don' see any in 'ere."

"He don' use it," I reply. "Don' believe in usin' poison to cure people."

"Bah," she mutters, and continues perusing the herb stock. Nemain says nothing, although I catch the smirk on her face.

"Aife?" Iwan is at the door. "May I have a word?"

I leave my sisters to stand beside him out in the evening mist, turned gold with the late sun. He studies my face until I am twingy with nerves. Only my mentor can make me quake like a leaf now. "Have I grown another face, er what?"

"Ya just seem..." He searches for a word. "Sharper."

"Birdlike, am I?" I ask nervously. Have I turned uglier? Do I have a beak? I touch my nose.

"Nay, only slender, like. Fierce." His hand clasps my arm reassuringly. "Like a warrior."

"I am Battle, after all," I grin.

We leave before the morning sun rises, many of us on chariots, the rest on horseback or on foot. My sisters stand at my sides as I lead, heading to the west. We will not fail. Not this time.

In all the preparations of battle, I had not been able to steal a moment with Rogan, although I had seen him in passing. I wonder what he thinks of me now that everyone knows what I am. I hope he is not frightened like my father, or angry as my uncle.

With blue on our bodies, swords and spears in our hands, we march on until the sun is well above the horizon, blocked by the thick curtain of clouds overhead. Nemain holds out her hand to stop our progress, and with the flap of wings, flies as a raven over the crest of the hills before us, before swooping back to land as a woman.

"The Cruithni lay ahead, sister," she report. I nod and turn to face my people.

"Our enemies lay just beyond this hill," I cry, my hooded cloak snapping in the misty breeze. "They don' expect us, nor do they fear us. But that will be their fatal mistake!"

A cheer rises up.

"They will regret their actions those last days. They will rue takin' our people. They will rue killin' our children!"

Another cheer rises. My pulse roars in my ears.

"Chariots!" At the word, the chariots climb the hill.

"Archers at tha ready!"

A group carrying bows breaks off and mounts the hill, spreading out in a line behind the chariots and warriors on foot. I make my way to the front of the group, where I mount my new horse. "We will not lose today, my friends!" I glance at my sisters, now circling in the sky above us. Power courses through my body. "The Cruithni don' stand a chance."

We charge. The tents of the Cruithni camp lay on a small hill, smoke rising from cooking fires. They are nomads, passing through and raiding as they do so. No more, I think. They will be no more. A horn sounds from the camp as my warriors ride down the hill: they see us, but it is too late. A few heartbeats later, and we are among them, running through the vast camp. Shouts ring out as we swing sword and staff, cutting down enemy after enemy.

I plow through a cluster of men, shouting out as I do so, my sword wedging through armor and cloth and bone. We have caught them during a meal; food plates and fires are trampled as chariots crush everything in their paths.

And then come the armed warriors, having reached their swords and bows. An arrow is sent straight to my horse's heart, and I am flung off as he falls. Shaking off the dirt and the daze, I stand, surrounded by the enemy.

"Come on!" I shriek. And they come. But I am faster than they – stronger, too. I dodge and swing, cut and jab. One after another, they fall before me. Untouchable, I tell myself. And so I move on, finishing off each of the warriors I face – it is a dance between my sword and I, perfect partners in perfect sync. Dozens, hundreds of them fall victim to my sword, and with each felled enemy, the strength in my arms only grows and grows. I can feel the fury of my people, a physical heat surging through me veins, and the fear of the Cruithni as they are slain. It only fuels my fire. My vision turns red, each new enemy a smear before me before they are cut down by my sword.

Then I hear a cry that shakes me from my rage; "I found tha prisoners!"

I run to the crier, and there they are, all the children and women who were taken, tied up to trees and gagged. The men and women guarding them fall to my sword, and then I turn my blade on the ropes holding my people captive. More warriors come to help me. "Get 'em out of 'ere an' to tha archers! Stay in a group!"

And I dive back into battle, spinning, dashing, unstoppable. We are winning. I hear many of the Cruithni shouting orders to run. We are beating them off!

I climb onto an empty chariot, the horses lying dead before it. And I crow, feeling the red-hot energy of Battle within me. "Let this be a lesson ta any clan that dares attack the Dáirine! You will be destroyed!"

I walk through the refuse left behind by the battle after the last Cruithni had fled or was slain. There are fallen warriors everywhere, both Cruithni and Dáirine. Iwan and some of the archers run from body to body, checking for survivors, tending to the wounded. Nemain and Babd are perched atop a tent, surveying with beady eyes. They wait for all the living to clear before escorting the fallen spirits away. I should be with them, but I am searching. Rogan was not among the warriors to regroup at the top of the hill.

He is out here somewhere.

"Aife!" Iwan calls. "Over here!"

I fly. I don't know how I do it, but between one heartbeat and the next I become the raven and fly over my broken obstacles and then drop to the ground beside Iwan. It feels more natural than breathing.

And so does my pain. I fall to my knees as I see the man laying on the ground. "Rogan, no."

A deep wound runs from his neck to his ribs, and although Iwan presses tightly on it, crimson seeps through his hands. It is like being that frozen form again, unable to move, unable to breathe. My hands shake when I cradle his face, tears burning my eyes.

"Rogan, my love," I whisper. His breath is so shallow, his eyes glassy with pain. "I am so sorry…" The flap of wings sounds, and I feel Nemain and Babd crouch beside me in their human forms. I look at them. My voice is weak. "How could this happen?"

They just look at me pityingly.

A sob chokes my angry words and I press my lips to Rogan's face. He is so cold. The faint glowing that comes from his soul is flickering, like the dead leaves. Again, I look to my sisters. "Can't we do somethin'?"

Nemain shakes her head. "He's nearly gone."

"A…"

I look down. Rogan's faraway eyes are fixed on me. "Aife…"

"Rogan! I'm so sorry," I sob, my voice choking out until only a whisper. "I'm so sorry."

The red outline fades, and is gone. A small orb floats out from his chest and simply hovers in the air. The body in my hands is still, and I feel hollow as I stare at the orb.

"Tis his spirit," Nemain says, but I am so distant, like I am dreaming, and all of this will be gone once I wake up. "He waits fer ya. We'll show ya our next step, sister."

Numbly, I nod. She and Babd stand and walk away, the orbs beginning to float after them. I make to follow, but Iwan's hand touches my arm and I stop. "Aife, I am sorry. He was a good man, an' I know 'e loved you."

"Please," I say, standing although the air seems unbreathable and the weight on my chest unbearable. I pull on my hood. "My name is Macha."

We take the souls to the woods, where the faeries will care for them in their afterlives. I stare at the orb that had been Rogan for a long time before handing it to a small, mouse-like sprite with green skin. "Care for it. Please." It winks and nods at me.

The sisters allow me to stop in my village before we move on. Everyone is celebrating the victory, but Brendolyn is waiting for me alone at the edge of the village. When she sees me, without hesitation she runs and embraces me, and I hold her so tightly I think we will never become unstuck.

"I will come back, I promise you."

She nods against my shoulder; I can feel her tears on my skin. "I'll hold ya to that."

Da is not there, but it is for the best. I cannot handle his strange looks and the fear that boils off him. Eventually I have to leave my birth sister for my immortal ones. We wander away through the wood, and I ask listlessly, "Where do we go?"

"Ready ta move on so soon?" Babd croaks, but Nemain throws her a glare and wraps an arm around me.

"Yer hurt will heal. Tis one o' tha beauties of immortality; ya have eternity. But heed what we told ya. Mortals will bring ya pain. They always do."

"Jus' don' worry o'er it, lil one." Babd pinches my cheek. "Soon ya will be occupied. There'll be prayers fer ya yet. And ever more battles fer ya ta win."

My lips perk up. I like the sound of that. Already my fingers itch for my blade, for the surge of battle.

The Incompetent Vampire

Bev Jafek

THE INCOMPETENT VAMPIRE

He was a skinny kid in his early twenties with very visible acne, emitting a cloud of halitosis, red-haired with the signs of early baldness, his blue jeans so old and crushed that they looked like gray foam and a strangely lumpy hoodie that fell from his head. A look of dismay was perpetually on his face, as though someone had just slapped him. He stared at an iPhone like all those his age but, unlike the others, looked up often, as though for anyone or anything that could save him from himself. I had no intention of doing so, but he immediately captured all of my mental and emotional faculties because he had just declared that he was a vampire and had the long incisors to prove it. I, on the other hand, was writing the Great American Novel and had concluded that, if one hoped to speak as directly to any reader as Hemingway had once done, one must know a great deal about vampires. Perhaps one must even have studied the whole menagerie of supernatural creatures that dominate our literature; those who, above all other beings, have no reason for being.

We were sitting together on an MTA train just out of Grand Central in Manhattan. His voice was soft so no one else could hear what passed between us. "I can only offer a bit of friendship, no blood, no bites, no hanky-panky," I said and asked if he was capable of sharing any part of a meal with me or perhaps some wine. He gave me a huge, yellow-orange toothy smile of relief and said he loved red wine. So, I took this raggedy kid home with me. He bumbled along in ancient gym shoes with holes in their soles and that terrible state of tooth decay, orange neon bright, in his mouth. The train stopped at Greenwich, CT, and from there I drove him to my modestly luxurious home that brought a great gasp of relief from him, as though he would take his salvation on any material terms. As I prepared my dinner, he began to drink wine in huge quantities like an alcoholic, and then the first rat came out of his hoodie.

"Please excuse me," he begged, and took fresh blood from the quivering, bewhiskered little animal while its eyes glowed with adoration. When I had finished my dinner, so had he; that is, he had collapsed in an alcoholic stupor on my living room sofa, and four rats hidden in his clothing had now offered their throats to him. They lay in many poses of rodent-transcending love all over his body, one pressing its face into his armpit, another on his chest gazing in awe, another rubbing its furry back all over the vampire's abdomen, and the last only two tiny pink feet for it was continuously burrowing into his other armpit.

Of course, I wondered what I had gotten myself into, since I had offered him a room to live in temporarily (he was homeless) before the first rat came out. "So," I said, "you don't return to your coffin, you have no problem with sunlight, you can drink plenty of wine, you have no capacity to mesmerize or influence people, and you have rarely if ever fed on one."

"You're so perceptive," he said in his soft whining voice. "You must be a great writer. Of course, I want to feed on people. My dream is to take a drink from Angelina Jolie and Hillary Clinton."

"You're shooting for the top. How will you lure those famous women into a bite or two?"

His voice became loudly whining, his words slurred from all the wine, and it suddenly struck me that, with his rats crawling and lolling all over him, he looked more like a huge, squirming human worm than anything else. "I know that Hillary Clinton wants me to bite her!" He yelled righteously. "I know that; I swear! She would be able to run for President again and again ad infinitum. I see no reason why such a powerful woman would not change the Constitution and be our leader for centuries, all without decaying like a dreadful, farting old dog the way Ronald Reagan did almost upon assuming office. I could offer her the dream of her own heart! How could she resist me? I only have to get myself close to her, somehow, and bite away." Full of dismay, I had to agree with him. I had a creature before me who was, perhaps, as poisonous as he was disgusting.

"And Angelina Jolie, too! Why not? She could live even more roles that she does now: ambassador, film star, film director, sex symbol, action adventure heroine, expatriate mother of foreign adopted children, mother of her own children and so forth. All of her roles would multiply in eternity. She could become the mother of thousands upon thousands of people and anything else she might dream up. She might even become more powerful than Hillary. Oh yes, there would be quite a contest between them in a century or two, and who would then be President over and over? I dare not speculate." His face suddenly became a parody of wisdom and cynicism. "Oh yes, they'd finally be running against one another. They'd let Cheatin' Bill pop but give the gift to Chelsea, who would be our greatest astronaut and space pioneer, walking all over Mars and even discovering and communicating with life on Europa. Only vampire blood can travel in space for such long periods without perishing. You see, they all want me."

I could scarcely believe that I was agreeing with him, but I was. "Why only women?" I asked.

"I'm just a plain old horny dude, man. I want to be intimate with all of them and any other luscious woman I find." Now he was smiling in admiration of the life he would lead, his eyes nearly closed in simple joy.

"Then why haven't you pulled it off? You say all these women and more are just waiting for you." I did not add, and why are you such a disgusting lump of creaturedom sacked out on my sofa, not having achieved a single thing in your life but a harem of devoted rats? The Great American Novel was hanging perilously in the balance. He erupted into tears and even started hurling his rats against my very clean and attractive walls. Supernaturally loyal, they all rushed back to him for more abuse. I watched him in fury and decided on a new approach.

"You're very tired, young vampire. Why don't you and the little rats just go upstairs and sleep? It's the small room on the left."

"You're so kind," he sobbed. "You must write very humane novels." In fact, I am known for vicious satire, but I accepted the compliment, since it meant that I would be rid of him for the rest of the night. He stumbled upstairs, his sobs stifling, the rats clinging heroically to his collar or ensconced in his hoodie. I heard him opening and closing the door and that was the last of him for one night.

I smiled and went into my study to write. My inspiration and ability were not improved in the least, but that was only to be expected. I still knew next to nothing about the man upstairs who carried the key to the future of literature. At last, I took off my fedora, short tie, widely double-breasted tweed jacket and slacks and snuffed out my Havana cigar. It is a costume I wear whenever I am working on the Great American Novel. Though I am not a sentimental woman, I must acknowledge that the GAN does not have the influence in our lives that it did in earlier decades. Ah, but I would change that, my vampire and I! I enjoyed another glass of wine and also retired. I had no fear of my guest. I had fully explored his limitations and absurdity and could imagine no power he might have over me. The only influence that would pass between us was the mystery that would lead to the resurgence of the American novel.

In the morning, I heard moaning alternating with chuckling. I knew he had found the wine cellar; that was a vampire given. As I came downstairs, he was opening the door to another ten or so rats. I noticed a smell of excrement coming from his room and was shocked. In full indignation, I addressed this immediately. "Since when do vampires defecate," I asked, "and who has allowed it in your room?"

A look of utterly abject despair and guilt came over his face. "I don't, of course," he said. "But the rats, you see, make imperfect vampires. They are not one of the higher species, so they retain some physical functions."

"Well, you'll clean it up immediately," I said. I may want to write the GAN but not so much that I would clean rat shit out of my home. Writers are sensitive souls. Everyone knows that.

Soon his room was clean again and he sat drinking, as usual, on my sofa. I tried a whole range of topics to probe his inner self – philosophy, current events, history, literature, sports, religion, new scientific discoveries, etc., and found that he knew absolutely nothing -- or rather, he knew wine, blood, rats and lust. I then inquired of his family life and possible intimate relations and discovered that he had, as a newborn, been left in a garbage pail by his mother. He was rescued by a religious couple; but, a short time later, they left him outside an orphan agency at night. Then one foster family after another brought him back and abandoned him on the steps, all at night, as though they feared something. He then suffered a long history of being abandoned at night until he associated it with the dark and was frightened by it.

"A vampire afraid of the dark?" I asked.

"Oh yes," he said with pathetic resignation. In spite of myself, I shed a few tears, then noticed that the rats were crying, too. This reminded me to stick rigorously to my task, for the GAN depended on it.

"What does interest you?" I finally asked. At last, he gave me his plans. He had found Hillary Clinton's speaking schedule on the Internet. He would go to Washington, DC for the event, be in the audience, and try any means of making direct contact with her. He

90

had been practicing running and leaping for many days. His eyes glowing with pride, he wanted to show me his skill. I said I believed him and that was enough. I didn't want to see this revolting human worm running and leaping about. So, I gave him his bus fare and he was off.

I then explored my feelings toward him, all I could sense of the psychology and manner of vampires, but could only come up with a distinct sense that it was wonderful when a vampire abandons you.

A few days later, the results of his efforts with Hillary Clinton were all over the media and Internet. At the close of Hillary's speech, he apparently sprinted down the aisle, leaped to the stage and stood before her. I did not hear what he said, but it was reported as, "I can give you eternal life if you will just let me gently bite your throat." An iPhone in the audience picked up the exact look on his face, which was tender and adoring. Hillary at first just stared at him in astonishment, then one of his rats came out of his hoodie to gaze on her magnificence, and two more rushed from his pockets to his shoulders for a better view.

Hillary emitted a great, throaty scream and, with surprising strength, picked up the podium and threw it at him. He stood there foolishly, never imagining that she had such physical powers, and ended up getting a podium in his gut as he fell off the stage, his rats shrieking in terror. He was then carried away by two security guards; and, after a day of questioning, the event was calmly reported by the media as one involving a mildly retarded individual with no ties to terrorism. When Hillary was later interviewed, her brow momentarily furrowed, and she dismissed it in a short sentence. "A President is ready for anything," she said.

Three days later, he was back on my doorstop. At first, I did not respond, but when he kept standing in front of my living room window and blocking my view of verdant nature, I did let him in with consequence only for the contents of my wine cellar. As much as my instincts told me that I should cut off all contact with him, my desire to write the G.A.N. eventually won out. "You can stay a few more days, and then I don't ever want to see you again," I said firmly. This pained him, but he drowned it in red wine as usual, which seemed to put his rats in a celebratory mood as well, no doubt the result of the mysterious blood connection between them.

"I will succeed," he said in firm though slurred words. "Angelina is next. I've hacked into her schedule and fortunately, she will be meeting with an African ambassador at the U.N. tomorrow afternoon at 2:30. Needless to say, I will be there. No one will ever expect to see me. If anyone thinks of me at all, he will assume that I have been institutionalized."

Again I had to agree: everything about him was unpredictable since it was also nonsensical. I found the implications of this annoying, however, since it implied that I was running a nuthouse when all I wanted was the renaissance of the Great American Novel. "Perhaps you should turn in early again and conserve your strength," I said, hoping that he would not polish off my whole wine cellar. He agreed with me humbly and I added only, "Make sure you've got the rat shit out of here before you leave."

Once more, I left him alone and resumed my writing that, if anything, had deteriorated. I hoped that this time, he got himself killed, since it might at least give me a moment of drama and the always intriguing last words before death.

In the morning, he was gone, and by nightfall he returned in even worse condition. His face was full of despair and seemed to have aged, more of his hair had fallen out, and a bit of blood dribbled from his mouth, not Angelina's but his own from the huge incisor that barely dangled from his upper row of teeth, probably the result of trauma and tooth decay. Soon, he would not even be able to bite, not even the rats, though one of them had just, in compassion, bitten itself and offered him its blood. It occurred to me that I had one insight regarding him: he did inspire loyalty and adoration. That much was true; but only from rats, which was of no use to anyone. I wondered when I would just throw him out, but I did want to hear what had transpired. Of course, he immediately began blurting away as he dropped onto my sofa.

Apparently, he had somehow gotten into the room where Angelina Jolie was speaking with the ambassador. He stopped for a moment, thrilled by the drama, power, and beauty of her presence. All of his rats came out of his clothes to see this radiant sight. Angelina was not horrified as Hillary had been and had a more worldly air and a dark, direct gaze that could probably stop an elephant. Still, he said, "Come with me into eternity and become even more than you have ever dreamt of being, all from my bite on your luminous neck." Something in her sumptuous dark allure had drawn more elaborate

92

words to his lips. He then leaped toward her and was felled by two expert karate chops. It had never occurred to him that she kept her body slender and desirable through rigorous physical disciplines.

Smiling confidently to the African ambassador, she said, "Let's find another room." As her glorious stiletto heels stepped over his crumpled form, she turned a last time, gave him a dramatically penetrating gaze with one eyebrow arched and said, "You poor sick puppy. Do yourself a favor and never come near me again." Then, the vision was gone, and he could only think, she'd have beaten Hillary in any race for the Presidency. She simply was our leader. But, the dream was impossible, never to be... He and his rats wept until they were all too dehydrated to continue. He returned here, he said, in a delirium.

His despair was simply impossible to tolerate. "Well, there's always Chelsea," I said, not believing a word of it. "You might have better luck with her," I lied.

"Nevermore, nevermore," he croaked like the raven.

"Why not, you idiot?" I had lost all patience and serious interest in him, but there remained a single grain of curiosity for I could not wholly abandon the GAN.

"I can't really offer anyone immortality. It's just a myth, a reason for me to get some blood and attention. I'm a vampire but also a fake. There are no real vampires. I get all kinds of diseases from sucking so much blood. I'll be lucky if I make it to fifty. Even forty. Maybe even thirty." I could control myself no longer. I picked him up by his collar and hoodie as well as his dissolving pants and threw him and all his rats out of my house. No literary glory to be was to be found there, ever.

I went to my writing desk and considered the abomination my efforts had produced. My leonine literary vision must clearly go in some other direction. I could only hope that I would find one. The GAN was perhaps something of a wraith in the night itself, becoming as supernatural as American literary taste. I continued sitting there in my fedora and 1940s suit, waiting, waiting. O the horror! The horror! I thought, but even that line was too famously used. I could only take another puff on my Havana cigar.

I Wish I Could Tell You

Steven Schwanitz

I wish I could tell you, that I was there to watch the strength of men prevail. I wish I could tell you, that when it was put to the final test, an alliance of the last free people held out against evil, and freed themselves. I wish I could tell you that I stood side by side with my friends, men and women that I'd come to look upon as family, to vanquish an evil and bring hope to a new age. I wish I could tell you this, but I can't. What I can tell you is that while man's vigor wasn't enough to stem the tide of evil, it never faltered, never ran screaming, and never shirked in the face of evil. I was there at the beginning of the end, and fate had it that I fought 'til the days of glory were gone, and all that we could hope for was an escape.

The war had started suddenly enough. The fragile truce between the free peoples, and the orcs of the badlands was determined to be shattered when raiding parties had been spotted across the border, and murmurings of the first orcish army in a century had started up throughout the region. The straw that broke the roof had definitely been the burning of the town of Yorksville, which was quickly followed by Argon and the small village of Lescria. King Mason Galahad quickly scrounged up a volunteer army to deal with the situation, 10,000 strong of possibly the only people who even had an inkling of what might happen if it wasn't stopped then. I was there to watch the carnage, our brave king, bold as the old tales led us forward. It never occurred to us that two more full armies of the goblins from the under kingdoms might be lying in wait.

I was one of the lucky few to escape that event, we quickly retreated to the nearest town on the border, determined to be dug in 'til reinforcements might be found. Somehow the men rallied around me to be their captain, in light of recent events, how could I say no? That battle was only first of a twenty year long war, our vicious enemy had spent the last 100 years building their forces, while we lay completely blind to the now obvious danger which could've been spotted so easily. Was it our greed? Our refusal to believe that we could ever be overcome? Maybe it was the sheer fact that an alliance with both the dwarves and elves were supposed to make us impenetrable, invulnerable even. The folly of humans was always said to grow too large one day, when our sins as a collective species would eventually overcome us. Woe that these last dark days would be mine to witness.

In the midst of such a time, one would think that he'd live his life in immense fear, that each day would be his last. The fact of the matter is my heart shriveled up the day my family was destroyed. I led a group of men from my village, the last few who'd left with me in that first rout. Everything was gone, these orcs leave no one alive. No survivors, they had no desire to but to eradicate everyone and everything in the allied lands. I found her, and my daughter, hung from the support beam in my home, which was the last thing that stood in that whole two story home that I'd built myself.

Twenty years of battle and blood, of fire and fear, of glory and grotesque fields. I fought in more fights then I can count, seen more men and women die then I can comprehend, I've watched our lines pushed back time and time again. Watched as our brittle alliance was forced into a corner, it had all led up to this fight. We couldn't fight on more than one fight any longer, and sent everyone left to The Heart of the Sunrise, the last free base, located in the center of a large ravine, with its back to the coast. The perfect place for the final stand of the free peoples. One battalion made from Elven archers, Dwarven Sentinels, and human warriors. Three hundred and fifty men and women sent to protect the several hundred innocent citizens, a list ditch plan to send several ships across the far oceans, loaded to the brim with supplies in an effort to hopefully find a new land, free of the corruption of the newly expanded badlands.

Our leader was none other than Orik Ironcleave, the last dwarven king, and somehow I'd been brought into the inner circle of soldiers. My place was on the wall, with my men, not here in a circle of pompous assholes, who's main concern was who among them was going to be chose to take the last few spots on the boat. The meeting was dull, and of no concern to me, I remember several voices speaking up in anger as I left my seat, and stormed outside. A simple glance over my shoulder showed the king had silence the anger with a simple wave, I'd fought alongside him several times, and I had come to respect the man, who showed more sense than 1000 other kings combined. The sky was dark, a great storm loomed on the horizon, and the men and women sat about in armor, a careful examination reveals that not a single face among them showed anything other than determination, backed by a simple yet prominent feeling of anxiety. It was the feeling that could only be shown before a great struggle, a fight of life or death.

They'd started showing up weeks beforehand, thousands at a time, a hundred armies of a hundred clans of goblins and orcs, their skin an oily black, and their armor a rough patchwork of bone and fur, their teeth too white to be human. The elves stood upon the outer and inner walls, several of the sentinels and warriors stood amongst their number, not because elven archers weren't capable warriors, we just needed them to stay behind their bows. I was to stand on the west wall, and stay in command of the soldiers. It was a war that built heroes, heroes of the new age. Several had made themselves fight to the end, and far too many had suffered for it.

Amongst our numbers stood many names, Orchid the Silent, an elven assassin, the only in their number without a bow. She'd proven herself in the battle of three cliffs, where she saved fifty innocent souls and wiped out four goblin squads, at the cost of her tongue, and a nasty scar on the left side of her face. The Stonewall brothers, dwarven triplets who were the last through the doors in the last battle fought in the underground dwarven kingdoms. Gerard Galahad, son of the human king, vicious with a spear and shield, he'd given up the crown when a true king had shown his face, king Ironcleave, he was 22, and has been said to have killed over a thousand orcs alone, easily one of the youngest on the field. There was the Hood, a former pirate captain, who always wears a hood, to conceal his identity. There was Grimm the engineer, Percival Blueheart, and a mysterious young elf that everyone simply called the Whisperer, an archer that supposedly held the goblins and orcs armies from advancing into the forest of the sleeping giant for the last 3 years, but when the call went out, he dutifully came to the fort, though he swore allegiance to no one.

So many others could be called upon, but I haven't time to speak for them all, neither do I have any right to do so. I am only a man, one of no importance in the grand scheme of things, the only thing that makes me stand out amongst my peers in my mind, is possibly the mace strapped to my back, a thing of dwarven genius, the spokes sticking off of it spoke a story of blood and anger that I dare not repeat to its fullest. Two handed and heavy enough to crush an orcs head beneath its bite, I could almost feel its eagerness to continue what it was made for. Some in my company had come to call me the giant's fist, though I couldn't imagine why.

The day seemed endless, and I couldn't even begin to count how many days we'd been stationed here, the two sides sitting in a vicious stalemate that neither were in any hurry to break. It wouldn't be long now, you could feel it in the air, and the goblin commander had arrived about a week back, a grotesque version of a man, The Weeping thing he was named, the very mastermind behind that very first rout. I could only pray that we met on the field once more, the first time he'd left me with a vicious scar across my now bald head with that demented scimitar like blade he carried on his person. He preferred to fight in the lines, alongside his men, not out of any kinship, but out of a bloodlust that distinguished him from other goblins in general, his particular brand of evil was something to be feared. Tonight would be the night, that much was clear by the torches of green fire that were lit in the camps closest to us.

The rain came as they approached the walls this night, a single wall of endless proportions, we stood firm in the eyes of our enemies, the boats were not off yet, we needed to buy them as much time as possible. The elves bows were strung, and it was well known that there would be no form of communication, there hadn't been in any of the battles previous. The one time we had tried, our commanding officer of the battle had been returned with his limbs in several rather small packages.

It seemed...different, this time. The people around me had the same look on their faces, as they had at any other time, but with the situation being what it was, you could tell that under all that determination, all that vigor and courage that shone bright in their faces, that none of them were at all ready to die. Prepared, yes, but not at all ready. Deep bellowing horns blared through the night, All in the fort tensed. I stood upon the Western wall, Mace in hand, the men and women around laced with steely savagery, and it was needed given the fight that faced us. I wish I could tell you that the battle raged for days. I wish I could tell you that each man and women killed over thousands of orcs a head, but I can't.

They stopped before the wall, menacing, savage. We let them sit for less than a moment, before the order to release the volley was given, the first line was down, but that didn't even seem to faze the rest. The world seemed to slow, as they rushed our walls, the ladders raised high. It couldn't have taken more than a few minutes, yet it felt like hours would pass before that night would end. I snapped myself out of a stupor when the first of the ladders crashed down directly in front of me. Hearing the grunting of a male orc as it quickly scaled the crude deice, I'd decided that I wasn't quite ready to face one head to head yet. I placed my foot against its top rung and pushed it off the wall, hearing several orcs squealing in fear as it tumbled to the ground, finished with a rather satisfying crunch. I look to my right, mace in hand, at Percival Blueheart, his longsword and shield created an immovable wall for the archers that he'd placed himself in front, easily slaying 5 of the orcs that had managed to climb onto the wall.

My mace sung as I used the handle to deflect the wickedly sharp blade of the orc that had somehow sneaked up behind me. I quickly bounced back on my left foot, and staved in its chest plate, as it struggled for breath, I took stock of just how tall these things truly were, possibly 6 feet and counting, the orcs weren't exactly difficult to spot. Yet at their full height they pushed 7 feet. A height which man had yet to reach, even I stood a mere 6' 2" tall, the direct opposite of the goblins, which barely stood at four and a half feet. I retched my shoulder, leaping away from the vicious swing of the two handed axe, almost cleaving me in half. Not one to be outdone, I quickly returned with vigor, as the Giant head of the mace caught the orc in the side, sending him over the side of the wall, and hurtling to his death. I felt a sharp piece of steel rap across my back, and spun in time to catch a gobbling which had sneaked over the wall at some point. I grabbed him by the scruff of his neck, nasty furry little things, and smacked him against the wall; the mace quickly finished the job.

My attention was dragged back to the pandemonium around me, as I realized with a certainty that we were quickly going to be over taken. A voice in the distance cried out the order that all on the wall had been waiting for, the retreat to the courtyard. As my compatriots filed down the stairs in an almost desperate panic, I stayed atop the wall, winding up back to back with Blueheart. We protected the staircase with a savagery unseen by the likes of goblins and orcs. His shield protected my lower quarters, and my mace tore through my enemies with a blood-lust. I brought the mace down atop an particularly unlucky goblins head, I watched without mercy, as it face caved beneath its weight. I heard a sickening cry, and turned my head to see what the Blueheart had done, and my look turned to horror, an orc had managed to get past his defense, and his blade dug deeply into the poor man's neck, his face a twisted mask of pain, the look in his eyes never wavered though. That look of hope that made him so famous never left his eyes, even as he dragged a blade across that orcs neck, with a vengeance I've seen all too often.

I quickly crushed the tow orcs that came rushing forward, my weapon singing as it did its deadly dance, and lifted the blue heart from the ground. He grabbed my hand in anguish, yet a smile resided on his face as his eyes grew dark. I had no choice but to leave him, grabbing his shield and sword in the process, and leapt from the wall, landing on the pile of orcs below me. I scrambled to my feet, to watch the carnage in process. The majority of our forces had built a wall in the courtyard, which was smaller than you'd might expect, and created the perfect dense before the barracks, which was the final stronghold, for on the opposite side lay the docks, and the ship with it. I fought my way through the crowds, somehow making it to the back of our forces, and handed Percival Blueheart's weapon and shield to a page, his wife and child would know that he'd died for a grand cause, one too large to be selfish about.

I spent no time rushing back into the fight, spinning my body in a circle, and wiping several goblins from existence, I could feel the air around me scream by, as a group of elves, led by the whisperer release a volley of arrows into the ever darkening crowd. I heard the Stonewall brothers and the hood fight a huge group of orcs by themselves at the forefront of the field. I even saw Orchid and the engineer eliminating target ways on the other side of the field, for just a moment, I felt an undeserved ray of hope enter my chest, and used the false strength to power my arm. A deep bellow came from behind the barracks, signaling the boats cast-off, our men fought ever so hard, yet it seemed the orcs were a little angrier then we had planned, to see their hard work slipping from their grasp. I've seen routs before, Hell, I've even been the center of them, expecting to get slaughtered like countless others, but I've never seen a vicious whirlwind of blood-lust run through a crowd like that. I watched as the orcs suddenly swarmed us, quickly swimming through our forces with ferocity of an angry bear. It was all we could do to push back into the barracks, and even then we had a hell of a time doing so.

I watched the whisperer die painfully, with a pair of orcish hands wrapped around his neck. The engineer was shot with fifteen arrows, and fell like the mighty elvish warrior queen Arya Swiftleaf. I believe I'd witness several goblins swarm one of the Stonewall brothers, a man whose name I'd never gotten the pleasure to learn. Taking stock of the men who'd managed to lock themselves withing the barrack was disheartening to say the least, maybe fifty soldiers, mostly dwarves, with only three of the remaining heroes left to lead them. Gerard Galahad, One of the Stonewall brothers, and Orchid the Silent. I took a step out of the back door, to watch the last boat to the foreign see drift away, and was thankful that at least some of our people were able to escape.

Shouts started up in the barrack, a quick examination showed two soldiers screaming at each, which in a situation like this wasn't all that uncommon. It would be an hour at least before they broke through that door, the majesty of dwarven engineering. I decided to skip the mighty speech, it was for those who had nothing to give themselves for, and I had a cause to die. My family is up in the sky-planes, waiting for me to join them. I sat and stared out at the water, memories flowing through my brain, every single event in my life had me to this moment, and eventually I ran out of memories, and was content to watch the water sparkle in the morning sun. The rain had cleared a while ago, and the grey clouds had rolled away. It was an absolutely gorgeous morning, and there was the reddest sunrise I'd ever been granted the pleasure to see.

I eventually started to hear crackings in the door, I left my helmet out on that dock, I would have no need of it now. I stood amongst the greatest warriors of our time, Orchid to my right, Stonewall and Galahad to my left, I watched as the door gave way, could almost see myself running into battles with reckless abandon, to my death. It didn't feel as glorious as the tales, but it did feel right, as if I'd been given a good death, for something worth it. I wish I could tell you exactly what had happened, that somehow our scrappy little outfit had won the day. I wish I could tell you of the songs that would be sung on the ship, or the tears our friends shed at the sight of our defeat. I wish I could tell you, but I can't.

What I can tell you is that I woke in a field of lush green grass, as long as the reeds in my hometown. I felt them between my fingers, and shed the smallest tear out of its simplicity. I looked to the sky, and felt the warmth of the sun on my face as I sat up. I checked my body, and felt every scar that I'd ever been inflicted with disappear at my touch. I watched as my armor vanish, and became a comfortable set of clothing, suitable for living at the coast. Felt the blood run from my body as it all washed away. I felt a tingling in the back of my brain, one so familiar and sweet that I wept like a child. I turned as saw my Wife, and my beloved child sitting in front of the tree in my long yard, smiling at me in happiness.

Eye of the Storm

Aaron Hodges

A pillar of smoke rose from the burning house. The roar of the flames was deafening. Heat scorched his eyes, but he could not look away. The blaze lit the night, chasing the stars from the sky. Amidst the fire, the silhouette of a boy appeared. He stumbled from the wreckage, clothes falling to ashes around him. Sparks of lightning leapt from his fingertips, leaving scorch marks on the tiled street. Soot covered his slim face, marred only by the trail of tears running down his cheeks. The wind caught his mop of dark brown hair, revealing the deep blue glow of his eyes. He wore an expression of absolute terror.

"Help me!"

Eric sat bolt upright, the nightmare tearing him from his sleep. He gasped for breath, eyes darting around in search of escape. A wall of vegetation loomed above him. The dark fingers of branches clawed at his clothing. He scrambled for his dagger, but it tumbled through his hands. He dove for it as it fell.

His knees hit the dirt, and with a sudden rush he remembered where he was. Eric took a deep breath; slowing his racing heart, and rose to his feet. The clearing had not changed while he slept. The trees still stood in a silent ring, their leaves speckled with the red and gold of early autumn. Where the canopy thinned above he could make out the blue sky, but below the dark of night still clung.

Eric shivered, wishing he had more than a holey blanket and a worn leather jacket to ward off the cold. Reaching down, he stuffed the blanket into his bag with the rest of his measly possessions – dried meat, a water skin, and the steel bracelet his parents had given to him as a child. The familiar dream clung to him, the boy's face lurking in the shadows of his memory. He knew that face. It was his.

A tremor ran through his body. He flung the bag over his shoulder with a little too much energy, determined to ignore the bad omen. Just through the trees was the Gods Road, and about a mile to the west was the town of Oaksville. There he would to make a fresh start for himself.

Eric paused long enough to pull on his travel worn boots and brush the leaves from his hair, then he was away through the trees. Excitement quickened his pace – this was it. Today he would end his exile. In the two years since his fifteenth birthday, he had wandered alone through the forests and across the plains of Plorsea. In all that time, he had spoken to only a handful of people. It had very nearly driven him insane.

The trees either side of the Gods Road soon began to thin, giving way to the grassy steeps of a valley. Eric squinted into the rising sun, straining for his first glimpse of Oaksville. A layer of fog clung to the hill slopes, but it was quickly fading in the rising sun. Buildings began to take shape – wooden houses with tall smoking chimneys, the three-pronged spire of the temple, an old castle set at the town center which towered above the town walls.

Eric's spirit leapt at the sight. Then the first gust of wind reached him on the hilltop, carrying with it the clang of a hammer and the clip clop of hooves. His nose twitched at the tang of smoke and humanity that hung in the air. The image of a burning house flickered into his mind.

He hesitated mid-stride. A voice whispered in his mind. Go back – it's too dangerous!

Fear gripped him. What if I'm not ready? His knees shook. His heart pounded like a runaway wagon on a cobbled street. For a second his vision swam, and he felt the warmth of tears on his cheeks.

Eric turned his head and looked back up the hill. The long grass rippled in the wind, the trees beyond shadowing the movement. The forest could offer him nothing more. He drew a breath of air and faced the town. He took a step forward. The terror returned. His chest constricted until he could hardly breathe, but this time he held his nerve. Eric walked down the valley towards the town gates.

Soon the outer wall loomed over him, its great stone blocks casting the path into shadow. Ahead a gaping hole in the stonework swallowed the road whole. A guard stood to either side of the gates, dressed in the chainmail and crimson tunic that marked the Plorsean reserve army. Each held a steel tipped spear loosely at their side and a sword on their belt. The one to the right spared Eric a glance as he passed by, then returned his eyes to the road. Until recently Plorsea had been peaceful. However, lately bandits had moved down from the mountains and were plaguing the countryside. At first they had only targeted travelers, but lately raids had occurred on some of the smaller settlements.

Eric passed between the open gates, and into the darkness of the tunnel. Moss covered the giant slabs of rock on either side of him. Iron grates, once used to pour burning oil down on invaders who breached the outer gates, spotted the ceiling. These walls dated back to darker times, before peace had come to the Three Nations.

With a deep breath, Eric stepped out of the tunnel and back into the sunlight. A bustling marketplace spread out around him. The air was heavy with dust and the stink of human bodies, and the buzz of a hundred voices assaulted Eric's ears. To his left bakers stood at their booths waving loaves of bread in the faces of passers-by. Elsewhere he could see butchers and jewelers, fishermen and carpenters, all chaotically crammed into the small square before the city gates. Each was doing their best to draw the early morning crowds to their stalls.

A nearby jeweler caught Eric's eye, and began motioning for him to look at the array of golden he had laid on a table. Eric smiled and shook his head, but suddenly the jeweler was out of his stall and moving through the crowd towards him shouting. "Sir! Sir!"

Eric shrunk back towards the cool comfort of the tunnel. His feet stumbled on the uneven surface, sending him tumbling to the ground. His head struck the cobbled pavement. A ringing sound filled his ears. Groaning, he looked up, straining to see through his spinning vision.

A face appeared above him. "Careful there, mate," the man offered a hand. Eric immediately recognize the western twang of a Trolan accent.

Eric took the offered hand and the man hauled him to his feet. He stumbled for a second, trying to regain his balance.

"That looked like a nasty fall," the Trolan offered. "You okay?"

The man wore a dark brown cloak, and towered over Eric's own five feet and seven. A poorly trimmed beard and mustache covered the lower half of his face. A broad smile detracted somewhat from the twisted lump that served him for a nose. His hazel eyes looked down at him from beneath bushy eyebrows. There were streaks of silver in his black hair.

Eric nodded. "It was my fault," he stuttered. "Everything is so… overwhelming."

"A country boy then?" He gave a booming laugh. "I remember my first time in a town like this. They stole every penny I had, not the pickpockets, those crooked merchants! Bought a dagger that snapped the first time I dropped it. These townsmen ill prey on the weak. Well don't you worry mate, us country-folk look after our own. The names Pyrros Gray, what can I do for ya?"

Eric grinned. The man's manner reminded him of the warm manner of people in his old village. "I'm Eric. Is there some place quiet I could sit for a while? My head is spinning."

"My pleasure, Eric. There's a tavern not far from here that's usually quiet at this hour. I know the owner, he won't mind you sitting down for a bit. Just follow me and we'll have you there in no time. Just try not to catch the eye of any of these vultures, or they'll soon convince you to trade everything you own for one of em statues that grants good luck with woman."

Pyrros set off through the crowd. Eric followed close behind, afraid to lose him in the press of bodies. His legs felt unsteady, and his head was beginning to throb.

A big woman stepped between them and thrust a wet trout in his face. "Cheapest fish in town! You buy!" She demanded.

Eric shook his head and side stepped the merchant, trying to avoid any further contact. She shouted after him, but he ignored her words. He scanned the crowd, trying to find Pyrros.

"Didn't think I'd leave you behind, did you?" Pyrros' voice came from behind him.

Eric spun around, relieved to see the bulky man right beside him.

Pyrros laughed. "So what bought you to Oaksville mate?"

Eric shrugged. "I wanted to start a new life."

"Well we'll have to see what we can do about that. Now come on, we're almost there."

A minute later they slipped into a narrow alleyway that twisted away from the marketplace. Tall brick walls hemmed them in on either side, throwing the alley into shadows. The drone of the markets died off as they rounded the first corner. Dead wood and discarded garbage lay in piles along the alley, but someone had maintained a trail through the mess that led deeper into the town.

Eric wrinkled his nose as they passed a wreaking pile of decomposing fish heads. He stepped around it and hesitated. "Are you sure this is the way?"

Pyrros turned around and grinned. "It's a short cut. The streets surrounding the marketplace tend to get so crowded you can hardly move. This way goes around."

A chill breeze blew through the alley. Eric felt the hairs on his neck stand up. He didn't like the way Pyrros was grinning. The man no longer seemed so friendly; suddenly the way he towered over Eric seemed threatening, and there was now a strange glint in his eyes. Eric's gut churned in warning.

"I think I'd prefer the crowd to this mess, thanks," Eric turned to leave.

Two men blocked his path. One spun a wooden baton in his hand and the other held a heavy club. Each stood a head above Eric. They were dressed in plain clothes, but the smiles they wore lacked any trace of warmth. A coil of rope slung over the baton wielders shoulder. They spread out to block Eric's only exit.

"Don't bother running, mate," Pyrros' voice now had a menacing tone to it. "You'll make this easier on everyone if you come willingly."

Eric half turned, keeping the other men in sight. "What do you want?"

Pyrros shrugged. "Fair trades not the only business that's booming. Slaves have grown popular in southern Trola. So long as we're discrete, and only take the ones no one misses, people turn a blind eye. You're one of those, aren't you mate?"

He shook his head. "No, my parents are waiting–" he was interrupted by a harsh cackle.

Pyrros scratched at his beard. "So you were lying about being here to start a new life, were you?"

Eric clenched his fists, tense as coiled wire. He glanced at the men behind him, gauging the distance between them. Fear made his breath come in short, ragged gasps.

"No, I think you're lying now, mate. I don't think anyone is out there waiting for you. I don't think there's anyone in the world that will miss you."

This can't be happening!

Pain pounded at Eric's head, but he fought it down. He gave Pyrros a last glance, then leapt at the man with the club. The thug lifted his club with a grin. A moment before he could swing, Eric dived sideways and twisted for the gap between the men. He almost made it.

A club to his chest stopped him cold. For the second time that day, he found himself flat on his back. Winded, he choked for air, the faces of the two men spinning above him. He could feel his anger taking hold. Overhead, thunder clapped. Drops of rain began to fall.

Footsteps came from nearby. Pyrros appeared overhead, a frown on his face. "The first thing a slave must learn is obedience. You disappoint me, Eric. I took you for a quick learner."

The man's booted foot came up and crashed down on Eric's stomach. The breath exploded from his lungs. Pain constricted his chest. He gasped, eyes watering, desperate for air. Inside, Eric felt the embers of his fury take light.

"Stupid boy," by now the rain was bucketing down, soaking through the clothes of his attackers. Pyrros' foot lashed out again, smashing into his ribs and head.

Eric curled into a ball as the assault rained down. He choked back his tears, fear and rage battling for control. There was a sudden roar as something within him snapped, giving way to the chaos of his emotions. A terrible power exploded through his mind, slipping from the darkest recesses of his conscious. He no longer felt the blows, or the rain, or the dirt beneath him. All that remained was an all-consuming hate; a need to lash out. A scream of torment echoed through the alleyway. The last barrier in his mind shattered.

Eric opened his eyes. Blue light lit the stone walls of the passageway, freezing the men in a sudden blue glare. He saw the hate in Pyrros' eyes turn to terror, saw the men beside him glance up, heard the crackling and smelt the burning as it came. Then the lightning struck.

The men vanished into the blue light, their screams cut short by the roar of thunder. There was no chance for escape. One second the three men were there, the next the lightning had consumed then. But it did not stop there.

With a deafening crack, the sky was torn asunder, and a hail of lightning was unleashed. The screams of the villagers rose above the crashing of thunder, as destruction rained down on the defenseless village. Splinters of wood and stone flew through the air as the blue fire tore buildings apart.

Eric struggled to his feet. His anger had vanished, his hatred spent. He stumbled towards the marketplace, mouth agape. Horror clutched his soul.

No, no, no, this can't be happening – not again!

Eric watched in horror as the lightning burnt a deadly trail through the marketplace. Booths exploded before its wrath, filling the air with smoke and debris. Dozens had fallen already, their clothes blackened and crumbling, their bodies broken. Gusts of wind swirled through the square, picking up tiles and rubble and flinging them into the air. The rain poured down, but even that could not wash the smell of burnt flesh from the air. Eric stumbled amid the chaos, powerless to save his hapless victims.

There was no escape from the storms fury. It tore through the market, an unstoppable force of nature. Eric fell to his knees, his tears mingling with the torrent of rain. Lightning struck his frail body, but he felt nothing. Bolts of energy danced along his skin, raising goose bumps wherever they touched. But he remained unharmed. He buried his head in his arms.

Why?

The thunder died away, leaving a devastating silence in its place. Eric could hardly summon the courage to look. At last, he opened his eyes. His gaze swept the wreckage with growing shock. There was not a stall left standing. Burnt beams and canvas covered the square. Orange flames were already beginning to spread. Bodies lay scattered amid the ruins, at times half-buried by the rubble. Eric choked at the sight, his mind rebelling against the truth.

This is my doing.

Movement came from his right. He looked across as a man struggled to his feet. Their eyes met. Eric saw the horror grow in the stranger's eyes. Eric looked down, and saw that lightning still played across his chest and arms. Noise was coming from elsewhere now, as more survivors rose to view the shattered remains – and to see the boy with lightning dancing on his skin.

Eric watched them, despair filling his heart. The faces of those around him were filled with hatred and despair. He had to say something, but could not find the words. His body ached and his muscles burned, but he struggled to his feet. A surge of blood rushed to his head. He swayed. Then, determined, he opened his mouth to speak.

An angry buzz of voices assailed him. To his left, a man drew a dagger from his belt. He started towards Eric. Another quickly followed suit, ripping a makeshift club from a pile of rubble as he approached. The broken ground crunched beneath their booted feet. Each wore a grim mask of determination. When they were a dozen feet from him they hesitated, eyeing him warily.

Eric struggled to find some words of explanation. He wanted to shout that it hadn't been his fault, that he could not control this curse. But he knew in his heart it would be a lie. He had known his presence was a terrible danger to all around him. A heavy weight settled over his shoulders. There was nothing he could offer these souls but his life.

More survivors had joined the first two men, arming themselves with whatever makeshift weapon was within reach. Each sported burns across their arms and clothing, and dark bruises on their faces. A fire burned in their eyes, fueled by the horror they had just witnessed.

Eric trembled, staring at the blades and cudgels held by men and women alike. His heart pounded in his chest. He clenched his fists, trying to ignore the hollow feeling in the pit of his stomach. His rib cage ached where the club had struck him earlier. Bruises from the beating were already starting to swell on his arms and legs. His mind shuddered at the thought of the pain still to come.

Cautiously, the survivors edged towards him, numbers fueling their courage.

Eric backed away, his own courage fading with each step. The villagers began to move faster, sensing his fear. He stumbled backwards over the rubble, unable to tear his gaze from the madness in the eyes of the crowd. He stumbled backwards over a pile of rubble and crashed to the ground. The shock lifted the spell. Eric scrabbled to his feet, and ran for his life.

Peak of the Clouds

Allison Wade

Fairies aren't meant to fly with wet wings. Her mother always said that during the rainy days, then she prepared a chamomile tea and sat next to her in front of the fireplace.

The fire was warm and pleasant, thought Nymphea while she rushed in the rain, but now the wood was so wet it wouldn't burn anymore.

The cold water bit her bones. The leafy branch she used for shelter was becoming too heavy for her arms and she had to let it go and watch it slide away with the stream flowing along the pathway. She landed for a moment on a big rock, just to take the leap and reach the mountain face that stood tall, bare, disappearing through the gray clouds.

She turned back to watch the valley, which had almost lost all its colors. The lake level had raised again during the night and the water overflowed, erasing the shores and reaching the village, filtering through the little roads and leaking in the basements of the houses, from time to time taking away some piece: a bowl, a chamber pot, a chair, an embroidered tablecloth.

The rain didn't want to stop. It had been pouring for months, washing away the joy of living and tearing off the strength from the bones. What was just bad weather seemed to have become a tragedy. They didn't know how it all happened and neither from where those thunderous clouds came; maybe it was just a twist of fate.

The elder fairies gathered in the big house, they arranged some makeshift shelters for the ones who had their house flooded, and decided that the only thing to do was to rely on the ancient magic. After choosing the fastest fairies, they sent them to the four peaks in search of the wishing dandelions. They had to wait a long time, because the season wasn't right, but now the spring had come and Nymphea was determined to find the flowers and save her home.

She had to reach the Peak of the Clouds, the highest of them all, so tall that it disappeared in the sky and no one had ever seen its top. They said that up there the sun was so hot and bright that it would burn the transparent and flimsy wings of the fairies, the air so thin that it would left them breathless.

Nymphea took a moment to rest. She felt frozen, her breath faded away in clouds of condensation, her soaked hair fell on her forehead like dark roots, her wings, wrinkly like crumpled parchment, felt uncomfortable and heavy, her back muscles were aching, and they were the only thing burning in her body, since she almost couldn't feel the tips of her fingers.

She closed her eyes, her teeth grinded for the shiver she couldn't control, she tried to take a deep breath.

You've got strong arms and sturdy legs, said her mother. Fairies are not meant to just fly, you'll become lazy and sickly if you use only your wings.

Nymphea looked up, following with her eyes the line of the rock face, memorizing the position of the ledges that looked more comfortable.

The white light coming from the sky made her sneeze. Oddly, she felt like laughing. When they were little, in the field behind the school, they always competed to see who was able to restrain oneself from sneezing while smelling the awful herbs infusion made by the teacher fairy, and they said one another, "Don't look at the light!" But the memory of the green blooming fields that now were flooded, made her heart tighten to the point it became a cold little stone. She shouldn't waste her time.

Planting her left feet on the first ledge, she gave a boost and stretched her arms to grab the rock. It was slippery and sharp. She tightened her grip and started to climb.

A hand after another, a foot and a slide, the fear of losing her grasp and the water, which lashed oblique and got in her eyes fogging her sight. But a little higher there was a small clearing, where she could make a stop.

She climbed with a last effort and finally was able to catch her breath. She laid down, on her back, covering almost all the flat space, squashing her wings, which remained a little bent and were hurting, but her breath was so heavy that she couldn't move and she rather suffer that small pain, just the time to recover, while the water poured down like needles pounding on her chest, it penetrated her lips as if to drown her or quench her thirst, or both.

Nymphea remained there for a long time, maybe she even doze off a little, until something, like a shadow, passed over her.

She jumped up, and almost fell beyond the border, and had to hold on to the rock with her nails.

The shadow in front of her was leaning out with curiosity. "What are you doing here?"

The fairy flinched, recognizing the language of humans.

It was a young man, dressed with animal skins, with a hood from which stuck out wet curls and a couple of eyes, blue like fleur-de-lis, like deep waters. "Are you a fairy?"

Nymphea stood up and flattened against the cold slippery rock face, like she wanted to hide herself, but she had no way to escape: below her there was nothing but the cliff she had climbed, and above, another vertical ascent from which he was barring the road.

The young man got near. Nymphea stepped back and her left foot missed the ground, she lost her balance and her body weight seemed to drag her down. She grasped with a hand but slipped on the sharp rocks, a burning sensation on her palm made her lose the grip; she moved her wings as fast as she could, but they were slow and numb and she felt like falling.

A strong hand grabbed her arm.

For a moment she was standing at mid-air, a foot on the rock, the emptiness below her, the cold wind swirling around her, it was like flying.

The warm hand pulled her up. Nymphea stepped back on the ground. But her legs were shaking and she fell on her knees. She stood there for a while with her heart pounding and her breath heavy. And that stranger skin touching her.

She looked up. Water eyes were still upon her.

"Are you all right?"

Finally, Nymphea nodded. She knew the language of the humans, her mother had taught her, because she was a border guard, even if her only contact with them was when the strangers trespassed the valley limits.

Nymphea didn't like the humans, they were rude and arrogant, and they always tried to go where was forbidden; if it weren't for the fairies' magic, they would have conquered the valley already.

Even if there were treaties going back to the beginning of times, stating that the humans were not to thread on the sacred land, very often the poachers climbed the mountains looking for ibex and wild goats to slaughter.

They weren't afraid to enter the wolves territory, as greedy as they were, they didn't have respect for anything.

Yet, that young human, even if he had frightened her, had just saved her from a fall that could have been deadly.

The rain kept pounding merciless on them. Nymphea looked at her hand and saw red drops staining her palm.

The human leaned over her. "Are you hurt?" Without waiting for an answer, he began to rummage in his leather shoulder bag and pulled out a piece of cloth that was supposed to be a handkerchief. He reached for her hand, but the fairy drew back.

"Don't worry, I won't hurt you, I just want to bandage that bad cut."

Nymphea stood for a moment, hesitating, but then gave up and showed him her wound.

He bandaged it with care. "Do you understand my language?"

Nymphea nodded, moving her head slowly, still wide-eyed.

"My name is Jaden," he said and then smiled. It was a smile so bright and kind that she was surprised. She didn't know humans could smile like that, she had always imagined them dirty and mean.

The fairy got up, leaning on the man's shoulder, her legs still a bit wobbly. She stared at him quietly.

"And what is your name?" He asked, finally letting go of her hand.

"Nymphea."

Jaden looked down thoughtfully, then turned back to her. "What are you doing here? Are you lost?"

She shook her head.

"Where are you going?" Now his smile seemed a bit cracked, obviously that odd non-conversation was becoming an embarrassment for him.

Nymphea realized she was being rude to the person who had saved her, and maybe she should answer. She pointed her index finger upward and looked at the clouds that hid the summit of the mountain.

"You're climbing up the top too? Well, this is a really strange encounter," he scratched his head. "I think we could make the road together, what do you say?"

Nymphea frowned, turned slightly, just enough to not lose the balance again, and showed him her wings, shaking them and scattering around raindrops.

"You're a fairy, I noticed, you know," he laughed. "You're not afraid of a humble man, right?"

"You have to be afraid," said Nymphea, slowly spelling the words and trying to correct her accent.

Jaden looked at her, puzzled. "You don't look so dangerous." He pulled out the stick that was tied behind his back and rotated it into the air. "I waded across a raging river and through the territory of the wolves to get this far. I will certainly not be scared by a pair of wings."

Here, now she recognized the typical baldness of humans. Nymphea tilted her head to one side as if trying to see him from a different angle, with a reproachful gaze. "Are you a hunter?"

This time it was he who shook his head to say no.

"Why are you here?"

"I have to reach the top," just that. He put away his stick and smiled again. "Do you think we should be going?"

Nymphea shrugged as Jaden clung to the rocks and began again to climb with surprising rapidity; it was evident that his muscles were stronger than those of a slender fairy, but she could not allow to be left behind. She returned to the mountainside to follow his steps. "What are you looking for?" She asked, already short of breath.

"They told me that on top of this peak grow dandelions," said Jaden, without turning back, continuing to climb, one step after another, tireless.

Nymphea gathered all of her energy to keep up. "Why do you need them?"

He stopped for a moment to catch his breath. "You're a fairy, you should know better," he turned his head slightly to look down at her. "Is it true that they grant wishes?"

Nymphea didn't slow down, determined to reach him. She arrived at his height, and stopped next to him. She leaned her head to the rock, closed her eyes, inhaling deeply. The water dripped down her back, under her clothes, slipping between the junctions of the wings, making her shiver. "It's the old magic," she whispered. "Nothing is truer than this."

He smiled in satisfaction and resumed to climb.

"Wait! What... what is your wish?" Asked the fairy, following him.

This time, Jaden didn't turn, nor slowed down. "My mother is very sick," he said only, with a grim note in his voice.

The atmosphere had become foggier; they were entering the layer of clouds, the air was thinner and the rain had reduced to small pins on their face. The human had vanished from her sight, hidden by the white and gray. Nymphea found herself disoriented, struggling to see the rock face and follow any direction, but she heard his voice out of nowhere. "We're almost out!"

Nymphea felt her heart sinking; she found the urge to climb higher.

Beyond the clouds, the world rekindled with light and color.

The sky was a turquoise that hurt their eyes, the sun was warm, the air was clean and dry, it was like being born again to a new life.

She found Jaden and his eyes of fleur-de-lis; the human had

found a solid support and was stretching out his hand.

Nymphea grabbed it grateful, flapping her wings to shake off the raindrops and give the push to the last jump.

Above them, they could finally see the top.

The fairy looked down instead, at the gray cloak that covered the valley. "The rain doesn't stop," she said sadly.

"Is that why you're here?"

Nymphea nodded.

"Then let's go," urged the human and found his way through the rock ledges.

They went up again for a stretch, when Jaden hissed, "Damn!"

"What?" The fairy didn't know that word.

"A griffin's nest," pointed the human. "And we don't have enough handholds to change the road."

"I can't see it."

"Now it's empty, but the mother could be around. We must move fast." Jaden slightly quickened his pace; Nymphea could hear his breathing getting heavier. She flapped her wings to help herself in the ascent; they were slowly drying and she felt them regain strength.

A screech through the sky. From a distance, a dark shadow was gliding toward them, like a brush stroke on a blue canvas.

"Don't move," whispered Jaden. "Maybe it didn't see us."

Nymphea pressed herself against the rocks, following the erratic flight of the bird with the corner of her eye. It was getting closer and closer, she could already see the white, patchy head; its strange cry, alternating grunts and whistles, resounded sharp in the empty sky, creeping under her skin and making her quiver.

It absolutely had seen them, and intended to defend its territory.

"Keep climbing, quick!" She said to the human.

Jaden didn't hesitate, but now the griffin had pointed him. It swooped down on him. It was big, its wingspan measuring almost a fairy and a half. It would have hurt him, maybe made him fall; Nymphea felt she had to do something.

She pulled away from the rock face, letting herself go down in free fall.

As she precipitated, she saw Jaden raising his left arm to protect himself from the beak of the bird of prey.

She closed her eyes and concentrated on the flight. She flapped her wings, faster and faster, forcing her back muscles to the extreme. Her body on fire. She was going down in a tailspin, cutting the currents, waiting for the right one, which would bring her back up.

She went almost to touch the clouds. Opened her arms and stroked them with her fingers, feeling them, impalpable as dandelions, but finally she perceived the friction that held her back. She flapped harder, gave a push with her arms and legs, like a frog emerging from the pond, and began to ascend higher and higher, freer and freer in the immense blue.

Jaden had managed to ward off the griffin, but he had lost his balance and half of his body was leaning on the void. The bird was going round to get back and attack.

Nymphea pushed more, gaining speed, and then stopped in mid-air, right before the human. She closed her eyes, concentrated, breathing deeply, letting her inner voice speak.

The fairies had a gift, to communicate with the heart of every living being, but only those who were wild and lonely were able to hear them, only those who were pure and not contaminated by unnecessary thoughts, only those who were free.

She outstretched her hands, with her palms facing upwards.

"What are you doing? Go away!" Shouted Jaden, but she didn't listen, she wasn't there at the moment, but in his heart. She could hear his heartbeat, his fear, his pain. She would have protected him, because that was the purpose of each fairy: defending life.

She radiated her message, which spread like a warm wind.

The griffin, returning in nosedive, came very close to her, but then veered sharply, touching her forehead with just one of its feathers. Then it flew away and reached its nest, perched among the sharp rocks. It remained crouched there, watching them with its crooked neck and black, curious eyes, which now didn't see them as a threat, but as a part of the whole, like a fragment of an interconnected world.

Nymphea turned toward Jaden, this time she was smiling and giving him a hand, helping him to regain his balance. "Let's go. We're almost there."

She flew next to him, while they completed their climb.

The top of the Peak of the Clouds was a piece of grass, green like a velvet carpet. Nymphea landed gently and held out her hand again, helping Jaden to get up.

The human laid down on the grass, exhausted, his chest getting up and down more and more slowly until his breath became regular again. "We did it," he said, looking at the sky, as blue as his eyes.

He sat up and took off his hood, showing his disheveled curls, the color of the corn. He looked at that small piece of land in the middle of the sky. "Where are the dandelions?"

Nymphea pointed to a spot behind him, a single flower sprouting from a tuft of dark green leaves, a white ball swinging in the breeze of the high altitude.

"There's only one?"

"Take it," said the fairy.

Jaden stood up, but turned towards the precipice. He looked down at the thick layer of gray clouds that covered the entire valley of the fairies. "You haven't told me yet what your wish is."

Nymphea approached, contemplating the view with him. "It's been raining for several months. The waters have flooded the valley; soon we will not have a place to live anymore. I was sent to clear the sky."

"Then you take it," said Jaden.

The fairy looked at him in surprise.

"You saved me from the griffin and for that I owe you. I'll find another way to help my mother, it's more important that you protect your people."

Nymphea turned around and walked the few steps that separated her from the dandelion. She reached down and grabbed the stem with two fingers. She picked it gently.

The flower produced a small flash of yellow light, which only she could see, the aura of the ancient magic that dwelt in the sap of plants, the one that healed wounds and cured diseases, the one that only the magical creatures knew how to use fully.

She returned to Jaden and handed him the flower. "You've saved me too, there is no debt between us. There are other fairies, who left, as I did, to climb the peaks. I'm sure they have found other flowers."

Jaden turned around and put his hood back on; he was going away.

"Wait!" Nymphea grabbed his sleeve. "Please, take it."

He looked at her thoughtfully. "Are you sure?"

The fairy nodded, moving her wings as if to accompany her resolution.

Jaden granted her a new smile. "Okay." He took the stem with caution and stopped, with the flower in front of his face, the fairy on the opposite side. His watery eyes stared at her calmly, as if he was meditating.

For a moment, Nymphea heard his heartbeat; she tried to read in that deep blue, but before she could grasp his thoughts, Jaden closed his eyes. He stayed so for a few moments, barely moving his lips to pronounce his silent wish.

He opened his eyes and blew.

The haired seeds scattered lightly in the air around them, the human breath stopped only when the last one was removed, leaving a bare and lonely stem.

"You think it will come true?" Asked Jaden.

"The old magic never betrays those who ask with an honest heart."

He walked to the edge and dropped what was left of the dandelion; he watched it disappear into the clouds. Then he sat down, with his feet dangling in the void.

"What are you doing?" Asked Nymphea.

"I'm waiting for the rain to stop."

"But..."

"Didn't you say that your fairy friends went to look for other dandelions?"

Nymphea nodded and sat down next to him.

"I'm sure everything will be fine."

The fairy felt a drop run across her cheek. She looked up but the sky above them was completely clear, it was her eyes that were wet. She wiped her tears with the back of her hand. "Thank you," she said.

"For what?" He asked with his usual smile.

Nymphea stretched her thin white hand, and gently put it in his rough and warm palm.

"For waiting with me."

Within The Forest

Sergio Palumbo

Over the last few months it had been reported that some young women had disappeared near the Mountains of the Night. There were only two small villages in the gorge there, and Marwen knew very well about the missing girls: she was native to one of the towns – Ltinw – which was situated almost at the foot of Mount Lush, close to the Woods of Ltinweharl.

As soon as their Sister-Superior heard the news of the first strange disappearances near their Fortress-Convent, she had become worried. But it was only when the remains of one of those unfortunate people had been found that the Congregation of the Blessed Sisters finally decided to intervene immediately. The woman's corpse had been spotted next to a small river, half devoured by some wild beasts, most likely exhumed from the bank by hungry animals. So Marwen had been sent there.

Marwen knew exactly how to move about in those surroundings, having been born in that area, efficiently managing the discontent already snaking among the local peasants. She knew that soon gossip and old wives' tales would be likely to stir up trouble for everyone, including officers of the law.

Marwen had already formed her own opinion of the bloody situation at hand and believed she knew exactly what her Congregation was going to face. At least, so she thought.

The region of the Mountains of the Night rose to the north-east, and was a twenty-day ride from the place where the Blessed Sister's Fortress-Convent was located. It was an isolated land, mainly inhabited by cattlemen, with no mining sites and far away from any of the main trade routes. As her mount approached the village of Ltinw, Marwen's heart almost broke. It had been a very long time since she had felt such a feeling inside. She looked over the horizon but the young woman couldn't see the precise place where she had been born and had lived until she was five-years-old. Besides, her home didn't exist anymore, having been burned to the ground twenty years ago.

The Sister could still remember that night, when the plunderers from the mountains nearby had stormed into the village - stealing, rustling and setting fire to many houses. In the end, once the counting of all the dead had been completed by the surviving population, the terrible truth had come out: her entire family had been wiped out because of the arson. Marwen was the only survivor out of all of them.

Not having any other close relatives, nor anyone else who could care for her, the child had been given eventually to the Congregation of Blessed Sisters. By tradition, the Sisters usually attended to unfortunate and lonely girls -- provided they were still young enough to begin school -- and welcomed them into their cathedrals. This practice was in order to make them unlearn everything they had studied before then, so they could be trained in the use of the magical arts practiced at the Congregation's Fortress-Convent. All the newcomers had to start to see the world with new, different eyes, laying aside their previous knowledge and developing their ability to evaluate every single object, all places, and every single person they were going to get in touch with, allowing their hidden qualities to finally be discovered and exposed. This was so they could seize the energy necessary to be capable of creating their enchantments and increase their skills, of course.

Marwen had been studying with her Sister-Superior for twenty years, and had become very accomplished thanks to her valuable teachings. She considered herself to be one of the most beloved of this mentor. The elderly woman had immediately seen in her a great potential which was to be developed thoroughly, with much devotion to duty and engagement.

Glad for the progress she had made during her training, Marwen often remembered the one day her Sister Superior commented, while inside the colonnade of their Fortress-Convent: "My dear, it was very beneficial for you that what happened occurred, so you would become one of our Congregations. Otherwise, your great potential would have most likely have gone undiscovered. You would never have been allowed to give so much to our kingdom if you had remained some poor peasants' ordinary daughter, this much is certain."

At first, the little girl didn't appreciate such talk, feeling uneasy and even offended at those indelicate terms, but with time she had come to fully understand their true meaning. Thinking again of all the lives she had saved so far, the important tasks she had completed while busy undergoing some very perilous assignments, today Marwen could inevitably value what her Sister- Superior had said.

"It's not for us to decide which people possess the gift of magical powers. It's up to Nature of course – and that woman has pre-ordained it. And that is the end of it; there was no way to change things, obviously." If only her coming to live with the Congregation hadn't occurred because of such tragic circumstances.

Seeing the houses and the wooden walls of her native village once again with her own eyes, Marwen almost gave a start and began visualizing the characteristic alleys and the stony fountains she had drawn water from when still a small child. But she soon regained her self-control thanks to her training and her ability to manage her feelings.

On behalf of their Congregation, the Sisters performed a very important duty which at times took them to the farthest recesses of the kingdom. Although formally at the Sun Divinity's service, they were used to acting in accordance with the Royal Judicial Order of the King. In this way they brought justice and peace, whereas the traveling judges weren't able to go due to remarkable distances or many dangers. This was especially true in cases where their actions would have proven ineffective given the peculiar matter dealt with, or most of all if it looked like forbidden sorcery or similar crimes had been involved.

The Sisters were perfectly able to carry out such tasks thanks to their skills and were proficient at resolving the rebellious acts made by heretical groups and bloody assassins. They were even better than regular troops - sparing the government the trouble of deploying militiamen that could be better used elsewhere, like sending them to defend the borders against the barbarians of the Western border, for example.

The perfect combination of their magical knowledge and their fighting skills made them experienced swordswomen and clever practitioners of spells. Anyone would have found great difficulty in challenging them. All of that wrapped them in a sort of reputation of invincibility, which undoubtedly commanded respect and fear, wherever they went.

Not all the Sisters were as tall, statuesque and beautiful as Marwen was and, any common woman would have boasted if they had possessed her curly hair, her blue eyes, or the wondrous face with delicate features she had. But it was mainly their traditional clothing which made them easily recognizable among the people while passing through: the red mantle along with the green leather cuirass allowed everyone around to easily identify them. In most cases just their presence was enough to have an easy resolution to any dispute once and for all. No one usually dared to defy or contradict them, unless he were a fool or stupid. They had been granted full powers, but it was rarely that any of them executed capital punishment, apart from a few terrible crimes where a lesson needed to be taught to the population.

Marwen couldn't tear her eyes away from her village, which lay in the distance. In her mind she kept seeing where her old home should have been. Twenty years ago, almost a whole lifetime, after all.

As soon as she arrived at the village leader's home, the young woman introduced herself and declared that she had been sent there under her Congregation's orders to solve the case of the female corpse found next to the small river and the other recent disappearances.

The old village leader – a man named Ulf who was about sixty-years-old, with grey-hair and an imposing beard, greeted her warmly. Marwen didn't have any memory of him among all the faces of the inhabitants the Sister remembered when she had been living in Ltinw. But she knew he should be a native of that place, given his local accent. The woman and the leader sat down in the entrance room where there were two plush armchairs near the window.

"Do you think all the other people who disappeared have undergone the same bad fortune as that poor maid who was found dead?"

"It's too early to say," Marwen replied, sipping the beverage a servant had placed on the table next to them and then handed to her. "But I don't doubt that this is exactly the case."

"Could the murderers be slavers? It might be they who took those women - maybe the one discovered dead just tried to escape or rebelled in some way," Ulf supposed, scratching a long gash on his face. The scar was seemingly more a result of some past fieldwork than a war wound. At least that was what Marwen thought.

"That's unlikely," she objected, "as they haven't operated in this region before. At the most you might think of some occasional plunderers from the mountains. They're used to robbing these lands at times." The Sister became thoughtful: she herself knew something about that.

"Well, then, is this your theory? Plunderers?" Ulf asked, frowning.

"Actually, no…But I can't tell you anything more at present. I need to gather evidence before I can say anything else."

"We'll be very glad to give you all of our help, indeed. The people are clearly upset, and resentment is already spreading inside the village, you know."

"I see, and I thank you for the assistance you're offering me. But now I must ask you to lead me to the house of one of the poor women who disappeared."

"Of course, Sister. We could start with Arlhenf's dwelling. She's a young peasant living just on the village boundary; she's alone and has no children."

"Perfect, I just don't want to cause more pain to her family."

"On the contrary, your presence in town will surely be of help and a cause for rejoicing! I'll order a man-at-arms to escort us immediately."

Just outside, they set off for the main street. Citizens were soon crowding in around them and watching inquisitively. It was clear that a Sister from the Congregation coming to town in order to make inquiries was a matter of relevance - her presence was enough to calm down the murmurings and pacify those seeking justice.

The dwelling they went in, more a sort of shack than an adequate house, was located on the eastern side of the village, which was an area comprised of woodworking shops stores and old sheds. Given the stench inside, it was easy to figure out that it had been a very long time since anyone had entered there.

Marwen headed in a resolute manner for the bedroom, followed by Ulf, while the man-at-arms kept watch outside the door. As soon as she found the right room, the woman saw some clothes inside a worn-out hope chest. She took a blouse and began touching it with the simple touch of her fingers. Then, the Sister opened her mind completely while her power arose inside, filling her body with many sensations, almost completely inebriating her senses.

"A steep slope, some steps forward, running fast, escaping in search of safety, escaping from someone. The legs suddenly stumble once, twice. The pursuer is very near; there is no place to hide. The weapon comes down as fast as a lightning, hits two, three times the chest, then keeps going at the tormented body and finally cuts the head in half.

"Just before the darkness falls over everything, in the distance the shape of a copper-beech tree, a huge verdant crown, is outlined against a full-blown yellowish meadow. A small river flows next to the wooden fencing, not far from a drinking fountain in ruins..."

That's it! I know where that place is...Marwen thought. It looked like one of the spots where her parents took her for water just before diner, when she was still living in the village. She had no doubt!

"Now I have what I was looking for!" The Sister exclaimed, suddenly going outside, still under intense meditation, both eyes wild. It was as if there was nothing else around, only her mind and

But there was no one else around who could help her to perform her duty. All day long she kept meditating in her room, tidying up her magical instruments and sharpening her sword. Late in the evening, she let her hair down, went down to the common dining room, had a full meal without any alcoholic drinks, of course, and then waited for half an hour before leaving the table. Eventually she set out, heading for the woods just outside of the village.

By then, it was already dusk. In an hour the countryside would be immersed in total darkness. While she walked alone across the meadows, in the still of the night, only cut off at times because of some rapacious birds whose sounds could be heard here and there, Marwen was well aware that, before going to face her opponent, she had to become stronger, and more protected.

So, she made all the preparations she had to and completed her best rituals. Some of them involved her fresh blood, too. Then the woman took her weapon up and set off for the trees nearby, heading for her destination.

"Enter a forest and the boundaries of any country are forgotten": so the saying went. "Enter this forest at night and leave aside any hope of surviving, if you are not well prepared," the woman thought it should say.

While going around at nighttime throughout the Forest of Ltinweharl, Marwen looked more pensive than ever. Such a place seemed to be peopled with many ancient trees, higher than the ordinary, almost shutting out the sky with their wide leaves, seemingly unwilling to reveal its secrets: this just looked like a perfect spot where somebody's thoughts could easily take flights of fancy. Those of lesser will would succumb to distracting thought. But, not Marwen, surely.

The thing that most worried her were the wounds she had noticed on the corpse unearthed the day before. Certainly, those had been made by means of an exotic cutting weapon. A blade foreign in origin...however, it could mean something else, something worse, as well.

Suddenly the Sister saw and heard movement in the undergrowth, turning immediately. The shadow of a tall and bulky man suddenly jumped out of an arched linden tree.

As she saw him standing before her, his curved long blade unsheathed, Marwen understood that the worst she could have imagined was in front of her: given its intricate luminous drawings her visions, out of time and space. Nothing else was more important, no feeling more absorbing or considerable than those. "Just follow me, mayor."

Ulf didn't say anything, restricting himself to pointing at the man-at-arms and gesturing for him to stay close to the Sister. They traveled along a path leading to the woods, breaking off just before a slope. Marwen then stopped next to a little fountain along the small river.

"We must dig here!" She cried out to the two men nearby.

"We'll need more help," Ulf replied, ordering his guard to go search for more men in town.

While waiting for the excavators, the village-leader wasn't brave enough to ask the Sister for some explanation. On the one hand, such a spot seemed to be without a single clue, it looked exactly like the rest of the meadow that lay between here and that nearby beech tree. On the other hand, the middle-aged man didn't doubt this woman's powers, nor did he want to call her actions into question, of course.

As soon as the excavators arrived at the spot indicated and started digging, a clump of curious people came to the meadow where the village-leader and the Sister were, just to wait anxiously. When the men had finished their job, to the common dismay, some remains came out from the hole in the ground. These were exactly the ones of the lost woman the peasants had been searching for, one of the many who had disappeared over the course of the last months.

Her chest had been torn open, and the heart removed. Likely eaten...

Suddenly, for Marwen, all was clear. Damn clear, unfortunately...

Still absorbed in such vivid images of death, Marwen's sensations were wobbly and mixed-up. It happened to her any time she was using her abilities in order to find the mutilated corpse of a dead man. It took a while for her to get used to the room the citizens of Ltinw had kindly provided for her. But only the dark of night was able to give the Sister some comfort, finally.

***

When morning came, her mind felt fresh and ready to face the new day ahead of her. Now the woman knew exactly what she had to do, the only thing was that she doubted she could do all that alone.

and ornaments, it was self-evident that the assassin handled the Sword of Blood, a rare magical weapon too strong to be faced even by means of her great powers. Such a sword had to be bathed in tears and blood of somebody, usually an adversary killed in battle or a prisoner sacrificed on purpose, in order to maintain its deadly power. It was perfectly capable of piercing the greatest armor. So, the man was a Follower of the Nocturnal Deities!

It was going to become an uneven fighting, for sure. But she would muster her best anyway. Like her elder Sister-Superior of the Fortress-Convent would say, on the battlefield, life is the sum of all your choices and skills, death the result of your blunders and wrong techniques".

"So, you are the Damned Warrior that has been roaming these lands!" the woman cried out, almost as a sign of defiance, continuing to stay on guard.

"And you must be the member of the Congregation I saw arriving at the village yesterday. I was spying the area because I didn't want to be caught by surprise." His voice was undaunted, both eyes icy, a pleased sneer on his full lips and the massive head shaved on top. He was a man about thirty-years-old, clad in black, and muscular, but his skin looked as white as though he were dead.

"Why do you harm innocent, helpless people? Why do you slay them? Isn't there any real adversary worth your attention! Or do you lack the courage to fight against a strong opponent, like me?"

"You must be speaking of those dead women, of course," the warrior replied, while advancing in circles around the Sister so to make her move, keeping her at a safe distance. "It's not as you think. We act like this on purpose! All our childish feelings: love, good will, compassion, fear. They have grown up along with our bodies, making us human, weak…but we need to be something more, superior beings! By killing some feeble and blameless women we show everyone we can get rid of the burdens of love, courtesy and pity and this way become Damned Bloody Warriors. By eating their hearts we bury our scruples once and for all, turning into emotionless men, finally."

It was following these words that the man moved in to attack. His enchanted weapon twirled rapidly, giving some powerful and forceful blows that made the Sister back off, so as not to get run through. On equal terms, Marwen hit back at his assaults, making up for all the wild attacks her opponent had struck thanks to her excellent technique, crisp concentration, and precision. The woman knew that such jumps forward and evasive actions were just the beginning of what she had to go through. The Eternally Damned Warrior was more skillful than this, she was sure.

He instantly stopped his lunges and the Sister thought that maybe she had been able to put fear in his heart. However, the evil grin she saw on his face immediately convinced her to the contrary. Maybe it was just that he liked this sort of fighting, thinking it was interesting.

Another fierce attack began and this time it forced the woman to be at her best in order to parry all the most dangerous blows. However, despite her goodwill, the woman proved incapable of preventing two downward passes from cutting directly into her mantle. One of them also pierced her leather cuirass, cutting into the skin on her left side.

As sure as hell, such a warrior was exceedingly very powerful and well trained! Besides, his sword looked extraordinary, and her blessed weapon was unable to crack it. If only she could disarm him by means of a smart move.

Now it was Marwen that started in again and chased him, trying to use all her experience and her most impressive blows before it was too late. She worried that she might get wounded because of her inattention and that might put her offside or thwart her. But everything was all to no avail, there was no way to beat that monster, not even by making a display of some usual spells of her, and she had really a lot of tricks stored up.

Sadly, there was nothing to be done.

"Your skills are not all that reliable," the man sneered in an arrogant way.

Marwen knew she had to end such a fight as soon as she could or it would be too late, her weariness was already weakening her body. Both legs felt like lead and the wound in her side was unquestionably throbbing. So, she assaulted him again, suddenly and fiercely, using her most powerful attack.

The sword swished from the bottom to the top, passing by her adversary's neck, only a span away from his hard, sweaty skin. Near. But not near enough, unfortunately.

On the other hand, the warrior moved forward with his enchanted weapon and pierced the woman's left shoulder in a bloody and agonizing way, causing another deep wound that forced her to immediately drop the sword to the ground.

At this stage the Sister, already feeling defeated and almost dying, just being on the point of letting herself pass out because of her lack of strength, raised some questions inside her mind. 'What is going to happen now that I've failed? What if such a bloody assassin has the upper hand because he has proven to be stronger, more resolute and more capable than me? What if the evil acts prevail over the good, over the right deeds?"

The Sword of Blood that belonged to her opponent was coming near...

'What about my mission if his training with martial arts wins out over mine? And what if no one else, after my death, finds a way to defeat such a warrior? Who will avenge the dead and bring justice to these lands? What is the use of possessing my abilities if this one wins in the end?'

And while Marwen was falling to the ground, meditating on all that, the warrior came raced closer and hit her violently again and again, inflicting many new wounds. It was obvious she would soon die because of a lack of blood.

Rejoicing for his win and sheathing his weapon, the man vulgarly smiled - making fun of the one defeated at his feet. He then turned to move along, leaving her exhausted on the ground without giving her the final deathblow, certain that soon nature would soon take its course.

However, he didn't get far away. When he arrived at the nearest pine, he felt himself stopped because of an invisible force that, incredibly, didn't let him go on. The man wasn't able to move away more than ten paces from that place, there seemed to be no way to go past this unexpected barrier. Then he got out his magical Sword of Blood again and began beating the invisible wall with all his strength. But none of it had any effect. And he kept beating and beating many times afterward that, but nothing happened.

What kind of a damn curse was this?

So the warrior backtracked, soon coming before the woman who was just breathing her last breath, between the pain and dismay.

"Just tell me, Sister! Why can't I go away from here? I'm speaking to you!"

It's because of the ritual I performed before fighting, just in case," her voice was faint now.

"How may I remove it? Tell me now!" The assassin exclaimed, towering over Marwen's dying body.

"You can't...it's linked to my own blood!"

"How can I leave?" The man repeated, as if he hadn't been

listening to her at all.

"You won't be allowed to."

At that point he rolled his eyes, hate-stricken.

The Sister, using her last energies, said, "You have a great strength, assassin. I can't defeat you, that's a fact. But I took some precautions before coming to fight against you. I sealed the boundary of this forest, in case I died because of you. My ritual won't let you ever move away from here, you're trapped within these trees! You aren't going to harm any other woman after me! Maybe you'll be able to kill somebody who enters into these woods by chance - but nothing else."

"You be damned! How long it will last?" The warrior yelled at her.

"As long as I lay dead...that is, forever!" And, that being said, she gave out.

So, the man turned around and around, looking at the outline of the trees standing all about him, hidden by the night. It was still hours until dawn. Finally he put his hands to his head, excessively despairing, and started yelling at the top of his voice.

He had already noticed that such an unimportant forest, lost near the borders of the kingdom, was already becoming entirely too small for him...

THE END

Locking Horns

Amdi Silvestri

Triumphantly, Erdengard jumped from behind the bushes and slashed the rope with his sword. The sharp buzz of Thornblade cut the stout hemp robe with the same ease as it had cleft trolls and sliced evil wizards open. The blade was seasoned and had tasted its share of both.

The prey sharply lifted its head and exploded into a run. But alas, it only managed to put down one of its front legs before the same leg went straight through the cover of leaves that had been used to cover a trap. Still majestically, it went on its knees. From above, a big cage made from sharpened stakes, landed in the soft soil and effectively put the prey behind bars. A blanket of birds rose in panic form the tree tops, darting here and there until dispersing into nothingness.

A smug grin slowly invaded the beautiful visage that was Erdengards. His blond, wild hair that no comb or brush could tame framed a wide jaw, a straight nose and eyes so incredibly blue that even his own mother whispered that they could only be sapphires put there by some benign power. Erdengards grin widened. Already, he could feel the satisfying weight of the duke's gold in his pockets. You see, Erdengard was an adventurer and he worked for anyone rich enough to pay his fee.

A swagger in his step, he entered the clearing and glanced at the old oak, that supported the rope. He followed the thick cord with his eyes, from the large branch to the top of the cage. The simplest of traps had been enough. It was almost too easy. He had pictured an epic chase unfolding, brimming with clever ruses and ingenious tactics. The way it was supposed to go down. But in the end he really did not care much. Noble deeds could make the hearts of women melt, but the sound of gold coins pouring onto a night stand would do it twice as fast.

From the cage the prey stared. Its golden eyes were sad, the pupils silver coins of longing and goodness. It was white, as white as a new tooth or polished ivory. The mane moved like a controlled thunderstorm across the chest and in its forehead the vibrating form of a twisting horn. It was shaking, but whether it was the product of fear or the inherent magic of the horn that made everything shimmer, was impossible to say.

"Gotcha," Erdengard laughed and hero-posed in front of the cage. Thornblade sliced the air in half with a whine, as he stuck it into the ground. Calmly he rested both his hands on the pommel.

The unicorn, for that was what it was, bowed its head so the horn pointed directly at him. So close he could see just how exquisite it was. Every twist and every groove was perfect. No chipping, no wear marred the beautiful surface. So delicately intertwining it was that it did not appear as something natural, oh no, instead it looked like something made by a true artisan, who had sweat for years and finally, when all was done, had planted the marvelous masterpiece in living flesh.

"Good knight. Let me go. I am not a creature that can live among people," said the unicorn, its voice resembling a row of silver bells caught in a sweet summer breeze.

"Let you go?" Erdengard laughed and shook his head. During his many adventures he had encountered much beauty and even more evil and the many years had made him all but immune to their effects. In the end, all that was, was money and gold pieces never asked stupid question like what was right and what was wrong. "I cannot let you go when I have caught you. You will be sold to the duke and for the rest of your life you will be standing in a golden cage in the middle of his garden. That is, unless, you can offer me a better deal?"

With great sadness the magnificent animal shook its head.

"I have no gold nor silver. They only thing I have is the purity of my heart and I can only share that with one who already has his own."

Erdengard barely paid any attention to the animal's words. In his mind he was already in the midst of planning how he would transport the unicorn and whether or not, he could squeeze the baron for an additional sack of gold. And if not gold, then something warmer and softer. He had caught a glimpse of the barons daughter sitting in her bower and he much preferred not to pay for his company.

"Well, then I guess we have nothing to discuss," he boasted and looked in the direction where he had put the cart. Many things could be (and had been) said about Erdengard, but going on a quest unprepared was not one of them.

"Yet, I am confused," the unicorn neighed. Somehow the statement managed to penetrate the goldadled brain of the adventurer, and he said:

"What about?"

"How did you catch me when you had no maiden by your side? I was so certain that I sensed a pure woman beneath the cover of leaves."

"A qualified guess that the legend was nothing but a hoax and it seems I was right. When it all comes down to it, you are nothing but a pretty horse with a horn in its forehead," he answered.

For a moment the unicorn pondered Erdengards words. Then it bowed its head in apprehension.

"You are right. It is nothing but an old wives' tale. You see, we had to come up with something, otherwise we could never live in peace."

A dangerous light flickered on in the deep recesses of Erdengards gemstone eyes. One unicorn was worth a lot of money. How much would two unicorns be worth?

"We, you say? So there is more than you?" He asked in an innocent voice.

"Yes," was the reluctant answer. "We are many, hiding from the greedy eyes of humans who only want to know us to use every part of us. Especially the horn. We have lived in peace for centuries but now you have caught me, and soon we will emerge from the fables and once more become fact. Then again, we will shortly be back in the fables, because your kind eat and abuse facts. Perhaps this is the right way to go. Over the years reality will once more fade and we will be nothing but dreams. And in the dreams we can finally be at peace."

A single tear fell from the unicorn's eye. When it touched the air it transformed into gold and with a soft tinkling, it landed in the vast, green carpet of grass. Erdengard followed the tear with his eyes. In the second it took for the tear to reach the ground, he had valued it to at least fifty gold pieces. Untouched by the unicorn's words he pocketed the gold tear and turned to the beast.

"Are all unicorns crybabies?" He asked.

"No," it answered and for a fraction of time something other than sorrow flickered in it's gaze. "We only cry when good is about to die."

"Too bad," said Erdengard. "Perhaps we could have made a deal if you were a whiner. Unicorn tears must be worth a lot to alchemists and other riff-raff."

The unicorn stood silent.

"But you say there is more of you. I might be persuaded to let you go if you told me where exactly the rest are. You see, I have nothing against you personally. You are money. But if you were to do business with me, at least you could save your own hide before somebody else saves it for you. And hangs it on his wall."

"I would never betray my kin," the unicorn answered and for the first time Erdengard looked it directly in the eye. "If I betray them, I betray everything we are and stand for."

The adventurer shrugged.

"Suit yourself. But before you make the final decision, I would like to tell you exactly what is going to happen. At first, you will be an exhibition piece. Insecure men will form long lines, future brides in hand, to check whether or not their brides-to-be really are virgins. Later on, your horn will be used to secure that wine, water or other drinks have no trace of poison nor venom. Seems like a breeze, right? Don't you worry. I have just described the first years," Erdengard laughed. He had the unicorn's undivided attention.

"When you start to get old they are going to cut off your horn, because you yourself are beginning to look unsightly and haggard. In the end they are going to kill you, of course, and if I know my fat nobility, then they will eat you because you never know? Your flesh might just grant special powers or prolong their greasy lives."

He rolled his fingers on the pummel of Thornblade while he spoke. It was an old trick designed to confuse and hypnotise any listener. For every sentence he brought to an end, the unicorn's eyes expanded in horror.

"At least they keep the head. Actually, that could be your chance of keeping your horn. They are going to hang it in the great hall, next to the faces of goblins and elephants alike. And perhaps they will not spoil your good looks. Perhaps, maybe, might. Such uncertain words, unicorn," he smiled.

Erdengard had seen it many times before. Headstrong younglings, chaste maidens, greedy merchants. They all had their precious principles and their convinced convictions. But when he told them of their future, what would happen to them, somehow all those misunderstood intentions seemed to falter and turn to dust. The unicorn was no different. Since it spoke it had to be a person.

"Your insides they will give to the alchemist and if you are a he, your castration is a certainty, nay, a tapestry of entertainment for a crowd. Why should they wait until after you are dead? It must truly be a sight to behold. It begs the question, horsie. Are you a he?"

The unicorn swallowed hard and nodded. Then it swallowed hard a second time and nodded again.

"Ouch. Not something I would like done to me. I guess you can all but forget about frolicking foals shouting and laughing, even whinnying your name, unicorn," he concluded and threw his hands up. "But if you are still not interested I will go and get the cart. It is very impolite to keep your future waiting."

"Hold on," the unicorn said, tossing it's mane. An unusual mix of a whinny and a cough escaped its throat.

"Maybe I spoke too hastily. I might be able to show you where the other unicorns are, but then you have to let me go. And just to be clear: My horn can in no way trace poison or remove it from any drink or food. It's useless."

Erdengard frowned. "Alas, what is it good for? Another fabricated tale from the mouth of unicorns?"

"Yes," nodded the unicorn. "Back when it all began people killed each other with weapons, not all this cloak and dagger-stuff. We had no way of knowing that poison would become fashionable."

"Works, does not work. I do not care much either way," said Erdengard. "The duke believes in your horn and when he finds out the truth I will be in the valley three times over, doing business. But you mentioned squealing, I believe?"

"I did." The unicorn let out a sigh. "It is for the greater good. But if I do this you have to promise me to tell the duke that we were the last. If you do not lie to him, he will just send out more men with nets and pikes, and soon we will be gone."

"You have a deal, my dear unicorn. Now, where are your friends?"

"Deep in the woods. Where a pure spring, ensconced by lady slipper orchids and wood sorrels, bursts from the rock and the air is as sweet as honey. But you cannot catch any of my brethren unless I am alongside you. They will smell you a mile away and, just saying so, it is not a particularly daunting task to accomplish," the unicorn said, wrinkling its nostrils in disgust. Erdengard inspected himself. Agreed, it had been a busy week and some of the troll blood could still be lodged somewhere in the chain mail.

"You did not smell me," he pointed out.

"I have had a cold and the wind was on your side. Besides, I was lost in thought. And I stumbled when I tried to run," were the avalanche of excuses that spurted from the unicorn's mouth.

"I had dug some holes. Quite cleverly so, if you ask me."

"I do not. It worked. Let that be satisfaction enough for you."

No answer came from Erdengard. He scoured the unicorn's eyes for information. Then he thought he struck something.

"Just a minute. Are your horsie friends not going to smell a rat when you come strolling in with me, a man most certainly not a virgin? Your treachery will shine through."

The unicorn scratched the ground with its front hooves and shook its mane.

"We are creatures of light and treason does not run in our blood. They will only believe that I have brought them a lad, lost in the woods and scared out of his mind. And we are not horsies! We are unicorns!"

"For a creature of light and la-di-da you took to treachery like a drunkard to mead," Erdengard remarked in a voice dry enough to soak a gallon of water. For a moment, their gazes locked, his sapphire blue with the unicorn's golden. Then he looked away. It was impossible to stare for long into those beautiful eyes. Even if it was true that the horn held no powers, he was not all that sure about its prying eyes.

"What I do is not treachery. They will go with you by their own accord as soon as you have sworn an oath to uphold your word. Because we are good we believe that a core of decency remains in every human, even I you, living as you do by the sword and misery of others," it answered poignantly. The unicorn reminded Erdengard of when he saw his mother last. She had been a pain in the ass, complaining how he never came to visit her even though she was in her frail autumn years and barely had the strength to chop wood and fetch water from the well. It had been a very short visit.

"Well," he said. "I can agree to that. But why did you try to pass one over me? All that shite about good and purity?"

"It was not trying to pass anything. I spoke to the good inside you, but apparently it is as deep underground as the gold of the dwarves."

"Dwarven gold? Do you know anything about that?" He replied greedily.

"No. I used a metaphor. And before you ask, it was not worth much either.”

“Then you will have to do,” Erdengard said. ”But a thought came to mind. You say that your horn does not protect from poison. Does that mean that you yourself are not immune to poison?”

“Yes,” said the unicorn. ”Why?”

“I just thought I would ask before wasting an arrow.”

Fast as a very fast rabbit Erdengard reached into the bushes, where he had hid, and produced three things. A bow, a bundle of arrows and a small flask. He took an arrow, pulled the cork of the flask with his teeth and then let a few drops of clear liquid drop onto the arrows head. Then he picked up the bow and nocked the arrow.

“I normally use this when I hunt bears. They fall asleep and are then much easier to handle. Of course, it cannot be all that fun to wake up and discover that your fur is gone,” he added and drew the bow. The aim locked on the unicorn.

“You are a bad person. Why are you doing this to me? I thought we had a deal?” The unicorn whinnied.

“We do have a deal. I just prefer to be somewhat more intimate with my business partners,” Erdengard replied and let the arrow fly. With a thud it pierced the unicorn’s thigh. It kept standing for a few seconds, then all four legs folded. The golden eyes battles fiercely, but lost. Silently the unicorn kneeled, then fell on its side.

“You have to get up early to fool Erdengard,” the adventurer remarked, before pocketing the flask.

“Wake up. We are paying your friends a visit,” bellowed a deep voice.

The unicorn shook its head. Something incredibly heavy was on its back and the smell of stale troll’s blood raped its nostrils. It tried to speak only to discover that something was in its mouth. Rope. Wrapped around the neck and held firmly. Someone pulled hard on the rope and the unicorn’s head jerked up. For a second everything was a messy blur before the world slipped back into focus.

“What have you done?” It spat angrily and tried to buck, to no avail.

“Bridled you. Together we ride to the pure spring and together we get your friends to surrender, volunteer, you choose the word. You thought that I would walk beside you? That would be an invitation to get trampled to death.”

“Only the champions of good must ride a unicorn. And we do not trample people!"

"Then you stare them down with your golden eyes. It is basically the same. Doing things my way makes sure that we keep our agreement, and afterwards we do not need to speak or even look at each other. And that is a promise," Erdengard answered and heeled the unicorn in the flanks. With a grand whinny of pain it broke into a stride.

They rode in silence for a while. Then Erdengard shattered the quiet with a question.

"What do you call each other? It must be really confusing if everybody is calling everybody else 'unicorn'."

"We have names. Like you," the unicorn spat without breaking its run. It was gaining momentum. The trees turned into a blur and behind them, a tunnel of leaves rotated in a spiral. It was fast. Really fast.

"So what is your name, unicorn?"

"None of your business," it remarked and tossed its mane, but Erdengard kept a firm grip on the makeshift reins.

"Have it your way, but I though we at least could make polite conversation."

The unicorn mumbled under its breath.

"What was that? Sorry I did not hear," laughed Erdengard.

He had tried many things, oh so many things, in the course of his travels. Worn down crypts to their bootlaces, slaughtered orcs and won more than his fair of bar fights, but he had never ridden a unicorn. The sensation was brand new. He felt like a child again and by the roadside of his experience he found a rare piece. The memory of his grandfather sitting in front of the fire and telling Erdengard of his adventures. Suddenly he remembered them all, the stories of heroic deeds and kindness, but somehow Erdengards own life had forked off in a different direction.

Something within Erdengard's chest transformed. His heart. Riding the unicorn was like a damp and dark veil being pulled from his eyes and he saw. He had been a scoundrel. Driven by greedy thoughts and golden glimmer, not by virtue like his grandfather. How often had Erdengard seen the glint of true thankfulness in the eyes of people? How often had they cheered his name in true recognition of his greatness and not because they had paid him to get rid of trouble? How many of the fair maidens (and the not so fair or maidens) he had bedded had given themselves to him in the name of love and not just because he was the hero of the hour? Suddenly he had a lump in his throat, one he could not just swallow.

Erdengard dawned on himself. He had never wanted to become what he was, but it was the roll of the dice Fate had given him. His eyes were open, filled with tears. Was it because his heart showed its true colors in his wondrous eyes or was it instead the whipping wind? It could have been both, but you decide. His grip on the remains lighter, his heels not digging as deep into the flanks. He opened his mouth to ask the unicorn to stop.

"We are here," said the unicorn and locked its hooves. Erdengard was catapulted from its back like a wounded crow. Somehow the forest had stopped, the sound of a spring reached his ears and a rare spark from the sun's rays reflected in the trickling water. Then he hit the ground, jaw-first, and plowed a groove lasting not less than two yards, before his body finally ground to a halt.

His face now a hideous and bloody visage, he spat out a lump of dirt and lifted his head. The unicorn had indeed brought him to a clearing and the air did taste a bit like honey. Bliss was written across the scenery in capital letters, but Erdengard only noticed the splendor for a scarce second. Then he saw the unicorns. Plural.

There were ten of them. Not at all identical but just as surely unicorns. All of them with their heads bowed, not looking at him. The only one that he recognized was the eleventh. First of all it stared intently at him and secondly, it was wearing a makeshift grime and harness. It was the unicorn and the look in its eyes was not at all kind nor forgiving.

"You were going to sell us to the duke for simple gold coins. You tried to make one of the true lights of this world betray his kind. You shot me and you raped your way onto my back. You, Erdengard, because your reputation runs faster than you, are one of the worst people we have ever encountered," said the unicorn and lowered its crest. A gust of wind made its mane billow like a banner.

"I am sorry," replied Erdengard and staggered to his feet. "I was filth, acting upon my own twisted desires but when you carried me on your back I could see clearly for the first time in many years. I understand now that I chose both wrongly and poorly in my life."

"I know. But your repenting has come too late, Erdengard. More than once you had the chance to let me go but you did not. You sealed your own fate. Now you have to face it as the hero you have always claimed to be."

"Sealed?" Erdengard said in a confused voice and stared at the unicorns. Not one of them had raised its head or acknowledged his existence. The animals were nothing but a fence. An ensorcelled fence constructed from magic flesh and closed metal eyes.

"You humans believe what you want to believe and forget the rest. You did not believe in needing a maiden to get to me, but you did believe that my horn could detect poison. You have done your research and perhaps, if you give it a try, you will remember other things those bestiary pages held," snorted the unicorn. The muscles in its neck were like thick rope.

Erdengard thought and thought. Tried to remember the wood carvings and the colourful illustrations. The endless tales spoken from dying and rotten lips in exchange for gold or mercy. Then it came to him. A grinding vision of truth. The oldest stories of creatures, not of good, but of necessity. Thundering hooves, blood and grime, screams among trees and then silence.

"It cannot be true. It must not," he said, his body trembling

An impossible smile landed on the unicorn's muzzle.

"But it is. Unicorns are many things. One of them is filled with rage. Another is that we carry grudges for centuries if need be."

"You cannot kill me," cried Erdengard in a voice armored in fear. "You are good. Good does not just kill. It is not allowed to." His hand found the hilt of his sword.

"You know what, Erdengard?" Asks the unicorn in a dragging voice, the smile morphing into a wide horse grin, showing a row of sharp teeth. "I am not that good."

Erdengard unsheathed Thornblade and swung it with all his might, but it was too late. For a second he had sensed good and ridden with the speed of thought. No sword chop, no arrow shot could move faster than that.

The unicorn's horn pierced his breast plate, went right through the leather armor underneath and forced itself into his body, below the heart. Like a little girl's doll, a mere toy the unicorn lifted him from the ground. An exploding pain bolted from his abdomen, as he slid down the horn, his own weight doing the pull and he only stopped when the unicorn's forehead forced him to. Clattering, Thornblade fell to the ground, its magic pointless. He coughed and covered the unicorn's neck in a sprinkle of red.

"I played your game right from the beginning. I knew what you would do. Every single word I uttered was nothing but a ruse. Do you really think survival goes hand in hand with stupidity?"

The unicorn bowed its head and he slid off, unto the grass.

"For good to prevail we ourselves must be more than good. That too is just one of our stories. Did you really think that the duke would have known anything about us, if one of us had not shown itself on purpose? What you remember now from the oldest and truest books is that unicorns are dangerous. They cannot be tamed and they know that violence sure as gold solves things. This is how we are and this is how you must know us."

"Have mercy," Erdengard begged and recognized the tone of his voice. The same that had lived in the voices of his victims, and he had given them none. The same amount would be given him.

"You will have no mercy, Erdengard. Only truth. The blood, pumping the grass scarlet. I taste its iron. Carnivores do not eat grass. They eat their prey," said the unicorn and reared its head. The rest of the unicorns formed a slow circle and the shadows of myth covered Erdengard in darkness. Silence. Only the trickling of water from the wonderful stream dared exist. Then, one by one, the unicorns opened their mouths. Their maws. Their eyes melted gold and silver.

Erdengard closed his eyes. But pain had no need to be seen.

ELIZA'S SHELL

CHANTEL BOUDREAU

Miranda breezed out onto the walkway behind the castle, trying to keep her spirits from sinking. She wanted a good look at the view of the beach in Feltrey one last time before she left, if she decided to go, to keep it at the forefront of her memories.

The beauty of the ocean there always made her catch her breath. Maybe it was the passionate energy carried by the strong winds and crashing waves that broke against the rocks there. A colleague from Alma, one of the other court mages, described the scenery in Feltrey as "intense". Maybe it was that intensity that Miranda treasured, native born to the city. Then again, it might just be the fact that the sea was in her blood. That was what her father would say.

It was a little chilly out, for so late in the spring. A salt spray blew off of the ocean, damp and brisk. Typical Seaforest weather, she thought as she hugged herself against the cold. How different would things be in Anthis? She had heard it would be a bit warmer, and almost as humid. She wrinkled her nose in distaste. She would be a day's travel away from the sea there, but the ocean on the opposite end of the land was different – tamer, with more traffic. Somehow it would not be the same. She was drawn to the savageness of this sea.

Miranda glanced back at the castle, warily. She had no choice in the matter, really. Refusing this assignment would be refusing to fulfill her duty to the crown. Failure to follow through on the prince regent's request would almost definitely bring about the end of her career as a court mage. As much as her heart told her to stay in Feltrey, her mind was insisting that she go, for the sake of her career.

Miranda sighed and shivered. Her mother had been right, she should have taken her cloak, but she had come out with exposed skin on purpose, wanting to feel the soothing kiss of the sea breeze on her face and arms. She had hoped it might settle her nerves. The trip would be a horribly demanding one, a real challenge and one she was not sure that she was capable of meeting. The sensation of the salt spray was nice, but it did not prove to be the antidote to her anxiety that she had been anticipating. She was still feeling extremely excitable.

She took a deep breath. She wished that she was not the court mage most adept with the portal spell. She had only made the journey to Anthis and back a few times – enough to give her the familiarity with the route that she needed, but not enough to give her the confidence that she could make the trip under the current conditions required. She would have very little time to rest between jumps, and no guarantees she would arrive safely. She would also be feeling panicky, making it more difficult to concentrate.

The university where the man that she would be escorting would be seeking treatment was half way around the known world. She would not be able to change her mind part of the way there, or she would likely have his death on her hands as a result. The decision as to whether or not she would refuse the prince regent's request had to be made now, before she had committed herself in any way, and she had only minutes to come to some conclusion. If she did refuse, it also might spell his death, as they would have to rely on a court mage of lesser skill who would have less chance of success.

Miranda looked down the pathway that led away from the castle and noticed a lone figure standing alone out on the shore. It was her older sister, Eliza. Unlike Miranda, Eliza was by profession an artist with no talent for the type of magic involving gestures and incantations. Hers was a different kind of magic entirely.

Eliza stood with her easel set up in front of her. She was using the special paints that Miranda had concocted for her. They began shifting shades slightly once they had been added to the canvas, breathing life into the oceans and the skies in her landscape scenes.

Miranda could still remember the day Eliza had declared her intentions to be a painter. Their parents were craftspeople by trade, a potter and a leather worker, but they made items with an express function, exploring their creative side by adding flourish to their designs. Eliza's paintings would be entirely decorative and her success subject to consumers' tastes. They warned her against following such an uncertain path and advised her to choose something more practical.

Eliza, however, would not be dissuaded. She started by selling her paintings in the marketplace. Business was slow at first, but Miranda's sister was talented, and she eventually gained enough recognition that the queen had taken an interest in her. Queen Mathilde had actually traveled with her entourage into the marketplace to get a look at Eliza's work firsthand. She had retained Eliza's services to enhance the castle decor on the spot. This had been the best exposure that Eliza could have asked for. Now her paintings were always in demand.

Miranda envied her sister. Eliza had never hesitated despite her odds. She had boldly pursued her dreams, throwing caution to the wind. Their father had described Eliza as being kissed by an angel, and blessed simply for trying.

Not that Miranda had ever tried to hide that envy. She agreed with her father; Eliza was exceptionally blessed. Her older sister could achieve anything that she set her mind to, no matter what the obstacles, and she seemed entirely immune to fear. Miranda longed to have only a tiny morsel of Eliza's calm and confidence, but aside from a few similarities in appearance, they were as different as night and day. For all of Eliza's ease, Miranda was equally anxious.

"How do you do it?" She whispered into the wind.

Eliza's self-esteem came naturally to her. The woman was tall and quiet, always at peace with her surroundings. Her inner strength and steadfastness reminded Miranda of a somewhat sturdy tree, but one willowy and flexible enough to bend with the wind, rather than breaking. She kind of looked like a tree in some ways too. Along with her height, her skin was pale, almost white, like birch bark, and her frizzy hair had the same rich colour of the autumn foliage of a red maple.

Someone called out Miranda's name from behind her. She twisted to look over her shoulder, still facing the shore. The man approaching was on the shorter side of average height with a young looking face and short brown hair. It was Duncan, another of the court mages.

"The medics have this fellow, this Renegade, almost stabilized. If you're the one going, you better be ready to leave in a few minutes. If not, you should inform the Prince Regent, so he can make a substitution." Duncan did not look pleased as he spoke. If she turned away from the task, he would be her likely successor, and he was not the type to say no, even though he wanted the job even less than she did.

"Stall! Stall!" Miranda's mind shrieked. She still remained undecided.

"I have to say good-bye to my sister, Eliza," she remarked, pointing at the lone figure on the shore. Duncan sighed, frowning slightly.

"I wouldn't leave the prince regent waiting if I were you," Duncan warned. "Make it quick." He disappeared back into the castle.

Miranda did not need further prompting. She was off like a shot down the pathway, and, reaching the end of it by the shore, began wading her way through the sharp-bladed marsh grass. She could feel the black, salty mud seeping in through her suede boots but she did not care. It might be the last time she would feel that cold, wet sensation. She took a deep breath, letting the ocean air tickle her nose before wandering out onto the sand.

She approached Eliza quietly from behind, watching her sister's slender hand whisk the brush dexterously back and forth across the canvas. Miranda might be the wizard in the family, but what Eliza did seemed to cast its own spell, especially with those marvelous paints. The paints, however, could not weave their magic on their own. They could only bring things to life if they looked real to begin with. Eliza truly captured the essence of the sea, even with ordinary pigments. She drew things out of the blank white canvas; the foamy crests of the waves, the soft roll of the surf as it broke onto the shore, the tide eroded stones that dotted the shore with their pale colours – they were all there. What had always surprised Miranda the most was her shells. Eliza's shells never failed to look like they could not possibly be paint and paper, as if you could reach out and brush their satiny surface with your fingertips, feeling their rounded edges.

Miranda wandered over to a large chunk of driftwood, and perched on its closest corner. It had been bleached by a combination of sun and salt, and had been worn smooth by the surf. She kicked at an empty periwinkle shell in the sand, trying to peer over her sister's shoulder at the artist's current piece.

Miranda did not speak to Eliza at first. It was more soothing to sit and watch her work. Her sister had been changing, but Miranda had not noticed until now. Her red wavy hair, tossed gently by the sea breeze, was framed by a touch of gray at the sides and silvering a little at the top. When Eliza smiled, the lines by her eyes and the creases at the corners of her mouth were much more visible. Time had been catching up to the older woman, and Miranda had not been around much to notice. How different would she be the next time Miranda returned, if she chose to go?

"They'll be waiting for you," the redhead finally said, fully aware that her sister hovered nearby. Her voice was low and gentle, but

Miranda had always had trouble reading any emotion from Eliza's words. "You don't want to disappoint the prince regent. This will be the opportunity and experience of a lifetime. Don't waste your chance."

So...Eliza already knew, but she and the queen spoke regularly so it was not that much of a surprise. Miranda did not respond at first, watching the gulls fly overhead. When she glanced back at her sister, Eliza was still painting, waiting patiently.

Her brow creasing slightly, Miranda gazed down the shore to her far left, past crown land. She could barely make out the small wharf that they had used as a diving platform during high tide, when they were children. They had always jumped in feet first, wary of the rocks beneath the waves, but Eliza had never hesitated, whereas Miranda had always been the last to get up the nerve. Miranda had been scared; scared of scraping her toes, scared of being pushed into the wharf by the waves, scared that the water would be too cold, scared of potential underwater creatures such as eels, crabs, or even sharks. She had often made up excuses as to why she should not go in, but Eliza had always managed to persuade her in the end. Miranda had never failed to have fun either, once she had taken that plunge. Maybe that was why she was here now. She was looking for that encouragement. Perhaps she really did want to do this, even if she had reservations.

"I'm scared," Miranda murmured.

Eliza nodded, still staring out to sea, her brush whirling rhythmically. It flickered in her hand, occasionally throwing off little dabs of shimmering paint. She chuckled softly.

"That's not a bad thing," she said, pausing to wipe a smudge of the magical pigment from her hand. "It will help keep you focused on what you have to do. It means that you will be cautious – that you are aware of the dangers involved. You know that you can't let that stop you. People are depending on you. Someone's life is in your hands."

"That's what scares me the most. You wouldn't understand. You've never been afraid of anything."

Eliza laughed, loudly this time. Miranda was taken aback. It was something that she could never recall hearing her sister do, not Eliza, the forever-soft-spoken. The older woman laughed for several more seconds before managing to catch her breath. When she finally stopped, she put the brush down and faced her sister.

"Do I seem that far from human to you? I've been scared out of my wits more times than you could ever imagine. I may hide my fears better than you do, but they're still there. We all have to make choices in our lives, Miranda, and we all face risk. If you never push yourself, if you don't take that leap of faith from time to time, you'll never know how much you could have actually achieved with your life. Don't settle. Make your life meaningful, even if it is only by inspiring others through the risks that you were willing to take."

Miranda did not know what to say. She had not been expecting this.

"How do you think that I got where I am today," Eliza continued. "It certainly wasn't by taking the path of least resistance. If that were the case, I'd probably be married with children, making bowls or belts with extra flourish and wishing my life away. Or maybe I'd be completely dependent on my spouse and even more devoid of self, wondering if I could have ever accomplished more, and regretting that I hadn't tried."

Miranda looked at Eliza's painting. The waves there tossed and swirled, lifted by the magic of the paints. It reminded her of the turmoil that seemed to toss and swirl inside her.

"Sure, you're scared," Eliza said softly. "But if you avoid doing this for that reason, will you be happy?"

Miranda shrugged.

"It's so much responsibility," she sighed.

"You can't escape the responsibility. If you don't go, and whoever goes in your place fails, won't you feel equally responsible? You are the best person for the job, that's why the prince regent chose you. You should also consider how much of a learning experience this will be for you, no matter what the results. You'll have fewer opportunities for that, as time goes by. Take it from me, as you get older, the years get shorter."

This still did not seem to sway her younger sister. Eliza pressed on.

"Imagine if I had abandoned my painting because I was afraid that I wasn't good enough. What if I had been worried that I was wasting my time? It was an investment of time, effort and faith, and it might not have paid off. But the flip-side was worse. I couldn't live my life knowing that I hadn't tried. There are no guarantees in

152

life, Miranda. When you get older, you'll be looking back at all your successes and failures, and you'll realize that you respect yourself more for your difficult failures than for any of your easy wins. That's life. That's where it counts."

Miranda glanced back at the castle. Eliza was right. She was burdened with that man's life no matter what choice she made, and she would hate herself for not trying, especially if he died.

"I admire you for what you will be doing," Eliza stated matter-of-fact, as if the decision had already been made. "I always wanted to travel, but I've had my obligations here. They won't last forever, and maybe when I'm done, I'll head for Anthis, too. Maybe you can tell me where the best sights can be found, so I know where I should go to observe and paint. You can be my inspiration – my muse."

Miranda stared into the sand. She was almost there, almost convinced, but there was still just enough doubt to hold her back. Eliza walked over and took a seat beside her, putting her arm around her younger sibling's shoulders. She took a deep breath.

"When I was eighteen," Eliza began, gazing up at the cloud-studded sky, "I had a choice of my own to make. Mother wanted me to apprentice with her. She would guarantee me work, security and some sort of future. She told me if I chose to walk a different path, she and father would be willing to support me for two years, while I tried to establish myself as an artist. After that, I would be on my own. That was the big question; was I willing to sacrifice my dreams for the sake of a sure thing?"

Miranda had been fortunate that she had never puzzled over what she would do. She had never been artistically inclined and had always shown a predisposition towards magic. That was one decision that fate had made for her. She knew that this made her the odd one out in her family, but she also had the feeling that her parents were proud of her nonetheless, intimidated, but proud. Eliza went on.

"I had trouble convincing myself that I could make it as a painter, and I almost caved to other people's doubts. It was never about whether or not I was good or that I had passion, but nobody seemed to think I would have the strength to survive that career choice. Only the best, they insisted, had any chance at success. It's highly competitive, I was told, and based partially on luck. You need to have the right pieces at the right time appealing to the right person's tastes, they said. Worse, success as an artist is fleeting, because people's tastes change all the time. Your work may just be a trend, a passing fad. All I ever heard was discouragement, and I had no one who wanted to support me, aside from you, little sister. Their arguments were breaking down my will. And then something happened."

Miranda had never realized Eliza had ever faced such a struggle. She had been too young, too oblivious, and too caught up in her efforts in learning magic. Finding herself in the midst of a new discovery, she listened attentively.

"I came out to the beach, to sketch and to clear my head. This was long before you gifted me with those glorious paints. I was scared – really scared. I was scared that if I followed my instincts, I would disappoint my family. I was scared that if I didn't, I would be miserable for the rest of my life. I was even scared that there was no right answer, and no matter what I decided, it would be wrong. That was when I noticed a hermit crab, just like the one in my painting."

Eliza paused and pointed at the canvas. The magic pigments had brought the creature to life, and it crept slowly across the sand in her artwork. Miranda smiled.

"It walked into the middle of the area I was sketching. I did landscapes only then and avoided painting living things. I even avoided painting shells, because they always looked too complicated. When the crab came to a stop in front of me, I realized that I would have to change an entire section of my sketch. I could move it, but if I did that, my own footsteps would disturb the sand there, and change things as well. Frustrated, I was ready to ball up the paper and just leave. But it got me to thinking," Eliza said. "I watched that little crab for about twenty minutes. Its tiny feet were moving, but it didn't go anywhere."

Miranda nodded. That was how she felt right now, stuck and flailing her feet futilely.

"Why wasn't it going anywhere?" She asked.

"It had caught its shell on a ridge of rock and it couldn't get away. Those crabs have a particularly vulnerable backside. They slide it into an appropriate-sized abandoned seashell for protection. When it gets too small, they find a new one. But the thing is, that shell can be as much a hindrance as it is a boon. It is security, but it slows them down, or in some instances stops them altogether. You can snatch them up more easily by that big shell, without worrying as much about being nipped by its pincers."

"Eliza," Miranda sighed, glancing back anxiously at the castle. Duncan would come looking for her again soon. "What does all this have to do with the decision I have to make?"

"I'm getting to that part. I didn't want to end up like that hermit crab. I could go with what was safe, but it would slow me down, and maybe catch me up so I would stop moving forward. I didn't want to stagnate. While I was considering all this, I decided to try something new, and for the first time, I added a living thing to my sketch. The difference was dramatic. I captured the image of that crab much more precisely than anything else on that beach. Chance worked in my favour that day, and I saw it as a sign. I stopped depending on the opinion of others to make my decisions. I did what was right for me. But more importantly, I stopped allowing my life to be governed by fear. You can't make this choice based on fear, or based on how it will impact your career – factors that have been pushing you in opposite directions. You have to follow what's in your heart. That poor poisoned man needs you, Miranda, and you know that you are the best choice. You don't need me to tell you that."

Miranda wrapped her arms around her legs and balanced her chin on her knees. That was the one thing that she was sure of, in this case. If this man died, she would always feel to blame, and the best way to solve this problem was to make sure he got the treatment that he needed, to oversee it personally.

A shout in the distance drew her back from her reverie.

"Miranda! The prince regent requests your presence immediately!" It was Duncan. That was it. There would be no more stalling.

"I had better go," she said. "I'll miss you, Eliza. It's a long way to Anthis, and who knows how long I'll be gone." There – she had spoken the words out loud. It was decided. Miranda stood to go.

Eliza reached up, grasping her wrist, and gave her a big smile.

"Wait" she murmured. "I have something I want you to take with you."

She reached into the pouch at her belt, and withdrew a large, white, pointy shell, the type hermit crabs preferred to house in. The back of the shell had been scraped smooth, with a miniature version of the water, the sand, the boardwalk, and the little salt marsh that separated the beach from the pathway to the castle, all painted there. The waves shimmered and rolled and a seagull soared circles in the tiny sky.

"A little piece of home," Eliza explained, "To take with you."

Miranda took it from her, nodding. She could not find her voice in order to speak. Her older sister leaned over and patted her arm.

"You had better go," she said. "They'll be waiting."

Taking a deep breath, and clutching the shell in her hand, Miranda turned towards the castle, and started to make her way through the tall, stiff grass. Now, she was ready to meet her fate, no matter what the consequences.

THE SONG OF SPENCER

DANIEL FRANKLIN

"FOR ROCHELLE, WITHOUT WHOM SPENCER WOULD HAVE NEVER EXISTED."

Spencer sat with her back against an enormous willow tree, as she often did. She was gazing out over the ruins of a forgotten civilization. They called this particular place "The Campus," although that term was foreign to her, an ancient artifact from another time. A breeze picked up, and she turned her gaze upward to watch the sunlight dance through the leaves. All was at peace, and all was quiet.

This was the calm before the storm.

Spencer arose with an almost ethereal grace. There was a way about her movements that seemed to defy gravity - more of an elegant flowing than the barbaric mechanical motions we normal people are subject to. She stretched briefly, allowing her arms to gently drop back down to her sides. She stood quite still then, listening. It was another six or seven minutes before the man showed up, some Lieutenant from some company in the Army. She had first heard his amateur footsteps fifteen minutes prior, tramping lost through the woods nearby. He had passed by her four separate times before he'd finally gotten his bearings (or perhaps good luck) and come to her. She had been waiting for him, and she knew exactly what it was he wanted.

He approached her, gave a respectful bow, and began, "My Lady, I haaa..."

His voice, and his breath, were immediately taken from him. He had heard stories, tales passed around the officers' quarters and the barracks where the enlisted lived, of the otherworldly beauty that was the Lady Spencer. They said her eyes alone could stop a dragon mid-flight from a mile away, and having come face-to-face with her legendary countenance he was immediately made a believer. Her eyes... there was an almost curious pulchritude to their deep turquoise hue, as if they were actually calling out to him. As soon as her eyes met his he was taken into them, lost in an abyss of divinity and grace and wonder and awe. He felt an irresistible urge to give himself to them, mentally figuring how much of his worldly possessions he could offer in exchange for just one more moment submerged in that angelic ocean of majestic allure. He began to wonder if his soul would have any value to her...

"Speak."

The Lieutenant snapped out of his thrall, startled. He was amazed at the sheer power behind her voice, that something so...

mighty could come from someone so fair...

"My Lady, I bring a message for you, from the Praetorian."

"Yes, you do," she sighed. "He is here."

Seemingly on cue there rang out a peal of thunder with such intensity that the poor Lieutenant was caught off his guard and thrown to the ground. As he opened his eyes he observed with more than a bit of wonder the Lady Spencer had been seemingly unaffected, having simply turned her head towards the direction the hell-roar had come from. There was a look in her eyes that bordered on mere exasperation... but how could that be? She of course knew what had caused that sound, she of course knew what its source had come to do in this land, and she of course knew that it was more than capable of annihilating them and everyone they'd ever known! He knew of the stories surrounding Lady Spencer and this... Jackson, if he was recalling correctly... but HE was here! And it was HIS arrival that horrendous roar had announced! Suddenly it occurred to him that he was no longer certain of just whom he should be more afraid... The Lady Spencer was on their side, but her power was almost as terrifying as-

"AZH A'THAN NAZH GIL, KYUM'B EYTH GHASHUL!"

The challenge entered both their minds simultaneously. It was of an ancient dialect, one avoided by the scribes of the time because of its darkness - there has never been any being of any good in this world who has spoken that language. In fact, it had never been uttered nor heard nor even spoken about for centuries until recently. Recently it had begun to be mentioned in hushed and alarmed tones, as stories began to filter in of its existence, that it WAS real, that it had returned... and the whispers began to speak of the one who had brought it...

"Azh A'Than..." The Lady muttered to herself, a mixture of disgust and hate slipping out with her words. "AZH A'THAN NAZH GIL!!!! K'YUM'B EYTH GHASHUL!!!! KYUM'B EYTH ICTHIIIIRRRRRRRRRRRRRRR!!!!!" The screams came from the writhing Lieutenant. With every word of the damnable language that escaped his lips, there was an accompanying blast of hellfire. It shot out his mouth and through his eyes and began igniting the flesh of his face. Spencer strode purposefully over, having seemingly materialized a Great Scythe from thin air, using it in one effortless, graceful arc to separate the screaming man's head from the rest of his body. There was a brilliant flash followed by a final crippling wail of anguish, and the Lieutenant's corpse lay silent and still. She eyed the Scythe, the blood of the man still boiling upon its blade. Her turquoise eyes reflected back at her as they watched it sizzling and popping until it finally cooked itself into the metal sheen. It covered up most of the name engraved upon the blade, and it was this that bothered her the most. She tore a piece of what was left of the Lieutenant's uniform coat off, using it to polish the burnt blood off of her Scythe so that its name was clearly visible again, and it read simply: Jackson. The Lieutenant's was not the first head Jackson had freed from the confines of its neck, and nor would it be the last. No, she thought, not by a very long shot...

More thunder.

The Lady stepped away from the smoking corpse, taking Jackson with her. As she moved forward, a large pair of wings slowly stretched out from behind her, finally extending to their full span. She stopped a little way from her beloved willow tree, allowing her wings to stretch and warm themselves in the dying light. An enormous, thick, dark cloud had begun invading the sky and had almost reached the sun. It would be dark soon, the calm would give way to bloody chaos. People would scream. People would cry out. People would die. Not even the knowledge of these things nor of the things to come could damage the resolve etched across the Lady's face. People would die, yes... and so would an ancient evil who long since should have begun his eternal burn in the deepest pit of Hell. But... better late than never...

Her wings moved, and the Lady was aloft. They pushed her through the sky, effortlessly and yet with a deadly determination. As she rose higher she observed her destination a full two miles south: a fiery crater, right in the middle of town. The courthouse had been split in two, half still standing and the other half reduced to a smoldering pile of rubble, flame, and corpses.

Though the sky overhead had darkened it was a little beyond midday, and where there were streets full of people shopping, working, or simply meandering, there were now people dying, screaming, or just simply lying, some whole, some not. Her keen eyes saw what her equally keen ears heard, the screaming and the ripping, the rending of flesh from bone, and the roars of the creatures decimating the town's populace. She searched as she began to close in, her wings bearing her at a rapidly increasing rate. Finally she saw it – a body, torn raggedly in half, each piece of the former person lying while he stood in between them, and his eyes were burning straight into hers. A slow smile pulled the corners of his mouth back, and each passing second revealed more and more teeth, like two long lines of fangs. Blood dripped from them, and as his breathing increased with the excited anticipation of meeting his enemy his whole form seemed to glow, like bellows stoking a furnace. His grin reached its full hideous breadth and he inhaled sharply, bellowing with such force that the heat of his infernal words hit her like a blast from a furnace, "KYUM'B EYTH GHAAASHUUUUUL!!!" Dark words with a darker intent, and the Lady grinned back. She, too, had prepared for this day, had known of its coming for four lifetimes. And hers was not a power to be scorned.

She continued to gain speed, and what had at first seemed to be an imperceptible glow about her began to grow, to amplify. Before long there was a pulsating brilliance coming from all about her, growing in intensity and speed, except for her eyes. The penetrating turquoise was beginning to fade, overtaken by the brilliant light emanating from within her, and they had begun to shine with the light of the sun. Her calm, angelic countenance was beginning to fill with all the rage of ages past as her lips began to curl into a snarl. Her beautiful lips parted and a thousand voices rang out like a hammer striking an anvil, "AZH A'THAN! I WILL BATHE IN YOUR BLOOD BEFORE THIS DAY IS OVER! YOUR CORPSE WILL BE STREWN TO THE ENDS OF THE EARTH WHILE YOUR SOUL BURNS IN TORMENT FOREVER!!!" The words rang out for miles in all directions, and as they reached their intended target his demonic jaws set and his eyes narrowed. He growled something incomprehensible and four dragons ascended from the ashes and blood that were now everywhere. They rose to match the Lady's altitude, and as they acquired their target they let out a roar, stirring up hurricane winds as they beat the air into submission, propelling themselves forward, eager to sate their bloodlust. The Lady, sizing up her new opponents, found that she shared their sentiment. She gripped Jackson tightly, feeling it hum in anticipation; it had not tasted the blood of a dragon in quite some time and it relished the opportunity. The Lady's glow turned into a menacing vermilion, and as her thousand voices let out a thousand roars she charged her unworthy foes.

The first fell quickly. It made the fatal error that was the full-on frontal assault, becoming intimately acquainted with Jackson as Jackson became intimately acquainted with its brain matter, spine, stomach, and intestines in one fell swoop. The Lady continued on her path in between the two halves of the dragon unfettered. The three remaining wisely took their comrade's foolishness as a lesson, two of them sweeping out wide in a pincer move as the third timed its advance so that the three would meet Spencer simultaneously. The Lady, more angered than concerned, suddenly flared her wings and wheeled to her left, heaving Jackson in a spinning wheel of death towards the dragon to her left. She turned to face the other two amidst the desperate roars of the beast's disembowelment. One reared its head back and bellowed a jet of brilliant white flame as the other dipped in low. Spencer quickly rolled to her right, and the resulting loss of altitude put her directly into the path of the oncoming dragon from below.

The dragon met her with open jaws, its saliva boiling as it growled in anticipation of finally devouring its hated enemy. The Lady was abhorred and feared by all from their realm, and for good reason – all, every single one of them, who ever met Lady Spencer in combat has died. Her destruction of their masses was known far and wide, tales of them passed down through their generations until their hatred for her was burned into their very existence. The monster's excitement grew as it approached – Spencer had not yet recovered from her near-miss with the hellfire, and she was close enough now that there was no chance for her to escape. The beast lunged forward, its eyes filled with anticipation... and then, suddenly, confusion. In place of its left eye there was a searing pain that tore through its entire head. Its jaws wouldn't work anymore. It tried to breathe hellfire in a panic, but nothing would come out. Its world then began to spin, and in the tortuous chaos it caught a glimpse of its body flying off into the distance, completely whole except for the ragged stump at the end of its neck. The last thing it ever saw was the chest of its comrade before its eye was smashed into the scaly armor, having been flung with terrifying force by the Lady. The dragon that the head crashed into grabbed it and threw it away in a fit of rage as it flung itself at Spencer.

She was surprised at the speed and ferocity of this last dragon.

Normally they were big lumbering behemoths, quite powerful in their own right but arrogant, mistakenly believing that their girth and might would be enough to destroy her. This one, however, whether spurned by the deaths of its comrades or drawing strength from some other unknown source, was proving a tad troublesome. It was faster than others she'd encountered before. Usually their primary method of attack was their jaws backed up by their hellfire, but this one had learned to use its wings to whip her about and attempt to disorient her. One of her aerobatic maneuvers found her upside-down in a diving evasion, and she was surprised to see a dragon's tale very rapidly approaching her face. She reached out and caught it, allowing its momentum to carry it past her as she twisted around it, wrenching it as hard as she was able. There was a dull ripping sound as the dragon was ripped downward and flung towards the ground, its tail listing off at an awkward angle.

It hit the ground hard, a visible shockwave traveling outwards from the point of impact. It tried to push itself up in a painful daze, but its front legs weren't working right. It looked around frantically for the Lady but couldn't seem to find her. Suddenly it became conscious of a distant roaring sound. It sounded almost like it was her, but there was something different about it... almost like-

KABOOOOOOOOOMMMM

The Lady hit her target with the force of a thousand avalanches. The crater that appeared when the dragon hit was expanded tenfold. The dragon was now but a stain on and in the hard granite beneath the soil, the shockwave of its demise traveling with such force that it circled the globe one and one half times before finally dissipating. From amid the smoldering wreckage that used to be the subject of horror stories all over the world, the Lady arose, her crimson glow more brilliant than ever. She lifted her hand upwards and Jackson came whirring out of the distance, returning to its Mistress. She wiped the dirt from her face and smiled. She had not had that much fun in quite some time.

Spencer caught her breath, and then turned to continue towards her true target, spreading her magnificent wings. As she completed her turn she did not have time to realize that Azh A'Than had, during the course of her battle with the dragons, made his way over and was at this very instant flying directly toward her. Her brain did not have time to acknowledge that his evil, twisted, leering face was now within six inches of hers, that she could smell his sulfurous, that her hair had begun to singe from the heat of his hellfire, that the acidic saliva that touched her face was beginning to burn, or that his claws had entered her chest before she was heaved up and flung into the air. She was a full mile away before her mind had caught up with what was happening enough to scream. It was another mile and a half before she regained her senses and realized what had happened. A half mile later and she was back in control of her trajectory. There was another three seconds to assess the damage done to her before a statue of a lion from the wrecked courthouse caught her in the back, breaking one of her wings and sending her plummeting back to earth. She lay dazed and very much injured for a few seconds, fighting off the gray building up around her field of view, threatening to send her into the dark abyss of unconsciousness. Her mind fought desperately to latch onto something, anything from this world and keep from sinking into what would lead to her very slow yet very violent death. And then her mind found something, possibly the most effective anchor into consciousness that she could have hoped for.

Azh A'Than had arrived, and he was laughing, a terrible sound that was like the lamentations of every man, woman, and child on Earth mixed with the beating of a million war drums. He then paused for a moment, watching Spencer as the full realization of what had just occurred was dawning on her, and this was the happiest moment of his life.

"Lady," he said, in a guttural tone akin to a lion who spoke only by snarling. "Or, at least, that's what they call you. But, as we can so clearly see, it would seem that it was a title given to you most... presumptuously." He advanced on her, or at least seemed to. The statue he had flung at her was lying several paces away from where she lay, having shattered on impact with the woman. He moved over to the pieces strewn about, and as he continued to speak he accentuated his words by crushing them underfoot. "This day has, as your people put it, 'been a long time coming.' It has taken me no small amount of time to build the power necessary to make this visit possible. Many of your people were sacrificed," He leaned in towards her and continued, "Many of your people were sacrificed in my name, and for every drop of blood they spilled I grew, my power grew, my divinity grew. "He stood back, observing the effect this news had upon her. Anguish was one of his favorite emotions, but he had never seen this particular kind. It looked like she was in immense pain, physically, emotionally, and mentally, but there was something more to it with her. He continued, watching her as she reacted to what he said, "If I were to choose my favorite moment… or rather, should I say 'moments'… from the last three centuries, I would have to say it would be that sound the mothers made, when their children were ripped from their arms…" He paused now to watch her, to relish in her torment. Her glow was dying now, and had calmed to a pale red. She was breathing heavily, but steadily. Her face was turned down towards the ground, and while he could not see her expression he could make out her tears as they intermixed with the blood on her face and fell to the ground. He thought he detected a faint sobbing, but he couldn't be sure… and so, he made sure, "No, actually, I would have to say the part I enjoyed the most, that I derived the fullest measure of pleasure and gratification would have to be the children themselves. Have you ever heard how loud they can scream when you have a large enough group of them together in the same place, enduring the same excruciating torment? Dismemberment? Evisceration? It's almost as if they were trained…"

He trailed off, for what he saw happening before him had come as a mild shock. While he was speaking he had continued his circle about her, crushing the rubble as before. He had just come full circle, and smashing the final stone upon speaking the word "trained." He turned his head towards her, and there The Lady Spencer now stood before him. She was panting heavily. The wounds to her abdomen were still very fresh, and she had just then been able to fight off their excruciating pain. Her right wing lay folded awkwardly down her back and it was missing a good portion of its feathers. Her left was partially stretched, intact but obviously damaged, to help steady herself. Her right arm had evaded injury, and it hung low and ready with a firm grip on Jackson. Her left she held bent in front of her with a clenched fist over her heart. It was badly bleeding but was yet still functional. Her legs held her up, slightly wobbly but strong, ready to pounce. But the most striking about her as she stood now was her face. Before, when she was fighting the dragons her face carried a fierce determination that was quite unlike the strong serenity she usually wore. Her mouth was contorted into a

166

hideous, terrifying, snarling thing of pure rage and hate. She was breathing heavily, and with each breath her glow began to return to full force, and then to be amplified beyond. Within seconds he was squinting under the onslaught of her brilliance, and all that was visible of her was a pair bright eyes ablaze with a strength born of pure enmity set in the frame of her once serene face. As the light continued to grow she opened her mouth, and the thousand voices rumbled through his very core, "The children? Do you mean the innocents? Those tiny creatures of ours who represent the pure embodiment of love?" He couldn't see, but there were tears flowing from her now, manifesting themselves as quick bright flashes as they left her cheeks and caught her light on the way to the ground. "Those tiny little creatures with whom our sole purpose for existing lies? DO YOU MEAN MY SON!?!?!"

The final statement erupted out of her like a volcano, and hit Azh A'Than with ten times the magnitude. He was knocked off-balance by its sheer power, and before he could fully regained his footing he took the full force of the vengeful Lady in the chest, who had leapt forward and swung Jackson, hitting him with the back side of the blade and sending him up and out into the dark sky. No sooner had he broken free from the bonds of gravity that Spencer was after him, running with an incredible speed until she'd caught up to him. She leapt high and then brought Jackson's blade down into Azh A'Than with such speed and force that a clap of thunder boomed out upon impact with the damnable creature. He was driven into the ground with such savagery that his impact carried him into the ground and down several dozen yards. Blindly furious that he may take this opportunity to escape, Spencer landed next to the hole and then dove in after him. She brought him out of his daze by landing on the back of his head, which gave an audible crack. She reached Jackson down, hooked him neatly between his ribs, and threw him back out of the hole. She leapt out after him, catching him in her hand this time and, planting her foot firmly into his face, thrust him back down to earth, landing on him as she did so. He bounced two times and then lay, bent awkwardly, on the ground. His breathing was ragged and laborious, his once fierce hellfire glow a fraction of what it used to be. His blood rushed out of him, collecting into a boiling pool all around his twisted body. Spencer bounced off of him and came to a stumbling stop several paces away. She caught herself, using Jackson as a support, and paused for a moment, breathing heavily. Her glow was faded as well, but still very much alive. She could hear Azh A'Than struggling feebly to move, but had also heard the sound his spine had made as it snapped upon being literally stomped into the ground. She took a moment to collect herself, and then turned to face the wretched creature. She slowly and carefully walked towards him, desperately trying to work her dizziness off. As she came upon him she gave him a mighty kick, putting him flat on his back. Spencer knelt down next to him, putting her face close to hers so she would be certain he heard her, "I heard about what you've done to these people," she said in a soft voice, accentuating her words by using Jackson to let a little more blood out from his chest. "I heard about what you have done to their children." Azh A'Than let out a small cry, like the whimper of a wolf, as Jackson dug just a little deeper into his chest. "I know you've been looking for me, planning for me, waiting for me all these many, many years." With a dull, slight sucking sound she extracted Jackson from him and stood upright, covered in wounds and dirt-caked blood. She began to very slowly walk in a circle around him, much the same way he had done to her. "I know all about you, Demon. Or," she smiled at him," at least that's what they call you. But, as we can so clearly see, it would seem that it was a title given to you most... presumptuously." She stopped and stood next to his waist, resting both of her hands on the bottom edge of Jackson, whose blade sat resting upon the ground, drunk and rich with his blood. Azh A'Than sputtered weakly and growled, "Son? Yes, I remember him, I think. He must have been the one begging fooAAAAAAAAAAAWWWWWWRRRRR!!!" The sudden scream came due to the sudden separation of his leg from his torso, achieved by one skillful upward turn of Jackson's blade. As he continued to scream Spencer stepped one leg over him so that each foot stood upon either side of his abdomen. A storm had broken out in the darkness overhead, and fierce orange lightning arced across the sky every second. Her glow had grown in intensity again with her anger, and in the brief flashes of lightning he could see her face, twisted in a menacing grin as tears streamed down her cheeks. For the first time in Azh A'Than's life he felt fear, and as the panic overtook him he began to blubber pathetically, "No! No, this isn't right! This cannot be! That was three and a half centuries ago! You're supposed to be gone! So much time has passed-"

"You fool!!" The Lady cried out with all the strength she could muster, "I AM TIMELESS!!" Thunder roared as the words left her, and as it rang out over the sky she brought her right foot up as high as she could, bringing it down in another clap of thunder directly onto the beating heart of her hated enemy. It exploded on impact, and as it did so a thunderous howl leapt from the monster's mouth, bellowing out with the wails of all those he tormented. The countless screams sang out for what seemed an eternity before fading into the darkness. Azh A'Than's glow burned out, and right as it did there was a massive clap of thunder overhead as the darkness parted, giving way to the warmth and the light of the afternoon sun. Spencer watched it go, feeling the warmth renewing the life in her. As the darkness finally vanished completely, she turned away from the wreckage and the rubble and began the long walk back to her beloved willow tree.

It was twilight now. Spencer reached over to prop Jackson up against her tree and then leaned herself back against it. She used it as a support so she could slide down into a sitting position. She was still bleeding from the wounds in her chest, and she was beginning to feel a weariness that she could not fight back. As she looked out over the ruined Campus she felt a sense of calm... the wrong done so long ago was finally avenged, and that brought her some peace. It was a thing that could never be properly righted, but at least she could sit with the knowledge that it would never ever happen again. As she sat she allowed herself to begin drifting off to sleep, when suddenly she heard a small voice, "Mom?..." She woke up quickly. It was a dream she'd had many times before, and each time was just as painful as the last. "Mom?" A quizzical look came across her face, and she looked around very much confused. "Mom!" There, again! She knew she heard it that time, and as she turned to look behind her her breath caught in her throat. There, impossibly... there he was, a face she had not seen for centuries and had yet spent all this time unchanged. It was a little boy of about seven years old, with brilliant blond hair and the most beautiful turquoise eyes she had ever seen. She stood up and ran to him. He ran towards her as well, and as they met she scooped him up and swung him around, tears flowing like rivers from both their eyes. She stopped and held him for a long time, unwilling to let go for fear that this dream would end.

Finally she held him back so she could look into his face, brush his hair, feel his cheeks, see that smile she had yearned for for so very long a time. "My love!" She said. "I've missed you so much for all this time! I never ever stop thinking about you, even when the pain is too much to bear... I-" The boy reached up and pressed his finger to her lips, silencing her. "Mom, it's OK, it's OK. I'm fine and happy, see?" He gave her a beaming smile and the tears started welling up in her eyes again. "Mom, I've come to tell you, it's time to come home!" She looked at him for a moment, flabbergasted. Home? But how could she take him home? He's been dead for so long, he hasn't been home for years and years and years... "Home? But... wha-?" "Ssshhhhh," he said. "No, not your home. This time, I'm taking YOU home." As he said this he pointed behind her, and she turned around to look. There she saw Jackson gleaming in the moonlight, still stained from the battle before. And next to her there she was sitting, still caked in blood and dirt. Her legs were stretched out in front of her, her hands folded in her lap, one wing folded neatly behind her while the other still hung broken next to it. And her face held the picture of serenity, the serenity of one who had worked tirelessly for an age and finally accomplished what they had set out to do. She looked at herself for a long time until it finally occurred to her what exactly had and was happening. She turned back around to look at her son with a slightly questioning look, and he nodded in confirmation. "Yes, Mom. You did what you were needed to do. And now," he said, taking her hand, "it's time to come home." The two walked, mother and son, Spencer scarcely able to allow herself to dare to believe that this was really happening. As they walked off towards the woods it was his glow that began to grow and illuminate, to amplify and encapsulate. It flowed over both of them and became brighter and brighter, and Spencer could feel herself brimming with the love and happiness she had so desperately longed for, for as long as she could remember. Then suddenly there was a bright flash, and they were gone.

They were home.

Fragmentations

EJ Shumak

Grec stumbled, nearly falling from the rail car. Two days earlier he had been rested and ready to work. Now, after the long grueling trip out to the rail head, he couldn't even remember why he had taken the job. Not that he'd had a real choice. It was a Royal project. The Princess and her royal father had made that quite clear. Grec wondered wearily if beheading could really be worse than what waited for him here.

At that moment, waiting with a grim watchful expression on his lean tan face, was Stebben W, a half elf and, according to the King, Grec's chief scout and problem solver. Small comfort, Stebben had certainly solved the previous field engineer's problems, he was dead. It made Grec real confident.

Stebben approached warily to catch up to him, "Grec? Grec Lawrence? It's good to meet you. I'm Stebben, Stebben W. I'm to be your scout," said the half elf, his slim hand outstretched in greeting. The half elf's cool slanted silvery eyes seemed to be mapping Grec's features, searching for clues to the man's inner nature. This human was to be his superior. "A bit unsteady, eh? You'll get used to it," Stebben said brusquely.

Grec nodded, then turned aside, concealing his dismay over the icy encounter. Half elves were notorious for stiff necked pride and hatred of "full blooded" humans. The two of them would be working closely, their very lives dependent on each other. He had hoped, had allowed himself to believe, that things would be different.

After a moment the scene before Grec's eyes came into focus. Now he was able to recognize the beauty of the land. The surface of the lake was suffused. A beautiful orange cast reflected the sunset. The foothills beyond the lake were every imaginable shade of blue and green. It had been a long trip, but it was much more than distance. He had not traveled just eight hundred miles -- he had traveled to a whole new world. It was pristine and pure, unspoiled by man and his needs.

"You okay?" Stebben asked.

"Just a little tired, and rail wobbly. Get me to my cabin and we'll talk," said Grec.

Stebben laughed, "Cabin? I don't know who you were talking to, but the King himself wouldn't rate a cabin out here. I can take you to the tent we share, if you'd like."

"Fine, fine, whatever. Just let me sit down on something that isn't rocking and vibrating, and wash the dust out of my throat."

"Right this way BOSS," Stebben said, putting an accent on the word as he cut through a group of dwarves hauling ties across the camp.

The camp was unlike anything Grec had ever seen. He had never seen so many dwarves in one place, much less working alongside men and, if he wasn't mistaken, even a few half orcs! Anything to do with orcs made him nervous. He was amazed they had made it this far without being raided. Why use half orcs when orcs are so dangerous, he wondered.

A set of three large tents stood just north of the main camp. Stebben led Grec to the middle tent, the largest of the three.

Grec studied the rigid set of the half elf's shoulders, "What's the W stand for?" Grec knew that Elfin law forbade the use of Elfin names by half breeds. The W could only represent Stebben's Elfin name.

Stebben spun around with fists clenched, his arms tight to his sides ready to challenge this "full blooded" human, field engineer or not. The half elf's rage was now fully apparent.

He was disarmed by Grec's warm smile and upraised hands. "Easy, my man. I meant nothing by it. I just thought we should get all the awkward stuff out of the way. My step brother is half elf. I have no prejudices."

"Then let's just say it stands for 'Wild', and you don't want to get me wild," replied Stebben. Silver half elf eyes met steady brown human eyes.

"Settled. It's been mentioned once and set to rest. I trust you'll accept my word on it," said Grec.

"Accepted -- and settled," replied Stebben.

"One more thing," said Grec. "I understand you've taken an oath to protect me with your life."

"True, though you might have reason to doubt its value. I also swore such an oath on KarlSon's life."

"You're still alive. They didn't denounce you. The blame must lay elsewhere," said Grec.

"They didn't tell you?" Asked Stebben, his silvery brows lifting in astonishment.

"No. They only said it was unfortunate and you weren't responsible. I took that as a bit of an understatement," Grec said

174

dryly.

"You have a right to know. You should have been told everything before coming here. I saw it. I was there and yet I could do nothing," said Stebben.

The half elf sat down on the edge of the planning table while Grec pulled out a canvas chair, preparing to sit beside him.

"Okay, I'm listening," he said.

"It was horrible," Stebben said, eyes glazed, looking inward. "KarlSon had been acting sick for more than a week, but he was still functional. Considering the stresses we were all under, especially him, nobody was surprised, or worried. We had lost the initial work crew along with a team of surveyors. They just never came back. KarlSon and I went up to investigate."

"KarlSon got killed up in the mountains?" Grec asked.

"No, but he might as well have. It was where it all started. There's really no way to explain to you... you'll think I'm drunk, or mad. I really don't know how to tell you," the half elf's voice began to shake.

"Just tell it as it happened," Grec said softly.

"We were set upon by something. I don't remember it, or rather I don't know what's memory and what's fantasy," he broke off and pressed trembling fingers to his eyes. Grec held his silence, waiting patiently.

Stebben drew a deep breath and seemed to calm himself. He resumed the tale in a dull monotone, "We had gone up to investigate the disappearance of the crew and surveyors when the sky closed, turned black, and a great wind came up. We were blown across the creek like dry leaves. The wind sucked the air from my lungs and I thought I would die. We awoke on the other side of the creek, covered in mud and slime -- exhausted."

"Odd," Grec frowned. "Could it have been a seasonal storm?"

The half elf shook his head. "It was no natural storm, of that I'm certain. KarlSon had horrible nightmares from that night forward. Neither of us could sleep more than two or three hours at a crack."

"The visions are gone now?" Asked Grec.

"Aye, the nightmares, along with the waking images, stopped when KarlSon died," said Stebben.

"How did he die?" Asked Grec.

"We were at morning mess, in the main tent with the whole crew. We had both had a horrible night. I had begun to believe, still do, that the nightmares were a suppressed memory of what happened to us up in the mountains. The nightmares were fragmented. Our memories were fragmented. That was how KarlSon died, fragmented," Stebben said grimly.

"I don't understand. How?" Grec asked.

"He started to shake," Stebben said slowly, the blood leaching from his face at the memory. Grec suddenly felt very cold, even in the summer heat. "Then the end of his left index finger just -- slipped off."

"Did anyone else see this?" Grec asked in amazement.

"Oh yes," said Stebben. "Everyone, Half orcs never miss a meal. We had the very devil keeping the men from deserting. Everyone wanted to leave, including me."

Grec leaned forward, listening intently, "Go on."

"It was as I said, KarlSon just fragmented. Pieces of him separated -- cleanly -- no blood, nothing. He just came apart. It started with his hands and feet, then legs and arms. Everybody was terrified, but we all stood there and watched it. There was a circle of people, ten to twenty feet back, watching him die, listening to him beg us to help him. I felt it in my mind, Grec. I felt him coming apart." The half elf appeared on the edge of collapse.

"Finish, I need to know," Grec said firmly.

"There's nothing more to say. He just kept coming apart. The word fragmenting says it all, actually, the Elfin word, frapice. He was frapicing, cleanly. You have to understand that it was clean. It was as if he was a hundred different creatures that didn't want to be part of the whole anymore. Chunks just kept coming off him, none of them bigger than his fist, and they slithered away. The pieces took on their own life and left, slinking into the woods. We all just stood and watched. Even KarlSon just sat there and watched. His head was the last to separate."

"You think he was conscious?" Asked Grec.

"Oh, yes. At the end, when only his head remained, lying sideways at the front of the mess table, he looked at me. He looked at me and cried out. The words just came into my head, 'Help me!' But, it was his voice. It was still him." The half elf fell silent.

"Tomorrow we're going up. I have to see this for myself," said Grec, knowing even as he spoke that there was nothing he wanted to do less.

Stebben got up, nodded curtly and walked out of the tent without a word or a backward glance. It was near dark, more shadow than light. Grec was left to ponder the future, alone in his new tent, alone in this new world.

Stebben was nowhere to be seen. It was dark here under the glowering trees, dark even in the midday sun. Grec wiped icy sweat from his brow with a shaking hand. He was scared, scared deep down, but why? He clasped his hand tightly on the hilt of his long knife and circled back towards the river, eager to be gone from these woods.

The foothills at the base of Cron Mountain were a series of progressively higher plateaus, reaching up towards the mountain face. Grec came out at the river, near the campsite of the surveyors and the initial work crew. He could feel their presence. He felt they were somehow still here.

Stebben, of on his own had found the campsite. He had been working loops from here to the mountain face and back again. The men had been missing for two weeks, and the camp had been abandoned, by Stebben's account, at least ten days. Stebben had tried to explain the feeling of loss and hopelessness here at the campsite, but now Grec felt it too, and there was no need for further clarification. Something was here. Something had taken the men, all of them, and it wasn't interested in giving them back.

Grec caught a glimpse of something bright in the dirt near the central tent. Walking over, he tripped on an abandoned stake and fell headlong. Brushing himself off, he knelt in the dust by the tent flap. Carefully brushing away the dirt, he picked up a safety talisman, or rather the remains of a safety talisman.

The green crystal was shattered with only a small point remaining imbedded in the bone mount. The mount was charred and there was a crack through the center. Grec laid the talisman in his hand, lifting it by the leather thong. It seared his flesh on contact.

Grec jerked his hand back and stared at the talisman. It was still hot, very hot, yet the leather thong was unburnt and cool. It was as if the heat was concentrated in, and restricted to, the crystal matrix and bone platform.

Grec carried the charm over to the camp stove and lowered it into an empty pot. It hissed as the crystal shard touched the bottom of the pot. Grec poured a cup of water from his water skin into the pot. Immediately the water began to boil and steam off. In the blink of an eye, the water boiled away, yet the bottom of the pot remained cool, save where the talisman touched it.

There was no transference of heat past the direct contact of the talisman. It had obviously been charred by a heat stone, or a heat stone curse. Grec carefully wrapped the talisman in a leather scrap, watching the inside char while the tanned outside of the makeshift pouch remained cool. He carefully placed it into his pack after securely tying the pouch shut.

In the right hands, this bit of strangeness might help lead them to those responsible for the disappearances and KarlSon's death. The talisman and the curse were so evenly matched that they canceled each other, perhaps indefinitely. Neither would be able to undo the other, and there would be a constant, though negligible, drain on the powers of whomever or whatever had cast the spell.

Grec started back into the forest to find Stebben. He had been gone far too long. Following their initial trail he became confused. Grec was no scout and the tracks and trails all looked pretty much the same. He walked in far enough to lose sight of the camp, only about a hundred feet in the heavy foliage, and started calling for Stebben.

A high pitched whistle from near the lower plateau cross drew Grec eastward. Grec found Stebben examining a small, crude campsite. It was much fresher than the one Grec had just left.

"What have you got?" Asked Grec. "I was getting worried about you."

"Stay back. I'm still checking tracks," said Stebben, warding Grec off with a gesture, totally immersed in his work.

Grec watched as Stebben moved carefully about the small campsite quartering it methodically. The coals from the fire were still warm, Grec could see that from his position on the edge of the small clearing, and there were pieces of bone and fur strewn about. There was also a wooden frame work, charred, to one side of the campfire, one that had been used to dry meat, as opposed to cooking it.

"This isn't a human campsite," said Stebben.

"There were dwarves in the initial crew."

"Right, some half orcs too, but that's not what I mean," said

Stebben.

"All right, what is it that you do mean?" Grec said impatiently. He had trouble accepting skills he didn't have, and couldn't understand. He was still unconvinced that tracking wasn't some sort of magic. It sure looked like it to him.

"These depressions," Stebben said, pointing to the ground, "are clawed out of the earth, and I mean CLAWED out. There are pug marks all over the place. Either we've got some awful smart catamounts here, or we've got a pride of catmen."

"Look, catamounts or pumas or whatever don't build fires, and I don't believe in catmen. I've never seen any. I think they're a myth," Grec said heatedly, wondering if the half elf was trying to pull something.

"Believe what you want," Stebben said coolly, rising and turning to face Grec. "You're as close to seeing them as you can get. They camped here last night. Believe it! A hunting party, three females and two males. They ate rabbit and smoked some to take with them. Believe it! They weren't human and they've got cat feet and cat claws and I don't find any forepaw scrapings, so you figure it out -- if you've got a better theory," Stebben said tersely as he kicked dust over the cryptic tracks and headed back towards the surveyors' camp without even a backward glance. "If I were you, I'd keep my mouth shut about this. We've got enough problems right now without spooking the rest of the crew."

Grec kept his mouth shut about the catmen and the talisman, and followed Stebben back towards the abandoned campsite. On the way, Grec, of course, felt that every bush concealed a catman, or something even worse, watching their progress. He had to work hard to remind himself that he didn't believe in catmen. He couldn't tell if it was paranoia, probably normal under the circumstances, or if this really was a very crowded forest.

Grec had grown up around magic users. They weren't common in humans, except for those of royal blood. Grec had just enough blue blood to get into court, and to believe most of what he heard about the royal sorcerers and sorceress.

Princess Teama was probably the most powerful sorceress in the three kingdoms, and he treasured the amulet talisman she had given him. He clutched it now in his free hand as they walked. He sincerely hoped his belief in her was well founded. He felt certain he would soon find out just how powerful the amulet really was.

As they reentered the campsite, a strange wind came up. Stebben walked towards the main tent, where Grec had found the burnt charm. Stebben screamed.

Grec ran over to him, staring in horror as a man's finger skittered rapidly back into the forest. The finger wore an Engineer's Guild ring. Grec recognized it. He had an identical ring on his own left index finger.

"That was KarlSon. It still has him. He's not even free in death," choked Stebben as he turned away.

Grec looked down and saw that the finger had been digging about in the dirt where he had found the charred talisman. Whatever had KarlSon, and probably the surveyor's crew, knew about the talisman and wanted it back.

The Icicle and the Ornament

P. C. Moorehead

The snow piled high, drifting against the windows. Inside the house, ornaments on a tall tree sparkled in the firelight. One of the ornaments, round and red, looked about. Above her hung a long, crystal icicle. The angles of the slender icicle caught the light from the fire and glowed in multi-colored hues.

"Hi there, how are you?" The ornament asked.

Icicle gazed down at her. No one had ever spoken to him before. "I'm cold, of course. How else would an icicle be?" A small red tint began to creep up his sides.

"You're turning red. You're blushing!" The ornament looked at him in surprise.

"I'm sorry. I didn't mean to embarrass you." She shrank back. "I'm always blurting things out before I think."

"Oh, that's..." The icicle hesitated, and then he realized she really was sorry.

"That's alright. I'm just not used to speaking, nor to having someone speak to me."

The round ball laughed happily. "Well, I love to talk," she burbled.

The icicle looked at her more closely. She's so pretty, he thought. A gold satin ribbon circled her middle, and shiny gold sequins clustered where she joined the branch.

A long red velvet ribbon, tied in a bow, held her in place.

"You're red all the time," he said to her. "You're lucky. No one knows when you're blushing."

Ornament looked down shyly. "I blush inside, especially when I'm teased. I'm teased a lot about my size. I'm a perfect circle. Any way you look at me, I'm round." Her dark eyelashes blinked against her red cheeks.

Icicle smiled. "It's alright for you to be round, just as it's alright for me to be skinny. I think you're perfect just the way you are."

Ornament fluttered her sequins. "Why, thank you, Icicle. That's the nicest thing anyone has ever said to me, but I'm not really so perfect. One year, on Christmas Eve, I was dropped, just as I was to be hung on the tree, and I lost a sequin. Then, in my childhood, a kitten batted me and pulled one of my ribbons. He was just a kitten though, and I forgave him."

"Is that the kitten over there?" Icicle looked at an old cat, snoozing in the corner.

"Yes, that's Fritz. He's never harmed me since that time. He was so afraid that he had hurt me. Now, he watches out for me. He makes sure people admire me but don't hurt me."

"You've been here a long time then. I just arrived. I came across the sea, on special order. I worried all the way if I would make it here without losing my point."

Ornament tittered. "Have you lost your point?"

"Oh no. I'm in fine shape, but I need careful handling. I used to hang on a beautiful chandelier in a grand old house."

"What did you do there?" Ornament asked.

"I shone for all the parties, the banquets, and the dances."

"Oh, that must have been exciting," Ornament smiled at Icicle. "Tell me, what was it like there at Christmas?"

"It was so happy. A tall tree stood in the great hall, and gifts wrapped in ribbons circled the tree. Ornaments hung from every branch."

"Ornaments like me?"

Icicle looked at her. "Oh, no, Ornament, they were pretty, but there is a special sparkle about you that they never had."

"Maybe it's my sequins," Ornament responded. "They sparkle."

"It's you," Icicle said. "It's the way you are." A tear welled up and rolled down his side.

"You're crying," Ornament said. "Have I hurt you?"

"Oh, no," Icicle responded. "Your friendliness has touched my heart. There were so many of us in childhood, there on the tree, and I looked just like everyone else. No one paid me any special attention. I always wanted to be different enough to be noticed."

"You are different," Ornament said. "Why, I think you're the handsomest decoration on the tree. There isn't another here like you."

"That's the way I feel about you. You're the prettiest ornament here."

"Thank you, Icicle," Ornament said.

Icicle looked at her shyly, then looked away. "It's been a long evening," he said. "I think I'll go to sleep now."

"Me too," Ornament replied, snuggling down on her branch. How handsome he is, she thought, and how nice! I hope he likes me.

The evening wore on, and the snow piled higher outside the windows. The fire cooled to embers in the fireplace, and the house grew dark. Everyone slept.

The next morning, when Icicle awakened, the sun was already shining through the clouds. Light came through the windows and glanced off his angles in pinks and yellows.

Why am I feeling so happy, Icicle wondered. Then he knew. I have a friend, a pretty friend. He looked down. Ornament was gone!

He looked around. "Ornament, where have you gone? Ornament, I miss you." The words surprised him. He had never missed anyone before.

Icicle worked up his courage and called to the ornaments on other branches. "Have you seen the pretty red ornament with the satin ribbon?" He asked. No one had. Ornament was gone, and Icicle didn't know where she was.

Outside, the snow began to melt. Icicle sank deeper into his branch. "Where could she be? What could have happened to her?" They had just met, and now she was gone.

The day stretched on. Icicle looked up hopefully each time someone entered the room. When the sun set, he sighed a long sigh and tried to sleep. He turned, dreaming of the cheerful red ornament with the happy voice.

The next morning, Icicle awoke, but he felt no warming sun. The room seemed cold. He looked down. Ornament was still gone. He shed a tear, and it dropped on Fritz, sleeping below.

"What's wrong?" Fritz asked, looking up at Icicle.

"I've lost my friend," Icicle said, "my generous friend."

"I know," Fritz replied. "I saw them take her away. They said she had grown too old for the tree. They said she looked shabby next to the newer ornaments."

"She's not shabby," Icicle said. "I thought she was the most beautiful ornament I had ever seen. In my childhood, there wasn't an ornament that compared with her, and I lived in a grand manor with a huge tree and many decorations."

"I know. I thought she was pretty too. I tried to protect her. I leaned against the mistress' legs and tried to get her to take me instead of Ornament, but she took her away anyway. She carried our beautiful friend out to the kitchen and put her on a shelf of the pantry cupboard. Ornament has had a hard time staying on that shelf. She's so round; she keeps rolling to the edge."

"Oh, Fritz, that's terrible. She must be so frightened. We must save her. What can we do?"

"Yesterday, I tried to rescue her. I jumped many times, trying to reach the ledge but my legs are old. I can't jump high enough anymore."

Icicle sighed, then brightened. "Fritz, would you take a message to her from me?"

"Yes, yes, of course," Fritz said.

"Tell her, tell her – that her new friend misses her. It's not the same here without her."

"Yes, yes, I'll tell her," Fritz said, getting up slowly. "I'm going out to the kitchen now for a drink of water, so I'll tell her on the way."

"Oh, thank you, Fritz," Icicle replied. "Thank you."

Fritz walked slowly out of the living room and through the dining area. Then he hustled into the kitchen as fast as he could go. Ornament was still there, struggling to stay on the ledge.

"Ornament, Ornament," Fritz called. "I have a message for you – from a friend."

"A message? From – from Icicle?" Ornament asked.

The old cat nodded.

"He's missed me?" She asked.

Fritz nodded again. "He says it's not the same on the tree without you."

Ornament smiled. "Oh, I've been so nervous, Fritz. Maybe now I can relax a little. I like Icicle, Fritz. Don't you think he's handsome?"

"Indeed, he's the handsomest ornament on the tree, and you're the prettiest," Fritz responded.

Ornament fluttered her eyelashes. "Help us, Fritz. I need to get back to the tree. Isn't there any way you can get up here and carry me back?"

Fritz looked at the high shelf. He knew that he couldn't jump that far. "I tried my best yesterday, but I just couldn't make it. We must find something, a step to which I can jump. Then, from that, maybe I can jump to the top, take your ribbon in my teeth, and leap back down."

"Your teeth, Fritz – they won't hurt me, or tear my ribbon?"

"No, I'll be gentle. I would never hurt you Ornament. I hurt you when I was a kitten, but I didn't know any better then. I thought you were so pretty. I just wanted to play with you. I didn't want to hurt you."

"Oh, thank you, Fritz. Now, would you take a message back to my friend?"

Fritz saw the dish of water waiting for him in the corner. "I was going to have a sip of water, but I'll go back now and give him your message."

"Would you – would you – tell Icicle that this shelf is lonely without him and that I hope to be back on the branch soon, talking with him?"

"Yes, yes, I'll tell him." Fritz sniffed in the direction of his water dish, then turned and hurried out through the dining area and into the living room.

Icicle watched him approach. "You saw her?" He questioned Fritz. "Is she alright? Did she send a message to me?"

"Yes, she did," Fritz puffed, padding closer. "She's alright, though she grows tired from trying to stay on the ledge. She's afraid of falling. She – she says the shelf is lonely without you, Icicle. She wants to be back on the branch, talking with you again."

"Oh, she's alright! How wonderful! Oh, Fritz, thank you, thank you. Now, we must find some way to get her off that ledge. It's too high, Fritz, for you to jump there?"

"It's too high," Fritz responded sadly. "In my youth, I could have made the jump easily, but now, now, it's too high for me."

"There must be a way. Think, Fritz. You know this house. Isn't there anything we can do? Isn't there some way that you can reach her?"

"I'm thinking, I'm thinking," Fritz said. His stomach growled. He remembered that it was almost lunchtime. His snack awaited him in the kitchen by his water dish.

"There's a way. I'm sure there's a way," Fritz said.

"Yes," Icicle answered. "There must be a way."

"I'm going for my snack now," Fritz said and padded toward the kitchen. He looked at the ledge as he entered.

Ornament, rolling to the edge, called out, "Fritz, did you see Icicle? Did you give him my message?"

"Yes," Fritz answered. We are trying to think of a way to get you down. We know there must be a way."

"Yes, there must be a way." She saw Fritz eyeing the corner of the kitchen. "Drink your water, Fritz, and eat your snack. You must be hungry."

"Well, I am, a little," Fritz said, biting into the snack. He finished it off just as the mistress entered the kitchen.

"Fritz, you ate your snack, at last. I was wondering if something was wrong with you. Well, you won't want lunch just yet. I'll put it out later." She crossed to the open doorway leading to the dining room.

Fritz stared down at his empty food dish, then looked around the kitchen. There must be something that he could push in front of the pantry cabinet, something he could use as a jumping off spot to get to the shelf where Ornament was. He sniffed the wastebasket, then nosed it. It didn't budge. He nosed it harder, and it banged against the side of the refrigerator.

"Fritz, what are you doing?" Mistress came into the kitchen. "What you need is a good nap. Then you'll start behaving like your usual self." She scooped Fritz up into her arms and carried him into the living room. She placed him on the rug in front of the fireplace and picked up her knitting. "If I hurry, I can finish this Christmas stocking in time to hang it by the fireplace tonight."

Her needles clicked away. Fritz' thoughts raced in time to them. The wastebasket might work, but he would need to push it closer to the cabinet when Mistress was out of the kitchen. If Fritz nosed it over, the noise would bring Mistress into the kitchen again. Fritz, in his mind, circled the kitchen, trying to think of something that would be quieter to move than the wastebasket.

"Psst. Psst."

Fritz looked up. Icicle motioned to him. Fritz rose and stretched, as though too warm from the fire. He walked over to the tree and curled up under it.

"Fritz," Icicle whispered, "have you thought of anything?"

Fritz rested his head on his paws and pretended to sleep. "The wastebasket is our only hope," he whispered. "When Mistress leaves this afternoon to pick up the children, I'll nose the wastebasket close to the pantry cabinet, leap to the edge of the wastebasket, and try to leap from there to the ledge."

"Won't the wastebasket tip from your weight?" Icicle asked.

"We have no choice. We must try it. It's the only way." Fritz responded.

"Alright, if it's the only way." Icicle's face drooped.

The needles stopped clicking. Fritz looked up. Mistress held the completed stocking before her. "It's just right, and it's just in time for Santa's visit," Mistress said. She put away the needles and yarn and called out to Fritz, "Lunchtime, Fritz, then I have to pick up the children at Grandmother's."

Fritz followed her into the kitchen. Ornament gazed down at him, and he tried to look brave. "It's alright. Everything's fine," he whispered to her. Ornament nodded.

Mistress pulled open a drawer and took a spoon out. She opened a cupboard and took out a can of tuna morsels. The doorbell chimed, and Mistress dropped the spoon on the counter. She hurried through the doorway toward the sound.

"Fritz, this is our chance," Ornament said. "Mistress left the drawer pulled out. Leap to the drawer, and from there, leap to where I am. Hurry, Fritz, she'll be back in a few moments, and we will have missed our chance."

Fritz eyed the open drawer. He hadn't leapt that high in a long time. Once yesterday though, he may have leapt almost that high.

Fritz pushed himself back against the far wall, took a deep breath, and rushed off toward the cupboard. A whirl of gray across the white tiled floor, he waited until the last moment, then, gasping for breath, he flung himself upward. His front paws caught the edge of the drawer, and he hung there, his back legs hanging loose.,

"Hold on, Fritz, you can do it. Hold on," Ornament yelled.

Fritz tried to swing his back legs up and over into the drawer. With one last mighty breath, he threw his legs over the side, and lay there, shaking.

Ornament looked at him from over the side of the ledge. "Fritz, you did it. You did it."

Fritz smiled at her. He tried to stand.

"Fritz, be careful," Ornament warned. "There are knives in the drawer. You'll cut your paws."

Fritz placed his paws between the knives and forks and stood, looking up at the cupboard wall looming above him. He scanned the height.

Ornament peered downward. "Fritz, hurry."

Fritz avoided her look. If I were just younger, he thought, I could do it.

"It's too steep, isn't it, Fritz?"

He didn't answer.

"I can't stand it here any longer, Fritz," Ornament cried out. She rolled back and forth, building up speed to leap into space.

"No, Ornament, no!" Fritz shouted.

"Anything, Fritz, would be better than staying here alone." She pushed again, gained speed, shot to the edge, and flew into space.

Fritz leaped. He caught Ornament by a strand, then she slipped downward through his paws. He hung on, a thread of her ribbon in his teeth, and the two dropped to the floor together.

"Ornament, are you alright?"

"Yes, Fritz, are you?"

They heard the click of the Mistress' heels as she crossed the hardwood floor of the dining room. Fritz picked Ornament up by her top ribbon and raced through the door, as Mistress entered.

"Ornament!" Icicle shouted, as Fritz carried her into the living room. "Fritz, you did it, you did it. You saved her."

They heard Mistress closing the drawer in the kitchen. She called to Fritz, "Fritz, come and get it. Lunch is ready." Fritz looped Ornament's ribbon over the branch next to Icicle. He pretended not to hear, as the two greeted each other.

"Oh, Icicle, I missed you so," Ornament said.

"And I missed you," Icicle replied.

"It's Christmas Eve today, and we're together," Ornament said.

"Yes," Icicle said, "we're together. That's the greatest gift of all."

They looked down at Fritz. "Thank you, Fritz, thank you," they murmured.

Fritz meowed softly. Light from the fire reflected from Icicle. The rainbow hues shone on Ornament's satin ribbon. "Yes," Fritz said, "that's what counts. It's Christmas Eve, and we're all here together."

-The End-

Nightmares

Emily Verona

NIGHTMARES

Let me tell you a story. It is not pretty. It is not sweet. It will not lift your soul, but send it screaming from this earth. It will not tug tenderly at your heartstrings, but rather rip them out one by one.

My brother used to tell me stories. The sinister kind. The sort you don't tell children as they lie in bed at night, tucked safely under the covers with a teddy bear crooked in one arm. I think he meant them to comfort me, to prove there was still an ugliness out there darker than the one we knew-to prove nightmares still existed beyond our very own.

So there he'd sit, my brother Dom, spinning tales late into the hollow night. And in these stories, everyone died.

It never seemed strange to me, it wouldn't to you either if it was all you'd ever known. He told me of rippers stalking children in the streets, thieves taken in by kind, fair ladies who would slit those stranger's throats in the dark of night. I'd sit up huddled with my back against the pillow, Thomas the Teddy Bear squeezed between my sweating palms, listening with the fierce attentiveness. He could have slit my own throat in those very moments and I wouldn't have even noticed.

There was one story in particular which he'd always return to, one that frightened him beyond all the rest. In it a boy stood at the edge of death, only death was a lake residing in the center of an empty field -- a lake filled with blood, vast as anything and darker than an open vein. The boy saw no fish. Not a single one, dead or otherwise. Instead eyes drifted across the surface, nerve endings swaying gently from side to side like tails swimming. Tongues littered the bottom of this lake in place of sand and hair ripped from the roots lay scattered where patches of grass should have grown.

The boy leaned in, tipping further and further over the surface of the blood in order to get a closer look. He feared the lake and yet it drew him in. Steadily. Slowly. Like a siren call. Then, rather suddenly, just as that boy was about to fall, he woke rapidly to realize he had not yet gone to meet death after all.

Dom would always grow grim as he told those last few lines, as if the boy's realization was in fact disappointing. His bright eyes would dim and he'd cock his head to the side dreamily until I'd ask him who the boy was and he'd just smile and shake his head. "Go to sleep Daniel," he's say, "Dream a good dream."

I'd always pretend to do as he said, rolling over in the bed and closing my eyes. I'd wait until he thought I was fast asleep and then I'd peek out from behind the covers and watch him cry. Dom looked funny when he cried, like a wrinkled mouse or an old sock. It didn't suit him, and yet he'd shriek silently into his arms from the far corner of the room. Every night. Without fail. Then, very calmly, he'd stop and stare into the darkness for hours. I never knew how long, for no matter how hard I tried I'd always drift off eventually, waking to the sight of Dom standing over my bed in the late hours of the morning.

"Would you like to hear a story?" He'd say, and I'd nod eagerly. The stories he'd tell when I first woke were always special, unique in that they were strikingly kind. Much like a dream, fragrant and frail and filled with beautiful things.

They were meant to give us hope, he'd explain, but only just a little. Enough to get by. After all, hope is a horror left untamed. It produces thoughts of freedom and joy and endless possibilities. We couldn't ever risk something like that. "In our hands," Dom would say gravely, "Hope is hell."

Some days my brother was too weak to tell me tales, or he'd go out for hours at a time without returning, leaving me in the dark quiet all alone.

I always tried to make up my own stories, trying to get them to be as good as his, but they never were. He had a talent for it-a true talent as some might say. Only no one ever heard Dom's stories. I was the only one to whom he'd speak about such things, partly because he had to, but mostly because he wanted me to understand.

I didn't know what exactly, to this day I doubt I ever will, but there something that he'd always wanted me to hear from him and him only. Dom never told me though. He never got the nerve.

Ultimately the fits became too much for him. They were the reason he left. No matter how he tried, he could not resist the call. My brother used to say he felt it in his temple-that when I was older I'd feel it too. A ringing louder than a scream. Shrill like a cry. Unforgiving as a blade pointed against the bone.

Soon he started to hear the ringing more frequently. He'd go out in the rain or at night, doing whatever he could to keep the sound at bay. He shook more violently each and every morning, his fingers thinning and trembling day by day. His stories grew less patient. His manner of speaking as he told them lost that careful

194

calmness. Instead when he spoke the sound grew hollow, as if he were hollering into an empty pit and enjoyed the distortion of his own voice as it called back out to him.

He'd always said that it would change him, but I don't think he really believed that until it actually did. Like all things, it happened slowly, so tenderly that by the time he'd become different neither of us were really all that surprised.

He stopped crying at night. It should have been the only sign I needed, but I didn't want to believe that the silence meant anything. I was too young to recognize the gravity of it. He stopped crying at night and began clawing at the walls, ripping his fingers raw and bloody under the nails. That lasted a short time. Then he started going out more. The stories had stopped by then and he'd return later and later, a stranger's long, fine hair clinging to his jacket or an empty wallet in his pocket. He never took the money, only the IDs. Dom piled them in the corner of the room, at first carefully, then carelessly, stacking them like empty dinner plates on a kitchen counter.

I'd ask him for stories, beg him at times, but he'd shake his head, mumbling that he was tired. Other times he'd turn against me, hissing that I should just shut my mouth and bide my time.

Eventually he ceased talking altogether, and five years ago to this day he walked out the door and didn't come back. He's out there now, as I'd always known he would be. He used to promise he'd say goodbye, swear it up and down. Declare our bond to be one of blood. One of meaning. No matter what, we were brothers and he would never leave without saying goodbye.

I shouldn't blame him for it, that sort of thing couldn't be helped, but it hurts all the same. He could have said a word, given a gesture suggesting that I look upon him more carefully that final night. He could have told me so I wouldn't wait and wonder and spend my time trying to recreate those stories of his. Those awful, cruel stories that made me feel so very at home.

He was sixteen when he left. I have three years to go before I hit the mark, only a few months really before the signs begin to show in me as they did in him. They haven't started yet and at times it feels like they never will, but I suppose that's how it was for Dom too. It didn't seem like it would take him. And then it did.

That's the way it has always gone and it will never stop. Never waver. We might have been only children when we were abandoned here, but it had been done for good reason and safe measure. You see, a demon is still a demon no matter how small. Our father had known this when he left us, or so my brother always said. He left us because he knew neither how to kill us, nor how to let us live in a mortal world with mortal souls. He'd loved us, he had, but it didn't matter that he loved us or that if we loved him. Sooner or later, evil would begin to mature in our veins, stretching out and taking hold, turning mere children into creatures behind human masks.

I've got three years left, maybe less, before I become a story, the kind told to scare little children in the night. It won't be pretty. It won't be sweet.

And if you're not careful, I will send your soul screaming from this earth or rip your heartstrings out one by one.

THE RECRUIT

BR SANDERS

Everything Valiyon did in the early days of the red elvish rebellion was about recruitment, right down to what she wore. Yes, the leathers were meant to protect her, but they were also meant to impress. They had to do both. It wasn't enough for them to be just functional. When Valiyon hopped out of the trees, she had to look like vengeance incarnate, like justice embodied. Or, at the very least, like someone quite dangerous.

Valiyon's leathers came from a dead human soldier she killed with an arrow through the throat. He was pissing in a stream away from his fellows. Valiyon killed him before there was any rebellion, back when it was just her and her anger to keep her company. She killed him, dragged him into the underbrush before anyone realized he was missing, and stripped off his leather tunic. She used her hunting knife to scrape off the human king's insignia and cut it down to her size; being a girl elf, she ran quite a bit smaller than that bastard. Valiyon turned that awful thing into a real beauty--a solid hunter's doublet, high-collared to keep anyone from shooting her through the throat, with give at the shoulders for extra range of motion so she could scale trees when she needed to. After cutting it down, there was enough leather left over that she could make bracers and chaps, too, which meant she was protected all over and still able to move freely. A good haul, that.

For years, Valiyon lived in those leathers. That armor was a part of her. Valiyon--the Mother of the Rebellion, that's how she was known. She birthed a daughter and a war both, and she did so in those leathers. Her armor started a high-collared fashion trend among the elvish neighborhoods in the cities, it's said. That's the point--what she wore mattered in terms of recruitment, and a war can't be won without bodies on the ground.

At first it was just bodies, just numbers Valiyon needed. Just anyone. Zealots, those with as much anger as Valiyon had herself, those who had lost as much as she had. It didn't take long before enough of those turned up that the elvish rebels had to divide up into a few different crews. After that, Valiyon went on the lookout for talent. To win a rebellion, a war needs more than just numbers. A rebellion needs talent among the rank and file: brilliant minds and brilliant hearts.

Valiyon used to recruit out on the front, wearing her leathers, dropping out of trees. Ten years into the way, she recruited with her leathers half undone, in a tent buried in the weirdness of the deep forest, tucked out of sight. Times began to change.

The trees of the sprite path creaked apart. Valiyon's right hand, Benno, stepped through. Valiyon smiled slightly--that her most trusted man in this war, a war for her red elvish homeland, was a blue elf, remained strange to her. But his loyalty was long ago proven, her mate Ben, despite the blue skin and black hair and weird tattoos which crawled all over his face and arms. Behind him came the recruit she wanted in my cell, this boy from the human cities, Vathorem. He was thin as a rail, orange-haired, freckled-- as red elvish as Valiyon was herself: a pure-blooded red elf. She noticed he wore a quilted high-collared vest, the kind of thing rumor had it was modeled off her own leathers. It didn't actually resemble her armor much in person besides the collar, but it made her smile a little anyway. The boy was large-eyed and grim-faced. He had a fresh wound on his cheek. "You should have my medic, Tayo, look at that for you," Valiyon said.

"I've been looked over," the boy said. "I'm all right. You had me brought here."

"I did."

"I'm guessing it weren't about this scratch on my cheek."

Valiyon nodded at a chair across from her. The boy did not sit, which irked her something fierce. Mother of the Rebellion, she was. He should have been gracious enough to sit when asked. She leaned against a nearby table. She noticed a bottle of whiskey and took a drink. She offered some to this defiant boy, Vathorem, who to her surprise drank some, as well. He seemed reluctant to give it back.

"You know the deal," she said. "Folks wanting to captain come through me."

"I don't want to captain."

"No, but your friend Li does." The boy stared at the ground between them, arms crossed tight against his chest, frowning slightly. "Came all the way from Susselfen, left his spy network behind and dragged you here with him. Should've heard him sing your praises. Should've heard him talk about the things you can do."

"Nothing redder than a lie," the boy said through clenched teeth.

"Ah, but your man Li, he's only half red elf, eh? That hair is dyed. I've an eye for it. He's too tall, too brawny to be one of us.

200

What's a halfie doing begging me for a captaincy?"

Vathorem looked at Valiyon, finally. A strong look, he gave her. An intensity, this boy had, like a cornered fox. "He's loyal. He's half-red, and you're questioning Li's loyalty, but you've got this big blue elf bastard dragging me to come have this chat with you?"

"Benno's loyalty is proven. I don't know Li from any soldier in the King's army."

"We ran a spy cell--"

"Not under my command, you didn't. You did that all by yourselves."

Vathorem shut his mouth and stared back down at the ground. His eyebrows drew together. "What did Li say I can do?"

"Said you can just about talk anyone into anything. Said you got some real useful skills."

Vathorem looked up at Valiyon. "I've seen your striker crew. Best of the best. Top pickings. Be straight with me. What is this?"

"Fine. I'll be straight with you. I need to see what it is he's bringing to the war effort. Sounds like you're the best he's got to offer. I want to see you in action. And, if you're good enough, I want you in my crew. That's the price of his captaincy."

"Do I have any choice in this?"

Valiyon smiled. "Of course you do. You can always walk away, boy. But if you do, not only are you walking away from the rebellion, but you're walking away from your friend. You walk away, and your halfie friend Li ain't ever making soldier in my army, much less captain. But of course you got a choice, Vathorem."

Strategically, it made all the sense in the world for Valiyon to stay out of sight and out of reach in the forest, but she hated doing that. She had come to crave the fight. Too many simple, easy days without danger made her uneasy. She stopped sleeping. She stopped trusting the world around her. She began to panic if she hadn't killed a human man in an army uniform recently enough. The rebellion stopped feeling real to her. That was one of the reasons she wore my leathers even when it seemed safe--to remind herself that it may not be. That the King's Army might be plotting an ambush on her. That none of the red elves were ever safe so long as any of the Royalists were out there still breathing.

"Are you good with trees, Vathorem?" Valiyon asked.

"No," he said. "I have trouble with concentration."

"Yet you want to be out here in the fray."

"No, Valiyon," he said. He plucked at the neck of a borrowed leather tunic. It was ill-fitting; already there was an angry red mark on his delicate skin. "Li is the one who wants to be out here in the fray. I was fine playing the spy back in Susselfen."

"Then you should've stayed in Susselfen."

"I did try to talk Li out of coming to this damn forest," Vathorem said.

Valiyon stole a glance at the boy. "Are you one of those? A lovesick follower?"

"Not how you're thinking, but in a sense, yeah. Looks like."

"I'm thinking whether you're in love him or not it always turns out the same. If you follow somewhere here, if you don't come here of your own accord ready to fight, you end up dying. Are you ready to die, boy?" Vathorem, this scrawny, grim-faced, lovesick fool, just laughed. Benno and Valiyon exchanged a knowing look.

"Where's the rest of your crew?" Vathorem asked.

"It's just the three of us tonight, boy," she said. "A quick in and out. So long as you keep your concentration, that is. Can you keep your concentration, Vathorem? Are you going to get me and Benno killed tonight?"

"I don't plan to, Valiyon," said Vathorem. "I'd rather not. To keep you alive I need to know what we're you're planning."

Valiyon buttoned her leathers up from left hip to armpit; Benno helped tighten the laces from her left shoulder to the collar. The armor was snug, not tight. She swung her arms out, testing her range of motion. "Benno, loosen the laces on my right shoulder, would you?"

"Yes, Val."

The leathers fit perfect after that. She was encased in the carapace, feeling ready for anything. No matter what this fool boy did, she had no plans to die that night. She restrung her bow and helped Benno into his armor. "Vathorem, you said you were a spy. Let's see if you were a good one. The three of us, we're going to infiltrate. If I have a single nemesis, one man I'm meant to kill, it's not King Marchaunt. It's this man, Vylan Worthis. You know of Worthis?"

"I can't say I do," said Vathorem.

"This bastard, he was a farmer. He was the one who started

all this. Riled everything up. He was there the night they burned Alamadour; he threw the first torch. He turned soldier. Been rising through the ranks these last ten yes. They gave him a manor house--Highsun Manor, he's named it."

"And this Worthis man's got what, army secrets in it?" Vathorem asked.

"I don't give two shits what Vylan Worthis has in his house. Maybe he's got nothing in it at all. I just want to burn it to the ground," she said.

"Then march on it with your crew. I don't see why you're dragging me into this."

Valiyon looked over at him. He stood there, fidgeting with his ill-fitting armor, a bad-tempered callow creature that disliked her as much as she disliked him. But mettle is meant to be tested, and loyalties are meant to be proved. "You man Li dragged you into this, not me. You let yourself be dragged into this when you laid your loyalty at his feet and he went campaigning for captaincy. He wants a crew of his own? He gets it by you helping me pull this off. Highsun Manor is to the south of us. Li says you have a sense of people, a sense of when people are around. Is that true?"

"Sometimes, yeah."

"Does that work on dogs?"

Vathorem looked over at her. The blood drained from his already pale skin, leaving him gray-faced. "Dogs?"

"He'll likely have dogs on the perimeter."

"I...I don't know about dogs. Never tried it on dogs. Not many dogs in Susselfen."

"Plenty of dogs out here on the war front, eh, Ben?" She said.

Benno looked up from a knife he was sharpening. "Plenty of dogs," Benno said with that odd forest accent he never did lose. "The army trains them, sets them loose on us. The fight is different than what you do in the cities."

For the first time, Valiyon saw the boy sweat. He lost his petulance, and fear crept into its place. "Dogs?"

"Dogs, yeah. What, you think the armor is just for show? You know how to shoot a bow, don't you?" Benno laughed behind her. "You know how to fight, don't you?"

Vathorem snatched the short bow from her hand. "I can shoot," he said.

"Here's hoping. Better watch out for the dogs." She held out my left bracer; showed him the teeth marks from the last time she tangled with a dog. "I still have scars from where the bitch bit through, but without the leather I might have lost my arm."

"Look, you can scare me off, but it won't change Li's mind. You can get me killed, but he'll just stick around, pestering you still about his captaincy," Vathorem said quietly. He fiddled now with the short bow. The way he messed with it told her he didn't know how to shoot that well, that he wasn't all that comfortable with weaponry.

"So, your man--"

"He's not my man. We're mates. It's not like that; I told you it wasn't," Vathorem snapped.

"My mistake. So, your mate offers you up to me like a lamb to slaughter and you let him? What's that about?"

"It's about the demands you placed, Valiyon," he said. He stood up and shouldered the bow. "It's about the choices you laid at our feet. Let's go set fire to this manor. Let's go." Vathorem stalked off into the dark night.

"Should I bring him back?" Benno asked.

"Nah," I said. "Let him wander. Let him spin himself out. What's your read on him, Ben?"

Benno was silent while he considered. A quiet man, her mate Ben. So quiet, so different than her--when he spoke it was always with honesty, always with carefulness. "My read on him is that he will not survive the night unless that would-be captain is right about his magic."

"And then?"

"And then we burn the manor anyway and carry the body back to his man. His man stays with the fight or he doesn't. If he stays, he's loyal. If he doesn't, he couldn't be trusted in the first place," said Benno.

"I thought so, too."

"But if this Vathorem has talents, and we get him killed," said Benno, looking up at Valiyon with unreadable, dark eyes, "then this test of loyalty comes at a high cost, no, Captain?"

She studied Benno's face. It was so hard to read. He was still so unfamiliar to her, even after years fighting side by side. A dozen times, at least, she'd saved his life, half a dozen, now, he'd saved hers, and still she couldn't read his face. "You think he's got some talents?"

"I think he is defiant. And arrogant." Benno looked out into the darkness where Vathorem had gone. "I was like that when I was very young. Whether or not his talents prove useful, I cannot say, but I do not doubt he has something."

There were dogs at Highsun Manor. Their howls and barks split the night air from a mile away. Vathorem cursed under his breath. "Steady on, boy," Valiyon said.

"How do you take down a dog?" Vathorem asked.

"By being quiet," Benno said.

"The same way you take down an army man," Valiyon said. "With a bow and some luck."

"A bow and luck," Vathorem said. "Two things I never seem to do very well with."

"Then all that magic your halfie came to me boasting about better pan out," Valiyon said. The boy muttered under his breath. Valiyon couldn't make out anything but the words 'focus' and 'forest'. Valiyon smiled into the dark night. Behind her, Benno let out a dry laugh. "All right. The plan is to push in and take out anyone in the manor. Set the place on fire and make sure the fire catches, then get out in one piece."

"What do you want me to do, Valiyon?" Vathorem asked.

"I want you to do whatever needs doing. Your mate Li says you're good at talking your way into places back in Susselfen, good at casing joints back in Susselfen. Use your magic." The dogs howled again. "Keep us alive."

The three of them pushed forward. Highsun Manor was a sparse thing, a rawboned farmhouse only just built on some hundred or so acres of land which had been stripped of trees but not yet plowed. It was just bows against the dogs that night, and Valiyon liked it that way. It made her blood run hot in my veins.

It took hard listening to get a bead on where the dogs were. Benno tracked them to a barn on the east side of the manor; the dogs ran in and out of it in a tight pack, cavorting in the moonlight, driven by who knows what beastly desires. "Vathorem, you stay here," Valiyon said. "You stay very still. Don't get yourself killed. Benno, up on the roof. I'll make one lap, and then I'm coming up after you."

Benno, obedient Benno, scurried off into the darkness. "What are you doing, Valiyon?" Vathorem asked.

"Shh," Valiyon said. She handed Vathorem her short bow and her belt quiver. She quickly braided her hair and tucked it into the collar of her leathers. "Keep your fool mouth shut or you'll draw the dogs to you. Stay here; stay still." And then she was off, towards the barn. The dogs howled and barked and made playful growls that echoed in the empty night air.

Then, they caught her scent, and the growls turned hostile. Their paws thundered against the hard earth of the manor's lands in unison as the entire pack came after her at once. Half a dozen hounds poured out of the barn door, tearing out after Valiyon. Their bodies were lean and rugged, dropped low to the ground for maximum speed. Their bared fangs flashed white in the moonlight. And she ran, oh how she ran.

Valiyon peeled around the corner of the barn, leaning into the run with her whole body, counting on sheer momentum to keep her upright. She heard the familiar faint whistle of an arrow fly through the air; she heard the whimper of one of the dogs as it wedged itself into the animal's flesh. Benno took out one, two more of the dogs. He wasted three or four arrows. The leader of the pack came at her, snarling, sniping. She ran as fast as her body would let her, her legs pounding against the ground, her chin held up high, her lungs gasping for air. The lead dog lunged, and Valiyon dodged, leaning to the left as the dog made its play. The dog crashed into the soil beside her. She gave it a fierce, quick kick to the nose and turned the second corner of the barn, leaving the dog whimpering in her wake. The rest of the pack hesitated for half a second, and Valiyon felt a margin of breathing room bloom between her and the pack as the lead dog shook its head and stood, recovering, clearing its head, and charging after her anew.

Benno fired off more arrows. Another dog fell. Valiyon spotted a window on the third side of the barn, a window that would serve as a good foothold and a viable way to scale the building. She took it. She left the dogs scrabbling and jumping after her. Her legs shook with exhaustion, but her arms were still fresh. "Ben!" She said. Within two seconds, he was at the edge, helping her up.

The remaining two dogs made a vicious racket. They were

whipped into a frenzy, throwing themselves at the side of the barn with everything they had, mad with grief and rage. Valiyon knew how they felt. She'd seen friends and lovers fall, ripped from life in seconds. She'd been ambushed like those dogs, had nights go from easy and meaningless to horrific in the space of heartbeats. She took Benno's bow. With two shots apiece, she had both dogs down. It took no more than ten seconds before the night was silent.

But it was no longer dark. The sudden raucous of the dogs and their sudden silence had roused whoever was in the manor house. Valiyon and Benno jumped down from the barn roof and ran back to where Vathorem still stood, white-faced. Valiyon took it for terror at first. But at second glance, there was something strange about the boy's face. There was something in the way he gripped her boy, about the tightness of his knuckles and the width of his eyes. He stood too still. Valiyon and Benno had the good sense to crouch, to stand loose and ready to run, but Vathorem was planted firm to the ground, wound tight and ready to snap.

Valiyon reached out to touch him. Benno caught her wrist and shook his head. He looked unnerved. "It might be a trance," Benno said.

"If it's a trance, then we leave him. A trance is a liability," Valiyon said.

"I can hear you," Vathorem said. It came out clenched, pained, a grated whisper. "You've jabbed some hornet's nest, you have. There's...what, seven? Eight? A bunch of them in there. Just waiting. I don't know for what. But they were so bored. They hope it's something like this. They're hungry for something like this."

"Give me my bow, boy," Valiyon said. A door in the manor house opened. A man in an army uniform came out, lantern held high. "Give it to me now."

Vathorem turned to face her slowly. His black eyes held endless depth, like a bottomless lake, like the weird wells they sometimes came across in the forest. "They will kill us and turn in our right hands for payment in town. Yours and mine. Benno's will fetch nothing. They'll be so disappointed by that. They have been so bored. Just posted here. They knew you'd come, though. They knew if they gave Worthis a plot of land that it would draw you out eventually. They just had to keep soldiers there."

Benno laid a hand on her shoulder. "Captain, we should--"

She knocked his hand aside. She took Vathorem's chin in her hand and dragged his face close to hers. His eyes began to focus. "Are you a double-crosser?" She hissed.

The boy quaked with fear. He twisted, tried to get out of her grip, but her hands were like iron. "I swear to you it's not like that. I know I--I was rambling, right? I--I do that sometimes. I know I do. I remember talking to you just then, I do, about the men inside, about the eight of them and their boredom, but I don't remember all of it, and now--you are nothing but rage, woman, it is *all you are* just that and your *pride, and I--*"

Valiyon threw him down to the ground. "Go back to your mate, Li. I don't want you in my crew. You can have him as your captain."

"He--he can have his captaincy?" Vathorem asked.

"If you make it there alive to give him the news, yeah, he can have it."

"What about you?" Vathorem asked. "Aren't you coming with me?"

But the army man had already found the first dead dog. He was already yelling to the others in the house, the others who were apparently bored and bloodthirsty. Valiyon ripped her bow and belt quiver out of Vathorem's hands. "Oh, no. No. I finish what I start."

And so she did. Using the door as a natural bottleneck, she did. It was quick work. They drew attention to themselves, with their loud voices and their lanterns. When one screamed and gurgled as the arrows pierced him, another came through the same door to see what the yelling was about. They had come with swords, not with bows, the stupid bastards.

They came out into the dark night with their useless swords drawn, without even their army-issued tunics on to protect them from her arrows. She left Benno behind to finish off the dying with his knife and dug around in the kitchen for bottles of alcohol with which to start the fire.

So the recruit hadn't worked out. Something better came from it; a kind of solace came from that night. Valiyon stood watching Highsun Manor burn until near dawn. She memorized every detail, every curl of the flames, every hue of orange and red and yellow. She wanted it etched in her mind, something she could draw on and dream about and sink into. She wanted the memories within her reach, as tangible and comforting to her as the leathers she wore every day, which gave her such a sense of safety. *Look at this thing I did*, she thought as she watched the flames consume Highsun Manor. *He burned my life to the ground, and I'm burning his to the ground, too.*

Bogerd's Bad Day

Robert Walton

Ilsa thumped Bogerd sharply between his shoulder blades. The blow was much mitigated by the tattered bearskin he wore across his shoulders. She hissed, "He's been gone since yesterday noon. Who knows what's happened to him by now?"

Bogerd glanced back at his wife and raised a lazy right eyebrow.

Ilsa snapped, "Don't you look at me like that. Karl's a responsible man, unlike others I could mention. He wouldn't let a wench or a flagon of mead keep him from completing a job. I sent him to collect the low-town rents. He didn't come back. You go and find him! Now!"

Bogerd grumbled deep in his chest, but no discernible words reached his lips.

Ilsa snarled, "Besides, he's your friend. Go!"

Bogerd opened his door upon a frosty Nordheim morning, far too early, far too frosty. He stepped out. The door slammed emphatically behind him. He grumbled to himself again and squinted his eyes against low, bright sunshine.

Nordheim's squalid, chaotic streets and alleys lay below him. Steams rose from unlikely places. Smokes, pressed down by the frigid air, hid in hollows and dips. Icicles glinted in the early sun like pristine diamond daggers. Bogerd surveyed all as he pondered how to get news of Karl.

Sigrid, the crazed witch, lived in low-town and knew all its dark-magical happenings. Bogerd chuckled. Her nightly habit of sailing the future's deep-misted seas through drug-induced trance would keep her warty cheek upon her warty pillow for some hours to come. She would be his last resort.

Gimp, the legless beggar king, would know of all the tavern happenings. He prowled the icy alleys on horny knuckles, propelled by arms thicker than most men's thighs. He took his tolls and ruled his luckless charges with fists much harder than iron. Bogerd patted his purse. Only silver produced fruitful words from Gimp.

Latifah, the displaced belly dancer, might have news of Karl. High town and low, she knew the secrets of Nordheim as did few others and she had a liking for the little man. As wide as Bogerd and nearly as tall, she dwarfed the wiry Karl. Still, in her heart of a thousand chambers, one of the inner ones was surely reserved for him. Her information, had she any, would be true. Bogerd nodded. He would begin with Latifah.

Bogerd sighed and checked his weapons. He pulled his long ax from its loop on the right hand side of his three-inch wide belt. He patted his short ax in its loop on the left hand side. Both boot knives, the throwing dagger and the long, heavy, close-fighting weapon, were ready in their sheaths. His brass cudgel hung from a rear loop. His garrote circled (partly circled) his waist. His short-bladed emergency knife was tied to the inside of his left thigh. These were his workaday town weapons. For true battle he also carried his war spear, a mace, a sling and lead shot and any of a variety of specialized implements which circumstances might dictate.

He hefted the long ax and paused. Vague unease slowed his momentum. He had no doubt that Latifah's facts were true. Somewhere in the gray dungeons below this wizard's tower, Karl awaited rescue. Bogerd cursed below his breath. "Wizards! Give me twenty screaming Mongol barbarians or thirty blue-painted Celts! Bah!"

Wizards, of which Nordheim had its fair share, usually kept to themselves. Bogerd knew nothing of this wizard, one Hanuman by name, except that he was middling high on their list of seniority. Further, he could imagine no possible cause for Hanuman's apparent interest in Karl.

What must be done, must be done. He rested the head of his ax on the ground. He took a deep breath and his shoulder muscles bunched as he swung the heavy ax with all of his might. The pike head of the ax whistled down and blasted into the triple heavy brass lock on the wizard's door. The lock disintegrated into three large fragments and numerous flying splinters.

Bogerd pushed open the door with his booted toe. Two gate-keepers, still fumbling with armor fastenings and carrying their short swords like bread knives, stumbled to a halt just before him.

Bogerd raised his long ax and said, "He's not paying you enough, boys. Drop your swords and I'll let you pass."

The tall (though he was a full hand-span shorter than Bogerd) guard replied, "Turn around, fat man. Leave. Master will bill you for the lock tomorrow."

Bogerd's long ax snaked out and punched the smaller guard squarely in the jaw with the blunt top of its head. The man fell like a stone.

Bogerd said, "He'll have a headache later. I may have to do

something more permanent to you, unless you drop that sword."

The tall man's eyes widened and he swallowed hard. He took a step back. Bogerd stepped forward into a wide hallway. A crossbow fired with a snap and a hiss. Its short bolt sped down the length of the hall and slammed into Bogerd's chest just above the edge of his triple-thick brass breast plate. It penetrated three inches of muscle and buried its not very sharp iron head in one of Bogerd's massive ribs.

Bogerd grunted, accepted the hurt and exploded into Berserker motion. Berserker rage is much misunderstood. It is less anger than it is demonic fixity of purpose. Bogerd attacked. He struck high with his long ax. The guard parried with his short sword. Steel shrieked and sparks flew. Bogerd struck low and again the guard parried. Then Bogerd's almost instantaneous backstroke took off his sword hand at the wrist. Sword and gripping hand bounced off the hallway's far wall. The man screamed in horror and fell.

Bogerd leapt over the sprawling, bleeding body and charged down the hall. The sands of a nearly empty minute glass measured the time he had to reach the crossbowman before that worthy was again ready to fire. He reached the hall's end with a few grains to spare.

He stepped to the left of the murder hole and flattened his back against the wall. He pulled his long knife from its sheath and waited. He heard a scratching noise, the scrape of vambraces against stone as the crossbowman brought his weapon to the ready. He leaned forward and drove his knife into the hole. It plunged into unseen cloth, leather and flesh. A muffled cry of pain and dismay sounded through the murder hole followed by the thump of a body hitting the floor.

Trusting that the crossbowman was sufficiently discouraged, Bogerd wiped his knife on his leggings, sheathed it and crossed in front of the murder hole. The hall turned right. He continued following it. After a dozen or so paces, he came to another right turn. Beyond the turn was a landing and two steep stairways. One led up and the other led down. Bogerd stopped.

The hallway was more than adequately lit by torches in wall sconces. The stairway on his left was also well lit and presumably ascended to the wizard's private quarters. The other stairway descended into darkness. Karl would likely be found downstairs.

Bogerd judged that even a wealthy wizard would be reluctant to pay more than three guards at a time. Any further defenses he might encounter would be of a magical nature. He nodded to himself and retraced his steps.

Bogerd returned to the wounded guard at the doorway. The man was seated on the floor. He cradled his bleeding stump with his good arm and rocked back and forth in misery. Bogerd knelt and gripped the man's injured arm. Blood pulsed from the wound. Bogerd wrapped a leather thong four times around the arm, pulled it taut and knotted it. The bleeding stopped.

Bogerd pulled the man to his feet. He said, "Come with me. It's not your day." Weeping quietly, the guard staggered ahead of Bogerd. Bogerd steadied him with his left hand. They reached the stairways.

Bogerd said, "We'll go down. You go first." The man sniffled. Bogerd prodded him with his ax handle. "Go ahead." The man leaned against the wall with his good shoulder and stumbled unevenly down the stairs. Bogerd waited. When the man's foot touched the seventh step, green mage-light flared. The wounded guard disappeared.

Bogerd blinked. Then he stepped forward. He knew that magical wards, once activated, must be recast. Hoping that he would encounter no more enchanted traps, he plunged down the shadowed stairway. It wound in corkscrew fashion through several turns to a wide door. The door was open. The room beyond it was lit by a single torch in a sconce high on the opposite wall. Beneath the torch hung Karl.

Wary of flanking knives and swords, Bogerd leapt through the doorway and whirled. No guards awaited him. He turned to Karl. The little man stood on tip-toe, his wrists pulled high and taut by iron chains. The chains were attached to massive staples just below the torch.

Bogerd said, "Karl?"

Karl raised his head and grinned. His voice cracked when he answered, "I wondered when you'd get here."

"Latifah told me where I might find you."

"Took you long enough."

Bogerd shrugged and winced when the crossbow bolt reminded him of its presence. "Not as young as I once was."

Karl's grin widened. "The wizard wants to meet you."

"Tell me later. Let's get you down."

Bogerd gripped his long ax with both hands, measured the angle of his stroke and swung. The ax bit through the soft iron chain and splashed stone sparks from the wall behind. Karl's left arm fell to his side. Bogerd swung again. Karl slid to the floor.

He muttered, "Thanks, Boss."

Bogerd nodded. "Hanuman will be down shortly. Can you move?"

"Give me a hand up, Boss."

Bogerd shifted his ax to his left hand, bent down, gripped Karl's belt and hauled him to his feet. Karl swayed, but remained standing.

Bogerd said, "Up and out, Karl. I doubt we have much time. One of the guards tripped a warding spell." Karl staggered toward the stairs. Bogerd followed him.

They were safe up the stairs, safe down the hallway, safe around the turn and safe past the still unconscious guard. Bogerd saw Karl stumble out of the open front door. He was within feet of the portal when a web of black silk enveloped him. He slashed at it with his ax, but his blade wouldn't bite on the silkiness. The web caressed, gripped and finally squeezed. Bogerd knew nothing more.

****

Bogerd swam deep in a dark sea. Shapes loomed; shadows menaced him but did not attack. He rose toward a wavering light. The light was a torch. Beneath the torch stood Hanuman.

The wizard said, "Ah, awake again."

Bogerd said nothing. He tried to move and discovered, not surprisingly, that he was lying on his back on a table bound hand and foot. His arms were chained to iron staples near his thighs. His legs were tied painfully apart, as if he were a dancer frozen in mid-leap.

Hanuman said, "That may be uncomfortable, but you needn't stay bound for very long."

Bogerd said, "What happened to your guard?"

Hanuman shrugged. "Oh, nothing terrible. The spell transported him to a dungeon cell. When I have time, I'll release him and then fire him. I'm not a monster. I do think I shall dock him his last week's pay. He didn't discharge his duties very well, after all."

"What do you want with me?"

Hanuman smiled. "You possess a magic talisman." He looked up at the ceiling and tapped his front teeth with an excessively long fingernail. "It is unclear to me how you came to possess it, but it is powerful beyond your imagining. Nothing like it has ever before come into the world of men.

Bogerd sighed. "The Brysinga?"

Hanuman nodded. "The Brysinga, Freyja's magical necklace, a goddess's greatest treasure. I want it. Of course, it will take decades of intense study before I actually dare to use it. Once mastered, though, its powers will make me supreme among wizards on earth. It might," he stared into distances invisible above and beyond Bogerd's head, "allow me to enter higher planes, undertake godly endeavors."

He looked directly at Bogerd. "So. Will you arrange for the Brysinga to be transported here?"

"No."

"Will you escort me to your hall and present the necklace to me?"

"No."

Hanuman sighed. "I thought as much. Therefore, I've prepared a little device to persuade you to cooperate with me."

Bogerd followed him with his eyes. Hanuman stopped and pointed to the distant ceiling. "If you'll glance above you, you'll note a large, razor sharp scimitar blade suspended from a pendulum?"

Bogerd said, "I see it."

"Good! Can you guess what it's for?"

"You plan to use it to convince me to give you the Brysinga."

Hanuman clapped his hands together. "Bravo! You are astute for an ignorant barbarian!"

Bogerd grunted. "Thanks."

Hanuman stroked his beardless chin. "I read across the worlds, across the ages. Pa, Puh, Poo, Poe. Poe." He raised a slightly crooked index finger to his lips. "Yes, Poe. It was Poe. This Poe fellow had a decent idea. I refined it, as you can see." He walked to the foot of the thick table on which Bogerd was bound. "You'll also note how your legs are splayed apart?"

Bogerd nodded.

"Notice how the scimitar blade is aligned with the midline of your body. When I depress this lever," Hanuman pushed the lever forward, "a concealed mechanism begins to function."

Above Bogerd the blade-tipped pendulum began to swing. With each swing, the blade described a wider arc through the shadowed air. A rhythmic, low-pitched whoosh issued from the darkness above.

Hanuman chuckled, "The blade descends a tiny fraction of an inch with each swing. I haven't timed it precisely, but it shouldn't take longer than a few hours before it comes close to you. You can deduce from the position of your legs what part of your anatomy will first be in jeopardy."

Bogerd said nothing.

Hanuman continued, "That string close to your right hand is connected to a bell in my chamber. When you decide to give me the necklace, just pull it. I shall stop the mechanism as quickly as I may." Hanuman turned, paused, turned back and looked at Bogerd. "You wouldn't want to save yourself all of this anguish and agree to give it to me now?"

Bogerd again said nothing.

"Ah, well." Hanuman shrugged. "I leave you to contemplate the consequences of willfulness." He turned and ascended the stairs.

Bogerd looked up at the blade. Still distant, it gleamed evilly in the torchlight. The steady whoosh of its passage through the air was already his least favorite sound, the sound of mindless, inexorable malice.

He glanced at the string next to his right hand. Iron cuffs circled his wrists. Short lengths of stout chain were welded to the cuffs and to bolts in the table on which he lay. He could move his hands a few inches in either direction. He could easily grasp the string and pull it. His hand remained still.

Bogerd had fought unnumbered desperate battles. He had faced defeat and death before. He knew the value of time. When you can win nothing else, win a bit of time. He closed his eyes, shut out at least the sight of the doomful blade. He prepared to wait for as long as he could.

His thoughts drifted to his grandchildren, little Olga and bouncy Fafhrd. Fafhrd was four and Olga six. He vowed silently to spend more time with them should he escape his present plight. He was wise enough to know that children learn little from instruction, but simply walking through a day with grandfather would live in their minds always. He opened his eyes.

The scimitar was much closer, only a few feet above his vulnerable groin. The fingers of his right hand twitched. Not yet. Not just yet. He closed his eyes again.

He thought of his youngest daughter, Gudrun. She'd followed her husband south to Arlane; a country of rains, forests and civilized habits. Bogerd wanted very much to visit her. He secretly doubted, however, that he could survive even a day in cultured Arlane. He would not be allowed to bear his personal weapons. Walking unarmed among strangers was far worse then being naked.

He opened his eyes. The great, dark blade now swung between his outstretched legs. It was within inches of slicing him open in the worst of ways. Bogerd reached for the string and pulled.

The blade continued its inexorable descent. Alarmed, Bogerd pulled the string again. Again. The blade did not slow. Bogerd glanced toward the stairway. Hanuman was there.

Hanuman steepled his fingers, pursed his lips and looked at Bogerd. At last, he said, "My curiosity may overcome both my better judgment and my humanitarian impulses. I really would like to see how my little creation will work. Surely you can afford a little blood?"

Bogerd glared at the mage with mingled despair and rage, but he did not answer. The blade whistled as it grazed the wooly hairs of Bogerd's breeks.

Hanuman smiled. "Don't be surly! You've cost me guards, spells and a good deal of trouble. Just a little discomfort on your part will allow me to calibrate the device."

A silver glow suddenly lit the stairway behind Hanuman. He didn't notice it. His attention was fixed upon the next stroke of the blade. The scimitar swooped down, cutting through Bogerd's breeks, cutting deeper.

Bogerd lurched against the chains when he felt the sharp blade's icy sting as it cut through the skin of his most intimate appendage. In horror beyond any he'd known, he watched the blade pause at the top of its backstroke. It paused and then swept back toward his helpless manhood. Bogerd closed his eyes and so missed the appearance of a giant silver hand.

The hand flowed like mist around and over Hanuman. It coalesced around the down-swinging blade. The scimitar slowed. Cracks, groans and grindings of gears sounded from above. The blade slowed further. Hanuman, fingers and thumb spread wide, gestured with his right hand. A red bolt of energy burst from his palm and struck the silver hand. The red bolt bounced off of the hand and dissolved into hundreds of yellow lightning darts. These darts zipped erratically around the dungeon. Hanuman gestured again and a transparent shield appeared in front of him. The silver hand gave one final wrench. The scimitar stopped inches from Bogerd's undefended groin.

Hanuman yelped as the odd lightning dart avoided his shield and struck home. The silver hand again became silver mist and settled over Bogerd. The chains holding him down dissolved. Stiffly, carefully he raised his right leg over the still menacing blade and rolled to his left. He rolled until he was sitting on the table facing Hanuman.

The last of the lightning darts sputtered against Hanuman's shield and fizzled away. Hanuman raised his right eyebrow twice. The shield disappeared. He slowly straightened and smiled. He said, "It looks as if we'll have to continue this experiment another time. I have urgent business elsewhere," He cast a black pellet onto the floor with his left hand. The pellet exploded into brown smoke. The smoke boiled up toward the distant ceiling. At its center an orange light glowed. "So I'll say farewell." He stepped into the orange glow and began to fade.

Bogerd reacted with characteristic swiftness. He snatched his throwing knife, left in its boot sheath by Hanuman in his arrogance, and cast it into the center of the orange glow. He was rewarded with a distant howl of dismay.

Karl's head appeared around the edge of the doorway. "You okay, Boss?"

Bogerd grinned, "Just barely."

Karl entered the dungeon. He held a long knife in his right hand and liquid star-fire in his left. He raised the white fire toward Bogerd. "I brought this."

Bogerd sighed, "The Bysinga. Its magic saved me."

Karl smiled. "Ilsa thought it might prove useful against a wizard. Guess she was right."

Bogerd nodded. "She was right. How did you get in here?"

Karl shrugged. "You know me. It wasn't any work at all to climb the wizard's wall and find an open window. I went back to the hall first to get some weapons and tools. Turns out all I needed was this necklace. You're its guardian and it feels the same about you."

Bogerd groaned. "Let's get out of here."

"Sure, Boss."

"Give me a hand."

****

"Your poor shoulder."

Bogerd said, "It's nothing, girl."

Ingrid dipped a clean cloth in warm water, squeezed it almost dry and wiped dried blood from Bogerd's arm. Her thick, blonde braids swayed as she worked. She leaned against him, pressing her deep, soft bosom against his elbow.

"Get your teats off Bogerd this instant before he faints from pain!" Ilsa rounded the corner in a swirl of furs and black shawl. "Don't you know where he got cut?"

Ingrid gaped with surprise.

Ilsa snarled, "Up, silly girl, and out!"

Ingrid shot to her feet as her cheeks flushed a delicate rose.

Ilsa pointed toward the kitchen. "Out!"

Ingrid flounced toward the passageway to the kitchen. She looked back over her shoulder and, when she was sure Ilsa wasn't looking, she stuck out her tongue.

Without turning her head, Ilsa snapped, "I saw that. Five bags of potatoes, washed and peeled, by mid-afternoon bell or I'll cane your skinny shanks, you nasty girl!"

Ingrid squealed and ran for the kitchen.

"Now!" Ilsa rubbed her hands together. "Let's take care of this crossbow bolt. Lie down flat on the floor."

Bogerd stirred uneasily but did as he was ordered. He said, "Shouldn't we leave it until Doctor Einar comes?"

"Nonsense! I've forgotten more about wounds than that fakir will ever know. This is a minor hurt, unless we wait to treat it." So saying, she placed her left foot against his chest, gripped the bolt's shaft with both hands and pulled.

What surely must have been the death howl of a pain-maddened wolf floated across ice-bound Nordheim. Old men checked the bars on their doors. Mothers held their babes close.

Ilsa shouted, "Stop your silly whining. It's out and the bleeding will slow as soon as I pour on my secret wound potion."

Bogerd gasped, "Not the wound potion!"

"Oh, be quiet! This will keep the wound from festering. It only stings a bit at first."

Again the howl of the tortured wolf floated across ice-sheathed roofs shining softly in starlight. Nordheim's denizens glanced at each other nervously, shivered and hoped never to hear such a desperate sound again.

END

The White Stag

Jacqueline Seewald

Steve hit the brakes hard and I was thrown forward. I cracked my head against the dashboard and felt foolish to not have buckled myself in.

"Are you all right?" Steve asked. He pushed his eyeglasses back on the bridge of his nose.

My head hurt right down to my teeth but I felt too embarrassed to make the admission. "Why did you stop so abruptly?" I tried to keep the irritation out of my voice.

"Didn't you see it?" I'd never heard Steve sound so agitated. His manner normally remained calm and collected.

"See what?"

"A white deer. It's standing in the middle of the road." His tone registered impatience.

I blinked and then observed what he was talking about. My mouth hung open in surprise. "I've never seen a deer like that before."

"Neither have I. Reminds me of something. Do you know the legend of the white stag?"

"No." I rubbed my aching skull, praying I hadn't sustained a concussion.

"It's one of the Pine Barrens' legends. They say if you see the white stag, it means someone is in danger. Like you could possibly die."

I felt a chill slither down my spine. I studied the deer. It was a huge white buck with massive antlers. The animal had pink eyes and ears. It must have been an albino. I'd never seen anything quite like it before. Did the deer have mystical qualities? It suggested something surreal. I thought of a unicorn, but that mythological creature had only one horn.

Steve and I were driving through the Pine Barrens of New Jersey. We'd been to Batsto Village to see the historic ironworks where cannon balls among other things were made and then supplied to George Washington's army during the American Revolution.

Batsto Village is a New Jersey historic site located in Wharton State Forest, part of the Pinelands National Reserve, a million acres of sandy soil set aside in the most densely populated state per capita in the United States. Supposedly, the Jersey Devil haunts these dark woodlands and has done so since Colonial times.

Steve is a professor of American history and loves the Pine

Barrens for the rich legends and folklore. He takes pleasure in telling me these tales. Since we're a couple, I listen with fortitude and feigned enthusiasm. According to Steve, scientists believe the Pine Barrens rose from the ocean over two million years ago, before the rest of New Jersey existed. It was an island with all manner of strange animals and unusual plants, a weird, magical sort of place.

Walking along the trails surrounded by the vast acres of pine, oak and cedar, I've found it to be a dark, eerie location. I can't shake the strange feeling of being unwatched by invisible eyes. And that feeling was stronger than ever now as we sat in the middle of a badly paved road replete with pot holes gawking at a peculiar white deer. Just as I was about to ask Steve why he didn't honk the horn, the deer disappeared. Funny though, I didn't see the white deer run off into the woods. It just seemed to vanish.

"That is what we call the natural supernatural," Steve said. "Awesome, isn't it?"

I shook my head and felt the pain surge again with a sharp electric jolt. "Weird all right. We better get going."

I was polite enough not to mention that Steve had gotten us lost after we left Batsto Village. It had started to rain heavily, a veritable deluge on this afternoon in late October—Halloween to be exact. The visibility, which quickly deteriorated, had become poor to nonexistent, and Steve made a wrong turn. However, he initially refused to admit that fact and kept driving along the unfamiliar road. Steve could be stubborn about his driving. He often turns off his GPS because he thinks he knows better. He is decidedly not a tech person.

"I need to look around for a moment." Steve stepped out of the car and walked ahead. When he returned, soaked and chilled, Steve actually smiled. "The white stag may have just saved our lives."

I thought he was a few slices short of a loaf. "Are you okay?"

"Better than okay. I'm going to turn the car around. We can't go any further. There's a small bridge crossing ahead and it doesn't look safe. I'm not an engineer, but it appears ready to collapse. Did I happen to mention that in Barrens legend, the White Stag is a ghostly white deer who helps travelers lost in the Pine Barrens like us? The deer can also prevent impending disasters."

"That sounds like superstitious nonsense to me--like the legend of the Jersey Devil."

Steve shrugged. "Legends often have their roots in fact. This one has it that the white deer once stopped a stagecoach from crashing into the Batsto River. It occurred in the Colonial era at Quaker Bridge when the horses of a stagecoach refused to go any further on a rainy night. The driver climbed off the stage and then observed a white stag standing in the road. It soon disappeared. Walking up the road, he saw that the bridge was out. The creature saved their lives. According to that legend if you see a white stag, it's supposed to bring good luck."

"Maybe we both just imagined it," I said, searching for a logical explanation. Since I'm a chemist by profession, I always look for more plausible reasons.

"Jennifer, you are a skeptic."

"I'm not a romantic like you. I believe in science, not myth."

Steve shook his head. "As Shakespeare said, there are more things in heaven and earth than are dreamt of in your philosophy."

"Probably true," I said with an amiable smile.

"But you still don't accept what we both saw with our own eyes?"

I moved my head from side to side which caused it to hurt again. "Perhaps."

"The Celts believed seeing the white stag indicated the other world was drawing near."

"A symbol of death? Not very cheerful. Concentrate on your driving, please." I didn't like the fact that we were out in the middle of nowhere surrounded by dark, eerie forest, a cathedral of pines. And this whole discussion was making me feel nervous.

"The white hart or stag is also found in Arthurian legends and eventually became a Christian symbol for Christ. It was also was the heraldic symbol of England's King Richard the Third."

"Correct me if I'm wrong, but that fellow didn't end up very well, did he?"

"You're such a negative thinker," Steve said.

"Just stating the obvious." I hated being lost and especially in the wilderness. Steve, however, seemed to take it in stride. "Would you like me to take over on the driving for a while?"

He glanced at me out of the corner of his eye. "Don't trust me, darling?"

"It's not that. I thought you might be getting tired."

"No, you didn't, oh ye of little faith, but I forgive you."

I let out a deep sigh and folded my arms over my chest. I was afraid if I didn't I would be tempted to strangle him. Steve's smug superiority annoyed me that much. "Admit it. You don't know where we are."

"Not a clue." He had the audacity to give me a smug smile.

"And that doesn't bother you?"

"We'll find our way."

I dug my nails into the bucket seat's leather upholstery and didn't speak for a time. Steve drove along humming cheerfully as if he didn't have a care in the world. I bit down on my lower lip until I tasted blood.

After a time, we came across what appeared to be a tavern sitting in an isolated location back from the narrow road. The sign above, which oscillated in the near gale-like wind, read: The White Hart.

"It's a signal for us," Steve announced.

"Strange, why didn't we notice this place before?"

Steve shrugged. "We probably rode right by not knowing it was here because of the rain. We were concentrating on the road ahead." He pulled over and parked by the side of the building.

I glanced around. "I don't see any other cars."

"Trust me. I have a good feeling about this. We'll get a drink, warm up a bit, and get directions back to the main road."

Steve got out of the vehicle and came around to my side. I found myself feeling dizzy and he had to help me out of the car. We walked inside a deserted building, or so it seemed. The place had the look of an old English pub. Everything about the tavern suggested yesterday. It made me feel uneasy.

"I don't think anyone is here. We should just leave." However, almost as soon as I spoke, a man came out from the back and approached the bar.

"What can I get you?" He had riveting sky blue eyes for a man advanced in years.

"Don't suppose you'd have tea?" I asked.

"Would a lager do?"

"That would be fine," Steve assured him. "Why don't you sit down, hon? You look exhausted."

My head hammered and so I kept as still as possible, seating myself at a rough-hewn table.

Steve proceeded to talk with the bar man. He told the fellow about our near accident. "Have you heard of any similar experiences?"

The man scratched his gray head of hair. "I have heard about the legend. That's how I come to name this place."

"I'm surprised you don't have more business."

The man smiled betraying discolored uneven teeth. "Folks don't come out much in weather like this. Of course, not many people live around here anymore. Ghost towns mostly these days."

"And ghost legends," Steve said.

"That too. We're known for the Jersey Devil, the black doctor, the black dog, the headless pirate, and the golden-haired girl. All famous ghost tales of the Barrens."

"And the white deer as well."

"That as well," the man agreed, filling two glasses with dark brew.

My head hurt so badly by now that I had to close my eyes. The room had started to spin as if something surreal was happening, almost as though I were living a bad dream that I couldn't wake from. The tavern had a sense of otherness. With a sense of urgency, I realized we had to leave. This was a place of the dead, of ghosts. The tavern was haunted. If we didn't leave right away, we'd be sucked into the vortex forever. I felt that death was in the room with us, ready to snatch our life blood and our spirits.

I stood up, unsteady on my feet, my heart pounding with a surge of panic. "Forget the beer! We need to get out of here. The white stag, it wants to take our lives."

"No, miss," the bar man said in an alarmed tone of voice, "the creature is pure. That's why it's white as new snow. The albino deer is a gift from the gods, mayhap God hisself."

Steve stalked toward me, his face flushed. "The white stag symbolizes the creative force of the universe. Can't you feel its energy? It's life itself."

"And also death," I said. This was Halloween, I remembered, a day of spirits when the dead returned to haunt the living. The room was freezing. I was freezing cold now too. My teeth chattered. I felt goose bumps form on my arms beneath my jacket.

"The white stag saved us," Steve said. "What's wrong with you?" He frowned. His elongated forehead wrinkled into a worried expression.

I shook my head and it spun again. I felt sick to my stomach.

Something was indeed wrong. "We must leave here," I repeated. "We need to go right now. We need to escape."

"All right."

Steve took my arm since I was moving toward the door with an unsteady gait. We hurried back to the car, the rain coming down again in torrents. The rain seemed to be the tears of heaven. They beat like a drum or a heartbeat with a steady rhythm on the roof of our car. The hypnotic sound made me feel so tired, so sleepy.

"Jen!" Steve was shaking me. "Jen, honey, talk to me. Wake up!"

"Stop that!"

"I'm sorry, but you hit your head and lost consciousness. I think maybe you have a concussion. Are you in pain?"

"My head hurts." My put my hand to my forehead and found a large lump had formed.

"You should have worn your safety belt."

"I made a mistake. But you shouldn't have hit your brakes so hard." I felt the need to defend myself. Hadn't we already had this conversation? I wasn't certain. My thoughts were fuzzy.

"I didn't want to hit the deer in the road."

"The white deer," I said.

"That's right. I'm glad you remember."

"You shouldn't have stopped at that tavern."

"What tavern? You must be hallucinating." Steve stared at me as if I'd grown two heads. "We're sitting by a washed out bridge. You blacked out. I've been waiting for you to regain consciousness. Maybe we better get you to a hospital. You're not yourself. You might have a serious concussion."

"I'm fine. Maybe a little confused is all. I have a touch of vertigo." Could the real world and the unreal merge together and create a different aspect of existence? How could anyone be certain what was reality and what was fantasy?

"I'm turning the car around. I remember where I went off and took the wrong turn."

"Yes, you took a wrong turn. Where's the white deer?" I said.

"Gone," Steve said. "Disappeared."

"Vanished?"

"Yep."

All I could feel was a sense of relief.

Howls in the Mist

Kenneth Caroli

"Nothing is what it is"

Jersualem had fallen to the Saracens! Talk of a crusade was in the air, throughout Europe. Pope Gregory called on all of Christendom to respond. Last autumn Prince Richard of England had been the first to take the cross. A few months later he was joined by his father King Henry II and Phillip Augustus of France. Finally, less than a month before, the Holy Roman Emperor, Frederic Barbarosa, had taken the cross at Worms.

Having just sailed south from Norway, Eirik Sigurthson had been in Denmark at the time. He'd sought work for his sword there but found the country at peace after several campaigns against the pagan Pomeranians. Yet, while he was in Copenhagen the emissaries of Barbarosa had arrived at the court of King Canute VI, demanding fealty. Frederic claimed sovereignty over Denmark.

The Dames denied him, refusing to send men for the army the Emperor was gathering at Regensburg to free the Holy Land. He planned to march over land through Byzantine territory. The Danish king allowed some of his nobles to join an international fleet headed to the crusade. But it wasn't due to sail for more than a year.

Eirik was too impatient to wait, despite Denmark being his late father's ancestral homeland. Sigurthson himself was an Hibernian* born near Dubhlinn. His family fled to Galloway in Scotland when the Normans conquered Norse Dubhlinn. Eirik hated the Normans and became an outlaw fighting them in Scotland.

*Hibernia is the Latin name of Ireland.

Although Sigurthson could most easily have joined Frederic's gathering forces, the haughtiness of Barbarosa's emissaries in Denmark reminded him unpleasantly of the way the Mormans treated the natives of Ireland during his boyhood. They'd enslaved the natives. So, the Hibernian refused to follow Frederic to war, even though planning to take the cross himself.

His hate for the Normans caused Eirik to avoid Normandy and England. They ruled Brittany as well so Sigurthson chose not to pass through there either, thought the Bretons were related to the Welsh and the latter to both the Irish and Scots. Despite their Norse descent the Normans were more French than anything else. They were oppressors wherever they went, as far afield as Sicily.

If he didn't go through Normandy, England or the Holy Roman Empire, only France remained. Besides, he didn't speak German. Eirik left Copenhagen on a Danish ship, landing in the county of

Flanders where he took to the land.

Sigurthson had always desired to see exotic faraway places that he'd only heard about in fireside tales. Most of those, such as Rome, Venice and Constantinople lay on or near the Middle Sea. That left him two main routes, both through France. Eirik could head for Marseilles or perhaps to fight the Moors in Portugal, traveling via Navarre, Castille and Leon.

Wherever he chose to go, his destiny hung over him like the proverbial dark cloud. There was no escaping it. Aelfriche de Gavin, a Norman lord from Scotland was responsible for the death of Eirik's parents. In revenge he infiltrated the Scottish court and murdered him.

But de Gavin resurrected as a demonic black hound. Eirik's sword proved useless against it. With no other choice Sigurthson resorted to prayer, which was unexpectedly answered, sparing his life. It was then that his unspecified mission had been laid upon Sigurthson's broad shoulders.

Tragically, though his undead foe seemingly could not take Eirik's life directly, de Gavin tormented him by attacking those the Hibernian held dear. The dread hound caused the death of his betrothed, Caitlynn, and the subsequent grief-stricken suicide of her brother, Gabhran. More recently, the beast slew his uncle after the battle of Momgravia Moor, when Donnall MacUilleam's revolt was defeated.

They all died solely due to their proximity to Eirik and his feeling for them. Their blood stained his soul, the guilt and loneliness eating at him like acid. How could he hope to destroy what was already dead? It made the Hibernian wary of letting anyone too close to him.

Reputedly, the Pope gave special dispensations to those who took the cross. The brawny Hibernian swordsman hoped to take advantage of that. It might be the only way he could escape the maw of Hell.

So, he had decided to take the cross himself. Eirik prayed that it could expiate the sin that had led to so much tragedy. Perhaps, his mysterious destiny awaited him in the Holy Land.

It seemed to be his best, if not his only option. But Jerusalem was a great distance away - a great deal might happen before he got there if he ever did. Would he survive to achieve his destiny or die in the effort? He tried to ignore the question.

Eirik had been riding for hours. The sun's golden orb was beginning to sink in the West. Only a few high whispy clouds obscured the fading afternoon light. Sigurthson's back hurt following a long day in the saddle. He was tired, hungry and thirsty. But there were no taverns nearby. Tonight, he would have to camp beneath the trees.

The forest rose up before him. The shadow of it's canopy fell across Eirik as he rode amidst the trees. Almost immediately it grew colder. Sigurthson huddled within his gray-green hooded cloak. Although it was spring, the winter's chill clung to certain places, especially by night. The day's warmth dissipated swiftly.

Once within the woods the darkness grew deep. The few dim lights from the nearest village and farms could no longer be seen. Loneliness settled over him like a pall.

Eirik was far from a home he'd probably never see again, with no one left there for him anyway. Now, he wandered alone amongst foreigners in unfamiliar lands. Once it was his fondest desire. But he was no longer sure what he wanted. Yet, he couldn't turn back. It was the only road open to him.

The blond giant, his azure eyes looking for a clearing to make camp. He used his knees to nudge his palfrey carefully through the gathering gloom. Its hooves clomped mournfully amidst the undergrowth. Eirik's booted feet hung nearer to the ground than had he purchased a war horse, as he was quite tall.

At first Sigurthson was a trifle embarrassed to be seen atop the shaggy little beast, instead of a stomping, snorting stallion. It had made him feel like some fat merchant riding to market. Yet, over the days he came to appreciate the sturdy mount, with its steady gait.

Battle chargers tended to be high-spirited, bred for short intense bursts of activity not long arduous journeys. They were also notoriously difficult to control... and very expensive. It was the cost which finally swayed him towards the palfrey. Eirik had only so much silver...

Wearing a new and a fine green tunic, news sword and scabbard slapping his right thigh, Eirik could pass for a nobleman, or maybe a young merchant. Further suggestive of an aristocrat was the signet-like ring he wore on his right hand.

While not a true seal ring, it did bear the insignia of Norway's royal house. It was a gift from Norway's king, Sigurth, Whose life

Eirik had saved. The sword, sheath and dagger which hung from his belt, were likewise royal gifts. The incident which had inspired the King's favor, however, was not widely known. To maintain his reputation amongst his peers, King Sigurth preferred to keep it that way.

Eirik's sudden inexplicable favor with the King resulted in whispers. The Hibernian's clearly Norse blood, combined with the odd coincidence that Eirik's late father bore the same name as the king, lead some to believe him to be a royal bastard. Though such an illegitimate son could rarely if ever inherit a throne, many could and did attain high positions...

Although the speculation was baseless Sigurthson did not go out of his way to dispel it. Eirik was wryly amused by the idea. Being thought a royal bastard gave him higher status than he would otherwise aspire to. For once it was nice to be looked upon with wary respect, instead of suspicion and disdain. It was a new experience for him and he enjoyed it.

Norwegian silver paid for his voyage, by ship, from Oslo to Copenhagen, the capital of Denmark and later from there to Flanders. It allowed him to purchase his horse, even to stay at several inns, rather than camping in the open. He ate better too.

Eirik had never been able to travel in such comfort before. The money wouldn't last forever. So, he figured that he might as well take advantage of it while he could. It might be a long time before he got the chance again.

At last Eirik came to a modest clearing. Above him the branches and leafy canopy thinned out. The sky was an intense blue violet, yet not the near black of full night. A few stars began to appear and the crescent moon rose in the east. Sigurthson reigned his horse to a halt.

Dismounting from the saddle he tied the beast to the closest tree, gently patting it. He took a biscuit from a small sack at his belt and popped it into his mouth, giving another to his mount. He had obtained them, as well as some wine, in the last village he'd passed through that morning.

Searching the ground Eirik gathered a number of fallen twigs and small branches. Placing them in a pile he removed two pieces of metal from his coin sack. Striking them several times together he finally achieved a spark and lit the branches afire.

Once that was done Sigurthson took the bag of wine from where it hung on the saddle. Sighing, he sat down, resting his back against the trunk of a convenient tree.

Rubbing his hands together for warmth, Eirik held them up to the flames. He exhaled as they soaked in the heat. It felt wonderful. Unstopping the wine sack, he took a long deep swig. He savored it as it went down his throat. A slight smile creased Eirik's lips. It did not last long.

Beyond the fire's glow, night had descended. The forest was quiet, aside from the crackling of the flames. The natural sounds, like night birds, were silent, alerting Eirik to possible danger. He was aware that the presence of humans sometimes caused animals to suddenly go quiet. Were they reacting to him? Or was somebody else out there?

Best to prepare, just in case. If it were due solely to him there was no danger. Yet, were it someone else Eirik had no desire to be caught unawares. He clasped the hilt of his sword and rose to his feet, eyes scanning the darkness, ears straining for any other sounds. When he heard them it was almost too late. Sigurthson withdrew his sword.

"He is on to us, my lads! Take 'im!' Shouted a voice from behind Eirik. Although it was said in French, the Hibernian's knowledge of the dialect of the hated Normans, revealed the gist of it. Under the circumstances, however, he might easily have guessed the meaning. The question uppermost in his mid was how many of them there were and where...

The campfire showed multiple shadowy figures rushing him from that direction. But Eirik had no chance to count them. He sensed rather than heard other attackers approaching behind him. The flames allowed Sigurthson to see the faces of a few of his opponents.

The men were dirty, with tangled greasy hair and beards. Their expressions were hard and determined. A couple were utterly wild-eyed. They wore leather jerkins, course frayed tunics and patched, stained hose. They wielded spears, axes and clubs. Only a couple of them bore swords. Their leader had a broken nose.

Their appearance suggested that they were simple brigands, as they had no armor, whereas swords were costly weapons, used mainly by nobles or professional soldiers like Eirik himself. Sigurthson only had his own blades by inheritance or as a gift from the Norwegian king.

"Pay no 'heed to 'e's pig-sticker," yelled the leader confidently." 'E may be big, but by the cut've 'e's clothes 'e's just some minor noble's son. I doubt 'e knows 'ow to use that blade of 'e's..."

The Hibernian smiled grimly in response. Eirik was tempted to answer but decided it wasn't worth the effort. He was better at understanding Norman French than speaking it, though so far he'd been able to make himself understood. Let these thieves be surprised...unpleasantly. Eirik would enjoy teaching them a bloody lesson.

Sigurthson didn't wait for them to reach him. Eirik leaped at the man, who had shouted, interpreting him to be the band's leader. He'd learned from experience that if you took down the head man, the rest might flee or at least lose cohesiveness. When facing superior numbers he needed all the advantages he could get. He raised his blade to strike.

The Hibernian's sword swung, slicing through the night air. The leader of the outlaws held up his own blade to counter the blow. Both men grimaced. Steel rang against steel. The others temporarily hung back so as not to risk harming their own leader. Eirik clenched his teeth...

Yet, in the very act of attacking the band's chief, Eirik had moved away from the tree he'd rested against, exposing his back. It had been an unavoidable risk. He was lucky none of the brigands were an archer...But two spears were thrown.

One of the thieves aimed his club at Sigurthson's head. Eirik sensed the blow just in time, feeling the movement of the air on his neck. He immediately shifted position to avoid the club yet could not afford to take his eyes off the sword-wielding leader. The club whistled past his right ear, just barely missing it. The blow impacted the Hibernian's right shoulder instead a spear flew over his head. The Thieves cried out triumphantly.

Eirik grunted in pain, his balance briefly thrown off. Sigurthson was forced to ignore the throbbing agony. He needed to regain his balance as fast as he could. Had he been wielding his sword with his right hand he'd have been dead. He still might be.

With difficulty he warded off another blow of the leader's blade. Eirik's foe hissed in frustration. He'd under-valued Sigurthson's size and allowed the Hibernian's youth to fool him where Eirik's prowess with a sword was concerned. It was a bad mistake.

The drop in temperature, after nightfall, caused a mist to form, carpeting the forest floor in it's clammy tendrils. The damp chill seeped into the marrow of Eirik's bones. The rest felt it too. The fo added to the lack of visibility for all concerned, diffusing the light from the fire.

Eirik was outnumbered, with no one to guard his back. The situation didn't look good, despite the lack of armor or quality weapons amongst his foes. The ground was uneven, the grass wet, the tree roots ever ready to trip him up... Instead, it was the brigand chief who tripped over a root as he made a lunge at Eirik with his sword. He almost fell to the ground.

The blade nearly gutted Sigurthson, tearing through his tunic, leaving behind a bloody gash. Eirik's own sword passed through empty air over his opponent's head. The Hibernian cursed, the cold air causing his wound to sting. He gritted his teeth against the pain.

The outlaw bastard shouldn't have been able to wound him to this extent so soon. His size, strength and skill ought to have precluded it. Though the leader might've been a war veteran, the others were half-trained peasants at best.

A fury took hold of Eirik. No mere band of thieves were going to be the death of him! Snarling angrily, a red haze descended over his eyes.

Sigurthson charged at the outlaw chief. The man tried desperately to fend the Hibernian off. The thieves' leader was shorter than Eirik and lacked the Hibernian's reach and swordsmanship. He would pay for it.

In his effort to parry Eirik's blade, the robber chief's own sword snapped in two, leaving him with only a sheathed dagger to defend himself. But the Hibernian gave him no chance to withdraw the knife. Sigurthson whirled and wove his sword around the chieftain's increasingly feeble defenses.

Unsure how best to aide their leader, the other brigands continued to hold back and watch. Eirik ceased defending himself, focusing upon attack alone. Yet, the thieves' leader was never again able to touch Sigurthson with a blade. The same was not true of Eirik.

He withdrew his sword. The man's eyes grew wide, stunned. His jaw dropped in surprise. He gasped futilely at this chest, as the

Hibernian stepped away. The sword fell from the man's hand and he collapsed to his knees. Then the chief toppled to the grass, his body obscured by the mist. The other brigand stared down at their fallen leader, incredulous and speechless.

"Which one o' you is next?" Eirik snapped through tight lips. He gestured at them with the point of his sword, whirling about to glare at those behind him. They eyed him, seemingly undecided what to do next.

The thieves were angry at their leader's death, greedy for the Hibernian's silver but leery of his sword. Their Former chief had held his place via his fighting ability. Eirik had therefore defeated their best man. None wished to join their chief in death. Nor did they want to acknowledge any one of their number as the new leader.

Eirik heard some incoherent mumbling. They spoke too softly for him to understand. He also couldn't tell which ones spoke as he was unable to see them all well enough. Their intent, however, soon became all too clear.

Several of them moved forward at him, from both sides, their clubs and axes raised. Sigurthson inhaled deeply and prepared to meet them. So much for beheading the serpent, Eirik thought...

The Hibernian fended off a blow by a club with his right forearm. The pain shot through his arm. But the club splintered on impact like kindling. It's wielder stumbled aside, thrown out of balance. The man gawked at the piece of the club still in his hand.

Sigurthson's sword then bit deep into the wooden handle of an axe born by his nearest foe, though not cutting all the way through the haft. The weight of the axe blade snapped the handle, flying off into the underbrush. The man cursed.

The axeman was as startled as his companion with the club. Both veered away from Eirik, eyeing him warily. After that the rest gave Sigurthson an equally wide berth. Although all glared at him, none tried to approach the Hibernian again.

Instead, they continued running away, swiftly melting into the fog and darkness. While the fight left Eirik winded and aching, at least he was still alive. Despite having driven them away, it somehow felt too easy.

Were they just too cowardly to risk serious injury to bring him down? Had killing heir leader worked after all, even with a delay? Did they plan to regroup again after he was lulled by their apparent retreat? All he had were questions, no answers came to him.

Weary, his breathing a bit ragged, Sigurthson sat down on the nearest fallen log. He shouldn't be so tired after such a minor battle. Eirik shook his head in annoyance. He was getting soft. As his pulse and breathing slowed he did his best to clean the gash in his side. Toi ease the pain he swallowed some wine which dribbled down his bearded chin. Unthinkingly he wiped it away with the leather vambraces on his right arm.

His thirst quenched for the moment, Eirik glanced down. He noticed that his coin purse was gone. The leather tie which had held the sack had been cut. The sack was gone...

"Damn!" Sigurthson hissed in self-recrimination. That was what that final attack had been about. They were distracting him while their cut purse did his work. The thief had done it too well.

During the fight, he'd made the mistake of viewing them as warriors, forgetting that they were thieves first, fighters second. His silver was what they were primarily after, not his life. They had fled upon getting it.

Doubtless, that was why they'd tracked him into the woods. It was his own fault, Sigurthson acknowledged. He had spent too freely, drawing the thieves unwanted attention. They had probably desired his gold hilted sword and dagger as well as the "seal" ring. But cutting the coin purse proved easier than getting any of the other items.

Eirik was tempted to track them anyway, to retrieve his silver, But he need to recuperate. The thieves knew this region far better than he. Sigurthson had survived without money before. He could do it again. Not that he had a choice.

Only the did the Hibernian notice the remains of his horse's tether, hanging from the tree to which it had been tied. The thieving bastards had stolen his horse too! He was going to miss his mount even more than the silver. He grimaced in anger and disgust. Without the silver Eirik couldn't buy another horse.

While more used to walking than riding, he had become fond of the sturdy palfrey. It was nice to let somebody else do the walking... or trotting for him.

Thankfully, he'd left the gold cross, given to him by his late father, within his tunic. The brigands never knew it was there. Had they tried to steal the cross he would've tracked them down and slain them all. The road ahead of him now seemed immeasurably longer...and harder.

Once away from the clearing the thieves came back together again. Though still in shock at their leader's death, they exulted in the coin purse and the horse one of them lead by the remains of its tether. They'd gotten what they came for. Yet, before they could celebrate too much they heard a wolf howl in the distance. The eerie sound echoed through the knighted woods. The moon glowed above...

Preoccupied, the thieves ignored it at first. Wolves were not uncommon in the forest. It was far off and alone. They were in a group and armed after a fashion, though two of them had lost their primary weapons in the final attack upon the bit outlander. They weren't afraid of one wolf.

Their attention was only gained when the lone wolf's howl was answered by a veritable chorus, which reverberated amongst the trees. The echoes made it difficult to tell how many wolves there were and where. The sounded as though they were all around- a lot of them. And they were getting closer... ever closer.

The thieves' eyes flitted about, scanning the shadows and fog. But they saw nothing. A single wolf offered no real threat. Yet, an entire pack was entirely different.

The howling few louder, mingled with growls and snarls. The group was surrounded. All grasped their weapons tighter, uncertain if or when the attack might come. Pierre and Andre had only daggers for protection, Henri his cudgel, Pasqal his sword. Reynald was grateful for his axe. None retained their spears.

Half hidden by the mist and undergrowth the glowing eyes of the wolves became visible. The howling of the pack ceased. But the snarling grew. That was chilling. There was no doubt that the wolves were closing in, encircling the band of thieves. Normally, not even a pack would dare approach armed men let alone attack them. During a bad winter, starving wolves had been known to raid isolated farms or villages, focusing on the weak. But this was not the depth of winter and they were not children, elderly or sick.

The pack gradually left the underbrush, their gleaming eyes the only thing that could be seen aside from their shaggy silhouettes. They were all fierce-looking muscular beasts. There were dozens of them, coming at the brigands from every direction. It was the sort of strategy soldiers might employ...not mere animals... Why would they do that?

"This... it is not right!" Snorted Henri uneasily. "These wolves... they should not act like this... it is not natural..."

"Loup garou!" Hissed Andre in wide-eyed terror. "They must be followers of Lucifer himself!'

"These woods – they 'ave always been said to be 'aunted..." Pierre shivered, suddenly pale beneath his tan. "Something attacks the village flocks and cattle... 'till now I never believed..."

The red maws of the wolves and their ivory fangs were revealed the closer they came. Saliva dripped from their hungry jaws. The animals padded. Towards their prey slowly, as if reveling in the thieves' fear. Seeing this the men moved closer together, back to back, facing outward at the cordon of wolves. Sweat, mixed with condensation on their flesh, hearts pounding in their ears. Apprehension of physical harm mingled with super-natural dread.

Suddenly, the wolves lunged forward en masse, as if let off an invisible leash. The thieves hardly had time to gasp collectively. Pasqal's sword, Reynald's axe and Henri's cudgel arched through the air almost in unison, desperation in their eyes. Pierre and Andre's daggers flashed.

Several of the wolves yelped in pain, falling injured to the ground. But others followed in their wake and after them came a third wave. While some snapped at the mens' legs their brethren hurtled upon the thieves, seeking to bowl them over by the weight of their impact. One leapt onto Pasqal's back doubling him over.

Claws scratched at exposed skin or eyes. Fangs chomped through cloth into the flesh, muscle and bone beneath. The men cried out in fear and agony, the assault upon them relentless. There was no time to think.

They could no longer coordinate a defense. It was each man for himself and none of them doing very well. First one, then another collapsed under the wolves' ferocious attack. It had ceased to be a battle, instead becoming a massacre.

When the last of the thieves fell there were growls, mixed with awful chewing and tearing sounds. Occasionally, the cracking of bone could be heard once the screams of the dying men ceased.

A few moments later, silence settled on the scene. The wolves raised their heads from their bloody feast, as if called, their pointed ears twitching. Then they all howled before dispersing into the woods. Silence... and death reigned supreme.

Eirik was grateful for the fire at least, and the wine. He wished that he had something to eat. The fight had left him hungry as well as aching. Then, he recalled the biscuits he'd bought in the village. They weren't much, yet better than nothing. The thieves had ignored the small sack they were in. Looking down, Sigurthson opened it. To his great surprise, he caught the glint of silver, not the biscuits!

The brigands made the same mistake he just had. They'd stolen the wrong sack! Eirik laughed wryly, at himself as much as the thieves. They were going to be surprised... Still, right at the moment, he half-wished they had left the biscuits instead. Out in these woods there was nowhere to buy food.

The Hibernian was weary. The idea of hunting in the dark and fog held little appeal for him. But it was that or go hungry. Standing once more he surveyed the forest around him. At first, Sigurthson saw only the vague silhouettes of the trees and the underbrush. Then, he was startled to notice a yellow-greenish glint staring at him. They were a pair of eyes in the underbrush, glowing faintly in the dying firelight.

It had to be some forest animal. Yet, if so, what kind? Eirik tensed in apprehension. Warily, he sought to unsheathe his sword, only to find his joints tight from being too long in one position. His muscles strained, un-cricking at last, yet too slowly.

A gray shape hurtled from the underbrush, its jaws wide, eyes gleaming. Its forepaws struck Eirik in the chest, pushing his back again the tree. The impact caused him to release the sword and scabbard, which fell to the ground. Sigurthson did all he could to keep the wolf's jaws from chomping into his throat...

The wolf snarled viciously, doing its best to sink its fangs into the Hibernian's flesh. Eirik was forced to use all his strength to fend it off. It seemed unnaturally powerful. Its muscles were lithe, its coat soft and silver as moonlight, with eyes that blazed like emerald fire. Despite the danger it represented, Eirik couldn't help but notice that it was a sleep, beautiful animal.

It reminded him of the wolf spirit that had saved him from the undead black hound, though the latter had blue eyes and pure white fur. Sigurthson felt the beast's glaring at him intently.

The two wrestled for what seemed hours, yet in reality was mere minutes. Normally, Eirik could've defeated such a creature, but hunger and exhaustion had taken their toll on him. The wolf, likewise, had the advantage of surprise.

Sigurthson grasped it by the scruff, gritting his teeth as he fought his way back to his feet. With all his remaining strength, Eirik threw the beast away from him. The wolf flew head over haunches through the air. It yipped in frustrated fury, crashing into the underbrush beyond the fire.

Eirik head it land more than saw it. In seconds it was back on its feet, on the far side of the flames. It did not immediately resume its attack upon him. It stood, four paws equally spaced, limbs rigid, glaring lividly at the Hibernian. The wolf bared its fangs, growling deep within its throat, reverberating in its chest.

Sigurthson and the wolf locked eyes. Eirik felt drawn into those yellow-green orbs, unable to look away. It was as if the beast would not let him turn aside or close his eyes. It was a strange sensation that the Hibernian could not explain, unlike anything he'd felt before.

Not only did the wolf gaze on him outwardly, Eirik could swear it was seeing into his mind. How that was possible he wasn't sure. Yet, it was there; psychic tendrils wrapping themselves around his thoughts, probing, searching. But if so, For what? He felt intense scrutiny, going through his memories.

It made his head hurt. Once the initial shock wore off, he tried to rally, pushing the invading presence from his brain. His late mother had always been able to tell what he was thinking and sometimes Eirik could read her thought too – when she let him.

Aeslynn told him it was the way of the fair folk, from whom she, and therefore Eirik, were descended. But his mother had always done it gently and never solely to spy on him.

This was a violent mental assault, an attempt to assess his entire past and way of thinking all at once. It was like having his mind flayed. It was not a pleasant experience. Yet, the more he focused his concentration, the less he sensed the foreign presence. Eventually, it was gone from his mind altogether.

The wolf made a snorting sound, shaking its head as if to clear it. He saw pain in its eyes. It blinked several times. Suddenly, it turned away from Eirik, facing the knighted woods and for a brief moment it glanced back at Sigurthson.

This time its expression was suggestive of curiosity and appraisal, rather than being threatening as before. When it returned its gaze to the woods, it quickly ran off into the velvet darkness. Eirik watched it go, baffled at the entire episode. What was the wolf anyway? It was more than a mere animal. But what?

Before long Eirik found himself beginning to drift off to sleep. Given what he'd already been through that night he fought the urge, afraid to let down his guard. It wasn't easy. He could barely keep his eyes open. Exhaustion... and the wine proved too much for Sigurthson and his head drooped, eyes closing, despite his best efforts.

Roughly an hour later there was a rustling in the undergrowth. Eirik was startled to wafefulness. Eyes widening, his ears pricked up. He straightened, gripping his sword's hilt in anticipation. What was it this time?

Eirik was stunned to see that it was the wolf. He expected a renewed attack. Sigurthson tensed, waiting. Yet, the wolf did not immediately attack. Instead, it moved slowly and quietly towards him, a rabbit in its jaws. With an even, purposeful gait, it came to Eirik's side of the fire. There it lay the rabbit down in front of him as though it was a peace offering.

That surprised him more than the earlier attack. He have never experienced anything like it before. Having given him the rabbit, the wolf returned to the far side of the fire and laid down there. It eyed Eirik quizzically, curious rather than threatening now. While grateful for the food the Hibernian remained wary. Not even a trained dog would do this without having received a command. Sigurthson had heard, however, that some cats did. But his was a wolf, not a tame cat.

Taking out his dagger, Eirik eagerly skinned the rabbit. Then he carved off some of the meat and tossed it to the wolf, before he began to roast the remainder over his fire. Since the flames had burned low Eirik threw some more branches onto the fire to stoke it. The flames crackled with renewed life.

Soon, the odor of cooked meat wafted through the camp, making Sigurthson's mouth water. He'd almost forgotten just how hungry he was.

"My thanks for the meal," Eirik smiled, tipping his head to acknowledge the wolf and giving a slight wave. Then he bit off some of the rabbit's flesh and began to chew avidly.

Part of him felt silly addressing the wolf. But the other half realized that he wasn't dealing with any ordinary animal. Besides, he had often spoken to his dogs and horses, even a few of his father's cattle, as a boy.

Never had a meal tasted so good to him. Sigurthson savored the smell and the juices of the meat, some of which ran down his chin. He wiped it away and gulped some wine to wash the meat down. He was more used to ale or mead. But the wine was growing on him.

"Sorry," Eirik chuckled. "I'm a messy eater..." he glanced at the wolf as he spoke. It did not appear to mind his lack of etiquette. "I'm neater when I'm not starving," he added with another laugh.

After the meal the wolf continued to lie on the far side of the fire, until the first hints of dawn became visible. Then it rose it its feet, eyed Eirik one last time and padded off into the trees. As it departed Eirik saluted it silently. It was a new day. Time for him to be off too. He had a long journey ahead...

As the sky brightened the trees remained in silhouette, though gradually emerging in pastel hues because of the mist. Beneath the forest canopy it was well past sunrise before the mist was burned away. The campfire had cooled to ash by the time Eirik forced himself to get underway. Since there was no particular place h had to be, at any specific date, Hibernian did not rush.

Eirik's boots crunched through the underbrush, which was relatively dry from lack of rain. He made no effort to move silently. Whom did he have to hide from? He'd already faced highway men and wild animals. Anyone nearby was liable to know the forest better than he did. Eirik laughed to himself grimly. Encountering oddities and danger was getting to be a habit... a bad one.

It felt as if some supernatural force knew where Eirik was going before h did and by what route. This force set innumerable deadly threats in his path, ensuring that Sigurthson would face them all. So far he'd survived those "meetings." Yet, for how much longer would that be true?

Was it all due to Aelfriche de Gavin, the Norman he slew three years before? Was it de Gavin's way of attacking him indirectly? Or was there more to it? On the other hand was de Gavin just another pawn thrown into his way by someone or something as yet unknown?

Who had enough power to do that? Why would they... or why bother with a person as insignificant as him? He was no king, philosopher or cleric, just a wandering mercenary. It made no sense to Eirik. Maybe, it was all just a coincidence.

Sigurthson hoped he didn't become lost in the forest. The areas of Scotland he grew up in had been relatively open and sparsely wooded. There was a modest path to follow. But it could hardly be called a road. It consisted solely of packed earth, without paving stones. Though free of trees it was encroached upon by undergrowth in places.

At least during the day the position of the sun gave him a rough compass. Beyond generally heading south, Eirik had no preset route. When the sun began to go down once more, the shadows grew ever deeper around him.

Sigurthson knew he had to start looking for a potential campsite. Earlier in the day he had stopped at a stream he had to pass and caught some fish for the night's meal. He still had a bit of wine left as well.

It hadn't been difficult to make a simple fishing pole. Then he took a metal ring that helped connect his dagger's sheath to his belt. The Hibernian bent the ring and sharpened it to use as a hook , a lace from his tunic provided a fishing line.

The time he spent fishing had reduced how far he'd managed to travel that day. Still, it would have to do. Although Eirik was lucky last night he had failed to prepare and refused to make the same mistake again.

As before, the Hibernian chose a spot near the base of a large tree, with a fallen log to sit on. Gathering sticks and branches Eirik built a fire. Then, he seated himself to cook his catch.

Though impatient to eat, he forced himself to endure the wait, without grumbling. Sigurthson completed his meal just as the last rays of the sun disappeared below the horizon. The evening mist began to coalesce once more. It created an odd, dream-like atmosphere that settled almost imperceptibly over Eirik.

Sigurthson's eyes flashed open, startled. The sun was streaming through the trees... wait! It was... a door? He must've fallen asleep. That was bad. He'd intended to remain on watch. Eirik was usually better at staying awake.

Yet, how could there be a door here? The Hibernian had been outside in the forest last night. Now, he saw heavy roof beams and a thatched ceiling above him, not leaves and branches. He looked about, sitting up. He found himself on a cot with dry stone walls around him and fire off to one side. It resembled a cottage like those in which he had dwelled back in Galloway. What was going on?

"Eirik!" A familiar voice called out, though one he had no heard in three long years. It was Caitlynn! His eyes widened, utterly stunned. It was impossible...his fiancé was dead. He'd seen her body himself, on the rocks below that cliff. Sigurthson stood beside her grave before he left Galloway.

"Are you ignoring me, Eirik Sigurthson?" Caitlynn yelled out to him, using his full name for emphasis. "It's time you were up! The sun's begun to rise already. There are tasks to be done today," an uncommon edge entered her tone.

A figure approached to stand silhouetted in the doorway. Even in shadow he recognized her. His heart beat faster. It couldn't be true... but he wanted it to be with every fiber of his being. His mind reeled. He must be going mad.

"How... how did I get here?" Eirik asked groggily, totally confused. "I was in a forest... in France," he blinked, shading his eyes.

"That's news to me," Caitlynn pursed her lips and placed her hands on her hips. "Ye' were here with me last night! An' how is it ye' made your way to France and back since then? It's dreamin' ye' must've been up with ye', husband! The day is nigh half over lazy bones!"

"You do... not understand," Eirik struggled for words. "You call me husband... you cannot know how much I have wished that was true. Yet, you were lost to me three years ago... the day Gabhran forced me to duel him. You ran to the cliffs... you fell... or tripped. You... cannot be here anymore than I..."

"An' yet here I be," she cocked her head sideways, raising one eyebrow. "I may not look my best, but do I look dead to ye'?" Caitlynn's annoyance showed. She seemed baffled by his odd attitude. Caitlynn looked troubled. " I was upset that day, torn between the two a' ye'. I blamed him but still loved him as my brother. I blamed myself for it all. I... didn't' look clearly where I was going. I did fall – hit my fool head. It knocked me out. But as ye' can see I'm very much alive. Ye' know all this – have known it all these years. Gabhren was there when I came to. I yelled at him... hit him. He apologized to me, said he'd gone a bit mad. Then he told you I still lived. Surely, ye' cannot have forgotten our wedding? No dream can explain that."

"Then, my aunt, and Gabhran, they are still alive? We are still in Galloway?" Eirik scratched his head in confusion. "Lord Locklann did not take over after Gillebride fell and Maelcolum was defeated?"

"Don't be daft!" Caitlynn rolled her eyes. "Of course they still live. The English king put Doncadh in power, to fend off King William. Due to their prior treaty William had no choice save to abide by the settlement. Lochlann was slain battling rebels in the north. With King Henry dead though, and Richard preparing to go on crusade, William may press his claim again. But the rebels still hold Inverness so perhaps not. We'll see. It has'na happened yet."

"What sorcery altered my memory?" Eirik shook his head in utter bewilderment. "Maelcolum was defeated by Lochlann eight months after the death of Gillebride. Lochlann crushed Domnall's revolt two years later. The Saseanach king let Doncadh accept the lesser title of Mormear, with Locklann became Lord of Galloway. After Domnall fell I had to flee Lochlann's hunters to Caithness and then Norway... from there I headed south not quite two months ago."

"Tis some imagination ye' have," she clucked in disbelief. "Now, out of bed wi' ye'! Enough a' your ruddy nightmares. There's work to be done."

"Aye," Sigurthson mumbled guardedly. "No doubt there is. I'll be out... in a moment me love. I apologize for my... flight o' fancy." Eirik tried his best to cover his disorientation. Had he indeed gone mad? Was he under some foul spell? Could it be de Gavin again? Which sequence of events was real?

Yet, did it truly matter? He had Caitlynn back! They were married! It was what he had most dearly wished. That made it difficult to believe. It was too good to be true. But it had to be real! It just had to Be! God, Eirik prayed, don't let this be a mere dream. Please, don't take her away again!

The days passed. Gradually, Eirik adjusted to his "new" routine, though his "real" memories failed to return. He had to restrain himself from following Caitlynn around, gawking at her, wanting to hold her every instant. Letting go of her each morning was torture to him.

But the night hours were glorious, even better than he had

imagined they would be. He could tell Caitlynn noticed his odd obsessiveness and the gaps in his memory. It clearly worried her. Yet, she rarely brought the subject up, perhaps hoping his memory would come back.

The Hibernian reveled in the chance to interact with his aunt Ethne and his uncles, Colum and Padraigh again. Eirik had missed them all and only now realized how much. To live amongst them all once more was like being in heaven.

Although much of the work was mundane drudgery, Eirik was able to fend off the boredom which assailed him. The alternate memories, from the "dream," slowly receded into unreality. Those memories had to be false. Everyone told him so.

The other choice was that he was wrapped in a fantasy. That would mean that those he loved were really dead and he was lone wanderer in foreign lands, without a home or family. If this was an illusion, let it continue, Sigurthson implored silently.

Yet, what of his "mission?" His dream diverged from realty after he slew Aelfriche de Gavin. That meant his life still had been saved supernaturally. His destiny remained to be fulfilled. But Caitlynn denied being chased by the Black Hound, though Eirik saw its paw prints that day atop the cliff. Could it be that he had imagined the hound too? If so, the whole quest for his destiny was part of a fantasy...

It made sense. Eirik always knew he didn't deserve divine intervention. Aside from that why would de Gavin be permitted to return from death as a harbinger of vengeance?

Conceivably Lucifer could do it. But why de Gavin? He seemed no more worthy of special consideration than Eirik himself. Sigurthson ought to have no higher than to live out his life amongst his family and friends. To believe anything else seemed foolish.

Despite that reasoning doubt continued to nag the Hibernian. Mostly, It was the almost paralyzing fear that it was the life he led now that was the dream. If so, at any moment, he might awake – alone and far from home.

Were that to happen he'd lose them all over again, for a second time. It would all be fresh for him once more... Eirik wasn't certain he could endure that. Death would be infinitely better.

"Eirik?" Caitlynn began tentatively. "I... I am with child," she smiled, blushing. "You are to be a father…"

The Hibernian's heart leapt. He could hardly believe what he'd just heard. When he thought he had lost Caitlynn, Eirik never expected to become a parent, as a wanderer he realized that he might sire children. But he assumed that he would've moved on well before he knew about them.

Sigurthson had no intention of settling down anywhere he lay with some wench… nor was he a monk, to remain celibate indefinitely. It might be a selfish attitude. But for him it was the only practical one. Now, that was all moot. Caitlynn was alive, bearing his child. The life of a wandering mercenary held less allure for him than it once had. The vision of a settled life, in Galloway, appeared far more viable.

"You are certain?" Sigurthson asked, haltingly, half-doubting it could be true.

"I am," she beamed with pride. "The child should come by late winter, if all goes well."

Eirik rushed to her and embraced her tightly, lifting Caitlynn's feet off the floor. "I love you Caitlynn Maenesa – more than ye' can know. You could give me no more welcome news…"

"Whoa!" Caitlynn struggled to get the words out, "I'm grateful you are pleased husband," she laughed. "Be careful ye' do not crush… us both. You forget your own strength."

Sigurthson himself blushed and loosened his grip. "Did I hurt you?" Eirik sputtered. "I am but a clumsy oaf…"

"Aye," Caitlynn nodded in agreement. "But ye' are MY clumsy oaf." They giggled together then kissed.

It seemed that the entire village had come to the small simple church to witness the christening of Eirik and Caitlynn's daughter, Brianna. Sigurthson could not remember having ever been so happy before. If only his parents were here to see it. He had to hope they saw it form heaven, though some claimed the dead slept until the "Day of Judgment." It was all too complicated for him.

It felt strange for Father Brian, for whom the child was named, preside over the ceremony. Though Eirik had always liked the village priest in the dream memories, which refused to fade entirely, Father Brian was dead… slain by the Black Hound. Of course, if de Gavin was never resurrected the Norman did not slay Father Brian.

250

Despite what reason told Eirik, seeing the elderly priest perform the christening gave him an eerie feeling he could not shake. It dredged up his fear that it was this life which was the dream instead of the other.

The sensation markedly increased when Father Brian requested Eirik's cross to complete the blessing. It was a reasonable thing to ask since the priest gave it to Caitlynn as a gift to protect Eirik, in his time of trial. It seemed only right to use it to bless Sigurthson's daughter.

Why should it bother him so to give up the cross? Yet, bother him it did. Somehow it just felt "wrong." Eirik had never removed it since receiving it. Although the reason for his reticence appeared to have been abrogated, his gut warned him otherwise. Even with Caitlynn, his family and Father Brian urging him to do it, foreboding slowed him in taking it from about his neck.

While suffering many dangers in the dream after receiving the cross, he had survived them against incredible odds. In his waking life his fortunes had improved greatly soon after he put it on.

He was reluctant to change that, even though no to seem selfish and foolish. The benefit of his new daughter ought to supersede any advantage it gave him.

"Why are ye' dawdling, beloved?" Caitlynn asked a half-hidden edge to her voice. "Give the cross to Father Brian. Everyone is waiting..."

"Just... reflecting on the night you gave it to me," Eirik fibbed. "You told me never to remove it. I'm reluctant to break my promise."

"You cannot think I considered such an occasion as this when I made that request?" Caitlynn shook her head in weary disbelief and frustration began to show on her pretty face.

"No..." he admitted. "I don't think you did," Eirik shrugged. "Nevertheless, it is a vow I made. I... I feel unable to break it. Since it was you I made the vow to, you can remove, my love, without my having to break my sacred promise. As you gave it to me I shall surrender it only to you."

Caitlynn rolled her eyes, letting out an exasperated sigh at Eirik's rigidity on so minor an issue. But she could tell that he was adamant about it, however silly it seemed. For her to refuse would be equally nonsensical.

"If it will let us complete the ceremony I will do it," she replied with obvious reluctance. Caitlynn appeared more uneasy than annoyed. Eirik wondered why. He'd expected anger not... fear.

Caitlynn reached out to take the chain, upon which the cross hung, from Eirik's throat. She did it slowly, carefully, avoiding the reflected glint from the polished gold. Caitlynn turned her face away from it, fluttering eyes half-closed.

Grasping the gilded chain Caitlynn held out her arms at full length to lift it over his head. The higher she lifted it the more sour her expression grew. If he didn't know better Eirik would've thought that it caused her physical pain. Why should that be?

Even odder was that Caitlynn was not alone. Father Brian and all the other attendees did their best not to look directly at the cross. Some just averted their gaze, others almost cringing away from it. Their faces were all distorted in a variety of ways, none of them pleasant. Several mumbled to themselves or inhaled in anticipation.

The reactions alarmed Sigurthson. His sense of unreality nearly overwhelmed him. As the glinting golden cross passed in front of his own eyes, his vision suddenly blurred. In a veritable flash, the scene before him changed.

One second he was in his village's church, the next he stood in a winter forest at night, lit by torches and surrounded by wolves, not people. Beside him was a young woman holding an infant. But it was not Caitlynn. The wolves glared at him, with growing hostility, baring their teeth.

The woman beside him was of indeterminate age, her skin smooth, features flawless. She might have been in her late teens save for her eyes which revealed hints of wisdom only age could confer. She had flesh as pale as alabaster, her long, wavy hair a gleaming silver white. Those large eyes, framed by dark lashes, glowed like green gems backed by silver.

"What... what witchery is this!?" Eirik gaped. "Has some spell been cast on me?" His eyes widened, stunned. With one hand Sigurthson reached for the hilt of his sword, the other clasped the cross before it could be fully removed.

Once he did so, the scene steadied and ceased to flicker. The church, Caitlynn and the villagers were gone. The knighted forest, the wolves and the mysterious woman permanently took their place. Winter's chill assailed him. The cordon of wolves snarled viciously, showing their fangs, yellow-green eyes glinting in the firelight. The

Hibernian stood, observing them warily, his booted feet braced wide, sword held out in front of him. The pack came ever nearer. They drooled saliva, savoring their trapped prey. The woman glanced towards them, raised one hand as if in command. "Leave him be," she ordered. "He is not to be harmed."

"Who... who are you... really?" Eirik barked accusingly at the strange woman. "What are these wolves here for?" he pointed at them with his blade. He continued to clasp the cross tightly, donning it once more. "Whose child is that?"

The woman stood even straighter than before, her beautiful face proud and unrepentant. "I am Selene de Ardennes. Some call me the Lady of the Wood; Daughter of Diana, the Moon Mother. Your people knew her as Dana or Anna. You Christians call her a heathen goddess. But she was the progenitor of our race. This forest is my home. I'm the last full-blooded child of Diana that I know of, east of the sea. I am the guardian of this forest. This pack is my family, my children. My father is known as the Green Man. He was the last true-blooded male of our kind. This child is our daughter – yours and mine. I have chosen to keep the name you gave her, if in French form . She will be called Brienne."

"Then... you took the shape of my Caitlynn? It was all illusion these past months?" It was more a statement of a fact than a question.

"Yes," Selene replied matter-of-factly. "Only that part do I regret. It was not my original intention to deceive you... or cause you pain. But I required a child to replace me, when the time comes. My life has been long, but it will not endure forever. You are alive now because I suspected you bore the blood of our mother in your veins. Upon investigation I was sure of it. The chances that I would encounter another like you again were not good. So, I made use of the opportunity fate had provided. I read in your mind your grief for that girl, your dedication to your 'mission.' I knew you would not stay here of your own accord. So, I took the only method open to me to do what I had to do."

"Witch!" Eirik spat the word. "You lied to me! Gave me what I most desired only to rip it away when you no longer needed to maintain the spell. What did you plan for me now?" He glared at her, grief etching his handsome fact. "The wound had begun to heal, now it has been torn open again."

"I am sorry for your pain," Selene responded sadly. "But I had no other way. Tonight, you would have joined the pack, as my mate. But I could not complete your initiation while you wore that symbol of your commitment to the new faith, and to the love you lost. You may still join us if you choose. Yet, while you wear that pendant I cannot compel you." Her tone was full of regret but also resignation. She eyed Eirik longingly.

"I might've refused you," Eirik grimaced. "But had you told me the truth perhaps I would've complied. You gave me no chance to decide. Instead, you pared my memories in order to achieve your own ends. How... when did you steal my thoughts?"

"Before we shared our first meal together," she answered cryptically.

"First meal?" Sigurthson was baffled. Then it dawned on him. She was a shapeshifter. "You were... that wolf?"

"I was," Selene acknowledged. "I have a dual form. I am as much wolf as human, as much human as wolf. But some of my children here have no human shape, only my sons, whose fathers were like you. Then I could teach them to transform."

"You said that I could have joined you," Eirik interjected. "How is that possible? I am no man-beat! I may be no saint but I have not sold my soul to Satan!"

"Nor did I," Selene interrupted him, with a dismissive gesture. "We are of an age before your god put on mortal form. There is no Satan as your faith understands the term, although extremely powerful evil beings exist and exploit your beliefs. I have tried many times to bear a daughter to succeed me. Always before I failed, birthing only sons. But the mother promised me a girl. When I encountered you I knew she had sent you for me. I was right," she nodded proudly to the infant she held.

"What did you mean by saying I could join you?" Sigurthson persisted. "You did not answer me."

"You bear the old blood," Selene shrugged. "If taught you could change. It would be harder than it is for me since your blood is mixed. But as my own sons learned so could you. In your mind I say your meeting with the spectral hound. The wolf – the one that saved you – was but an aspect of yourself."

"You mean heaven did not save me?" Eirik screwed up his face, not quite understanding or ready to believe what she'd said. "It was
254

all naught but pagan magic?"

"Only in part," Selene objected. "We are children of the One above all as surely as you. He made us what we are. It was mortals, who feared us, that said we were demons – offspring of your Satan. As we are what we are so are you. It is within you and it is not evil. I do not know how the wolf appeared as you were not taught to change and it was separated from you. Someone, possibly your god, permitted it to separate from you and to temporarily take physical shape. I will leave it to you to decide whom it was. Yet, this I do know. It is why your foe avoids you directly. He fears that aspect of you might manifest again and it is stronger than he. That is why he settles for attacking those you care about instead."

"Then I defeated de Gavin myself after all?" he asked suspiciously.

"Yes," Selene answered. "But still with help, since you did not know how to access your other shape. Your destiny still holds if that is your real question. I sense that too. It was another reason I knew you would never stay..."

"What of the child... my daughter?" Eirik's gaze locked onto Brienne. "Now that I know of her, despite how she was conceived, I would not simply abandon her, though I have nothing to offer her. Maybe this was what I was meant to do." Leaving now made him feel guilty.

"You are welcome to stay, as I said before," Selene smiled wanly. "It would please me to have you at my side. But you could never forget how I once deceived you. The grief for your beloved is still too fresh. You could never love me, now, as you loved her. Your destiny is real, and I think it does not lie here, much as I might with otherwise. Equally real is your restless nature. The time may come when you are ready to settle down. But this is not that day. In time you would resent me, resent even your daughter for keeping you here. Keep us in memory. Try to forgive me for what I was forced to do. The face was your finance's. The love was mine. Perhaps fate will bring you this way once more. Until then you are free to go."

"If you are certain," Eirik shrugged, feeling pulled both ways.

"I am," Selene looked away wistfully. "It is... as it must be."

The sun was high overhead. It shown through the bare canopy of the trees. Eirik shivered a bit, even beneath his cloak. His boots sank into the powdery snow. The Hibernian's breath misted in the air, as he walked, a newly carved stall in hand.

It was an odd, eerie feeling for him. It felt as if he drifted off to sleep in spring only to awaken in winter. Last night I was April, this morning it was February. In little more than a month it would be a new year.

Sigurthson wondered, idly, if the crusader fleets had set sail yet or the armies marched. Oh well, he thought, he would inquire in the next village... one way of the other he would reach the Holy Land... in his own good time.

Hard as it was to do, Eirik realized that there was only one way he could go on. He had to put his memories in the past and leave them there. He had no home because there was nothing and no one left to return to. Caitlynn wouldn't want him to pine for her forever. His grief helped on one save de Gavin.

Part of him would always love Caitlynn and miss the Galloway he grew up in. But both were gone for good. Eirik had to look to the future, allow himself to have one. Until now, Sigurthson had held himself aloof, moving physically but frozen emotionally. That could not continue.

This was his life, not some lengthy epilogue. Eirik had to start living it. That would be the best way to defeat the hound of vengeance. The Norman could only torment him if he allowed it. The Hound is dead! Long live the Wolf...

The Lioness of Afsana

L A Knight

She comes out of the desert dust and violent heat haze, sword-slim in Bedouin black. The Dasht-e Lut desert unfurls behind her like a tawny carpet; the city of Turan sprawls out before her, hewn from the jagged teeth of the Purza cliffs at the desert's edge. The people within mill about like ants. It is market day.

Her name is Rāzādi. She has made this name her own over centuries, shearing away the excess syllables with the weight of years and wanderings until it a simple name, a clean one without the threads of her old life dragging behind it to give her enemies a target. She has traveled far to find this place.

There is something precious to be found here.

A sandstorm has died away mere moments before her arrival at the edge of the city. The people there stop and murmur at her passing, and they shudder, because no mere mortal can survive the blasting storm winds and biting sands that can strip flesh from bone in mere moments. They step aside as she glides through the streets.

Only one is foolish enough to approach. A young thief lurches out of an alley, face smudged with sweat-mud and hands greedy and grasping for the jeweled hilt of the Persian akinaka at her waist. Her fingers close like iron shackles around his wrist.

She could break it with a brittle snap like cracking a branch in half. Rāzādi thinks this without emotion as she stares down at the thief-boy who has turned so pale in her grip. His cheeks are smooth of even the dreams of beard; fear turns his eyes to black glass. His wrist-bones press into her palm like pebbles against the tender sole of a foot—knobby and too sharp. She can see his ribs through the holes in his shirt.

He reminds her of a story she once told, long ago in the days of her mortality. Maybe that is why she gentles her grip just a little.

"Tell me—are you hungry, boy?" Even after all these years, there is still a bit of the sultana in her voice.

The child nods but says nothing.

"I swear I will not harm you, and I will see you well fed, if you come with me and tell me what you know of the beast-market in this place. So do I swear by the Sorceress of the Sands, Zāl bint Saēna."

The moment she speaks the name of the Sorceress—the foster-daughter of the sacred Simurgh, captain of the desert-faring djinn ship The Nest, and a very dangerous woman—the boy relaxes. It is well known that unlike her foster-mother, Zāl bint Saēna often makes port in mortal cities at the edges of her desert. Swearing by her name and breaking the oath is little better than suicide for most.

Rāzādi doesn't bother to enlighten the thief-boy that the Sorceress of the Sands is no match for her. Mortals, even ghūl-cursed and with a desert-demon crew at their command, rarely are.

She lets the boy lead her to a dining house—more a jackal den than an actual eating establishment, though she can sense no deceit from the child. He is quiet as shadows when he slips through the front door. Sand crunches under his bare feet and Rāzādi wonders if human children are hardier now, able to bear the desert heat baking their skin when they walk. She has a sister who always complained that her feet were roasting in her sandals as a child.

She cannot think of her sister without thinking of her purpose here. Somewhere in this city is a piece of glass no thicker than a hair and no longer than her little finger. It shimmers and dances with light, with magic. Its power carries the stinging spice scent of sandalwood and sun-baked sands. She has only seen this sliver once, before the breaking of her world, but she can sense it near.

Once she finds it, if it is not surrendered peacefully, then she will listen to the music—the symphony of cracking bones and the percussion of blood dripping into the dust. She will put an end to the cowardly thief that stole the last shard, just as she has ended all thirty-nine of the thieves that came before. And then she will go to the beast-market and do what she has come to do.

Years of sandstorms have polished the gopher wood doors to marble smoothness. The thief-boy is polite for an urchin and holds the doors wide for her.

Rāzādi slips into the shadowed interior of the dining house. Her eyes adjust instantly, from falcon's gaze to bat's, taking in the darkness and separating the shadows. The heaviness of her akinaka is a reassuring weight against her thigh. The short, defensive deer-horn blades—crescent moons of djinni steel polished to silver brightness—are hidden amidst the metal accents of her leather vest.

The first time she wielded the deer-horns in battle, dark blood breaking the gleam of argent light on the steel, was after the thieves came. She took the first of the broken glass pieces then, wiping away a smear of blood with a bit of silk and tucking the shard against her heart where it could not easily be stolen.

Forty thieves were a match for Rāzādi then, but one by one she has hunted them and taken back what they stole. The last of them—ancient, tired with the weight of stolen years—is no match for her now.

Carousing men at gambling tables and the soft murmurs of paid night-flowers fall momentarily silent as she lynxes past. She can smell the salt-blood sting of fear like molten copper when she brushes by. In their hearts they know her, though they cannot really see her face or even the body hidden under niqāb veil and robes; only her slim hands mark her as female, and the niqāb also hides her hair, masking the captured stars in her hair—the telltale sign of her true form.

Coins pass quickly from hidden purse to hand to wooden counter.

"A private dining room," she says, and the jowly proprietor doesn't argue with the iron in her voice or the glitter in her eyes. He leads her and the boy to the back with enough bowing that if she wasn't used to it by now, it would be tedious enough to fray her temper.

She orders a countryman's meal for the boy; even if the proprietor tries to pass off bad meat or other food, nothing should make the child ill—not in her presence. She demands only a pomegranate for herself and a leg of desert hare, well done, with a glass of sweet plum wine. Rāzādi doesn't speak until the chubby little man has gone to see to their meal.

When she sits in the simple chair, her body flows with the grace of a queen taking her throne. The boy does not move. She nods to the other chair.

"You make me tired watching you," she says softly.

There is fear in the boy. Rāzādi finds she dislikes the idea that this child should fear her. What she was and what she is now are both displeased; he does not know all the ways she can hurt him. All the ways she has learned to kill men. She does not want him to know.

"Sit down, tifl." She calls him child because he has given her no other name.

He sits, watching her with more wariness and more wisdom

than the fools who simply tense when she draws near. His eyes dart around the room; it wouldn't surprise her if in that split second he memorizes every possible means of escape. He cannot know that she is the child of the wind, with lightning in her blood. He cannot escape her if she chooses to give chase.

Rāzādi has not needed to chase anyone for a long time. She is a slow but patient predator. It is easy for her to simply run her prey into the ground over weeks and months and years of dogging their steps, their constant hungry shadow.

"They sell exotic beasts here, do they not?"

After a moment where she can see him weighing every possible outcome of every possible answer, he nods. Rāzādi is reminded of herself in her youth, a simple spinner of tales thrust into a world where every dawn could kiss the nape of her neck with a quick death and every falling dusk brought pleasure chased closely by icy panic. Maybe that is why she decides to feed him. Why she begins to consider just how helpful a local urchin can be as a spy and errand-boy.

"I know that young boys like to look, even when they cannot touch."

So do young girls. As a mortal child, she looked often enough at the beautiful things that came to the sultan's palace. As her father's daughter, she had the privilege. None could know how those beautiful things and all the burning questions about them that she carried for years inside her would one day save her life not merely once, but again and again. None could know those things—firebirds and peacocks garbed in rainbows; grinning hunchbacks and an assortment of fakirs; sorcerers with their spells and alchemists with their potions and engineers with their tools; clockwork toys from the West and Shaolin wizardry from the East—would one day allow her to break one curse and lead her on this quest to break yet another. A quest that has consumed more than five centuries of her long life. Five centuries of searching, and hope touched by despair.

The boy nods again. He hoards his words. He knows the power of speech. She wonders if he knows that she, too, understands this precious secret.

It hurts to keep her voice serene, disinterested, when she asks the one question that sears her with desperation and that hope hovering on the edge of devastation.

"Have they a kardagan stallion amidst the lovely peacocks and tame leopards?"

When the child nods this time, each bob of his fragile skull sends a shock of pain rippling through her heart.

A kardagan. There is a black djinn-horse in the beast-market. After so long, she has come to the end. The last piece, and her final quarry, are both within reach. Both within the walls of this very city. Half a day in Turan, if that, and she will finally be finished with it all.

"This is for you," Rāzādi says. Her voice betrays nothing. She slides five copper coins across the table toward the boy. Any more than five coppers and he will become a target for the scavengers that prowl the streets, ravenous for little urchins come into some good luck. "For your information. You have my thanks."

He scrapes the coins off the table and into his hands so quickly, one might think they are sweets and he a normal child hungry for goodies. She holds up another coin. It winks in the light filtering through the closed shutters, shiny and new. His eyes track the coin as she moves her hand carelessly through the air. Eyes nearly black with hunger, but not greed. Poverty has not taught this boy greed yet.

"I will give you fifteen more if you swear to aid me this day. Go to the beast-market and learn the fate of the kardagan. Tell me how it is being treated. If it is being harmed or is hurt in any way."

If the slavers or beast-masters are mistreating the kardagan, if he has been harmed, Rāzādi bint Jaffar bint Lamassu of Afsana will teach them what true fear is. She can feel the first slivers of rage slicing through her, prickling the tips of her fingers, melting into her blood like sweet poison. She tucks the fury away, an ember she saves but can bring forth to blazing whenever it is needed.

"Why do you care?" It is the first time the boy speaks, and Rāzādi finds herself smiling for no reason at all. It has been a long time since she has talked with a child. "Do you want it for something?"

Her smile slips. "I want to set him free."

"Why?"

Rāzādi's fingers curl. Her nails bite deep into her palm, but she is careful to draw no blood. If her blood touches this place, it will spark a fire that cannot be quenched. People will die. This child could die. So she is careful to keep her fingers loose enough that when her nails bite deep, her skin never breaks.

"Because he was not always a beast in a cage," she whispers. The stories in her voice weave together, a thousand and one nights of stories and then more, a lifetime of stories, a thousand and one lifetimes because she is no longer human, and neither is the djinn sultan who is also a kardagan. "Because I know his name. Because I will not see him broken." Never again will she allow anyone to break him as the one who came before her once did.

"Do you know him?"

Perhaps she should chastise the child for his impertinence…but if the djinn-horse who is also a man had chastised Rāzādi's little sister for her impertinence centuries ago, Rāzādi would not be here now to save him from the last of forty cowardly thieves.

"I alone know him," she says, and she realizes wistfulness and longing have parted her lips in a smile that shows her teeth. She wears the niqāb, so the boy does not see. If he did, he would be afraid. He has never seen a lioness smile. "And he alone knows me."

There is silence for a long time. At last the boy says, "I'm Aldīn."

"You may call me Rāzādi."

Their food comes then, and the boy is too busy pretending to be a ravenous dog consuming everything in his path, and there are no more questions. Only a sound she has almost forgotten—a hungry boy-child intent on food.

Rāzādi sips her wine and crushes the tart pomegranate piths between her teeth. When the boy tries one and makes a face at the juicy biting sweetness of it, she has to swallow the small laugh caught behind her lips.

It has been a long time since she has been able to laugh.

She sends him into the city when he is finished, bound to her by a promise she knows he will honor because she has seen into his heart; bound to her also by fifteen copper tethers that to him must seem like riches upon riches. A treasure trove.

They are to meet again at the dining hall come dusk. When the child returns, she will caution him about spending it all at once. He is wise beyond years with living on the streets but he is still a child and Rāzādi will not always be here.

Always she has loved children. First her sister, who begged a little girl's boons of a murderer in order to help Rāzādi break a curse and save her own life. Night after night her sister lisped so sweet and soft, Tell me one more story...

Her sister saved her then, a child asking a child's question of the one they love best. Her own children saved her after, when the curse realized what Rāzādi and her sister had done. For love of her, fought for after more than a thousand nights, their father would have resisted the spell on his heart. For love of them, he hadn't needed to. The curse crashed against the walls Shahryār painstakingly built around his wife and two children. Hurtled against them like a hammer against crystal, but the curse was the one to shatter.

Rāzādi has always loved children. This boy slipping quiet as a snake along the streets of Turan reminds her of that.

Perhaps when this is over, she and Shahryār can have another child.

For now, she has one more piece to find. One more shard to slip into place. She reaches inside a secret pocket of her robe and curls her fingers around the slenderest of glass bottles, blown thin as gossamer or spider's webs, a special bottle that would glitter like diamonds if she drew it out.

There are two openings. One is stoppered with faceted glass. The other stopper is missing a piece. An impossibly thin length of braided black horsehair—or something so like horsehair that one might mistake it, if they did not see the luster of midnight pearl and desert moonlight—is slipped through the break.

Rāzādi wears it around her neck beneath her niqāb, close to her heart.

It pulls her toward that missing sliver. She can feel it, like a heartbeat in her mouth. Like the moonlight on her skin that first night with Shahryār, before Rāzādi asked for her sister and began a deadly game of words. She can smell it, sweet as plum wine. She has the nose of a lioness and the magic of what she has become since breaking the curse on her husband. She lets both guide her through the city.

Sometimes fear is an instinct lacking in the foolish. Rāzādi's own instincts tell her that this is well, because that stupidity cannot be allowed to poison the rest. So she doesn't really mind when two men slip out of an alley as she passes and take up step behind her.

She will not draw her akinaka for this. Her deer-horn blades will be enough. It will be quick, and efficient. Her black robes will show no blood.

When this is over, when she has broken this last curse and restored what once was, she and Shahryār can go back to the desert, to the dreaming city of Afsana. There will be no more killing for a long time.

The quickening of footsteps sends her spinning and dancing between wicked, curved blades anxious to pierce her skin. Battle is a dance, sword work a tapestry of quicksand steps and thundering heartbeats and a faint dew of sweat as her deer-horn blades shine, gilded golden with sunlight. Her wings, tucked away beneath her robes, burst free in nova flares of brilliant crimson and aurulent star fire. She is leonine power and queenly grace. She is the Lamassu, the winged djinn-lioness of the desert, and she ends these greedy murderers with quicksilver strokes across their vulnerable throats.

Only a few drops of blood touch her. They are invisible against the black. She wipes her blades on her robes, tucks away her wings, and continues following the call of the sliver.

The last of the forty thieves is waiting patiently for her in a private courtyard just as the sun touches the tops of the buildings. It is a simple enough thing for Rāzādi to slip inside unnoticed by the guards.

The thief is not alone.

Rāzādi studies the woman with the glass shard on a hemp cord dangling from her fingers. A typical Turan beauty, all sable hair thick as an Arabian wolf's winter fur and eyes that glitter like a cobra's. No sack of bones, this woman. She carries the muscle of a sand sailor who's charted the shifting sea of the Dasht-e Lut for years; she is beautiful with the strength of the desert. A small sword hangs at her side. If Rāzādi chose, she could shatter the blade to fragments of broken steel with a single stroke of her akinaka.

It is what she wants to do. The coppery tang at the back of her tongue, salt-sharp with the flavor of rare-cooked meat, is the thirst for blood. Her wings are hot under her robes, sun fire sweet and anxious to taste air once more.

But the body-servants arrayed around the thief give her pause. The cruelty sharpening the thief's smile sends a chill prickling down the back of Rāzādi's neck.

"Give that to me, and perhaps I'll let you live." It is what Rāzādi said to the other thirty-nine that stole into Afsana that night and destroyed the twin-mouthed djinn bottle it has taken centuries to piece back together. None of the thieves ever took the easy way.

Neither does this thief. She clutches the final shard, the thing that gives her immortality and beauty. The thing that prevents Shahryār from taking his true form again, until all that has been broken is mended. She gives the order to attack.

Her servants rush Rāzādi, bristling with talwaars and scimitars bared like iron fangs.

Only then does the akinaka leap into Rāzādi's hand. Its name is Nyazadi, the name of her sister who saved her life in bygone days with love and courage, and it is never to be drawn from its sheath. It comes not when called but only when needed, and now it whirls in the battle dance with a mind of its own. The sword knows what it wants—to protect the one who wields it. Rāzādi merely has to hold on, wings flaring wide, and let it dance.

The courtyard stones, once ivory dusted with golden sand, run red when the dance is ended. Nyazadi flies back to its sheath. Rāzādi wipes the sweat from her forehead with the back of her wrist and turns to the thief-woman.

She bites back the savage oath that tries to fly from her lips when she sees the woman is gone, vanished away during the fight.

There is the sound of flesh slapping flesh, a woman's startled cry. Rāzādi lunges for a shadowed opening leading out of the courtyard as footsteps echo on tiles. Her deer-horn blades are back in her hands; they will do for the fortieth thief.

Her weapon halts at Aldīn's throat. Realization crystallizes in Rāzādi's mind in the split second as her blade softly parts the first layer of skin—he has followed her, either returning early from the beast-marking and crossing her path or having never gone at all. The boy swallows, a glimmer of true fear in his eyes. A single drop of blood trickles down his throat from the shallow cut she has made. But those dark eyes flash to the wings burning at her back.

Is that understanding in his gaze?

The thief-woman hides behind him. Her own blade is poised to thrust through the thin back and find the young heart. A sneer twists her lovely face.

"I've had centuries to learn of you," she hisses.

Rāzādi whips the blade away from the child's neck and steps back before her fury can poison her judgment. Aldīn is a child. He is a child. But the forty thieves had had no qualms about murdering the children who got in their way at Afsana. Why should things be different now?

"Centuries to learn the weaknesses of the beast hunting us all down one by one. Your precious sharaf is a waste, Šahrāzādi; it holds you back."

Rāzādi's eyes widen. Her teeth clench at the insult, but she does not recoil at the use of the name she has given up centuries ago.

"My honor is no waste and no weakness. Release him."

"Only if you swear you'll no longer hunt me," the thief insists. When Rāzādi says nothing, she presses the point of her blade into the child's back. Aldīn gasps and tries to escape the sword's bite. "Swear it on the Sorceress of the Sands, or the bratling dies now."

"I found him," Aldīn says then, almost too softly for Rāzādi to hear. But if she can scarcely hear him, the thief-woman hears nothing. "And came back to find you. I saw you walking and I followed you." Hesitation, a tightening of those young, scared eyes. Aldīn whispers, "He looks bad, my lady."

The sword-point digs a little deeper. Aldīn gasps, bites back a whimper. Rāzādi trembles with the choice before her.

Once, Rāzādi was Šahrāzādi, sultana of the star-kingdom of Afsana, the one who ensnared a king with one thousand and one nights of stories and broken the curse laid on him by his first wife—a curse of ice-cold heart and emptiness, a curse of madness and fear and loneliness. Even now she loves the king who has been cursed anew with the breaking of the twin-mouthed djinn bottle she has spent so many years making whole again. He is the one she has sought all these centuries.

But this child is bound to her, even if the bond is one of copper barely two hours old. Her promises to him are still warm in her mouth.

She is Lamassu, the winged djinn-lioness of the desert, protector of children.

He is only a boy, and so young.

"I swear," she whispers, and her heart splinters like breaking glass, "on the Sorceress of the Sands that I will hunt you no more if you release the child unharmed. But know this." Her voice burns with a cold deeper than any found in the Dasht-e Lut. It is a cold from the dark places beyond the stars, a cold only a Lamassu can endure for long. Aldīn shivers, and so does the thief-woman. "If he is harmed in any way, any way at all, I will kill you. And your death will last a thousand centuries."

The thief-woman smirks and begins to loosen her hold. She lowers the point of the sword. Rāzādi will make no move on her; an oath has been sworn, indelible as the living starlight spells bound in her bones when she became sultana and something other than human.

It is Aldīn whose eyes blaze, Aldīn who makes his move the moment the sword no longer needles into his back. He shoves at the woman, panicking, screaming like an ifrit intent on burning the world to ash. He slaps at her face and hands. Anger and a child's terror mingle in his face. Rāzādi can see that the thief-woman remembers the words of the Lamassu's oath well. The boy cannot be harmed, in any way, or her life is forfeit. So she only raises an arm to shield her face and scrambles away while the boy shrieks like a mad thing.

When the thief-woman is gone, Rāzādi stares at Aldīn. There is something hollow and puppet-like about his movements, his screams.

"When you're quite finished?"

Instantly Aldīn stops screaming as if he never began. He grins, impishness and a missing tooth and an invitation to praise him for some secret cleverness. He holds up a hemp rope with a piece of glass strung upon it.

Rāzādi's jaw goes slack. She is immortal. She has seen the fall of cities and even an empire or two. But she does not expect this.

"How did you…?"

How did she forget that Aldīn survives on the streets by picking pockets? And that even a street child may understand the honor code of sharaf?

Her promises to him are still warm in her mouth. Do his promises to her still sit hot on his tongue, reminding him that she has paid him a day's wages and holds more for him yet? Reminding him that she has put food in his belly and did not cut off his hands for trying to steal from her, though the law gives her the right?

Did he do this for fifteen more coppers? Because of sharaf? Or because he recognizes the lioness in her eyes and the star fire in her wings, though he cannot see the sharpness of her teeth or the glittering stars that cling to her hair beneath her niqāb?

Does it matter why? There is a bargain between them. She knows now he will honor it. And she knows she will owe him a debt all of his days, and love him for it.

He hands her the corded glass. "What is it?"

She reaches beneath her niqāb and withdraws the broken stopper, pulling it from the slim kardagan-hair braid around her neck. She makes no move, but the glass shard rips away from its hemp leash, slicing through the fibers like a hot sword through silk, and slips into place with a crystalline tink and a spark like a tiny star bursting.

"This," she whispers, "is the stopper of a djinn bottle."

Once, long ago in a hidden desert kingdom where demons of wind and sand and sun, flesh and fire and steam still walk and the stars themselves make their secret homes when the sun chases them from the sky, a sultan of the djinn and his sultana were attacked by forty thieves howling out of the desert and sweeping through the streets. They crossed swords with marids and ghilan, ifrits and jinn, but the sultan plunged into the battle with the slashing iron hooves and spearing obsidian horn of the kardagan, the djinn-horse. And in the battle, the twin-mouthed bottle that bound the sultan and his wife was shattered, sundering King Shahryār's ability to return from kardagan to humanoid form. The pieces were stolen and scattered across the desert, across the world. And so five centuries passed.

Now the djinn bottle in the secret pocket inside Rāzādi's robe is made whole again, and so is the sultan's power.

"Where's the djinn?" Aldīn asks breathlessly, for this is the stuff of legends and he is all afire to see more of it.

Her smile is all teeth, sharp and fierce. She can feel the heat of her wings burning delicious against her back beneath her robes. Nyazadi shudders in its sheath.

"The beast-market. Let's go get him, shall we?"

The slavers and beast-traders flee before the glorious sweep of her wings, blazing like the sun, scorching the sand under her feet. Aldīn keeps his distance, but he is smiling. He is a child, and it pleases him to see adults make fools of themselves as they scurry

270

away like frightened mice.

Rāzādi is not smiling when she finds the kadargan trapped in his cramped cage atop a low dais. Though tangles mat his ebony mane and tail, though white scars mar his midnight coat, she recognizes Shahryār in an instant. It is a knowing that shivers through her bones and burns in her blood hotter than any fire. A knowing she first felt when he looked on her as his bride and the curse splintered the merest bit.

Djinn-horse. Kardagan. A black unicorn.

Shahryār.

Her wings, spread wide to drive back any who would stand before her, droop to the sand and melt it to glass. Aldīn dodges backward to avoid the molten spread. The hot glass does not bother Rāzādi.

Shahryār's head hangs so low, the spiraling obsidian horn spearing up from his forehead gouges into the sand. He snorts and heaves a sigh, but does not look up when she approaches. It is only when she speaks, soft and low and so sweet it makes him ache with memory, that a shudder ripples through him.

"I have come to finish our story. I bring you a happy ending."

He lifts golden eyes to her face. Raises his head and steps toward her. He can barely move an inch inside the confines of the hot, iron bars threatening to crush him, body and soul. But his horn touches her shoulder. That simple touch pierces her like a lightning bolt, like a sword. She brushes her fingers beneath his chin.

"You will find the djinn bottle is whole again, my lord. You can take your true shape again. My love...step down." A sob roughens her voice. Her fingers clutch at the iron lock and her nails bite deep into the metal as if it is soft clay. Rāzādi wrenches it away. Rips the door to the cage wide and steps back, throwing out her arms.

"My sultan, Shahryār ibn Shazaman ibn Kardagan, step down! You are free!"

And when he steps down, he is not a djinn-horse any longer. Not now in this moment when all he wants is to pull Rāzādi into his arms. Now he is a djinn in the shape of a man, dark hair tangled and burnished skin bearing so many new scars, too thin and too worn, eyes shining with unshed tears. Now he is Shahryār, king of Afsana. Rāzādi steps into his embrace and he holds her as he has not held her in five-hundred years, and though he is weary and worn, he is all strength, all summer warmth, all tenderness when he presses his lips to her temple. His mouth just touches the smooth skin bared by the niqāb, a shock of memory and heat. Rāzādi presses closer, grateful for his arms at last.

"Kheili dusset daaram." There is more power in those simple words, I love you, than in all the magic of the desert and the djinn. Neither of them knows who says it first. It does not matter. Like a spell, it gains power in the repeating. "Kheili dusset daaram."

At last, her quest is finished. At last, she can go home.

The desert on the edge of Turan is quiet, and so too is the city, save for the shush of wind over the dunes stretching out for fathoms toward the west.

Just beyond the city's edge, Aldīn lays his hand against the strong shoulder of the ivory lioness standing with her fiery wings outstretched, careful of the mortal boy at her side. The sun seems to flood each dancing, fire gold feather with wild life. White stars sparkle like diamond dewdrops along the short, silky fur. Her eyes are dark as midnight, glinting with more stars like flecks of molten gold, and soft with something so like a mother's love that Aldīn catches his breath when she turns to him.

She saved him once. Risked her quest to do it. There is a bond between them. She can see he understands this when she looks in his eyes. He is young, but he wise for all that.

Rāzādi looks to Shahryār, in kardagan shape once more, all darkness and power. His horn glistens like black glass in the sunlight. Her sultan knows her thoughts. He nods to her. This boy had a hand in freeing him from the curse that bound him to this shape. A child, but wily, he helped prevent Rāzādi from carving another scar into her heart when he pick pocketed the fortieth thief. Honor demands Shahryār pay the debt.

But it is Rāzādi who says, Come with us to Afsana.

She can see her words pierce his heart like an arrow. He is shocked by the offer. But where else is he to go? Back to a life alone on the streets of Turan? Risking the cruel bite of the sword if ever he is caught?

Rāzādi cannot leave him behind. Not now. Copper and promises and the knowledge of what she is—Lamassu, protector of children, beast-queen of the sands, the golden-eyed granter of a young heart's wishes and sultana of the dreaming city of stars—binds them together. No harm will come to him in the desert. Not in her presence. She will protect him on the journey.

And the thief-woman may seek him as the years catch up to her and her long-held beauty begins to crumble like old stone. She may remember that this boy was there the day her immortality was stolen from her.

Rāzādi will not let her harm the child, either.

Come with us, Aldīn.

"I will come," he murmurs after what feels like several small eternities.

So they walk across the Dasht-e Lut to Afsana. To the desert city of stars and dreams, the city of myths and legends. The city of a thousand and one eternal Arabian nights.

THE END

PUNCH!

SHANE PORTEOUS

The clouds were swirling, looking like white puffs of smoke being consumed by a hungry drain. This caused the blue of the sky to have a flashing effect, both irritating and mesmerizing; it was hard to look away. Of course for her everything was hard to look at, her eyes had opened like cleaved wounds, the flesh underneath reddish and glazed over. With a mouth as dry as stone and a head full of pounding rocks, Escara knew she had drunken wagons worth of wine and her body was suffering from it. As was her memory, she remembered little about the night before, a veil of purple covered every image her mind could conjure. Her long flowing hair, the colour of larva, really did look like it had spilled from a volcano, its ends sticking to the ground around her.

She looked away from the spinning sky and upon her own body, many leaves were sticking to her skin. Smelling the air she was grateful that the scent of vomit wasn't all consuming, the leaves had stuck to her because of their sap and not her own rejected bodily fluids. This was a good thing, considering she couldn't place where she had left her clothes. Though her memories were distorted she could piece enough of last night together to know what had happened. She had passed out on a cloud, somewhere in her slumber she had rolled off of it and crash-landed in the mortal realm. It would certainly explain why she was now laying in a crater; leaves and what remained of trees were both under and around her. It seemed she had landed on a forest, one that would take decades to grow again. Being a goddess definitely had its advantages but even divinity was responsible for their own behavior. She had no dominion over nature and was quite sure she would get a stern talking to from the gods and goddesses who watched over the forests and fields of the world. Not that it really mattered too much to her, only the king of gods could really dish out the kinds of punishment gods were afraid of. Still it was in her best interest to get going and return back to the heavens.

Sitting up her head felt like it was ready to explode off of her shoulders and she closed her eyes in a bid to ease the tension. It helped a little but she remained horribly hung over. She casually brushed the leaves out of her hair and spat several times in a bid to rid her mouth of the rotten taste that dwelled within. There were no lakes nearby, just a dull looking series of plains and mountains, meaning she had no way to look at her own reflection. She would worry about her appearance when she found her clothes, which she guessed were still upon one of the clouds.

Closing her eyes again she ran her fingers through her hair once more stopping to pluck at her earrings. It had been a habit her mind had claimed many years ago, back when the king of gods had given them to her as a precious gift. She could feel the right one, the warm enticing metal of a decoration that only gods could forge. When she tried to feel for the left, the ear lope felt naked. Her eyes burst open once more, widened in concern as she felt every inch of her ear. The left earring was gone and in spite of her aching body she quickly crouched, rummaging through the leaves in a bid to find it. This was bad, she could deal with the stern yet ultimately harmless warnings of the other gods, but their King was a different matter. Any gift he bestowed upon you was to be considered sacred and irreplaceable, a decree that was irrefutable. Escara was well aware of what happened to the last god that had lost such a gift. Even through a haze of wine the memory was clear to her and she shuddered while thinking about. She had to find it and frantically she began searching the crater.

The leaves and twigs looked like they were caught in a windstorm as she rummaged through them all. Her movements were fast enough to keep everything in the air, making the crater completely bare, yet not an inch sparkled meaning the earring wasn't there. 'Dam it,' she groaned, her normally harp-stringing voice sounding more like the grunts of a farm animal. She tried to concentrate on the last time she had touched her earring, but couldn't place it specifically. There was a chance that it was up in the clouds somewhere. Escara was notorious amongst the other gods for skipping her earrings across the clouds like stones across a lake when she had had too much to drink. And she drank too much almost every single day. But she didn't want to risk returning to the heavens without that earring, there was no way of knowing when the king of gods would summon her for another meeting. Contemplating her options she stood up, taking a long strained breath. She attempted to scan the fields in search of something shiny. It was barely mid-day and the sun was out in full force. Even hung over her eyes were sharper than an eagle's. Still she was sure to be thorough, too many had paid the price of arrogance and she didn't want to be amongst them.

Spinning on her heel seven times in every direction she finally did see something in the distance. It shone for only a moment, but she remembered such a sign.

'Thank the gods,' she said smirking, often thanking herself in the same way mortals did when fortune smiled upon them. From such a distance it looked like the earring had fallen upon a mountain, a large looming formation that stood taller than most of its kind. But as long as the sun was shining she would always have a fixed destination. Relieved greatly, she had taken two steps before the smirk was slain from her lips. She blinked several times, contemplating that her wine warped mind was conjuring illusion. The mountain was moving and even from such a distance the ground beneath her shook slightly. She narrowed her vision, hoping to make the image clearer. It helped enough for her to make out the mountain had a head, an enormous collection of slopes and teeth, seemingly the size of the moon. She sighed deeply, now knowing what she had done. She had played pin the earring on the monster last night. It was a game she only played when she was drunk enough to silence all of her common sense. She would watch the realm of mortals and for reasons her sober mind could never conjure she thought it was amusing to hurl the earrings at the great monsters of the world to see if they would stick.

'Well at least I won the game,' she said sarcastically, doing her best not to allow the weight of the situation to crush her spirit. Promising herself that if she got the earring back she would never play the game again she began running in the monster's direction. Her speed was astounding, she could easily outrun an entire volley of arrows, turn around, catch them all and then hurl them back at the archers who had fired them, all without breaking stride. The world around her became a blur but not because of her induced state, she was moving so fast that even her sharp eyes couldn't see the world clearly anymore.

Because of her speed it only took a few moments to be standing in the shadow the monster cast. It was enormous in every sense of the word and within its shadow, night seemed to fall upon the world. Her eyes ascended slowly up its massive frame, beginning with its forest-sized feet, the monster was covered in scales, each one the size of a boulder, spikes the size of large hills decorated parts of its anatomy. Amongst it all she could see her earring, shining in a gray-scaled abyss that was the monster's right shoulder.

The behemoth had its back turned to her but she had a way to see its face. She created a whistle from her lips loud enough that the air seemed to shimmer around her, as if unable to comprehend such a sound completely. She remained calm as the monster turned, creating a series of earthquakes under its step. Seeing its face now, the monster had eyes the size of lakes, teeth as tall as pillars. Its head was the very embodiment of monstrous; even the most twisted of minds would struggle to find any beauty in such a mug. Yet Escara stood casually looking into its eyes, they were blood-red and not because the monster was hung over.

'Sorry to bother you,' she began, her own raised voice causing rocks to smash together inside her mind. 'But my earring seems to have been lodged in your shoulder. I honestly don't know how it got there, but you see I am going to need it back. So I am going to have to climb up you. But my sense of balance is a little off today so I need you to stand still for a little while, pretend to be a mountain; you're certainly big enough to pull off such a disguise.'

To this the monster merely stared, drool falling from its mouth like title waves. Though lakes of saliva were now forming around her, Escara didn't flinch, patiently waiting for the monster to respond.

'I can assure you the earring doesn't look that great on you, it just isn't your thing. You're clearly more of a fire and brimstone kind of creature, I think that would be fair to say.' The monster stared for a moment more as Escara didn't look away from its gaze.

'I apologize for the inconvenience; I will try not to take too long.' The monster bellowed out a roar, a sound that seemed to make the whole world cower in fear. She could feel the sound reverberate in the wind causing her hair to flail like it was drowning. Yet her eyes didn't even narrow as she said, 'I am sorry I didn't quite catch that, do you mind repeating it?'

The monster raised its hand and clenched a fist. Creating a shape the size of a comet Escara continued to stare as suddenly the monster attacked. It's fist really did move with the speed of the comet, its arm like gigantic flames, followed the fist as it came crashing down upon her. The impact could be felt for a thousand miles, the ground breaking and cracking like over-cooked clay. A wind more powerful than any offspring of a tornado sliced through the air. But the effect of the impact didn't stop there, the wind and quaking were too powerful for the surrounding mountain peaks to endure. They crumbled like sandcastles against the might of the blow as a single loud cracking noise exploded through the air. It sounded like lightning punishing the ground, only the noise was a thousand times more intense.

With what passed as a smile on the monster's enormous mouth it slowly rose its fist, glad that it had silenced that tiny annoying thing. The smile disappeared, turning into a frown as its gigantic eyes widened almost beyond comprehension. Not only was Escara still standing, there wasn't so much a strand of hair that was out of place, let alone a single scratch or blemish anywhere. She looked exactly as she had before the blow had been delivered. She stood staring up at the creature for a long moment before her expression soured slightly.

'What was that?' She asked, a little unnerved. Like there was a hook tugging at the side of her mouth her lip then curled. 'Was that an attack?' The hook vanished being replaced by a chuckle. 'It was? Wasn't it?' The chuckle became all out laughter, before she shook her head and took a breath in order to get control of herself. 'Something your size should be able to attack a lot harder than that!' She couldn't help but begin laughing again as the monster watched on confused. 'Here,' she began, the humor still clear in her voice. 'This is how you land a punch,' she said casually clenching her hand into a fist. She moved with speed no mortal could match as she struck the monster's foot. There was no great gust of wind, no mountains crumbling, no lands shaking, but the punch was more impressive than those three feats combined.

Instantly the monster was taken into the air, moving like a boulder flung from a catapult. The roar of the creature couldn't be heard, it was moving too fast for the wind to capture the sound. It continued to rise, its entire body stiffened by the pain the blow inflicted as it soon vanished from sight, seemingly swallowed by the sun itself.

Not once did her gaze narrow or flinch even as the full might of the sun rushed her vision. A slight smile did appear on her face when she rose her hand, catching the falling earring. Placing it back into her ear she was ready to return to the clouds, already thinking about her next jug of wine when she noticed she wasn't alone.

She could hear see a whole army worth of soldiers, men and women draped in armor, soot and dismay. Their once proud faces were filled with bewilderment as thousands of eyes were upon her. Scanning across her surroundings Escara could see flames, damaged dwellings and a whole plethora of destruction. She had wondered where the smell of fire and blood was coming from. She stared back at the soldiers, most of who looked at her and then up towards the sky. It was a surreal moment for each of them, Escara meanwhile was now thinking about where she had left her clothes. As one the army moved forward, across the gap of space where the monster had once stood. It wasn't an organized march of attack, but a creeping crawl fueled on by confusion and disbelief. With a good ten feet between them and Escara, the army stopped and just stared.

'She defeated the monster?' A soldier gasped, pointing a finger towards her. The question was answered only with silence as they continued to stare, wide-eyed and wide mouthed.

'That means our town is saved?' A woman warrior asked, everyone else remaining in a sea of shock.

'The monster is defeated, our town is saved!' Judging by the decorations of his armor, the man who had proclaimed this was an officer of some kind. His voice carried with it enough authority that the silence gave way to an echo of cheers, line after line of soldiers raising their weapons triumphantly. Escara raised an eyebrow, trying to piece it together, her mind remained full of cobwebs. Amongst the throngs of cheers an older knight stepped forward, removing his helmet with a trembling hand, his eyes were water-filled.

'How can we ever thank you for what you have done, that monster has been terrorizing our town for decades.'

Escara finally pieced it all together. The sheer size of the monster had kept the town completely out of her view. She had no idea that it had been in the middle of a rampage. She felt like chuckling, but she bit her lip to prevent that from happening. She thought about asking for clothes, though the few garments she could see under the rows of armor wasn't appealing. When not another word was spoken she realized every soldier was waiting for an answer.

'Um...live well,' she said with an edge of uncertainty. Unlike most of her divine breed she had never been particular good with speeches and spreading words. Not knowing and really not caring about having something else to say she nodded before turning.

She had taken two steps before she looked back and said, 'Oh, I think you should know that the monster will fall back to the ground in a few moments...' She could hear a whole stream of gasps and whispers from the army but paid little attention to it. 'Probably will land right on what is left of your town...so you might not want to be standing there when it returns.' For her warning she just got plenty of blank stares before collectively the whole army raised its head and looked to the sky. A second past and suddenly the whole army spoke up in a chorus of screams and bellows.

'Will you not save us?' The old knight asked, his beard dancing to the tremble of his lip. Escara looked him in the eye before casually raising her head, before looking back at him and then raising her head again. When she looked back a third time she could see the fear and hope in his eyes. She could tell this man was no coward, he was brave, a valiant warrior, a man of honor, maybe even a true hero.

'Nah,' she said finally. For a long moment there was silence again, she casually studied every gaze and couldn't find a single blinking eye anywhere.

'Please you must help,' the knight begged.

'This town is our home, my grandfather's grandfather's grandfather's grandfather helped build it with his own two hands.'

'There is nowhere else for us to go, the other villages don't have room for us!'

Many other soldiers either begged or protested for her help, she heard them but wasn't really listening.

'Well anyway, as I said before live well,' she said now thinking what was the point of putting on clothes? She knew where a good keep of wine was in the heavens and was fairly sure she hadn't gotten into it the night before.

'Wait!' A voice said, putting an end to the series of gasps and shudders that filled the army. Unlike the voice of the knight, there was no authority in it and still it cut through the other sounds like a sword through a book. Escara watched as a male, as scrawny as he was young, push through the ranks, most were too engrossed by her to notice him pushing them out of his way. Though he did wear simple armor, it was obvious this teenager was no warrior, he didn't carry himself the way knights did. Chances were he was a squire.

'What is it?' She asked, the tone of her voice was hard for the army to comprehend, how could one be acting so calm after what she had said?

'I heard what you said to the monster before you…sent it up into the sky….'

She didn't believe he was lying, a good sense of hearing was quite valuable to a squire, knight's always demanded urgency whether in battle or having their boots shined and would punish any kind of tardiness from servants.

'If I show you a real punch will you save our town?'

If the very stake of the town hadn't been on the line and this had just been a bar room proposition, many of the knights would have joined Escara in her long chuckle. But she soon noticed that the boy didn't waver, his eyes full of determination. Intrigued Escara turned back around to see him face to face, or rather face to chest considering how short the squire was.

'And who are you going to punch boy?' It wasn't meant as a threat or warning, but her voice remained strained from the hard night of drinking.

'If I can make your nose bleed with a punch do you agree to save our town?'

Escara smiled at this, at the least the boy believed himself. She glanced to the knights who watched on, amused by the dread that painted their faces. When she looked back to the boy she shrugged. 'Sure why not.'

The boy bit his lip, taking a sharp breath as he nodded.

'Would you like me to kneel, give you a chance to strike me between the eyes?' She asked, taking a tiny amount of delight in the absurdity.

'No, no,' the boy said. 'Standing will be fine but I must ask that you stay in one spot and don't move until I get back.'

'Fair enough,' Escara said shrugging once more. The boy nodded before turning on the spot and running back through the army.

'Gain way!' He called out again and again.

'Where are you going?' The old knight bellowed.

When he didn't respond Escara decided to. 'The boy probably just needs a good run up, wants to make the punch count.'

When the old knight looked to her there was anger in his eyes, but after seeing what she was capable of, he didn't act on it.

The army had parted now, leaving a very crooked gap between

two sides as every head was turned to see where the boy was going to. After a long moment the heads began to turn back to Escara once again.

'Excuse me,' another knight said gracefully, he limped away from the crowd towards her. His limp probably had more to do with a recent injury than age or birth defect for the rest of the man was strong and fairly youthful. She looked him in the eyes as he hobbled to be within reach of a conversation with her.

'Am I right to say that you are a goddess?' The limping knight asked.

'I am,' Escara said, the colour of her hair being a dead giveaway.

'I swear to you without one word of a lie, this town has always made tributes to the gods, we have prayed when we are meant to, we constantly visit the temples that we built to honor the grants of the gods....' He stopped for a moment to allow Escara to listen to the murmurs and see the nods of the rest of the army. 'I promise you there isn't a disbeliever amongst us, we have done everything that the old teachings taught.'

She knew what he was getting at and much like the boy she didn't believe he was lying. 'And which gods do you worship?' She asked.

The question seemed to throw the knight for a moment, but he recollected his thoughts. 'The gods of the woods and the winds, the gods we should worship.'

Escara smiled upon hearing this, wondering if he had mistaken her makeshift garments of leaves. 'Aye,' she began, not seeing deceit in his eyes. 'But what are their names?' She asked. The knight took a deep breath as the whole army watched on silently.

'Kumo, Neskin, Deerie, Trok and Calious. The Gods and Goddesses that have watched over us since the dawn of time.'

Escara kept her smile as she could feel every set of eyes boring into her. 'Than why don't you pray now to them, see if they will come and help you.'

She chose to ignore the chorus of gasps that filled the ranks. She didn't particularly get along with any of those gods and goddesses, this wasn't the first time she had fallen onto one of their forests. She found herself pondering now over which mortals worshiped her and where were they located. Normally she paid little attention to anyone's prayers to the extent she now had to think long and hard about what she actually was a goddess of. Before the answer could come to her she could see the squire approaching. He was moving slowly and carefully, apparently he hadn't tried to get a good run up. It was only when he came close enough that she saw what he was holding in his hands. He raised his hands up to her but not in any kind of attack, allowing her to get a good sight of what was in the goblet. The smell more than the colour of it, hinted at what it truly was.

'Morsetin punch, the finest in all the land.' The boy began, his eyes still burning with determination. This brought a large smile to her face, it was rare for mortals to do something so unpredictable and clever. She glanced to the old knight and still could see the anger in his eyes. Clearly this didn't impress him but Escara thought differently. Being quite familiar with many types of alcohol she knew that certain mixtures could cause noses to bleed. But it was obvious this boy had no clue just how much she could drink, normally it would take an ocean worth of wine to give her a nose bleed. Still she took the goblet, wanting a good belt to tie herself over before returning to the heavens. As the goblet touched her lips and she began to drink, her gaze was drawn to a yelling man. As he hurriedly moved out from the ranks he raised a finger to the boy.

'You better not have laced that with poison!'

'That would be very stupid!' The boy replied, showing an anger not normally seen in a quiet squire. 'I want her to save our town, how can she do that if she is dead?'

The question was answered by the man lowering his head and returning to the crowd. The urgency of the situation ensured the squire wasn't reprimanded as they all watched in a hushed silence.

Their grim reality was strengthened when darkness consumed the sun. Escara was the only one who didn't raise her head as the monster began hurdling back towards the earth. Panic filled every man and women there. Not everyone was paralyzed by their fear, some would have ran if they believed they had any chance of escaping the creature's fall, for it was moving with the speed of an arrow. All eyes were back upon Escara again, watching and waiting to see if she would save them. She remained only concerned with tasting the punch, running her tongue across her teeth, savoring the flavor in her mouth. As one their eyes ascended once more seeing that the monster was getting closer and closer. Now Escara began to smell the punch, savoring the scent like she was calmly sipping on brandy. The monster was so close now that the sound of its descent could be heard, a strange bellowing whisper like noise, both quiet and loud.

Now there was not an inch of the sky that could be seen, the yellow of the sun and the blue of the sky had vanished from vision. Escara puckered her lips, her mind deep in thought about the flavor. Many now began to close their eyes, accepting that they would meet their end here and now. But the boy watched her without blinking or breathing. With the monster only now the height of a tree above them, tears began to flow as men and women both hugged each other tightly.

When it seemed that they would indeed all be crushed Escara rose her hand, catching the beast within her palm. She held onto the mountain of the monster like it was the weight of a mere pebble as she took another sip. With a small trickle of blood falling from her nostril Escara said, 'Not bad.'

The Trailblazer

Lincoln Law

The desert continued on forever, and where forever ended, the desert continued.

Esmond stood at the foot of a mountain, surveying out across the dunes, stark gold against a blackened sky. Somewhere to the north of here lay the Dragling Canyon, and in that canyon was a town, famous for its wellspring. He had offered to wait for his client there, but she had been adamant she would come to him. He would meet her at the base of the mountain at midday. Despite the overcast sky, the heat fell heavy upon him, weighing him down.

A small grey jitterrat scampered across the sand from the base of the mountain. It leapt onto Esmond's staff, spiraling around it, its feather-like tail waving about madly.

"She's late, Lymon" Esmond said, glancing at the jitterrat.

Lymon looked across at Esmond with its dark eyes.

"Should've made her wait in the town," Lymon replied, in a voice that was uncharacteristically deep for a creature so small.

Exactly what I was thinking, Esmond thought. When he replied to Lymon, though, he only gave him a sarcastic stare, and returned his attention to the dunes.

"Did the letter say what her business in Rarelane was?" Asked Lymon.

"Of course not," Esmond replied. "No questions asked, no information given; that's the rule. I wish she didn't have to go there, though."

"Don't like Rarelane?"

"It's not that," Esmond said. He donned a wide-brimmed hat. "It's the distance. Longest distance between any of the cities in the demonlands. Only thing stopping them from building some kind of way station out here is the distance. There's water in the Dragling Canyon, and there's water in Rarelane, but in between, there's only sand and demons."

Esmond adjusted the duster he wore, undoing the buttons in accordance with the heat. He kept the coat on, despite his discomfort.

A shadow appeared in the corner of his eyes. He turned suddenly, eyes darting to the solitary figure approaching from afar. She wore trousers and a plain canvas shirt, her auburn hair tied back. A few stray strands found their way out of the band, though, and waved about her face as a wind rose, announcing her arrival.

Esmond let out a sigh of relief as the wind blew towards him, bringing with it a welcome sense of cool freshness. It then brought a mouthful of sand, but that didn't bother him as much.

The woman carried a pack with her, and Esmond assumed it had all the supplies he had requested in order to allow the crossing. There would be water and food, and a handful of coins as payment as well. Those were the rules: he blazed a trail for her, the companion brought the supplies.

"She's a pretty one," said Lymon, whispering into Esmond's ear, like a conscience demon. "If I had my body back..."

Esmond glared at the jitterrat. It annoyed him how honest Lymon was sometimes. It annoyed him even more how right he was.

"Well you don't. You're a jitterrat." He paused. "You do know I could have killed you rather than sealed you in this body?"

"And yet you showed me mercy," Lymon replied. He leapt from the top of the wooden staff, onto Esmond's shoulder, nuzzling his head into his neck with false affection. "And for that I thank you."

"Shut up."

Lymon scurried into the collar of Esmond's duster to keep out of sight and to get out of the wind and sand.

"Are you Esmond?" Asked the woman once she was close enough to speak.

"I am," Esmond replied. He moved towards the woman, his coat billowing in this newfound wind. He extended his hand to shake, and she returned her own. She didn't look delicate at all. She had a firm grip as she shook Esmond's hand, and kept eye contact with the man. She had pale violet eyes, but a hard face. Below that, though, Esmond could also see a real beauty to the woman. Something motherly and kind. She was probably somewhere in her late twenties, and yet it seemed trouble had worn her down. She looked tired like she had not slept well recently, her eyes drooping with dark shadows. Esmond imagined this had something to do with her traveling to Rarelane, but he didn't ask. He never asked.

"I brought water, as you asked," she said, unslinging her pack. She opened it, revealing water skins, and below that, crusty bread and cheese as well as some dried meat; probably hare. It wouldn't be nice eating, but it would be eating, and that, for Esmond, was better off than most. The woman gave the bag a shake, too, and he heard the characteristic jingle of coins.

"Good," he replied, nodding. He reached into his pocket and

pulled out a golden pocket watch. It was a quarter past noon now, but that wasn't what he looked at. On the other side of the watch was a compass. He sat it flat in his hand, checking where north was.

"This way," he said, pointing in a direction perpendicular to the way the woman had come, away from the mountain. "Let's go."

The woman seemed a little taken aback by Esmond's bluntness. It took her a moment to follow, and a moment more to catch up.

"Isn't it polite to ask someone you're traveling with their name?" Asked the woman.

"I'm not traveling with you," he said flatly. "I'm a trailblazer. I'm…trailblazing with you. There's a difference."

"Smooth," whispered Lymon into his ear.

"What if you need to ask me something?" She asked. "Or call out to me?"

"Then I'll say woman or girl or something. Names are for people who care for one-another."

"Well my name is Asta," she said, "and it's a pleasure to meet you, too, sir." Her tone was fiery, perhaps even a little sarcastic.

"That's nice, girl, now come along."

"Be polite," Lymon muttered, his voice only just audible over the wind. "She seems like a nice girl. How long has it been since your wife—"

Esmond cut him off. "I told you to shut up, so shut up."

Asta, still staying a few steps behind him, said, "You talking to yourself? You know, in the Old World, talking to yourself was the first sign you were going mad?"

Esmond sighed. "I suppose we're all a little mad." And with you around I suspect it will only worsen.

The group continued on into the desert, the wind continuing to whip around them. Esmond thanked it for the way it held off the heat, but hated it for the sand. He supposed sand in this case, though, was the lesser of two evils, and so he trudged onwards with Asta in tow.

Night fell a few hours later. The heat left almost as quickly as daylight did, but the wind stayed behind, unwelcome on the cold, desert nights. They found a rocky overhang under which they could set up camp. It was sheltered from the wind—which had, apparently, decided to worsen.

"Will we be safe here?" Asked Asta, as she lowered her own pack onto the ground.

"We should be." He examined the rocks for searmarks, where demons had pressed hands or feet or claws. "It doesn't look like a lair of any kind. There are still a few days till the new moon. That's when the cycle peaks."

Asta looked comforted, though not entirely relieved.

Asta helped Esmond light a fire by collected dead bits of wood from around. Trees weren't tremendously common out in the desert, but common enough to allow for a fire. He cast a fire spell to ignite the wood, though it was difficult with the cold.

They settled down on opposite sides of the fire. Esmond pulled his coat tighter around him, buttoning it up the front.

"You aren't cold over there?" He asked, nodding to Asta. Trousers and a shirt couldn't have been tremendously warm.

"I'm fine. Don't really feel the cold."

She sounded certain of herself, almost cavalier. That was enough for him.

While sitting around the fire, gnawing on hare meat, Asta began to ask questions.

"What's the jitterrat for?" She asked.

"Peaceful company," Esmond replied. He hoped that was hint enough for Lymon to stay silent.

"And are you married?"

"I was married," he replied.

"And where's your wife?"

"Elsewhere."

"And does she worry about you at all."

"I said were married. Past tense."

"Yeah, so does she worry?"

"She doesn't know."

"She's dead," said Lymon.

Esmond could have picked up the jitterrat and flung him into the fire.

"Did that jitterrat just talk?"

"It did," Esmond said, "despite me telling him to keep his mouth shut."

"So much for peaceful company," Asta said. Esmond couldn't help but laugh. "Where'd you pick him up from?"

Esmond sighed. "I suppose we could do something to pass the time."

Lymon scurried down his arm and onto the sand. He circled the fire and clambered onto Asta's boot. She picked him up with a gentle touch.

"Are you sure you're not cold," Lymon said. "Your hands are freezing!"

Asta simply laughed.

"He was a demon attacking a village," Esmond began. "A conscience demon, as a matter of fact."

"Conscience demon?" Asked Asta. "I'm sorry, I'm not familiar with those. We mostly deal with sand and shadow demons in the canyon."

"They're not particularly common. They have no true physical form, really. If you were to look at them, you'd see a flicker of light. Nothing else. Makes it easy for them to go by undetected. A blur in your vision…it just looks like a stray thought, really. But they latch onto your mind and alter your decision-making. Tell you to go left when you want to go right. Have you slice into flesh when you want slice a carrot. Simple decision-making and morality. And yet they can be deadly. They feast on confusion. They take someone's intention, and do the opposite. You see that's how possession works. They wrap around a heart and change intention. That's what demons do; they possess. It's what they feed off. Conscience demons just happen to feed on opposites…on change and possibilities."

Lymon looked up to Asta, black eyes glimmering. "The human subconscious is a delicious thing."

"So how did you catch him?" She asked.

"I had him latch onto my own mind," Esmond said. "It wasn't particularly hard. Once he was in there, I somehow managed to overpower him. I cut away that part of me he was stuck on and put it into a jitterrat."

Asta cocked her head. "Don't you trailblazers kill demons?" she asked. "Isn't that…the whole point?"

"Well yes, usually, but because this one has no real physical form, it would take a complex procedure to do so. You'd have enough trouble keeping him contained, let alone disposing of him. There's that, and also the fact that a conscience demon with me could come in useful."

Asta looked down at the grey jitterrat. "But would he even listen if you asked him to do anything."

"We have an agreement of sorts."

"What's the agreement?"

"None of your business."

Asta frowned. Lymon returned to Esmond, scurrying into his pocket.

"We should sleep," Esmond said, rolling over, resting his head on his hands.

"Goodnight," Asta said.

Esmond didn't reply.

The following morning, Esmond woke to the sounds of shifting sands and smashing glass. He sat up suddenly, recoiling at the sight before him.

A fyreworm snaked barely a mile away through the sands. Its body shimmered with a deep, molten heat, which turned the sand to glass. As it trailed along, though, its tail whipped about in its wake, breaking the glass, shattering it into shards as large as a man's body.

"Fyreworm?" Asked Asta nonchalantly.

"Yes," Esmond said, not meaning to sound as surprised as he did. "How did you know?"

"We have them go by the canyon sometimes. They never come in. I think it's because they don't like the shadows."

"They don't," Esmond replied. "They like the sun. Keeps them hot."

The worm disappeared below the sand, leaving a great, glassy tunnel in its wake.

"We have to get moving. Come on."

They packed up camp, leaving the fire smoldering in the sand. Any demons wandering the desert would be drawn to it, instead of them.

The group crossed through the sand, towards where the worm had dove.

"Why are we going this way?" Asked Asta. "Wouldn't it make sense for us to go…elsewhere?"

"It's demon-forged glass," said Esmond. "I can't take much, but it's useful when battling demons." He found a shard, which was spiked on one end, yet bulbous and round on the other, like a knife. "This should do nicely." As he held it up, he examined the streaks of darkness within the perfectly clear glass.

"See those flecks?" He asked, pointing at the glass blade.

Asta nodded.

"They're actually parts of the demon. Like smoke from a flame, or condensation from cold. It just so happens that these flecks contain aspects of the demon. That one was a fyreworm, so those flecks can create fire, should we need it." He tucked it into the pack. "I hope we don't though. Come on."

For most of the day, the wind continued to bluster, billowing out Esmond's cloak, threatening to blast his hat from his head.

"Bloody wind," he muttered, holding his arm up to protect his face as the sand blustered in his face.

"Sorry," said Asta.

"It happens," Esmond replied. He pushed onwards, through the sand. "It what we deserve for deciding to go through the desert."

He checked his compass-watch, nodded eastwards, and began in that direction.

As they walked, Asta sang a song of some sort. She hummed it mostly, though occasionally she whistled. It sounded sad… apologetic almost, but Esmond didn't ask into it.

That night, when they made camp, they set it up beside a large boulder. It didn't protect them as much as the overhang had, but it kept some of the sand out of their faces, and allowed a fire to burn. Asta watched in amazement as he again used his staff to ignite the flames.

"So how come you need that spike of glass if you can do that with your stick?"

"It's a staff," he corrected, throwing a handful more wood on the fire, "and I need the spike because the fire that comes from that will be useful for killing a demon. I don't need to kill a demon every time I light a fire, do I? I just need enough of a spark to light some dry wood. Demons…are much…trickier. I mean, the amount of energy I would expend on a single spell would probably kill me. We can't have that."

"Then why didn't you grab more of the glass?" She asked.

"Well if it breaks," he replied, "or if the two glass shards struck one another…the result would not have been pretty. They're volatile things. I've seen them do terrible things to man if used incorrectly. A single tap..." he banged his staff against the boulder and a shower of sparks fell from the tip, "...and it can tear a person to shreds."

Lymon leapt from his shoulder, twirling about in mid-air, before he hit the sand with a light thump. There, he lay for a moment, feigning death, before shaking himself to functionality once more.

With that piece of knowledge, Asta shuffled away from the pack, hesitant to even grab the food for the night from within. Once again, Esmond marveled at her ability to brave the cold without even a coat. Her shirt was only thin canvas, and yet she didn't show any hint of shivering. She began to hum that same song again. She picked up where she had left it off. Still, it sounded repentant... rueful, like it was a song that begged for its own forgiveness.

"There's more to you than meets the eye," Esmond said from across the fire. He rested his arm on his knee, removing his hat and sitting it beside him. "Isn't there?"

Asta appeared taken aback, the song stopping abruptly. "What makes you say that?"

He smiled, knowing he was right. "The way you act," he said. "When I first saw you, I was expecting someone more...delicate. Everyone is. For someone who's running from something, you are certainly braver than first impressions. You're the first person who I've guided across the desert here who hasn't run off screaming at the first sight of a fyreworm. You're the first person who, after the first bluster of sandy wind, hasn't had second thoughts and returned to town." He leaned in closer to the fire. "For someone who's asking me to guide them through the sandy desert, and on the eve of the new moon, you're awfully calm." He leaned back haughtily. "That and you're not cold. There is no way in hell you aren't cold!"

"I thought you said you don't like to get to know your passengers," she said.

"I don't," he said quickly. He took a moment, staring out over the desert. "I make these rules for a reason. But you," he turned back to her, staring into her eyes, "you're different. There's something about you that tells me to ask you these things. There's something I need to know here."

Asta was silent. Her expression was stony. Sad. Troubled, even. Esmond would have smiled in triumph were it not for the way she stared at him now. She looked almost sick, like she was ready to empty her stomach.

"A demon killed my family," she said quietly. "A wind demon. It swept into the village on a strong breeze one morning and tore apart my house...my family. The following night, it tore up another house and then another the night after." She paused here, biting her lip. "It hasn't appeared for almost a month now, but I can...feel that the demon's going to return. You said they're most active on the night of the new moon, so I guess I got out of town quickly enough."

"So why Rarelane?" Asked Esmond.

"It's as far away as I can get from the village," she said. "I could have picked Kirville or Rockston, but they weren't far enough away. I needed to put as much distance between me and the canyon."

"You picked a good time for it, then, what with the new moon tomorrow night. We won't get into Rarelane until tomorrow afternoon, so long as the weather stays as good as it has been, and so long as no demons attack."

"I'm surprised we haven't seen more," Asta said, staring out over the desert. "I expected more, truthfully. The whole point of you trailblazers is to keep the demons away, and I haven't needed you once!"

Esmond laughed. "That's because I've been keeping the demons away." He then laughed again, louder this time. It had been a long time since he had laughed that loudly, and he doubted he would again any time soon.

"Well I've told you something about me," Asta said, "now it's your turn to tell me something."

"That's not how this works," Esmond said, rising suddenly. He turned away from the fire, surveying the desert. In the very far distance, he saw the shimmering body of a fyreworm as it snaked its way through the dunes. Its body glowed in the night a deep, bloody red. Fissures of gold broke out across its length. Its body hissed in the distance with each blast of pressurised heat it released.

"That is how this works," retorted Asta, rising up herself. The wind lifted suddenly, blustering with an unusual strength.

"Well what is there to know about me?" He asked. "What could you possibly want to know that would make this a fair trade?" He stopped, bowing his head.

"Your wife," Asta said. "What happened to her?"

Esmond's heart stopped in his chest. He took in a deep breath, accidentally inhaling sand. He coughed and spluttered his guts out, thumping his chest with a heavy hand.

"I'm sorry," Asta said. "I shouldn't have...never mind."

"Don't worry," Esmond said, waving dismissively.

For a time there was only silence between them, and the distant cracking of cooling glass.

"But what did happen to her?" She asked.

The jitterrat scampered across the sand, up his leg and to Esmond's shoulder. Esmond glanced at Lymon.

"Conscience demon," he replied in a dead monotone.

Asta fell silent. Her breathing stopped. Esmond felt as her eyes deflected elsewhere. Even the wind seemed to silence itself, leaving Esmond alone in his quiet remembrance. She didn't ask anything else.

The following morning, both Asta and Esmond were quiet. They were on the final leg of their journey today and as far as Esmond was concerned, he would be quite happy to see her go. The crossing had been without incident, but he had grown far too comfortable with this woman. Once she was gone, he could get back to his time with Lymon only. This was why he didn't have company too often. This was why he hated people. They asked questions, tried to make friends, when all he wanted was a quiet place in the world where he could settle down and live out the rest of his days.

Thankfully, though, Asta was silent for the remainder of the trip. Night began to fall as they neared Rarelane. With this darkness, though, came a stirring in the desert. There was no moon in the sky, only gloom and the occasional star, sneaking a shining glimpse through the clouds.

The wind, too, decided to grow restless, carrying with it sand and debris. Asta seemed untroubled, but Esmond held up a hand to shield his eyes from sand.

"We should stop," called Asta, her voice almost lost to the wind.

"No! We're nearly there!" Called Esmond. "We have to keep going!"

"I think we should stop," said Asta. "I...I...I...."

But she never finished that sentence.

"Asta?" Esmond cried, turning around. The woman was barely visible through the sand and the black of night, yet somehow he was able to see a small silhouette. It was hunched over, groaning loudly. "Asta?" He asked again. Still no reply. Lymon was shivering on his shoulder, muttering something.

"Demon," Lymon whispered. "Nearby." The jitterrat shuffled deeper into Esmond's coat.

"Where?" Esmond asked, squinting through the sandstorm. It had grown stronger in the last minute, howling like a sandy devil.

"There," said Lymon, his body becoming utterly straight like a plant, pointing into the depths of the storm.

A tornado of sand whipped up around Asta. Esmond began to flee when the tornado started to shimmer, flashing with sparks of flame. The flames were gold and scarlet, flashing to brilliant life for a moment before they disappeared into the funnel of wind. Asta screamed, her voice somehow heard over the heat and wind.

"Wind demon," Lymon said.

"You don't think I don't know that already?" Cried Esmond. He gripped his staff tightly. He wanted the demon-wrought glass spike, but that lay in the pack and Asta had been the one carrying that.

"ASTA!" Cried Esmond, turning around. He was sure she had already been whipped up by the demon. He imagined now her body being found on a dune somewhere, thrown miles from where she had stood before. No one could survive a direct strike from a wind demon.

"You think it followed her?" Asked Lymon.

"I imagine it did," Esmond replied. He turned now, believing he had enough distance between him and the demon. Without the demon-wrought glass, he wouldn't be strong enough to kill the demon, but he could send it running.

The tornado continued to spiral, as a great, draconian shape appeared within. A pair of wings emerged from the wall of the storm, both white and opaque like glass. Within those wings, Esmond saw a channel of vein-like rivers of blue power, flowing and pulsing. A long, spined tail emerged next, filled with holes that whistled as the wind blew through them. And then finally the head, attached to a long, swan-like neck. Its body was feathered with glass-like spines, all of which howled whistled and howled.

Esmond fought the desire to cover his ears as he stared into the glowing, white eyes of the wind demon. The beast flapped its wings, chiming a painful chord. Then it roared, its cry like a screech. It took to the sky, carried on a current of air it summoned with its call.

Esmond gripped his staff tightly. He raced across the sand, facing the sand and the beast, refusing to remove his gaze. He struck his staff on the ground, once near enough to strike. A flash of light, a flip in the air, and he beat at the demon's tail. The staff sung against the glass, chiming in harmony with the whistling. The demon screamed, though.

As he sailed, though, his eyes caught sight of the pack on the ground. The demon-wrought glass lay within. There was no sign of Asta, though. He felt a pang of sadness. This is why it's bad to care.

There was hope, though. If he could get to the pack, he could take the spike and kill the demon. He wasn't able to get Asta to safety, but he could kill the demon. He could find a small, merciful happiness within that.

He gave it no chance to retaliate with that barbed tail. He spun around, the second his feet hit the ground, lifting the staff up to block as the beast made a swipe at him with its wing. Wood met glass, flames spewed from the place they met, and again the glass sung. And the song was familiar.

I know that song, he thought. It was a sad tune. Apologetic.

I'm sorry, he heard, whispered on the wind, in a voice he knew.

The demon hung in the air, peaceful in its flight.

The demon isn't chasing Asta, he thought as he heard that song again. That same song sung by Asta. Asta is the demon. It's possessed her. It killed her family.

He raced for the pack while the beast was calm, snatching it out from underneath. The glass tail struck him, though, throwing him aside. He struck the side of a dune with a loud thump, forcing the wind from his lungs. He held the pack in his hands, though. He hugged it fast to his chest as he caught his breath. He threw open the flap, reaching in, finding the demon-wrought glass within. Flecked with red, but otherwise perfectly clear, the spike seemed to hum in the presence of the demon.

Lymon scampered up to him, climbed up his leg.

"She's possessed," said Esmond.

"She's doomed, then," said Lymon.

With the spike in his hand, Esmond understood what Lymon meant. Asta's soul and the demon's soul were intertwined. That was how possession worked. If he struck the wind demon with the spike, then he was striking Asta, too, and she would surely die.

"This is why I try not to care," Esmond said. "This is why I keep my distance." He swore quietly.

The demon flew at him, its glass talons bared, singing all the while.

"Asta!" He cried, leaping out of the way. He held out his staff, feeling as it beat against the glass. Sparks rained, scattering on the sand.

The beast seemed to listen, stopping for a moment... but only a moment. It was quick to swoop in again for another air strike.

I can't kill her... but the demon... He lay his body down in the sand, keeping his head down. Lymon fell beside him, hiding beneath his hat. Esmond looked up at the jitterrat, and an idea struck him.

"Lymon, remember our agreement?" He asked.

"Of course," Lymon said, poking his head from out underneath the hat.

"I need you to keep it," Esmond said. "I'm trusting you'll do the right thing. I need you to stop...that." He pointed at the demon.

It swept over them, its talons slicing the air frightfully close to Esmond's neck.

"Of course," Lymon said.

"I need you to do this!" Esmond said. "I need you to keep your bargain."

Lymon's face showed little expression, but in those eyes he saw a mischievous glint.

"Lymon!"

"Afraid to trust a demon?"

Esmond stared at the jitterrat. His heart felt impossibly unsure of his actions, but it was, in truth, the only possibility.

"Of course I am," Esmond said, over the whistling storm. "But that doesn't mean I don't."

He pulled his staff up from his side, gripping it tightly. He whispered into the wind, summoning a spell of unbinding. Then, he tapped the jitterrat. The small, grey rodent began to shudder, its body bubbling beneath its fur as if its insides were boiling. The creature's eyes bugged out of its head. It squealed and ran about.

I trust you, Lymon, he thought, as he watched the jitterrat begin to fly. Don't betray me.

Asking a demon not to betray him? He might as well ask the wind to stop blowing, or the stars to stop shining. He'd have a better chance at those, at least.

Lymon's body fell away like a cocoon breaking, the layers of skin and muscle, blood and bone falling away, leaving only a glimmering speck of light, barely the size of a dust particle. It hung in the air for a moment.

"Lymon." His brow furrowed, Esmond said with a warning tone.

The light disappeared suddenly, Esmond's gaze rising to the wind demon. It seemed to have stopped its flight. It roared, but was cut short, like it was choking. Esmond watched as Lymon wrapped itself around the demon's heart, choking its intentions away from it.

If he could change the demon's mind, he might be able to stop the demon from killing that night. Then, once the possession had ended, they could continue to Rarelane. His job would be done. What Asta did from there was up to her.

But something was wrong. The demon struggled to stay airborne. It fought to scream.

It wrestled to stay in possession of Asta.

Of course! Esmond thought, slamming a triumphant fist into the sand. He's changing the intention of the demon. He doesn't want it to not attack. He wants it to stop its possession. He paused, realising the implications. He separating the two hearts so that I can kill just the demon. He hadn't even thought of that. Conscience demons worked entirely on intentional opposition. The demon's drive is to possess, so he was making it do the opposite.

You are brilliant, Lymon, he thought. "Brilliant."

Sure enough, the two beings separated. The bird, hanging in the air by strength of will alone, shuddered as a collection of cracks opened up across the beast's torso. A few moments later, this glass torso smashed and out burst a woman. Asta.

Now, he thought, taking a deep breath in. He gripped the demon-wrought glass spike and charged at the demon. He hit the staff tip on the ground, giving him a burst of energy, bouncing him off the surface. He sailed through the air off that beat and slammed into the demon's body, stabbing at the glass with the knife.

The glass struck the demon, shimmering a brilliant gold. It sung.

A blast of heat.

A wave of light.

The sound of glass smashing.

And then darkness.

Esmond awoke on the sand, as the dawn light began its rise over the eastern horizon. It took a short while for his memory to return, but he found it shortly.

"Asta!" He cried, lifting himself off the ground. His body ached, his clothes were charred, the stubble on his face burnt away. "Asta!"

"I'm here," she said. The air was still this morning. For the first time since leaving the canyon, the world was silent.

"Thank goodness." She had a handful of minor burns on her body, but nothing that time wouldn't heal.

He couldn't feel Lymon nearby, though. For the first time, he was alone. Truly alone.

"Let's get you to Rarelane." She nodded.

He dropped her off outside the city, just outside the gate. The walls protecting the city were made of grey stone, the gate itself a thick metal barrier. As he neared, he took note of the demon glass embedded into the metal, wondering what wards were placed on them. A small part of him—the part he felt was left by his time spent with Lymon—wanted to test them.

"This is where I leave you," he said. He removed his hat and nodded a polite farewell.

"Thank you," Asta said, gently. On their short walk since morning to the city he had explained what Lymon had done, in fulfilling his contract, and in separating the demon from her. He explained how he used the glass, and how, if she saw a doctor within, she would be quite all right and those burns would not turn septic.

"You going to be all right?" Asta asked, turning back from the city gates. "I mean…you don't have Lymon any more."

"I'll be all right," Esmond said. "I'm meant to be alone, anyway. Trailblazers…we're a solitary sort. I'll be fine. My job's done. Now go."

She nodded, turning to the city. The gates opened before her, groaning on iron hinges. It wasn't a grand city inside, like those hinted at when speaking of the Old-world. But it was a city, filled with people, and life. Esmond stared down that wide boulevard, at the tree growing in the centre of the street, marveling at what good staff wood that would be.

Someday, he thought, turning from the city and from Asta. He stepped down the rocky hill, returning to the sandy dunes and the desert that stretched on forever.

Wisps

Michael Tager

As the light dimmed, Garth eyed the game trail he'd been following. He had a brace of hares slung over his shoulder already and, if he hurried, he'd certainly make it back to more familiar surroundings before night fell. It wasn't wise to stay out too late this far from the village. The wisps, while not dangerous, would certainly delight in leading him far astray. They were said to be men who had given their soul to the Fae.

Garth didn't believe about the souls, despite what his grandfather had told him, but he still didn't want to find out, or test the wisps by following. He'd learned his way around the woods in the past year, hunting with his sling. If he ever became lost, he'd find his way home, but he had no desire to put up with the jeers that would follow if the will-o-the-wisps. He was better than a silly Imperial.

He'd just decided to head home when he a wisp popped into existence, just off the dirt path beneath his feet. It hung in the air, glowing in time with Garth's breaths, illuminating a scrap of fabric half-hidden by an ivy-covered branch. He'd encountered many wisps in his time and they all functioned the same: fluttering about, attempting to confuse and befuddle. But this one did none of that, but simply floated, pulsating. Despite his better instincts, Garth stepped closer, his eyes adjusting to the light. A few steps more and the wisp disappeared, just as he snatched the fabric from the branch.

It was a long strip of red kerchief, darkened and torn by the elements and the years. "Grandfather," Garth muttered. He wrapped the kerchief around his hand, eying the forest before him. One year ago, Garth had watched as his grandfather packed food and supplies for a week's stint in the forest surrounding their village, the northernmost outpost of the empire. "I know the woods, boy, don't you worry. Who taught you after all?" His grandfather had laughed, tied a red bandanna on his bald scalp to protect from the sun, strapped his old imperial battle-axe – from his soldier days – to his still-strong back and walked through the home he shared with his son and grandson. "I learned what I know from your grandmother, bless her soul." He stopped at the doorway and turned. He had a pack slung about a shoulder and Garth could see more kerchiefs, tightly bound into a ball.

Facing his grandfather, Garth saw the map of his own future: the same dark blue eyes, the same bushy eyebrows, nearly identical stocky frames. He wondered just how much of his grandmother was in him. He'd heard rumors that she was Fae. All he knew was that his grandmother had disappeared shortly after giving birth.

"I'm going to find her," his grandfather said. "I think I know the way this time." He smiled and waved and never returned.

Just as Garth finished wrapping the scrap of red around his large palm, the wisp returned, floating soundlessly between two poplars. Clutching the fabric, Garth shuffled toward it, through thick underbrush. Small thorns from wild roses and brier patches tore at his leather vest and sturdy trousers. The wisp continued to wait until he nearly reached it before fading into the shadows. He waited for it to reappear and regarded his surroundings.

Deep into the wild forest, further off the well-traveled animal trails that the villagers traveled, he stood on the lip of a valley. Hearing rushing water, he made his way down the steep hill, keeping his feet by digging into the hard earth with his fingers. The great river that cut the forest in two, separating the Fae-lands from the empire, shouldn't be here, Garth thought, continuing to follow the sounds, through the untamed foliage. Soon, he stopped and scratched his thin beard. "What is this?" He asked the wisp as it appeared. It illuminated the large, lichen-covered marble bridge that spanned the wide, rushing river.

According to legend, bridges connecting the empire to the Fae lands used to be regularly spaced along the rushing waters of the unnamed river. Soon after the Great War in which the Fae took their independence however, a great wind rose and rushed through the forest, tumbling each bridge into the waters below. The bridges would have been marked by a circle within a circle within a circle, the symbol of the old world.

"They represent forever," his grandfather once said as he smoked on his pipe. His white eyebrows bulged above his pale blue eyes. "The people of the old world were sure they would stand the test of time, that nothing could disturb their dominance."

"And what happened?"

Grandfather smiled. "Something disturbed them." In his hands, he had turned over a tarnished belt buckle, emblazoned with three circles, one inside another.

Centuries of leaves had fallen, burying the bridge several feet deep in rotting flora. Garth scraped detritus away from the bridge's edge with the toe of his leather boots, then with his hands, until the white rock of the bridge was exposed. Each stone was marked with the three circles of the old world. "Shit," he said, resting his back on the bridge wall.

That it still stood after a thousand years, he could barely comprehend. The layers of dirt he'd unearthed had turned up animal bones, desiccated fabric, even old coins and a metal belt buckle, nearly obliterated with rust. Grandfather was right, he suddenly realized, standing and stepping onto the bridge. He must have found it before he left.

Garth tested the bridge, gingerly at first, then with more confidence. They made well in the old world, he thought. The walls of the bridge came to his chest and were thicker than the walls of the home he shared with his parents and Grandfather. It spanned the entire river, perhaps one hundred yards across. The waters rushed quickly below. Large boulders broke the water, black and jagged. No one had tried to swim the Nameless River in decades; most, Garth included, could barely keep their head above water for long enough to bathe.

Beyond the bridge was an ancient road of cobblestones, half-covered by dirt. It was even, unbroken after countless years. Plants grew between the stones but had barely budged the stone. It was hard walking on the dirt paths of the village, as pitted and hole-ridden they were. The old world path, however, seemed nearly perfectly preserved.

The sun continued to fall and more wisps appeared, first a handful, then dozens and finally more than he could count. He had never seen so many before. Closer to the village, they came out in ones and sometimes twos. Most villagers ignored them, used to their ways, but the garrison of guardsmen was made of less stern stuff. New recruits were constantly disappearing, only to be found days later, wandering and dehydrated. Once, one turned up in the middle of the village, nude but for his cape.

The soft purple light of the countless wisps fell on the road, lighting it into the distance as it gradually rose and fell from sight. The wisps behaved as he'd become used to, darting from place to place, never staying still, their light casting ever-changing patterns of shadows on the ground. But they did not fade from sight and the path remained well-lighted. Game trails ran parallel for a time before veering off, but none crossed over. It was if the animals shunned the way.

Garth gripped the red fabric, indecisive. He knew he should return, come back when the light was out. But can I find it again? He doubted it.

"Grandfather must have come this way," he said. While he stood, debating, he saw another wisp glow into being. It was off the trail far away from the other and it hovered next to a pile of rubble. From the pile, a scrap of red hung limply. When he gasped, the wisp disappeared, as if in response. He had left the trail and was besides the pile of stones before he knew it. Picking up one piece to tug out the fabric, he turned it over in his hands. The stones were ancient brick, of strong, fine material. The same material as the road. What used to be here? He wondered.

When Garth was ten, grandfather had taken him exploring in nearby caves, just south of the wide river. They yielded riches for a boy: an ancient spear, mostly rust and rotten wood. Some silver coins with lilting script, nothing like Imperial marks. He asked where they'd come from, what they were.

In the forest, Grandfather explained, were countless relics of the old world, left alone by the Fae for lack of need. It had been a thousand years since the end of the war; much had been destroyed by time. "On our side of the river, we come across their remains: pieces of road or rusted metal. I bet on their side there are more, much more." He paused and sucked on his pipe, blowing fragrant smoke. "If only we could find one of those bridges; one must still be intact."

Ten-year old Garth had protested. "Some say that the forest is. That animals walk like men and women made of wood take your member and your soul." He continued, unconsciously aping the style of the minstrels who occasionally visited the village and told the tales. "They say that the 'wisps lead you off to the God of the Forest. They say that The Forest Lord is a deer with the face of a lion. Or a great eagle with a bear's body."

Grandfather grew quiet as they sat in the shade of an oak. It was dusk and the wisps began to appear in the shadows, glowing with their purple light. "I saw it once," he said. "When your grandmother left."

The old man shook his head and continued. "It had great antlers and the body of a man and it took her from me. She was in a clearing, far in the east, following the wisps. I saw it from a distance." He closed his eyes and said no more.

Garth replaced the scrap of red in case he got lost. "That's good enough for me," he said, returning to the road. Before he set out, he draped his nearly-forgotten hairs on the side of the bridge, checked his sling, belt knife and the flagon of water attached to his belt by string. When satisfied, he took a deep breath and set out.

After several minutes of walking, turning deeper into the woods, the path eventually forked. Garth stood and pondered: both directions looked the same, nearly featureless. One ran a little bit uphill, the other into a slightly more densely wooded area. Otherwise, they were identical. He scratched his chin until he noticed, tied to a low-hanging branch, another weather-beaten kerchief. "Thanks, Grandfather," he said starting uphill.

The path grew hilly though still densely forested. Twice more the path branched but each time, Garth found the red banners marking the way. The second time, he'd almost given up, unable to find anything. He stopped in the middle of the path and rested his face in his hands, unsure of which way to turn. The whole world was awash still in soft purple light, the sky hidden by foliage

After a moment, one wisp darted into the middle of the path, flickering about his face. The others remained on the side of the path. "What do you want?" He asked. "He was here, I know he is," he said, as if the wisp could understand. The excitement he felt overwhelmed logic and prudent fear, but now that he couldn't find his grandfather's last marker, caution came back to his mind. "Help me or not," he said, waving his hand before his face.

The wisp, darted around his hand and floated to the fork, glowing brighter and brighter as it did. Garth followed the wisp when it delved off the track and fluttered about a mound of earth. "Do you want me to follow you?" Garth asked. His voice sounded loudly in the still, dark night. For the first time, he realized that he hadn't heard a single animal since crossing the bridge.

He shrugged and continued. "In for a penny," he muttered, stooping to the ground and pawing at the earth. Soon, he revealed a soggy cloth, black with dirt, but still showing vestiges of red dye.

He turned to the wisp and smiled. "Thanks," he said. The wisp glowed once and drifted back to join its fellows along the road. He wondered, as he started down the right fork, if maybe the wisps had been trying to lead people here. They seemed awfully behaved.

The further he walked, the more he came across. At first, he'd see rubble along the side of the road, bits of old world homesteads, perhaps. But as he continued, he saw vine-encrusted signposts dotting the path in regular intervals. They were written in the ancient language, he saw when he stopped to tear vines off of one, the familiar three circles making their appearance. He wished he could read the text.

In the stories the villagers told, the Fae-lands were filled with treasure looted from the humans. But grandfather had told him something else. That the only treasure the Fae had that wasn't theirs by right, was an old pendant that the ancient rulers had worn. It had been lost centuries past, before Grandfather's grandfather had been born. It was made from fine material, amber mixed with steel. It was said to harness the wind and rain. One day, the ruler of the country went into the woods himself, some said because of the wisps, some said because he found a sign of the old world.

"He never came back," Grandfather had said. "That was before the Empire came and conquered what was left of the old world: a few villages, nothing more. I wonder what would have happened, if we had had the sigil, the pendant. Would we be part of the Empire now?"

Crumbled brick walls bordered empty fields that had once been cultivated; wild wheat grew in one, apple orchards in another. The higher Garth went the more remnants of buildings appeared. Most had once been small homes, none grandiose. Clumps of foundations rested along a stream and, near another field, were the remains of what had probably been a manor house. Despite his vague unease, excitement rose. What was Grandfather leading him to?

The night wore on and the path grew steeper. A peculiar calm fell over Garth the higher he climbed and the darker it became. The path continued to be lit by the purple light of the floating wisps. The piles of dirt and leaves grew sparse and the white brick of the road gleamed. This is what Grandfather saw, he told himself. He imagined the excitement in his grandfather's stomach as he trod the same path, what his grandfather hoped for.

After a particularly steep hill and a sharp turn around a smooth, round boulder the size of a mule, the cover of the forest actually came away entirely to reveal a breathtaking vista. For miles around the forest stretched, vaster than Garth had ever imagined. The way south – toward home – was obstructed by the woods, but to the north, the panorama stretched to the horizon and beyond, seeming to melt into the stars and risen moon. The treetops glowed purple and a sea of will-o-the-wisps lit the night sky. "The old world?" He whispered.

He shook his head and followed the path around the bend of the hill. Abruptly, the road tilted downward and ended at a long staircase with tall guardrails, tarnished by time. Vines grew over the top of the stairs, enclosing it entirely. Running his fingers above his head, Garth felt a thin metal trellis over which the vines grew. "Hello?" He called into the staircase.

One of the wisps again drifted in front of him. "You again?" He asked, recognizing it by its static movement. The wisp glowed, then darted down the stairs. He followed, ducking.

He took the steps quickly, the bare stone firm and clean of debris. After the fiftieth step he paused to rest his aching feet. After the hundredth, he still could not see the ground. The wisp hung in the air just before him, glowing. "I'm coming," he muttered.

After the three hundredth step, he emerged from the stairwell. He was at the base of a hill, before him a vast pile of ruins. The outermost building had been a tower. A tattered red handkerchief flew from a ground-level window.

The wisp entered the ruins. Garth followed, swinging his head to take in his surroundings. The further he went, the less-decrepit the buildings grew. They were all made of the same white marble, marked with the three circles. Soon, he stopped before a pristine-seeming building, a sign hanging from the front. He couldn't read what it said, but he recognized an inn when he saw one. No light shone from the windows and, when he ran a finger down the heavy oaken door, he disturbed a fine layer of dust. He turned to the wisp.

"What do you want from me?" He asked. "What is this?"

It shone brighter and pulsed in rapid waves. He sensed that it meant no harm.

His voice quiet, he asked, "Do you know where my grandfather is?"

The light contracted to a tiny circle hanging in the air. Then it drifted away, toward the center of the ruins. "Why should I follow you?" He asked. It didn't stop, but floated through a narrow alley between thick buildings that rose to the sky.

The alley ended in a broad thoroughfare; across it, the wisp darted into another alley, which turned into a street. He followed, the buildings crowding each other, all empty. When the alley turned, he turned, seeing the wisp just ahead, pulsing, waiting for him to approach before it took off again. The cycle repeated many times, until he was hopelessly lost. He stopped and rubbed the heel of his palm against his eyes when he turned a corner to see an empty courtyard, no wisp to be found.

"I can't believe it," he said. He'd lived among the wisps for his whole life. His grandfather – and everyone else– had warned him a hundred times to never follow the wisps. And yet he'd done so, further than he could imagine.

Garth took a deep breath, feeling a strange surge of joy. He savored the taste of the night air. He had discovered something! He had followed his grandfather's trail and stood in what could be the ancient city of the Fae. He'd get home if he had to bull through the forest itself. He'd be able to tell everyone. "I'll find you another time, Grandfather," he said.

He turned to leave, hoping to find his way back when the wisp appeared before him. It pulsed once and then came close, so that it nearly touched his nose. This close, it emitted a faint heat. "What?" He asked. "Tell me."

"Turn around, boy," a deep voice said...

He hadn't really looked at the massive courtyard before. It was larger than he'd thought, big enough to fit his entire village inside. The space was defined by four towers in the corners that gleamed in the moonlight. They looked new, unlike the crumbled pillars or stairs leading nowhere that littered the landscape. In the center was a stone dais with marble steps. And in the very center of the dais was a throne.

The throne was made of granite and marble; gold gilt along the edge. It was polished and clean, free of the contamination of the years. An old man, though still powerful and strong, sat dressed in a woolen robe with a simple golden circlet around his dark gray-and-red hair. His eyes were deep-set and flickered green, a thin smile on his lips. From his head sprouted a set of majestic antlers,

310

also a dark green. An amber pendant hung around his neck. When he beckoned for Garth to approach, he knew he was looking at the King of the Forest.

The Forest King rose, a smile on his face, and raised his hand. Garth stopped. Around him, in the shadows of the courtyard, Garth saw countless eyes, almond shaped with vertical slits, the dim light reflected in their pupils. "Why are you here, boy?" He asked. His voice was cracking ice.

He managed a squeak. "I'm looking for my grandfather." Garth paused. "He left us a year ago. I've followed his tracks."

The Forest King laughed and sat. He clicked his fingers and the wisp zipped over to him, settling by his ear. It was if the king was listening to it speak.

"Did you ever think he might not want to be found?" The king asked as the wisp rested near the king's antlers.

"I – no –it led me here." Garth pointed at the wisp. "I thought my grandfather sent it."

The king nodded. "Maybe he did, in a way. But did he want you to come for him?" Again, the king snapped his fingers and from the shadows strode forth a woman, lithe and fit, with long blonde hair and angular features. She wore a shift of leather and leaves, and downy fur ran along her bare arms. Her steps were graceful. Something about her was familiar. She strode to the Forest King and touched his arm.

Suddenly, she pointed at Garth, speaking in a guttural language he did not understand. The king nodded, his grin widening, showing square, yellowish teeth. "Come closer, boy," he said, his voice ringing. It was deep and powerful and it reached Garth's belly, twisting it in knots.

Garth was afraid he'd lose control of his bladder in the surge of fear. His journey through the darkness and ruins suddenly seemed an idyll.

Each step seemed to take a year but soon enough, he was at the foot of the throne. Close up, they seemed less human, more fearsome. When the woman smiled and Garth saw tiny fangs protruding from her mouth. The wisp now seemed to dance weaving through her long hair.

Garth focused on the King. With every step, the King had smiled broader and stood taller. He twirled the pendant around his neck and touched the woman. "He is blood," she said, nodding. "It should be his." She walked down the steps to Garth and took his hand, kissing the tips of his fingers. "Yes, he is blood indeed."

Confused, Garth attempted a bow. He flushed at her harsh laugh.

The Fae-woman turned and loped back to the shadows, the wisp following. While Garth waited, fighting confusion and fear, the King stood. From his back, he took up a battle-axe, polished and shining. He threw it into the air with one large hand and caught it by the handle. He extended it to Garth who took it, despite its weight. "From your other blood," he said.

He knew immediately that the axe was his grandfather's.

The King smiled again and touched the pendant. It was amber, bound by iron. "Well, boy?" He asked. "What say you?"

Garth let the axe slide from his fingers and watched the wisp float back from the shadows. It whirled around the forest king's antlers, resting finally at the pendant. It glowed.

"What about the pendant?" He asked. He wanted to ask about his grandfather. Where is he? He wanted to scream.

The forest king frowned. "What about it, boy? It is not from your blood."

"It's ours, though, isn't it? It belonged to our village and was lost. My grandfather told me." His voice quavered and his hand twitched toward his belt, to his slingshot.

Glowering, the forest king stood and stepped down from the dais, stopping one step away from Garth. He radiated an intense heat and smelled of deep musk. The wisp hovered by his shoulder and the forest king snorted, swatting at it with a massive hand. "Your grandfather is well-informed, it seems." Again, the king swatted at the wisp, ineffectually. "What of it?"

"I want it back." He thrust forth his chin, set his jaw. "It's ours."

For a moment, Garth was sure he was finished. The forest king's eyes glowed red and he raised his hand, his fingers ending in long, thick black claws. Garth backed up, plucking his sling from his belt and filling it with a small stone. He swung it around in a tight circle.

The forest king stared at him before his eyes opened wide and he threw back his head in laughter. "Go ahead, boy," he said. "Do your worst."

Garth released one stone, then in quick succession two more.

312

They flew straight and true. The first bounced harmlessly off the king's chest, the next off his shoulder and the final off his temple. The king blinked at the last and grinned.

"No one has ever…," he began. He returned to his throne. The wisp hovered by his ear and again, it seemed he listened. Finally, the forest king grunted and touched the pendant. He removed it and tossed it at Garth, who snagged it with one hand. "The man who gave it to me begged for his life. You fight for yours. I am impressed." He paused and waved at the wisp, which faded into the night. "You are the second of your blood to impress me."

Garth carefully put the pendant around his neck. He felt the heat within. Ignoring it for the moment, he lifted his head. "What happened to my grandfather? I need to understand."

The king frowned, unused, it seemed, to questions. "It is not my place to tell you if the old man didn't."

Garth closed his eyes. "Please tell me. What happened to my grandfather?"

The Forest King's frown deepened. "Your understanding does not concern me." He stood as if to leave. The Forest King was massive, as wide across as any two men from the village and tall as a horse, corded with muscle. And I threw pebbles at him.

He swallowed and raised a hand, "Wait, sir."

The Forest King stopped and turned to face Garth, his eyes wide and filled with incredulity. "You dare?" He asked, making a fist with his hand. Vines, thick as Garth's thighs, burst from the ground before him, wrapping themselves around Garth's body and lifting him aloft. "I am not your servant, human. You are here in breach of the treaty, suffered to live only because two of your blood in my service requested a favor." The king stepped from his dais and gazed at Garth, his eyes ice. Even held aloft, Garth was a head below the king.

Without breaking eye contact, the king lifted one arm and peremptorily waved to the shadows. His head free, Garth craned to see the spindly legged thing that approached. It was even taller than the king, but willow-thin and covered in bark. It had an ethereal, alien beauty.

"If this boy ever returns," the Forest King began, "you are tasked with bringing him directly to me for … punishment." He smiled. "Do you understand, elf?" The thin creature nodded, bowed and returned to the shadows. The lord then waved his hands, the vines drooping to the earth with it, releasing Garth heavily to the ground. "Your blood won't save you next time, my servants or no." Garth bowed his head and nodded.

The Forest King sighed, covered his mouth with one suddenly-disinterested hand. "I tire of this," he said, snapping his fingers a third and final time.

The pendant grew bright and overwhelmed Garth. He knew no more.

When Garth woke, he was astounded to find himself on the middle of the bridge, wrapped in leaves. The rising sun shone through the leaves above. Grandfather's battle-axe lay propped up against the railing, blades obscuring the triple-circles. He sat up and rubbed his eyes. A single 'wisp hung in the air, despite the early morning sun. "Grandfather?" Garth asked. It flickered once, twice, and then was gone. Garth touched the pendant, wet with the morning dew.

The bridge ended just beyond him, water rushing below. It was an even break, like a giant had cut it with shears. Garth frowned and stared at the opposite shore where, even through the dark, he saw a slim figure with blonde hair disappear into the woods.

He hoisted the axe onto his shoulder and left the bridge. "I'm going home," Garth said, to the creatures he felt watching him. Confident now, he raised his voice. "And tell my grandfather I'll see him again," he said to anyone who listened.

LIGHTS OUT

TINA ANTON

Dakari Williams looked up from the bright florescent screen of her laptop. A shadow had crossed the edge of her vision, but nothing appeared to be outside the window. She ignored the lingering sense of someone watching and turned back to her blog post. It had been "lights out" for nearly an hour in the girl's dorm, but Dakari's contraband laptop was purring happily in the sliver of space between her bed and the wall that was just big enough for her, several pillows, and an energy drink she had bribed another girl to smuggle inside school grounds.

Everyone else was fast asleep, their breathing deep and even, but Dakari wasn't like the other girls. She had Big Plans and New Ideas and the world needed to hear about them. Her blog, The Dakari Report, covered all types of conspiracy theories and any creepy news story that had been even partially substantiated. People needed to know that there was more to the world than what met the eye.

Another large shadow flickered in the peripheral of her vision and the teenager bolted upright, glaring at the darkness like an old foe. Huffing in quiet frustration at her own childish fears, she went back to typing. Phantom spider legs crawled over her skin and Dakari had to shake off the sudden thought that someone was behind her, poised to strike. Just to be sure, she glanced over one shoulder. A blank wall stared back at her widened gaze.

There must have been a stiff breeze outside, because a tree branch skittered across the dorm siding. Except the sound seemed to be coming from inside. A soft sskch, sskch, sskch trailed along the floor. Still typing, Dakari tensed and carefully pretended not to have seen the man-shaped shadow that loomed over her bed. Fingers shaking uncontrollably, she opened the chat room for her blog forum.

TheDak: Help ME! Someone is in my room call the police.

She typed the message hoping that the active chatters would take it seriously.

SlenderMain: Omg are you okay?

69down: ???

creeper2012: What?

FrankenStaink: Is this a joke?

The responses flashed to life across the screen. Dakari felt her chest tighten.

TheDak: Call 911!

Just as she pressed 'enter', the shadowed form lunged forward. Her heart thumped hard against her chest and Dakari opened her mouth to scream, but no sound came out. A skeletal black hand reached out from the man shaped form and caressed her face. Ice cold fingertips ghosted over her open lips, moving smoothly past bared teeth to explore the inside of Dakari's mouth. She couldn't move. Something had frozen her body and for a moment she wasn't even sure if she was still breathing. The hand moved down her throat. Dakari's gag reflex ignored the violation as if it were not even happening. Salty tears rolled down her cheeks and into her open mouth.

A sharp pain shot through her chest and then everything changed. Her body was no longer frozen and a horrified scream clawed past her teeth. The hand and shadowy body had vanished and so had the dorm room. Dakari looked around herself and saw nothing but rolling, wheat colored sand dunes stretched from horizon to horizon. She was sitting in a dip between two dunes. Heated air fell over her in waves and she felt sweat begin to bead her forehead. Dakari wiped a hand across her face and stared in horror when it came away smeared with blood.

She stood on unsteady feet and turned in a full circle. There was nothing, but sand, for as far as the eye could see. Dakari sank back to her knees and stared in horror at her crimson stained hands.

"Don't fear, child. You need only wake," a matronly voice spoke from every direction at once.

Although she looked around wildly for its source, Dakari could not find the speaker.

"Who's there?" Dakari demanded, voice wavering. "Show yourself!"

A stiff breeze, smelling of heat stone, blew grit into the girl's eyes and hair.

"Wake up. You need to wake up," the voice grew fainter and then vanished.

Sweat slid down Dakari's cheeks like salty tears. Her breathing was coming quick and it felt like any second her heart would burst out of her chest. Then Dakari felt the pain again, a sharp ache that pulled her into darkness.

Dakari screamed, the sound choked and muffled – barely any sound at all. Her mouth was propped open by the dark, cold hand.

318

Somehow, the desert was gone and she was back on the floor between her bed and the wall. Blue light from her laptop splashed across the profile of her attacker. Dakari's eyes widened in horror. She recognized the dark specter now from images online. It was The Sandman, a mythical creature or so she had always believed.

"He-phb!" She screamed against the cold flesh, hoping one of the other girls would wake and turn on the lights.

The only weapon that worked against The Sandman, according to the myths and legends she had read, was a bright light. Her laptop's pathetic glow probably didn't even sting the creature. The girl began to struggle, attempting to shove the black arm away, but it was no use. The creature was unmoving, expressionless and inhumanly strong.

Then the desert was back and Dakari was on her knees coughing, clutching at the air in front of her face where the arm had been. Now there was nothing but overheated air which she sucked deep into her lungs. An inkling was beginning to form in Dakari's mind about what the desert meant, but it was too soon to know for sure.

"Little one, fight it. There is enough light within you to call off the darkness," it was the same matronly voice from before whispering on the hot breeze.

"I don't understand," Dakari said.

Tears of fear began to fall, unnoticed, down the girl's trembling face.

"Think, child," the voice chided softly, "why does The Sandman live in darkness? What is in that black place that light cannot reach? Why is light such a powerful weapon?" The questions grew louder and more firm with each pause. "Why target you out of all the girls? Think, child."

Dakari squeezed her eyes closed and clapped her hands over her ears. It was the teenager's habitual way of blocking out distractions. However, the baking heat was impossible to ignore. With a whimper, Dakari lowered her hands in defeat.

"Tell me the answer," the girl begged.

Silence, broken only by the whistle of the wind through the dune valley, filled the world. Dakari almost decided the voice had been nothing but her imagination when it finally replied.

"Your memories, child. They are brighter than any light in the world. Use them."

Then Dakari understood. The Sandman was feeding on her fear, somehow, and she needed to overwhelm the creature with brilliant sense memories. This realization confirmed her suspicion that the desert was in her own mind – a construct created by The Sandman to trap her until her body had been drained and left for dead.

"Wake up, child," the unseen woman urged.

Whatever The Sandman was doing to her body, it hurt - sharp, aching pains in her chest. It felt like something was being dislodged. Dakari focused on the pain and darkness fell over the world. She was back in the dorm. By now the disorientation of moving from one setting to another was less of a mental blow.

Dakari bit down as hard as she could on the hand in her mouth. It was like trying to bite through cold metal, but she didn't release her jaw. The girl's nostrils flared as she drew in quick breaths. She still smelled heated rocks, the scent coming from The Sandman. Dakari saw a quick vision of the desert, but she refused to be drawn back into that illusion.

Bright memories. Bright thoughts. Dakari needed to blind The Sandman to interrupt his feeding. It didn't take long for her to settle on an appropriate memory. March 17th , 2005. The day Dakari would never forget. Focusing on every detail of that happy day, the teenager let herself get lost in the memory.

The Sandman recoiled, it's arm pulling out of her mouth. Dakari felt a thrill of victory and shot to her feet, stumbling over the corner of the bed to reach open space on the other side. The light switch was barely ten feet away. Dakari ran. An ice cold, vice-like grip stopped her abruptly, her feet leaving the ground for a moment as she became enveloped in a backwards hug from the specter.

"No!" Dakari's screamed hoarsely.

Several startled gasps came from beds around the room.

"What's going on?" A sleepy Debbie Small asked.

The Sandman turned, Dakari still held firmly in its arms, and the smell of desert sand intensified. A mist seemed to fill the room. Dakari blinked, her eyes stinging suddenly. Not mist, tiny granules of sand. Debbie and the other girls instantly fell back asleep, their slumbering bodies just lumps in the almost complete darkness.

"C'mon! Please!" Dakari begged. The girl coughed, fiery sand cutting into her throat with each inhale.

None of the other girls stirred and the dorm mother had almost slept through a hurricane the year before so Dakari didn't hold out any hope that the old woman would come to the rescue. Hacking coughs turned into gagging. The teenager felt like she had inhaled at least a cup of sand into her lungs. Her chest was tight under the intense grip of The Sandman. It was all Dakari could do to keep breathing.

Grasping for a happy memory, Dakari found one and latched on. A brilliant pink sunset coloring the last of the summer roses, she could still smell their sweet scent. She had been truly in love with nature that evening. Warmth spread through Dakari and her forced breathing evened out.

A screeching wail, sounding like a dying cat, came from The Sandman and it released the teenager, stumbling back into the wall. Dakari kept the happy memory on the forefront of her thoughts. She felt stronger already, less afraid of the monster in her room. If she could wound it, she could stop it.

Lunging toward the light switch, Dakari's heart nearly stopped in her chest when she felt it under her fingertips. Flipping the switch, the teenager watched as The Sandman recoiled with more shrieks of pain. The shadowed form turned transparent and then flickered several times before disappearing into thin air. Dakari stared at the empty spot near the wall where it had been. What felt like a lifetime passed before she was able to move again.

The shaken teenager left the lights on for the rest of the night.

<p style="text-align:center">~~~~~</p>

Dakari complained of feeling sick the next morning and was let off classes for the day. She watched the other girls wake, dress, and leave for breakfast. Nothing appeared out of the ordinary. Dakari tried to convince herself that The Sandman and the desert had all been nothing more than a waking dream brought on by an overactive imagination and too many late nights blogging about the paranormal. No matter how hard she tried, the girl could not convince herself. If it wasn't for the scratchy pain in her throat, she might have imaged the entire ordeal, but there was no denying that something had caused the bone-deep pain in her chest. She could still feel those cold fingers whenever her eyes closed.

When she finally dragged her body out of bed to get dressed for the day, Dakari was shocked and dismayed to see bruises forming around her waist. The teenager shook her head, changed and then collapsed back on her bed. It was too insane to be real.

Checking to make sure the dorm mother was not in the building, Dakari moved to the slit of open carpet between her bed and the wall, holding her laptop on crossed knees. She hadn't worked up the courage to go back online the night before, after the entity disappeared, but now she signed onto her blog's chat room.

FrankenStaink: Holy shit! Are you okay D? We were all so worried.

TheDak: Yeah I think. Actually not really. There was something in my room last night. Something inhumane.

69down: I thought it was a rapist murder dude?

TheDak: So did I...but...it wasn't.

FrankenStaink: What are you saying exactly?

TheDak: I think it was the sandman. It's too strange to explain on here, but just believe me...it was the sandman. I'm afraid it will come back tonight.

69down: haha! Are you sure you didn't just get bit by too many bedbugs? LOL

TheDak: I'm serious.

FrankenStaink: What are you going to do if it does come back?

TheDak: I don't know.

Dakari leaned her head back on her shoulders and stared up at the ceiling. She thought about what the strange woman's voice had said in the desert, 'Why target you out of all the girls?", and the answer suddenly came to Dakari. It was because she had the most fear. She fostered it each day and night when she read and shared urban legends. Fear of the dark, the unknown, the monsters roaming in the shadows. Dakari slapped a hand to her forehead and groaned. The Dakari Report was basically a big neon sign flashing 'come get me' to The Sandman. Dakari felt stupid for not having realized it as soon as she had felt it feeding on her fear.

The teenager signed off her site's chat room and then opened a search engine. With over twenty thousand results for 'the sandman', Dakari clicked on the first link. It showed a time line of the Sandman myth throughout history. There were always two constants: The Sandman used sand as a weapon and it could also control sleep, inducing dream states. Dakari assumed the desert she had been thrown into was a dreamscape The Sandman controlled. That didn't explain the mysterious woman's voice, but dreams could be odd things and some things were hard to explain in ordinary ones. The next twenty websites showed that there was no known way to kill The Sandman. She would have to improvise.

Closing her laptop, Dakari determined that the only way to beat The Sandman, if it returned, was to show it that she had much more bright, happy memories than fear inside of her thoughts. If there wasn't enough fear to feed it, then the creature would go away. At least, Dakari hoped that would be the case. Determined to defeat The Sandman if he returned that night, Dakari decided to rest up while it was still light outside. Hiding the laptop under the edge of the bed, the teenager curled up on the top covers and let her tired body fall asleep.

~~~~~

The girls started trickling back into the dorm after dinner so Dakari allowed herself a little more time to sleep. As long as the others were awake there would be plenty of lights on all throughout the dorm. Lights out happened each night at 8:30 and was always accompanied by a building-wide alarm chime. Dakari would rely on that to wake her up on time. Luck was on her side, because, several hours later, the familiar chime woke Dakari from a sound sleep. Debbie Small, the diminutive teen from southern Texas, was making some last minute changes to her bedding before turning off the lights.

"Are you feeling better?" Debbie asked when she noticed Dakari was awake.

"Yeah. Sleeping really helped," Dakari said.

"That's good." Debbie smiled and walked over to the night switch. "Night, everyone."

There were echoes of 'night' from all around the large dorm room before they were all plunged into darkness. Dakari's heart slammed against her chest and she bit back a whimper. It took a few seconds for her eyes to adjust to the darkness, but when they did she looked at every shadow and corner with suspicion. She was ready to face the monster and drive it away for good.

The teenager didn't have to wait for long.

She felt The Sandman approaching, goosebumps flushing up and down her arms, and closed the laptop. It was just her, the creature, and pale moonlight. The world's blandest battle field. Dakari smelled the desert before the dunes suddenly appeared. She
~~~~~

found herself transported away from the dorm room and into her mind.

"You can win this fight, child. Be strong."

"Who are you?" Dakari asked.

A patch of air in front of the girl shimmered for a moment and then a noble looking woman in a blue robe and veil appeared. "I am you, child. The part of your mind which no darkness can ever reach."

Dakari shook her head in disbelief. "This is too weird, even for me."

The woman laughed softly. "Go slay the proverbial dragon, young one. Even if you never see me again, I am always here to protect and help you." Without another word, the woman faded into nonexistence.

Suddenly filled with a bold, righteous strength, Dakari took a calming breath and focused on peaceful memories. The desert instantly disappeared, replaced by the dark dorm room. The shadowy shape of The Sandman had drawn up to Dakari's right side where it crowded next to her without touching. She seemed to have spooked it. Combining the creature's weaknesses, Dakari thought of the brightest, happiest day she remembered. A flood of positive emotions burst from her chest.

An animal scream erupted from the shadowed creature and it flew backward, bouncing off a wall, and fled into the hall. Tasting victory, Dakari pushed off her bed and ran after the creature. She needed to make sure it never came back. The Sandman stood in the middle of the hall.

"You never come back here. There's nothing for you here," Dakari commanded. Her whole body was shaking and her pulse thudded in her ears. "Leave."

She thought of golden leaves shinning in the sun on a cool fall day, the way they blanketed the city in such beautiful colors. This memory brought out another screech of pain from The Sandman.

"Leave!" Dakari yelled, pointing an unsteady finger at the creature.

The Sandman seemed to balloon into an oversized form, looming ominously. Dakari refused to waver. Biting her lip to stop any internal fears from surfacing, the girl continued to run through all the bright memories she could find. After several slow moments,

324

The Sandman collapsed back into its original form with a whistle of air that blew Dakari's hair around her face.

Any sense of dread The Sandman might have caused for her earlier was gone. It was nothing more than a shadow that couldn't hurt her or anyone she cared about. Clinging to that sudden certainty, Dakari glared at the creature.

"Leave," she said for the last time.

The Sandman twisted into itself until there was nothing but a tiny floating black ball. A sharp white light exploded from inside of it and the creature was gone. Dakari breathed heavily, numb with relief. She knew, somehow, that it was gone for good. She had beaten it.

"Good work, child." Dakari's inner voice was so quiet as to be nearly unintelligible, but the girl heard it and smiled.

Dakari returned to her dorm bed and opened her laptop. The browser was open on her chat room. She typed with twitching fingers.

TheDak: I did it. The Sandman is gone.

Phantom's Sting

Nicole Lavigne

Amrita Quarekall tilted her head down. The hotel door opened and a cool night breeze teased a lock of long, dirty blonde hair from its fastening to fall into her violet eyes. She let out a slow breath. Red aces, nine and ten of diamonds, and king of spades. She flicked a glance at her remaining opponent. She folded her cards, placing them on the table with a resigned sigh. Through her peripheral vision she tracked the location of bystanders. *Don't get backed into a corner and never show your whole hand,* those were her mottos. A card grazed her wrist as she exchanged the king for the ace of clubs tucked up her sleeve.

Their eyes met. She straightened in her seat as though suddenly self-conscious. His face was frozen in that arrogant grin. Amrita knew his type, that slightly condescending look. He wore a lavender-grey suit that complimented his iridescent green skin. His mouth twisted in an indulgent smile, flashing sharp teeth, before he raised his glass for a drink.

Amrita took a sip of her own drink. Flashing the breltaki her best shy smile, she threw some coins to the center of the table. With a manicured hand, he counted out the coins to match her bet. Then he pushed the remaining neat stacks of his money forward. Her hands itched. She shrugged her shoulders and smiled at him.

"Well, it looks like I'm out. I can't match that." She started to stand.

The breltaki raised a hand.

"Just a moment. Perhapsss an arrangement can be made." He controlled the characteristic breltaki lisp well, but it slipped out now and then.

She waited.

"If you win, you take all the money. If I win…" He paused. "If I win, you must take my cursling."

A chill ran up her spine. Amrita scanned the air around the breltaki, not that she would see anything. Her throat grew dry as she descended back into the whirlwind of emotions her first cursling had pushed her into: fear, disgust, self-loathing. It had nearly won, nearly convinced her to kill herself. It was self-defense. She repeated the words that had, at last, saved her sanity and her life. *It was self-defense.*

"But if you are too afraid…"

His voice snapped her back to the present. His eyes mocked her.

She gritted her teeth and grabbed the extended hand.

"Deal."

For an instant her hand turned to ice, then fire. The feeling spread up her arm to her heart. An eerie glow surrounded their clasped hands. It soaked into their flesh, sealing the bargain. They released their hands. She sat down and picked up her cards.

"Ladiesss first."

She placed her cards on the table. The breltaki nodded.

"A most impressive hand."

Amrita reached out towards the pile of money.

"But-" her hand froze. "I am afraid, not quite as impressive as thisss."

He laid his cards out. Royal Flush, spades. She bit her tongue. Revealing the king of spades up her sleeve would only prove that she had cheated too.

The air to his right became hazy. It condensed, becoming misty and darkening until the vague twisted form of a twisted, black humanoid crouched on the ground in front of her. Its face had two depressions where eyes would be. Nothing looked out from them. The darkness of its lower face parted revealing razor teeth.

Amrita suppressed a shudder, focusing her attention on the man who had beaten her.

"Congratulations," she said, her voice flat.

He began carefully counting his winnings. Thus dismissed, Amrita left the table, ignoring the cursling trailing behind her.

Amrita slammed the door to her rented room. The cursling crept through it, unperturbed. Amrita rounded on it.

"Who was that? Who was that guy and how did he beat me? Nobody beats me!"

Its featureless black face turned up at her. The mouth opened in a malicious grin.

"Nobody of any interest or particular skill."

Amrita snarled. Her hand whipped out, grasping the black thing about its tiny neck. She flung it at the wall. It floated through it only to come slinking back, cackling.

"Little Amrita," it taunted, "all she wants is to be the best. But you're a second-rate hack who has just gotten lucky. Your life is empty."

Amrita reached for the cursling again. Her hand passed through it, earning her goosebumps.

"You left behind the only person who could have ever loved you."

"Shut up."

It chuckled. "Worthless, that's what you are. What would Miriea say if she saw you now?"

~~~~~

Crystal blue eyes watered. Miriea's delicate hand held Amrita's in a vice.

"Please," Miriea sobbed, "don't go."

Amrita's own voice caught in her throat. "You heard Ravienne; she'll turn me in or kill me if I don't leave."

"You didn't mean to kill that client. She has to understand that."

Amrita shook her head. "She won't risk this place on me. Besides, this is my chance to get out of here, before she finds out... If she knew what I really am, she'd never let me go."

Their eyes met in the silence, clear blue and deep violet.

"Come with me."

Miriea looked away. "She'd send someone after us. This is your chance, not mine."

Amrita pulled her lover into her arms. "I'll get the money and buy your freedom."

Their lips met. Amrita pulled back from the kiss before her resolve could falter.

~~~~~

Amrita blinked back the tears. "I was worthless when Ravienne owned me, not anymore." She turned her back on it and undressed.

The cursling's face cracked in an evil grin. "At least you were an honest whore. Now you're a cheap con and a coward."

She slipped into the tiny cot. When she shut her eyes, a pair of crystal blue waited.

~~~~~

Daylight shone through the worn curtains. Amrita crawled out of bed, not that she had been able to sleep. Walking the two steps to the small table, she examined herself in the mirror that stood on it. Her eyes were bloodshot and ringed with dark circles from the lack of sleep. She poured water into a small basin and splashed her face. She rubbed her eyes before checking the mirror again. The redness faded and the black rings softened.
~~~~~

"Going to tuck your tail between your legs and look for an easier target?"

Amrita shook out a sleek black dress from her pack. The shiny satin hugged her hips down to just above her knees while a slit revealed the flesh of her left thigh. She brushed her hair, twirling the brush to give her hair a gentle curl. It shone golden. The cursling's eyeless face followed her movements. Amrita applied a pale blue powder to her eyelids; they started to look midnight blue instead of violet. She stained her lips red, dabbed a drop of jasmine oil to the nape of her neck and strapped on a pair of black heels. When she left, the cursling followed.

She stalked confidently, hips swaying, down the road to the upscale hotel at the other end of town.

Amrita sauntered up to the bartender, flashing him a smile.

"What can I get for you?"

Amrita leaned over the bar, giving the man a view of her cleavage.

"A moment of your time."

He smiled.

She took a seat on the stool next to her, crossing her legs to let the slit in her dress fall open.

"I was wondering if you could help me."

"Anything for you."

Her fingers touched his hand gently. "I had a feeling I could count on you. I met a most intriguing gentleman last night, but unfortunately we didn't get a chance to chat properly. He mentioned that he was staying here."

The bartender's smile fell.

"I have a business proposal to discuss with him."

The young man's eyes perked up again.

"What's his name?"

Amrita blushed. "You know, for the life of me I can't remember. It's embarrassing. I can tell you what he looked like though. He was a very distinctive gentleman: a breltaki, very sharply dressed."

The bartender nodded. "That would be Sikader Boixade. He had a meeting with someone this morning. I could go and tell hi-"

"No, I'd hate to interrupt his meeting. But you can tell me what he drinks."

The young man took a bottle of expensive whiskey off the shelf behind him and showed it to her. She nodded. He poured some into a crystal glass.

"Two please."

He poured a second. Amrita opened her clutch. The young man's hand took hold of hers.

"It's on the house." He winked.

She leaned over the bar and kissed his cheek lightly. Sliding off the stool, she tucked the clutch under her arm and picked up the crystal glasses. With a final bat of her lashes, she sashayed away, settling at one of the tables to wait. The cursling crouched atop the small table in front of her. Amrita stared past it, unblinking.

"He's not the type to hire cheap out-of-practice whores, so what is the point of this charade? You've already proven that you can't con him."

Amrita's eyes narrowed. She swirled the glass of whiskey in her right hand and brought it to her lips.

A door opened from further back in the building and voices emerged. Amrita recognized one of them as the breltaki's. She turned to watch as he approached alongside a man whose expensive suit didn't quite fit over his protruding belly. Amrita's eyes followed Sikader, darting up and down the length of his perfectly-tailored suit. The scotch rose to her lips again as she watched Sikader and the other man walk past, still in conversation. The breltaki's mahogany eyes remained focused on his companion. Several feet away they shook hands and the other man waddled out of the casino. Sikader remained. His head turned to look over his shoulder at Amrita. He walked to Amrita's table. His eyes slowly swept the length of her body before he spoke.

"I do not believe that we have had the pleasure of meeting."

"Not yet, Mr. Boixade."

"You know my name."

"I make a point of researching potential clients before approaching them. I waste less time that way."

The breltaki's eyes narrowed.

"My name is Zaphira Ordan." She set down her glass and raised her hand. He took it in his green one and brought it to his cold lips.

"It is a pleasure Mz. Ordan."

"Please, call me Zaphira."

He sat in the chair next to her. Amrita held out the untouched glass.

"Might I offer you a drink?"

He accepted and took a sip. "You have excellent taste Mz. Ordan."

"Zaphira. As I said, I do my research."

"Yess. And what sort of clientele are you looking for exactly?"

"The rich kind. And in that respect I also have excellent taste."

He accepted the compliment with a subtle nod.

"For what sort of businesss?"

"I sell property, Mr. Boixade."

He sipped the whisky. "Well, I am afraid to let you down, but I am not in the market for any property, and particularly not in thiss area. I am just passing through."

"I understand that, but I assure you that this would be worth your consideration."

"Why is that?"

"A man such as you knows a good deal when he sees one and takes advantage of it."

Mahogany eyes stared down blue. His glass clinked on the table. Sikader stood.

"Thank you, Mz. Ordan, but as I said, I am not in the market for any property, no matter how good the deal is. I wish you luck in finding another buyer. Good day."

"I already have, but I thought that I would give you the opportunity first before he arrives tomorrow."

"What is so special about this property, or are you just desperate to sell it before you get caught in something?"

Amrita downed the remains of her whiskey. She stood, setting the glass on the table. She walked up to Sikader until their bodies were a breath apart.

"If you want to know what is so valuable about it, then you will have to come see it for yourself."

She stepped around him, letting their shoulders brush. The cursling followed her. She gave a wink to the bartender as she left the building. Outside, she pulled a long, black cigarette from her clutch. Lighting it with a match, the clove smoke surrounded her as she counted. Sikader emerged; the cigarette was half finished. Men usually didn't take that long.

"Can I offer you a cigarette Mr. Boixade?"

He looked her up and down again, even slower this time.

"Show me the property. Thiss had better be worth my time."

The carriage came to a stop alongside a mountain. Sikader's face peered out.

"I am not seeing anything to impresss Mz. Ordan."

"Nor should you, yet, Mr. Boixade. Now, if you will follow me."

He stepped out from the carriage, sneering at the dust his feet kicked up. The cursling crawled out after him. Amrita watched it from the corner of her eye. She led Sikader back around the mountain the way they had come. The cursling had lost interest in taunting her; its empty sockets locked instead on Sikader.

"We have to go through here. It will get a little tight."

She slipped between two rocks. Sikader followed, with the cursling trailing him. After a couple of feet, the path seemed to come to an end. Amrita took a sharp turn, pressing against the rock wall. The passage twisted and turned, making it impossible to see it as the mountain closed in around them. She felt her way forward in the darkness. At last the passage opened up. She heard Sikader emerge behind her. Crouching, she felt along the ground for the lantern she had left there. Light filled the room.

The walls glittered in the light. Sikader's attention turned towards the glimpses of color sparkling from the black walls. His face remained neutral. Amrita sauntered past him. She rubbed her hand against the wall. It came away covered in a fine pearlescent dust. Sikader grabbed her wrist. Amrita winced as he crushed her hand.

"Yess, I see now why you would research potential clientss so thoroughly." His grip tightened.

She nodded to the wall. "Break off a piece. I always check beneath the surface."

Sikader grabbed an offshoot of rock with his free hand, snapping it off. He crumbled it easily, turning it to more of the pearlescent powder. His face remained neutral. He raised his hand closer to his face, appraising the powder.

Sikader's free hand gripped her throat, pressing her against the wall of the cave. The cursling bounced around the cave behind Sikader, knocking rocks to the ground as it crashed about. Sikader turned at the sound. His eyes returned to Amrita.

Amrita's vision started to go dark. She saw Miriea's tear streaked face on the day they parted and her heart broke again. I'm sorry.

Sikader released his hands. She collapsed to the floor, coughing.

"I wish you the best of luck selling this property, Mz. Ordan, once I inform the sheriff about your deception."

He started to walk away.

"Wait," Amrita rasped.

He stopped.

"I have another buyer."

"Not once he finds out that you planted the dust here."

"What will that gain you?"

He turned, a wicked smile on his face. "It is the right thing to do."

"You could help me sell it."

"And why would I want to implicate myself in your little scheme?"

She shook her head, pushing herself upright. "Compete with him to purchase the property, drive up the price. I will give you a part of the profits. If he backs down first then you will keep your money."

He considered for a moment. "I will take sixty percent."

"Fifteen. It's generous."

"You call that generouss?"

"I set this up. I put in all the work. There is no risk for you, all the risk is on my shoulders. All you have to do is show interest and improve the bid. I could still do this without you and keep everything for myself."

"If you get caught and mention my involvement that would implicate me as your accomplice. That is a huge risk."

"Fine, twenty-five."

He tsked.

"Thirty."

"You are wasting my time, Mz. Ordan."

The cursling hung from the ceiling, eyes darting between her and the breltaki. She sighed.

"Forty."

Sikader stepped closer until he had her backed against the wall. She could feel his breath on her cheek.

"Because I am feeling generous today, I will accept."

He didn't move. Amrita decided to try a different approach to regain her ground. She leaned into him slightly.

"How did you know?"

His eyes sparkled with mischief. "You should never try to con a con artist, Mz. Ordan, especially not one so much better than you."

Amrita forced a smile past gritted teeth. Her eyes remained locked on Sikader's. "I was right."

"Right about what?"

She cautiously raised a hand, running a finger just above the sleeve of his suit but not touching him.

"I knew there was ... something different about you." She chewed her lip. "That's really why I wanted to bring you here."

"Is that so?"

His hand caught her wrist again. Amrita gasped. He kept the pressure firm, enough to make the newly-forming bruises sting, but not hard enough to cause further damage. He pinned her hand against the wall.

"I guess my curiosity got the better of me," she breathed.

His other hand lightly traced up her thigh before grabbing her hip and slowly grinding her into the rough stone behind her. Amrita caught the snarl rising in her throat and turned it into a purr.

"And are you pleased with what you discovered?"

She nodded dreamily. "You are good."

"Yess. I am."

Amrita tilted her head forward to kiss him.

Sikader released her. She bit back the sigh of relief.

"Let uss go," he said, his voice cold.

~~~~~

The cursling leapt atop the desk in Amrita's room.

"I told you that you weren't good enough to con him," it taunted.

She checked the bruises around her neck, wincing when her fingers touched the skin. She sighed, glancing down at her bag.

"You almost got yourself killed."

"What do you care?"

It snarled at her and knocked her makeup case off the table. She dampened a cloth with water and began removing her makeup. The cursling studied her. Blue eyes returned to their normal violet hue. As she brushed her hair, the golden curls smoothed out, growing dull and dark. She tied it back low with a strip of leather. Stripping out of the slinky dress, she donned a pair of roughly worn khakis and a men's brown shirt. She massaged her face, looking in the mirror. Her face plumped and her skin became olive toned. The
~~~~~

cursling fidgeted.

"You're a changeling."

"My father was a changeling."

It grinned wickedly. "That would have made you a much more valuable whore than a con artist."

Amrita stopped, her eyes losing focus on the present. "Ravienne would have never let me go if she had found out, no matter who I had killed. It was my only chance to get out of there." She shook her head, snapping back to the present moment. "And it's not a thing someone advertises if they want to live their own life, or live at all."

Glancing back in the mirror, she checked her handiwork. She headed down to the gambling tables for the evening.

~~~~~

Amrita sat at a table at the hotel, sipping a cup of dark coffee and waiting for Sikader and their mark, a gentleman by the name of Galen Virago.

She kept her eyes on the door, watching the cursling through her peripheral vision. It watched the door for a few moments, then glanced at her before turning towards the stairs of the club for a moment where Sikader should emerge from his rooms, then glancing back at Amrita before returning its attention to the door. Then the cycle would start over again. She didn't remember her first cursling behaving like this.

Amrita filed away that thought as a portly gentleman in an expensive suit approached her. Amrita stood, smoothing her dress.

More conservatively dressed than the previous day, she sported a burgundy dress with a short collar, covering the bruises around her neck. Her low heels and lipstick matched it perfectly. A wide, silver bracelet hid the bruises on her left wrist.

"Mr. Virago?"

"Ms. Ordan. A pleasure to meet you at last." He shook her hand.

"The pleasure is all mine." She motioned to the chair next to hers as she sat. "Would you like to take a seat while we wait?"

"Wait?"

"Yes. Someone else has expressed some interest in the property. I hope you don't mind, but he will be joining us for the viewing."

He cleared his throat. "Yes, well, I suppose that would be most efficient."

Amrita nodded. "True." She leaned in, whispering. "I also thought
~~~~~

you might like to take stock of your potential competition."

He chuckled. "Very thoughtful of you, Ms. Ordan."

She lightly touched his hand with hers. "Please, call me Zaphira."

The cursling sunk deeper into its crouch, reminding Amrita of a dog protecting its master. She half thought it would growl.

"Ah, and here is your competition."

Sikader flicked a glance to the neck of her dress and the bracelet. He smiled. Amrita suppressed a shudder and smiled back.

"Good morning, Mr. Boixade. This is Mr. Virago. Mr. Virago, this is Mr. Boixade."

They shook hands, staring each other down.

"If you gentlemen don't have any questions first, we can be on our way."

Galen nodded.

"After you," said Sikader.

~~~~~

The driver circled the property, pausing to allow Amrita to point out its various features. The cursling crouched in the center of the small carriage. It ignored Galen. Amrita resisted the urge to pull her feet up out of contact with it. The driver passed the entrance to the cave as before. Amrita led them back and through the hidden passage.

"This last feature, I think you shall both find of particular interest," she said, lighting the lantern.

Again the walls glittered in the faint light. Amrita ran her hand along the surface, showing them the pearlescent dust that came away on her skin. Galen ran a single finger on the wall. He sniffed, then tentatively touched the tip of his tongue to the powder. He nodded.

"I see, yes. It is a good piece of property, albeit further away from the city than I would prefer. This," he said, raising his finger, "would raise the value however."

Sikader turned to him. "What is it that you intend to do with the property, if you don't mind my asking?"

"I build casinos, Mr. Boixade."

Sikader nodded appreciatively. "I see. How much business could you really hope to get with that distance to travel?"

Galen looked at Amrita wistfully and shrugged.

"That is a consideration, however, your casino will bring a lot
~~~~~

more business to this city and it could quickly start expanding and crowd you. Build here and the city will have some room to expand to you and you have room to grow as well. Just think of it, having your casino and its own little network of attached businesses, either owned by you or renting your property. And with the distance to the city proper, people will be less likely to go wandering away to spend their money elsewhere."

Galen nodded. His eyes focused on that imaginary casino.

"Yes, it has a unique potential there."

"It has some very long term potential," Sikader conceded. "But it may never attract enough business out this far for this city. It is a gamble, Mr. Virago. Are you a gambling man?"

Galen grinned at Sikader. "True success, Mr. Boixade, demands a long term perspective. I may leave most of the gambling to my customers, but I am not afraid of taking risks."

"Does this mean that you are interested in purchasing, Mr. Virago?" Asked Amrita.

Galen addressed her without turning away from Sikader.

"It does, Ms. Ordan."

"As am I."

Amrita permitted herself a slight smile.

"Well then, we shall have to see who is willing to make the best offer."

"What is it that you do, Mr. Boixade, that you are so interested in this particular piece of property?"

"My business is my own, Mr. Virago."

"Well, your business will have to be quite lucrative if you hope to purchase this choice piece of property. I know mine is."

"I can offer you ten grand, Mz. Ordan."

Galen smirked. "Twelve."

"Fifteen."

"Twenty."

"Twenty-five."

Galen looked his competition up and down. He winked at Amrita. "Forty."

Sikader's brows rose.

"I know what I want, and I always get it."

Sikader glanced at Amrita. "Well, I shall not stand in your way then, on thiss matter. The property is yours."

338

Sikader tipped his head to Galen, then Amrita, and left. A dark shadow slinked out after him. Galen turned a triumphant look on Amrita.

~~~~~

"Forty!" Amrita exclaimed, throwing her purse onto the table in her room. "I wouldn't have gotten Galen even close to that without Sikader."

The cursling sat on her bed, twitching.

"You're going to keep it all."

She sighed. "I wish." Her fingers reflexively touched the bruises on her neck, causing her to wince. She shook her head. "No, it would be too risky to try and slip away with all of it. Still, sixty percent, that will last a good long while."

"Especially on your own."

Blue shifted into violet. She went quiet. "I can't risk going back for her unless I know I have enough."

"Supposing she is even still alive," the cursling needled. "On the other hand, she could be so broken by now that she will hardly cost you a penny. Not that you will survive to make the attempt anyways."

Amrita scoffed. "I've got nothing to worry about. I get the pay from Galen, give Sikader his share and then change my face and boot it out of here."

"He'll kill you."

"When he finds out I planted the dust? It will be a while before he figures that out and I will be long gone. He will never be able to track me down."

"Sikader." The cursling's raspy voice almost quivered when it whispered the name.

"He has no reason to kill me if I give him his share."

The eerie, featureless face stared at her.

She removed the cuff from her wrist, letting her skin return to its natural state, revealing the bruise. "Ok, he might want to renegotiate his take." She sighed.

"He will kill you and take it all. You would be better off running."

"You don't know that. And I most certainly will not run. I invested a lot of time and money into this. I will not walk away empty handed."

"He always kills them," the cursling said softly.
~~~~~

Amrita studied the creature. It seemed unsettled. It hadn't been as intent in its taunting of late.

"What makes you so sure?"

The cursling mimicked Sikader's voice perfectly. "Forty is a nice little sum, almost makes up for enduring the little bitch's presence."

Amrita considered this for some time. It could be lying. Maybe this is just some new tactic of torment. Making me walk away from a take this big would fit.

"What do you care if he kills me anyways?"

It fidgeted. Amrita watched with growing interest.

"What happens to you if I die before you get me to repent?"

The cursling began to shake.

I see. She considered her options, discarding one potential plot after another. "Will you help me?"

"How?"

She sighed. "I admit he's too good for me to deal with myself. He'll be watching me, I'm sure. But if you could slip something into his drink..."

The cursling shook its head fervently.

"I'll buy a sleeping drug. His attention will be on me and he can't see you. It will just knock him out long enough that I can get away safely. I will leave him his share."

The cursling didn't respond.

"It's the only option, because I will not walk away."

"He will come after you for trying it."

Amrita concentrated. She shrunk two inches, her skin darkened till it was almost black. Her hair retreated into her scalp until it was short and scraggly. Her jaw broadened, her features becoming more angular while her muscles swelled and her breasts flattened. The transformation complete, a stocky young black man stared at the cursling. Her voice was deep when she spoke.

"That will be very difficult for him to do."

The cursling watched her. Slowly, she transformed back to her original appearance. Her heart raced, her back grew damp and her legs were shaky. She leaned gratefully against the desk.

"So will you help me, or will you take the risk that Sikader will kill me?"

Finally the cursling nodded.

The cursling's empty eyes watched as she handed the money over to the shop owner. She slipped the small envelope into her pocket, her finger brushing the edge of a matching one.

The cursling followed her through back alleys to her room. Reaching into her pocket, she pulled out one envelope and pushed the other in deeper. She placed it on the table.

She changed into a slinky dress, midnight to match her eyes once they shifted from violet. She brushed her hair until it turned golden blond with soft curls. The cursling studied the envelope while she completed her transformation.

"Ready?"

It nodded. Amrita opened the envelope, tipping out the tiny white pill. Two shadowy fingers picked it up. It disappeared in the cursling's grasp.

~~~~~

A server led her upstairs to Sikader's room. He knocked. The door opened, revealing a large, tastefully decorated suite and the breltaki. He motioned for her to enter. The cursling slipped through her legs and crawled up the wall. Before the server left, she turned to him.

"Could you please send up a bottle of champagne?"

He nodded and retreated.

As the door shut, Sikader raised one eyebrow at her.

"To celebrate," she said.

"It is done, then?"

Amrita slipped the packet of bills from her purse and dropped it on the table.

"It's all there."

He couldn't hide the sinister edge to his smile.

The young man returned. He set the tray with a bottle of champagne and two glasses on the hardwood desk. Sikader dismissed him.

Sikader popped the cork on the bottle and filled the two glasses. He handed one to Amrita. She forced her eyes to remain focused on the breltaki and her breathing even. In the corner of her eye, the cursling watched them. One shadowy arm reached forward, hovering above their glasses as they clinked together.

Amrita raised the glass to her lips. Sweat dripped down her back. Sikader waited. She smiled and downed her drink. He did the
~~~~~

same, then set the glass down on the table. A toothy smile spread across his green face.

Sikader lunged at her. He grabbed her throat, knocking her down and landing on top of her. Her head slammed against the floor. The glass shattered, shards cutting her hand. Stars danced before her eyes. She clawed at his scaled hands with weak fingers.

Sikader's grip relaxed and his weight collapsed on top of her. Amrita gagged. It took a moment for her to regain her breath. She rolled him over. She sat up.

The cursling vibrated on the table. It jumped to the floor and approached the breltaki. Amrita pushed herself up onto the bed as it inspected Sikader. It turned on her.

"You killed him!"

Amrita's voice was hoarse when she spoke. "You're the one that poisoned him."

It leapt at her, scratching her chest. Amrita fell back onto the bed. She tried to grab it, but her hand passed through it. Its fingers sharpened and jabbed at her eyes. She squeezed them shut. Cold passed through her eyes into her skull.

The sensation stopped. The only sound was that of her heavy breathing. Amrita gulped, wincing at the pain in her throat. She opened her eyes.

Black smoke dissipated. The cursling was gone. Amrita released a shaky breath. She collected the stack of money on the table and left.

~~~~~

Amrita's carriage pulled up in front of the old saloon. The sign was faded and the place looked worn out, but she recognized it. She stepped into a swamp of memories. Stomach lurched. Feet faltered. Mind raced. Is she still alive? Will she still want me? She gulped down doubts and pushed through the doors.

A weathered Ravienne put on her brightest smile. It dropped a second later.

"Amrita," she snarled.

Amrita smiled. "Ravienne, so good of you to remem-"

Ravienne pulled a shotgun from behind the counter and leveled it at Amrita. "I told you never to show your face here again."

Amrita took half a step back.

"What do you want?"
~~~~~

Amrita tossed her small purse on the counter.

"What is it?"

"Freedom."

Ravienne hesitated. "Your mother died years ago."

"I know," Amrita whispered. "It's for Miriea."

"Leave. Now."

Amrita took a half step forward. Ravienne cocked the gun.

"She hates you."

Amrita's shoulders slumped.

"Rita?"

Amrita and Ravienne turned towards the timid voice. A curvy woman with fiery hair and haunted crystal blue eyes stood on the stairs.

Tears welled in Amrita's eyes. She nodded.

"I... I never thought I would see you again."

"I'm sorry it took so long for me to co-"

Miriea shook her head. Amrita looked back to Ravienne. She nodded at the purse.

"It's twenty grand. That should be enough to buy her freedom."

The shotgun lowered. Ravienne nodded. Amrita sighed. She headed towards the door. A delicate hand took hers. Miriea smiled up at her, eyes glistening.

"Thank you."

Amrita pulled the redhead into her arms, kissing her hair and cheek.

Of Silver and Moonlight

Robert McGough

A pair of horses threaded through the thick nighttime forest, one a dozen feet behind the other. Riding atop the dark brown mare in front was Boris, the kings most fearsome wolf hunter, a gaunt man with a shaggy black mane of hair like the creatures he hunted. A thick drooping mustache split his face beneath deep blue eyes which constantly scanned from left to right as he slouched in the saddle. He rode under his mud-splattered cloak as if on the verge of sleep, it pulled tightly around his shoulders to keep out the chill night air.

Behind rode his apprentice, a boy of 14, Valko Nayden, one of the Kings foundlings. As animated as his master was still, the youth was constantly turning this way and that in the saddle, trying to peer around him at all times it seemed.

Their winding path through the forest at last found them where the trees thinned and the full moonlight shown through more readily, dispelling much of the darkness. Ahead Valko could see that the woods ended, revealing a low hill covered with grass turned blue in the moonlight. From his front Boris called back in a low soft voice. "Be still now boy. Now is not the time for curious glances. Make me proud."

The youth stiffened instantly, and straightened himself up in the saddle. He kept his eyes fixed steadily in front of him, though he longed to continue glancing about. Boris's word was everything to the boy though, so he obeyed without question.

As they broke free of the forests gloom Valko noticed a small fire had been lit on the hilltop. It was little more than a speck at this point, but he could see vague shapes peppered around it, some moving, others not. As they drew closer he was able to tell that the fire was in the center of a ring of standing stones, and a half dozen men and youths stood around the light it provided.

As they neared a voice boomed out from fireside and a massive swarthy man wearing dingy furs stepped toward them. "Boris!" He called over his shoulder. "It's Boris and his whelp, last as always!"

Boris slipped from the saddle and the two men embraced. "We traveled far Sergei Dor." He laughed, pretending to reel. "Bah! You are as foul smelling as ever! Standing by you is the closest to death I have been in years!"

Valko clambered off his horse as the rest of the grown men came out and met with his master. They were a rough looking lot, wearing wolfskins and carrying all manner of wicked looking weapons that glinted in the firelight. Most were heavily scarred, a sign of how dangerous the craft of wolf hunting was, and none were close too as old as Boris, who at 35 was practically an old man in the craft.

The youth walked past the men into the ring of stones. Each was over fifteen feet tall, and covered with runes that no man in the Konislund had ever been able to read. They were roughly hewn from dark grey stone, though the runes were cut neatly, and deep. As he passed through his hand brushed against one and he found it warm to the touch, having soaked in much of the suns warmth over the day.

These rings dotted the land, predating the coming of the Mayur to these shores, though those who made them were long dead it seemed. They were regarded as lucky, thought to hold onto forgotten magics. Towns were often built nearby for this reason, and in his time Valko had seen several other rings like this.

Behind him the men roared with laughter, but Valko had eyes only for the five youths his age that stood near the fire. Apprentices like himself, they too were foundlings, and considered each other the only family they had ever known. Grins devoured cheeks as they ran in to clasp hands with him, parroting their masters without realizing it.

There were four boys: tall, lanky Lazlo, Jaromir the only blonde to the others browns and blacks, Milos the runt of the pack, and Dejan, the biggest, just like his master Sergei. The girl, Ludmilla was a quiet, dour girl with deep scar on one cheek, the product of the bandit attack that killed her family. Together they had been given over to the wolf hunters at age 8, the traditional age of apprenticeship for foundlings. They had once numbered 7, but then wolves are a dangerous prey.

He knew them better than anyone save Boris, and he loved them all, and was proud of how far they had all come. Over their six years they had learned tracking and trapping, what plants healed and which ones could kill, where to seek shelter, and how to avoid dark spirits. They still had much to learn, but for their age they were fast becoming masters of the craft.

Behind them the welcomes were winding down so Valko hurried back to grab his horse's reigns, and along with his masters, guided them to them to where the other horses stood, chomping grass beneath a scrub oak. By the time he had returned to the circle each master was standing before a stone, his hands on his apprentices shoulders, facing in towards the fire. The boy rushed over to his spot in front of Boris, a bit abashed to be the last.

As soon as he felt the calloused hands of his master on his shoulder he felt a change in the air. The wind began to blow a bit harder, whipping the flames into a fury of dancing fire. There seemed to be a hint of lighting in the air, like that before a storm and Valko felt his flesh begin to tingle. The boy suspected there was magic at play here, but how, and what kind he knew not.

Boris spoke, his voice echoing around the stone ring. "Tonight you will be tested. If you pass, you will be granted to rank of journeyman, and brought into our mysteries, and taught the secrets you must know."

Valko yearned for that rank so badly it kept him up at night sometimes. He could tell from the looks in his fellow's eyes that they wanted it just as badly, tinged with wonder at what was to come. Never before had they all been tested together like this.

"In the valley below is what remains of the village of Fulksbad. Its history is dark, having turned to the worship of evil things, and for that the fury of the Forest King was brought down upon it, with the death of every soul within it." Boris paused, licking his lips. He rarely spoke, and Valko could tell that this speech was trying for him. "That should have been the end of Fulksbad, but the people had made a pact with a Dark One, granting them a sort of unlife each full moon. Tonight their spirits roam its streets, looking for those who serve the Forest King, to take their vengeance upon. You will go into the chapel at the center of town, and return bearing a token that Sergei placed there this morning with your name on it. Return with the token or don't return at all."

Broad Sergei stepped out from behind Dejan pulling a bundle from under his cloak. It was sackcloth wound tight with thin rope, and squatting down he unwrapped it, laying it out across the ground as he did so. Inside were six gleaming silver daggers, each about six inches long. They were clearly quite old, but well cared for, and Valko could tell they were honed to a razors edge. The big man stood and walked around the circle, handing one to each of the youths as he did. In the distance the rumble of thunder could be heard, low and powerful, causing a couple of the youths to jump a bit, which elicited a slight smile from Sergei.

Valko got his last, relishing the feel of the well-made hilt in his hand. He felt Boris remove his hands and saw him walk into the circle. The man pointed down the hill, into the darkness that their light-blinded eyes could not penetrate. "Those daggers will protect you from the spirits."

Boris looked around the circle, turning slowly and locking eyes with each apprentice in turn. When at last he faced Valko, he raised his fist. "Go!" He bellowed, slamming his fist into the side of his leg.

As one the youths sped off in the direction that Boris had pointed. Valko being on the far side from it was last, but he quickly caught up to the rest and in fact passed Dejan who was already beginning to wheeze a bit. "Sergei been letting you ride too much brother!" Shouted Milos at the hulking youth with a wink. Dejan made an obscene gesture back.

The initial mad dash had slowed as the group began to set a more sedate pace. They assumed the loping run they had been taught, much like that of the wolves they hunted, a run designed to devour miles with minimal energy spent. It was easy going as they went down the hill, and soon their eyes had adjusted to the darkness. Valko could begin to see the vague outlines of what must be the outskirts of the village, coming out of the gloom and slowly coalescing into familiar shapes.

The light of the moon began to grow fainter as wisps of clouds started to pass over it. Valko could feel the coming storm, that thickness of the air coupled with the steady rumble of thunder. Distant flashes of lightning could be seen now, and he worried that it would be on them before they could complete their task.

The faded remains of a dirt path seemed to sprout from the grass, and as one the pack of youths began following it. Focused on their breathing the joking and talking had stopped, and eager eyes pierced the gloom surrounding them. A ruined farmhouse and outbuildings rested to one side blocking the view of the town proper, while the other held a shattered wagon with only a pair of wheels remaining. Valko thought he saw the faint glimmer of moonlight reflecting off of the towns tall steeple over the collapsed roof of the farmhouse, but couldn't be sure.

As the group followed the track Valko at last could see into the main bulk of the town. Moonlight filled the narrow valley, giving the dozens of buildings that sat there an almost spectral glow. He could see that violence had clearly been done here, as many of the buildings were burnt husks, rotting timbers jutting up with charred tips like spent matches. Near the center of the town he could see the chapel, a stone building that was mostly still intact. It looked to be a straight shot down the dirt track, with nothing between them and their goal.

From the front of the pack Jaromir, always the swiftest of the group, looked over his shoulder and laughed. "Looks like easy pickings tonight! We'll be back before Sergei Dor has time to eat all the food!"

They all began laughing, even Dejan who wheezed, "I…hope… so… I'm… hungry!"

Just then blonde Jaromir stepped from dirt track onto a worn stone road. Immediately a horrific wail split the night. Coming from all around the ruined town, seeming to pour forth from dozens of throats came a ragged cry. Valko froze, listening as the sound, so full of pain and rage, washed over him, chilling him to the bone.

In front of them, silvery wisps that were almost foglike began seeping up from between the cracks in the stonework. Valko could see over a dozen of the clouds forming, the closest barely ten feet away. Within the mists he could see the vague outline of human shapes, arms stretching out towards he and his friends.

Valko called out, "Knives!" As he pulled his own from his belt where he had tucked it. Around him the rest pulled theirs as well, and each began to assume a fighting stance as the mists edged closer to them. The group pulled in tight to form a wedge, ready to protect each others flanks as they had been trained.

As the silvery clouds moved closer the shadowy figures within them became more clear. Dressed in simple peasants clothes, each wore an enraged look on its face, and a number of lethal looking wounds. They glided over the stones, looming tall above even Lazlo who was over five and half feet tall. As they closed, their mouths contorted and that horrible wail echoed forth once more. The steadily increasing wind, sign of the coming storm, whipped through their forms swirling the mist around them.

"By blade and claw!" Yelled Dejan lunging towards the closest of the spirits, dagger jabbing out to slice through the being. The silver knife passed through it as though he had stabbed air, leaving the ghost unaffected. The heavyset youth jumped back, slicing out again as he did so, with equally as little effect as before.

Valko lashed out at a rapidly nearing spirit, a blow that would have split wide the belly of a living creature. Instead the ghost silently hurtled closer, arms outstretched. He stepped back away, bumping into scrawny Milos behind him. Two more rapid jabs did just as little as his first, and the fear which had flirted with taking the fore within him at that first wail, now burst into full flame. The silver daggers did not work as they had been told, they were left defenseless in a town of the dead.

"Run!" Valko shouted as he tried to dodge the attacking spirit before him. Before he could get completely clear its spectral hand grazed his left shoulder as he ducked. He felt his whole arm go numb then, with only a feeling of bitter cold flowing through it. Arm hanging limply to his side he cleared away from the grasping arms and began sprinting towards the nearest ruin.

He could see that the rest of his friends had also scattered, with Dejan having thrown Milos over his shoulder. Valko was thankful the ghosts moved much slower, and prayed that Milos was just unconscious, not dead. The road looked to be filled with dozens of the spirits now, blocking the way to the chapel. The youth swore and tucked the dagger back into his belt with his good arm as he sprinted away.

He reached the ruined building and bulled through the rotting doorway, slamming into it with his numb arm in an attempt to save his good one any damage. The door fell to pieces as he entered the only room the house seemed to have. The roof was partly caved in, blocking most of the room and any possible exits it might hold, but towards the back he could see a pair of windows big enough to fit through.

He paused long enough to look through the doorway back out into the street. He caught a glimpse of lumbering Dejan ducked down an alleyway, but the rest of his friends were out of sight. Several of the spirits were following after him, their misty forms blowing in the rising wind, low moans rattling forth from within.

Dashing across the room he threw up the bolt securing the windows shutters and shoved them open. With his useless left arm struggled a bit to get through, but before any of the spirits could get close enough to attack he made his way out. He found

350

himself standing amidst a cluster of buildings. The moonlight had completely disappeared he was dismayed to find, the thick cloud cover having finally filled the night sky while he was inside.

A flash of movement caught his eye and he readied to sprint away, before he realized that it was tall Lazlo. The youth was signaling for Valko to come to him, waving his arm quickly with a look of fear on his face. Without a pause he sprinted towards him, trying to keep low and out of sight.

The narrow alleys between the tightly spaced buildings were overgrown with weeds and the detritus of the ruined homes. As Valko rushed he was forced to jump over a pile of rotting boards, a nail catching on his pants and ripping a large tear in them. HE didn't bother to slow to inspect the damage, as before him Lazlo interlocked his hands to make a step to help shove him to the roof.

Placing his foot it the cupped hands he used his momentum and the wiry strength of his friend to vault up high enough to pull himself up onto the roof with his good arm. The wood groaned beneath him but held as he reached down to clasp the reaching arms Lazlo, a task made doubly difficult due to his dead arm. Straining with effort they managed to get him onto the roof as well. Panting with exhaustion they lay flat as Valko saw the spectral figures that had been chasing him pass through the wall and enter the alley a few dozen feet away.

He held up a finger to the tall youth, signaling him to be silent. Watching quietly he saw the ghosts wander the alley for a bit, steadily expanding their search by threading in and out of the walls of the adjacent buildings. He gave thanks to the Powers that they never seemed to look upward and soon they had passed on out of sight.

"Seek height, right?" Said Lazlo.

Valko grinned and nodded. Their masters had drilled that into them countless times. In over your head with the wolves? Seek height. "Are you ok?" Valko whispered.

Lazlo nodded. "Why didn't the daggers work? They just kept on coming."

"I don't know," he said, shaking his head. "I hope everyone else made it ok. I saw that Milos was down…I hope he's alright."

"Dejan will look after him." Lazlo looked around. "I think we can go from roof to roof to get to the chapel. Shall we try it?"

Valko looked around. The spirits were gone, but he had a feeling they were merely waiting. He did not relish the thought of stepping back down onto the ground, that was for sure. Rising to a crouch the boards groaned ominously beneath him. "Yeah, but we need to be careful. What roofs are left aren't going to be very sturdy I think."

The pair began creeping over to the far edge of the roof. Valko was relieved that it held their weight and he hoped that they would continue to be lucky in that respect. He fingered the dagger in his belt, considering dropping it in an effort to shuck as much weight as possible for the jumps ahead, but at the last moment decided to hold on to it.

Reaching the edge he looked around. He could see no spirits nearby, though out in the main street he saw a few of the misty forms gliding back and forth seemingly aimlessly. The ledge of the next roof was only six or seven feet away, an easy jump under normal circumstances, but he was leery of getting too much of a running start. Looking over at Lazlo he asked "Ready?" Getting a nod he took three steps back and lunging forward leapt the gap.

With his arm flailing limply behind him he wobbled a bit, but managed to land safely. If anything this roof seemed even more sturdy than the last he was relieved to find, and a moment later his friend landed beside him. A quick glance showed that none of the spirits seemed to have noticed, still drifting, almost as if blown by the wind.

It had grown so dark that he could barely see the surrounding buildings and the closest bit of the main street. A patter of raindrops began falling, fat and cold. Valko swore and began treading over to the edge to try for the next jump. He was almost there when a jagged thrust of lightning split the sky, giving him a split second of light with which to see.

A few buildings over he saw Ludmilla, moving in the same direction they were. He thought she saw him, as she had been looking over her shoulder when the lightning flashed, and he hoped she would wait for them. He told Lazlo what he saw, and the two began hurrying faster, hoping to clear the roofs before the rain made them too slick.

The next jump went as smooth as the last, and the one after that found them sharing a creaking roof with Ludmilla, who as dour as ever seemed outwardly to be nonplussed by their arrival. Valko knew her well enough to read the subtle body language to know that she was relieved, but also knew better than to call her on it.

"Took you guys long enough," she said as she walked towards the next ledge.

Lazlo rolled his eyes. Valko walked alongside her talking softly. "Another dozen roofs or so and we will be near enough to the chapel to make a run for it I think. I figure Dejan and Jaromir are headed that way with Milos, maybe we will all get there around the same time."

Ludmilla just shrugged and leapt to the next building without saying anything. Shaking his head Valko followed. As he reached the apex of his leap he glanced down, and for a split second he saw a small upturned face, streaked with tears. It so startled him that he landed wrong, having to tuck and roll to save himself from being injured. Ludmilla was already heading to the next edge, but he called her back in a low voice. Lazlo landed next to them just then.

"There is a kid in the alley," said Valko. "Looks like it's hiding in a rain barrel."

Ludmilla looked aghast. "We need to help it." She went for the edge by Lazlo stopped her.

Holding her by the arm spoke just loud enough for them to hear. "What the hell is a kid doing here? It's got to be a demon. It's a trap, can't you see."

Snatching her arm away she glared at Lazlo. "Don't touch me."

While they faced off Valko walked to the edge of the room and peered down. Sure enough, hiding in a slowly filling rain barrel was a small boy of about six who was quietly crying into a blanket. He turned back to his friends.

The rain was really starting to come down now, hard enough he had to speak up to be heard over the sound of it drumming on the roof. He could barely see more than ten feet in any direction as the pouring rain began drenching them. "I don't think he's a demon Lazlo."

The tall boy glared angrily at Valko. "How do you know? And even if its not, how can we get it without climbing down? Those ghosts will be all over us if we try."

Valko looked down. He could not see any of the spirits, but in truth there could be a dozen within twenty feet of them and he would never know in this driving rain. He glanced to Ludmilla who was staring at him pleadingly. "It's what my master would do."

Lazlo snarled. "Boris Dor is not here. We have a mission to do, and I am not going to risk my rank on what is likely some demon."

Valko reached out and placed a hand on his tall friends shoulder. Before anything more could be said he took a step and jumped down to the ground below, Lazlo's curses following him down. "Make for the chapel, I will meet you there!"

The boy cowered in fear within the barrel, so Valko made a point to put a smile on his face. "My name is Valko. Come with me, and we will find your parents, yeah?"

The boys lip quivered. "They went with the ghosts...they left me."

Valko blanched inwardly. If they spirits had gotten them, this child was an orphan now. "Come on, lets get you somewhere safe, what do you say?"

Through the sound of the storm he thought he heard that frightful moaning, but he could not be sure. He knew he had to hurry, so with his good arm he reached into the barrel, snaking his arm under the boys arms and pulling him out. He set the boy down and kneeled. "Climb on my back, lets go for a ride."

The small child wrapped his arms around Valko's neck and together they took off down the alley. They had almost made it to the end when Lazlo and Ludmilla thudded down next to them. The tall boy pointed down the alley where a spirit was passing through the wall coming after them. "Run!"

Together they sprinted into the road heading toward where they thought the chapel was. Vague shapes formed in the downpour around them, ethereal moans echoing strangely, threading through the almost constant booming thunder. Lightning flashes bounced through the raindrops, causing an almost dizzying cascade of light. Valko prayed they would not run into one of the misty forms in their blind flight, but dared not slow his pace.

Carrying the added weight of the child had Valko's breath coming in ragged hitches. He could feel the boy burying his face in the crook of his neck, hiding from the horrors of the night as all children did, buy not looking. Legs pumping tiredly he tried for another burst of speed as he began lagging behind his two friends.

Just then Ludmilla leapt back, almost slamming into him. In front of her loomed one of the ghosts swinging blindly for them, its swirling form windblown and reaching. Lazlo tried lashing it with his knife, but as before it had no effect. Instead his hand was touched by the fell spirit and he dropped the dagger, his hand gone numb.

The group veered to run around it as it glided after them, but their speed held them in good stead once more and they broke clear of it, hopefully losing it in the storm. Moans came from all sides now, but thanks to the storm they could not be sure from exactly where they came from.

Though it was hard to tell through the storm Valko was sure they had to be getting close to the chapel. He desperately hoped so, because he was very sure if they did not reach it soon he would be forced to slow down, a move he felt sure meant death. He was about to call out to Lazlo, to see if he would carry the child for a bit, when several dark forms emerged from the gloom. Valko started to reel before he realized that they were solid, human shapes and not those of the spirits.

It proved to be Jaromir, who was carrying Milos over his shoulder, while Dejan limped beside them. With a sigh of relief the two groups met. Lazlo and Ludmilla threw arms around the injured Dejan and reunited at last they all moved as fast as they were able towards the chapel. Thankfully Valko could now see its stone walls looming out of the darkness, the steps leading up to its vaulted double doors just a few feet away.

They hurried up the rain slicked steps as quickly as they could, bursting through the open doors into the chapel. Lazlo turned and with Dejan's help forced the rusted doors closed while Valko set the boy down on the only pew that was still intact.

He turned to the rest. "By the Forest King, that was insane. I've got a dead arm, who else is hurt?"

'Turned my leg when I fell through a roof. Damn thing just gave way out from under me," said Dejan. He pointed to a bloody spot on his leg, which was roughly bandaged. "Got a bit of wood through my thigh too."

"Milos is unconscious," Jaromir said as he lowered the youth to the floor. "I can't wake him."

Valko swore, and looked around the room. There were piles of ruined pews, and on the far end sat an alter with six candles burning on it. They were arrayed around a massive wolfs head, a common symbol of the Prince of Night, one of the two main gods of the Konisland, though this one had no teeth unlike most.

Ludmilla was peering out through one of the shattered windows. Solemnly she turned and spoke. "They are coming."

"What the hell are our masters thinking sending us in here with no weapons!" Dejan roared, grabbing his dagger and flinging it at the far wall where it sunk into a timber. "We're doomed."

Ludmilla faced out to watch the approaching spirits. "They never said they were weapons you know, they just said they would protect us."

Dejan pointed to Milos. "He look protected to you?"

Valko, ignoring them, ran over to the altar, hoping something there would be of use. In front of the each of the candles was a small stone with their names on them. Other than those, and the statue of the wolfs skull, there was nothing. "Do you guys remember anything else they said? There must be something."

"Just that stuff about the town turning evil," said Lazlo.

"They are almost here," said Ludmilla, backing away from the window.

Inside Valko's mind, something clicked. "If they changed gods, why is the Lord of Night statue here?"

Jaromir huffed. "Cause the army of the Forest King put it there, duh."

Valko felt around in the mouth of the statue where the teeth should have been. "Why did they put one in with no teeth though?" His hand felt several holes spaced around the jaw. Pulling the dagger from his waist he slipped it into one of the holes where it clicked perfectly into place. "Put your daggers in its mouth! Hurry! If we can rebuild the statue, maybe the ghosts won't be able to come in! It'll belong to the Lord of Night once more!"

"That's crazy…" said Jaromir, but before he could finish Dejan and Ludmilla were pushing past him to put theirs inside. Hearing the moans right outside the walls however he scooped up his and Milos and tossed them to Valko.

"Guys…" Lazlo's voice was quivering. "I lost mine."

Everyone stared at him in horror as behind him the first spectral form slipped through the wall, its arms reaching out towards the youths. Valko frantically pushed each of the daggers into the waiting holes, but nothing happened save the ghost getting closer and being joined by a trio of other spectral forms. The youths began walking back to the far wall.

Valko felt a tug at his sleeve, and looking down he saw the boy child. "Mister...here." In his tiny hands he held up a dagger, similar to the ones they youths had been carrying. Valko knew it was not Lazlo's but praying fiercely he dashed forward and jammed it into the last open hole.

Instantly the eyes of the statue began glowing with a dark black light, and with a sound like a the howl of a wolf, the spirits were blown from the building. The youths rushed to the windows and looking out they could no longer see any of the spirits. They began whooping and yelling, clapping each other on the back. Valko turned to find the boy to thank him.

"Hey, where is the kid?" He asked. Everyone stopped and looked around. The boy was nowhere to be seen.

Ludmilla walked over to where the boy had last been. Lying on the ground was a small woven circle of ivy, the traditional symbol of the Forest King. She picked it up and held it out to show the rest, who stared at it with mute fascination. With a shrug she slipped it into her pocket and scooped up the stone with her name on it, blowing out her candle as she did so.

Mouse

Roselyn Perezv

I sit on the rocks watching the swirling water work itself into lather. It is unusually warm as I ease my blistered feet into it. I watch it wash away the dust and gravel that pricked like tiny knives. Each little stab wound leaving droplets of blood, like breadcrumbs to mark the places I've been. If I were to turn I'd see them, fresh as the dew on the grass. But there is no looking back, not for me. Instead I dip a hand in the water, and let the salt sprinkle my fingers. Lifting it out, I sample them. It is an acquired taste, but I am a fast learner.

Without further delay I push away from my perch and into the waves. The current snatches at me eagerly, dragging me out and in. Despite myself I start to struggle, gagging at the salt filling my throat. Above me a gull screams halfheartedly, as my head bobs in and out of the water.

I've lost all sense of direction; even the sky starts to dissolve into the water. Seaweed wraps around my wrist like a reassuring hand, as I sink. There is an incredible pressure inside me, as if I'm being collapsed, to make room for something else, which is as it should be.

Abruptly my body begins to float, by no will of my own. The pressure is on me again, only it's different somehow. Backwards. I'm back to where I started; coughing out everything I'd taken in. There is a mermaid sitting a few feet to my right, checking her reflection in a mirror and running a comb through her nearly luminescent green hair.

"Did you just save me?" I ask incredulously. She nods happily and smiles stunningly at me.

"Why?" I try to shout, but my voice cracks and it sounds more like a sad squeak. The mermaid only shrugs and hands me the mirror. It is surprisingly heavy, made out of gold and shells which I can only describe as fantastic, pearls the size of my thumb encircles the glass. In the center of all this extravagant beauty my reflection confronts me; my hair is a black, tangled, unruly mane, my hazel eyes are shiny with anger and unshed tears, the scar above my left eyebrow is visible even now that all the color has drained out of me. It hurts the way only scars can, reminding me that the past is something I carry always. I wipe my nose, my boxer's nose as my mom used to call it, but of course that is a gross exaggeration. It is a fine nose, even if it is slightly crooked. Still, it is plain to see that I am no mermaid. I pass the looking glass back, and try to stand up.

What I want to do is storm off indignantly; taking the tiny shred of dignity I have left with me. But, my legs are still too weak to support me, so what I actually do is fall back onto my butt. I sulk in silence for a while, as the mermaid pretends to look in the mirror as if what she wants is to make sure she looks as flawless as she remembers. What she is actually doing is tilting the mirror slightly so that she can watch me, and covering her grin with a delicate hand.

"You can leave now you know. I won't jump again. You did your job, so you can just be on your way." She looks wounded, her smile wavering and then fading altogether. I feel as if I've just kicked a puppy, and open my mouth to mumble some kind of apology when she leaps back into the water with a splash that hits me like a slap. It doesn't bother me all that much seeing as I am already soaked, and honestly what is a little slap in the grand scheme of things? A caress really, I think as I place a hand over my scar.

This is the edge of the world, at least for me. What can one do when they try to fall off the ledge and find themselves thrown back, but dust themselves off and go home? I try standing again, my legs wobble, but support me. It looks like I'll have to look back after all, more than that; I'll have to retrace each agonizing step. I put on my shoes, and wrap my old, but warm, cloak around myself, pulling up the hood. There is a mask inside the left pocket, and I slip it on. I'm someone else now, it's easier than people might think, this hiding your real face.

There are two things I really excel in; blending into any shadow and observing. That's why most know me as mouse. I must rely on my talents now more than ever, because they are close and now that I have no choice but to return they must not catch me.

Traveling is not an easy business. So, I tell myself a story to drown out the protests of my poor abused feet.

"Once upon a time, in a tiny village near the tremendous castle, there lived a little mouse who wished more than anything to be a lion. Foolishly, she crept into the lion's den for a chance to admire their great size and beauty. In that moment she again wished to be a grand and noble lion, before she found herself caught between the lion's claws." I tell the story out loud, and am pleased to find that the mask has changed my voice as well as my face. The sudden sound of baying dogs quickly dashes any pleasure, however. Dogs are not like people, they're not fooled by clever masks, and they smell what lies beneath. I look around, but there is only barren land on either side with shin high grass peaking up sporadically from the rocky ground.

Three enormous black hounds appear on the horizon, their paws devouring the distance with a determination that is almost elegant. They pause as one at the alarmingly close sound of the horns, and sing out a throaty response that falls over me, colder and wetter than any wave. My legs are wobbling, and I know running is not an option. I watch them descend on me, the slobber on their teeth reflecting the light, and creating pocket sized rainbows that disappear almost as soon as they form. I could reach out and snatch one up, they are so close, but then they move past me. Perhaps, the sea has washed the scent of me away.

The horn blasts again and now the four horseman are visible. The last rider carries a huge black banner with a roaring lion on it, the wind making it almost appear alive, and hungry. I leap out of the way as the first three; dressed in dark armor, ride past me in a rush to catch up to their hounds. The last one reins in his horse beside me. He wears no armor, but there is a long sword with a roaring lion's head on its hilt, strapped to his side. His face isn't familiar to me, but it has the royal features, delicate and rugged at the same time. His eyes are brown instead of the deep blue of most of his kind, but there is no mistaking his bloodline, he is a lion, and so, my mortal enemy.

"You, girl what is your name?"

"Rachael Trench, if it please my lord," I lie and give a deep curtsy that almost sends me down on my butt again.

"Well, Rachael Trench, we're on the trail of a dangerous trader. Sophia Streams, commonly called Mouse. She is accused of spreading venomous lies about our noble king, and leading several treasonous uprisings against the royal family. You didn't happen to see her, did you?" He raises an eyebrow and there is a slight smirk in his words.

"No, My Lord, but I heard her village and most all her family were destroyed by our sweet king. If it was me I'd drown myself and save our king the trouble."

"Yes, but mice are vermin, and vermin aren't that easily eradicated. She's easy enough to spot though; pretty in an offhanded sort of way, except for that scar and odd nose." There is no mistaking his smirk now, as I try not to stiffen at his words.

"I'll definitely be keeping a look out, My Lord." I say through clenched teeth, he nods and starts to nudge his horse forward, but stops and looks back,

"Oh, and if you do happen to see her tell her that all the main roads have hunting parties patrolling them." He digs his heals into his horses side and just like that he's barreling away from me, the banner looking like a lady's kerchief waving farewell.

There's a cluster of skeletal trees hunched together off in the distance, I head for them, and try to puzzle out what just happened. As I walk beyond them the land becomes greener, and soon I am at the edge of the dark woods. These trees are tall and muscular, boldly stretching out their limbs in invitation, or challenge. The royals and their men avoid this place, and when they do enter, stumbling and rattling in their heavy armor, the stoic silence of the woods unnerves them. But I feel right at home as I slip between two hulking trunks; there are a million shadows here, and I am familiar to them all.

It will take twice as long to reach my village, or what's left of it, but from there it is a short way to the kingdom, and I will be in my element. I stay on the inner border of the trees, peeking through the branches occasionally, and keeping an ear out for patrols. A large border town is visible ahead, and I watch the activity around it: bakers and vendors load up their carts and yell back and forth to each other and the people passing by, children dash between streets and alley ways chasing dogs, goats, chickens and one another, young girls with pails and baskets move arm in arm around the corner, disappearing into a building. It seems a pleasant, prosperous place at first glance, but an astute observer would catch the hungry, ragged look of the children and the animals, the anxious slant stares the girls throw from side to side as they clutch each other, and pass the charred remains of a pyre on the town square. Four soldiers ride into the town, thankfully they have no hounds. They stop to shout questions at people, then rush on, scattering the people and animals, trampling whatever isn't fast enough to get out of the way. Even with all this, or maybe because of it, I consider going into the town and finding an inn.

"I'd wait for dark if I were you." The voice comes from right beside me, so close that the words toss a few strands of my hair into my face. I flip the owner of said voice over my head and onto the hard ground in front of me. In a single motion I pull along dagger from beneath my cloak and point it at the neck of the lion with the brown eyes. He's winded, but tries to sit up. I press the point of the dagger down until I draw a spot of blood. That convinces him that sitting up is a stupid idea, and he lies very still on the forest floor. With my free hand I pull off my mask, so that he'll see my true face before he dies.

"Congratulations, Lion, you've found the vermin. What a shame it will be you, and not me who dies, but you know how hard we vermin are to eradicate."

"I never wanted to eradicate you; I'm here because I want to help you."

"Help me right into my noose, I have no doubt."

"If I wanted you dead I could have captured you when we met on the road, or I could have run my sword through you just now instead of giving you some friendly advice." I scoff at his words, but my dagger wavers. I step back, but hold the blade at the ready.

"Why would a lion want to help anyone, especially me?" He sits up and rests his chin on his hand, in the posture of thought.

"Let's see: I suppose we should begin with the fact that I am not a lion, oh, my father was king third of his name, conqueror of nations, lover of battles etc. but, my mother was a dairy farmer's daughter, milker of cows, and changer of chamber pots. There is no one my half-brother hates more than me, except maybe you."

"I thank you for your kind words, and friendly advice, but I am a solitary creature by nature. I hope you understand," I turn away from him and start towards the town.

"I do, because so am I, which is why I know we'll make an excellent team. My name is Daniel by the way." He smiles brilliantly, and ignores my withering look.

"I know this town quite well, the Inn is disgusting and lice ridden, luckily I have a friend who will take us in I'm sure," he says falling into step beside me.

"I have no problems with lice, I've dealt with worse." The Inn is just around the corner, and I head for it, stopping short as I spot the soldiers standing around the entrance loudly interrogating the people inside. A fat soldier steps into the street, mopping his face with a handkerchief and blowing his nose. He glances my way, and our eyes lock just as I realize I've forgotten to put my mask back on. His face acquires an alarmingly bright red hue, and his mouth yawns in a cartoonish expression of astonished outrage.

"This friend of yours, where did you say he lived again?" Daniel takes my hand and rushes in the opposite direction.

"This way," he huffs as we dart through a narrow alley hand in hand. I'm disconcerted by how natural having Daniel's hand on mine feels, but the soldiers heavy footfalls are close, so I hold on and let him lead me through winding streets until we reach the heart of the town. There is a sea of people and they crowd around us, slowing the soldier's progress, and stepping aside quickly to let us pass. I'm surprised, but Daniel just winks riley at me. We reach a large ramshackle house, and Daniel leads me around to the back.

There is a stable close by, and a well off to one side. Daniel gives the door three rapid knocks. An enormous bearded man opens the door wearing an equally enormous Viking helmet, complete with bull horns. He snatches Daniel up, and for a moment I wonder if he's going to eat him, but he only wraps him in a huge bear hug.

"Well I'll be damned, Martha it's the cub!"

"Yes, well so much for discretion Daniel says, as he tries to free himself from the big man's arms.

"Well, come in then, if you've got to have things kept quiet like. He ushers us inside and slides an iron bar across the door.

"Sophia this is, Bull, the finest sword smith in all the land, and one of my oldest friends. Bull, this is—"

"Mouse, as I live and breathe, I never thought I'd be receiving the people's queen under my roof. I am truly and deeply honored," he says as he drops to one knee and bows his head.

"What? What is he doing?" I ask, truly horrified.

"When my half-brother took the thrown and abused his power and his people there was only one person who dared speak out against him. You led your people to declare themselves sovereign, and when soldiers came to reclaim your people as slaves you fought."

"And lost," I add.

"Aye, that you did, but you showed the rest of us that we didn't have to cower in a corner and take kick after kick, like beat dogs. You gave the people hope and we want you leading' us. You're our choice not a cowardly king that takes everything we got, and beats us for not having more for him to steal." We all look up at Martha's words. She's carrying a basket like the ones I saw the girls holding. She sets it down in front of me,

"Look here, these are all the scraps of metal and brass that the girls and children collect and bring here for Bull to turn into something to arm the boys and anyone else that's willing to fight when the time comes."

Bull points proudly to a pair of wicked looking knives hanging on the wall, "Them's Martha's. She can slice the meat off a man cleaner than any butcher preparing a roast, and throw them farther and faster than any man can run."

"I'm not looking to be Queen, or to lead, I am just looking for revenge. Daniel would be a better choice to succeed the throne anyway."

"Did you see that pyre out there in the square? That's all that's left of a young girl caught bringing supplies here. They tortured her trying to get her to tell where she was takin' them things, and who else was helping take supplies. God only knows what all they did to her, and how she survived it, but when they dragged her up to tie her to the stake, naked and bloody she looked the executioner in the eye, and real quiet at first said, 'The lion will fall to the mouse.' Again, and again she said it, louder each time. Even as they lit her up she yelled it, and the people started yelling it with her, until a soldier drove a spear through her heart, and more soldiers rode through the crowd striking and trampling anyone that didn't get out the way quick enough. So, you forget your revenge, this is bigger than all that. This is about that girl and all us like her. You lost your village and that's a hard thing, but we're your village now and we need you." Martha's words move me more than I want to admit.

"Where do you fit into all this?" I ask, Daniel. To my further horror he unsheathes his sword and kneeling presents it to me.

"I would be honored if you would name me the first knight of your court." I look at their faces and register the truth in their words. Their trust settles on me and I have no choice but to nod.

"Take me to the square; I want to see it for myself." Without another word, Martha pulls a lantern from the wall and we follow her out. There's still enough light out to see by, but the last of the sun has disappeared, taking all the color from the sky and casting the world in a deep gloom. It seems fitting as we gather around the charred remnants. My eye catches on small fragments of bone scattered among the cinders, pale and delicate, but defiantly standing out among the ashes.

After a moment I say, "A soldier saw me today. If they sound the alarm the King's army will flood the city. He can't know where I am, not yet." Martha hands the lantern to Bull and pulls out her knives, and Daniel unsheathes his sword. We watch them ease effortlessly into the shadows, before returning to Bull's home to watch and wait.

Sometime just before dawn, Daniel arrives bloody and exhausted. We rush him inside, and I examine his injuries. Martha isn't with him. Bull and I wait for Daniel to speak, our eyes asking what our mouths refuse to.

"We killed all of the soldiers at the inn, but one of them, the fat one that saw us, went ahead to send word to the capital. We thought we might be able to cut him off, but the hunt for you is better organized, and manned than I imagined, because we ran right into troops headed for town. Martha saved my life," he pauses and puts a hand on Bull's shoulder, "I'm sorry Bull, she didn't make it."

Bull shrugs off Daniel's hand, "If the king had any doubts about Sophia and the revolution still bein' alive, he's got his answer and I need to get workin'. It's what Martha would want me to do." The big man's voice breaks when he says his wife's name and I feel as if I've fallen back in time to when people were losing their lives and families because of my act of impotent bravado.

"He's right," Daniel says, "The best way to honor Martha is to fight even harder." I don't respond and he takes my chin in his hands.

"Don't doubt yourself, Martha didn't, and neither do I. You are our queen. Now the war has started and we must be ready."

The war has indeed begun; the king sends his army to overwhelm the town. We are hopelessly outnumbered, but Daniel is a fearless warrior and leader. The king's army falls back further each day, and more and more men are crossing over to fight against the crown.

On the seventh day of fighting a messenger arrives in a royal coach. He pulls up in front of Bull's home and takes a box down. It bears the royal seal on the sides. He informs us that it is a gift for me from his highness. He says this with a stutter and a nervous glance at Daniel and Bull. Daniel wants to send it away unopened, but I want to see. Of course, they insist on keeping me away from it until they are satisfied of its safety. Bull gives the terrified messenger a hard shove and motions for him to get on with it. The poor man leans down and lifts the lid off the crate. His eyes bug out, and he jumps backwards so quickly that his foot hits the side of the box and knocks it over. Martha's head, dipped in tar, rolls out and lands with her facing me. Her face is as fierce and stalwart as it was in life. Not even death could take the fight from her. The men are cursing, and shouting, but I don't hear them. I stare at Martha's head and hear her words to me as if she were speaking them from where she lies,

"We're your people now and we need you." I nod at, Martha, finally I know what I must do. I look up to see, Bull lifting the poor messenger up by his neck.

"Let him go," I say, and they all turn to me.

"You will go to the king and tell him that I wish to respond to his gift in person." The messenger bows and scurries off. Daniel opens his mouth to say something but I cut him off.

"Get the horses and men ready. I want to leave as soon as possible."

We are lined up outside the castle as Richard rides up. He looks like a descended angel, but of course demons are just fallen angels after all. He and his men stop a few yards from us. We say nothing for a moment, just glare at each other from across the distance. Finally I say, "Too many good men and women have died on both sides. I come with an offer to end this."

"The only offer I'll accept, my frightened little mouse, is you're complete surrender." I ignore his haughty tone and press on, "We settle this in single combat," he perks up at this, and his arrogant smirk is more than I can bear.

"That suits me. I believe you know who my champion will be." The king gestures a rider forward, and I see that it is Sir Garret Frost. Most know, Frost as the Glacier, because you don't realize how enormous he really is until he's right in front of you, and then it's usually too late. And, the man is as cold as his name; he kills men and swats flies with the same indifferent expression.

"It will be my honor to put the glacier's head on a platter for you," Daniel says, but I hold up my hand for silence.

"No, my people have fought for me and now I will fight for them.

What do you say we fight our own battle, Richard? No armies, no champions, just you and I finishing what we started."

"Kings do not fight loathsome pests; Sir Frost however is quite adept at eradicating your kind. Tell me, how many of your family did he slay again? I resist the urge to charge him and tear into him with my bare hands. Instead I smile,

"You're too afraid to face me then? Behold, your king," I shout with mocking deference, "His royal highness, King Richard fourth of his name, King of cowards." A roar of laughter erupts, most of it coming from my men, but some of Richard's camp was joining in as well. Then all at once the chant of, "King of cowards" comes from every one of my soldiers, so that it is one single accusing voice branding him.

"Enough!" Richard cries, and I know I have him.

"I accept your challenge, unfortunately for you; I am not as gracious as Sir Frost. Your death will be a long and painful affair."

"I guess your highness hasn't heard the prophesy, "The lion will fall to the mouse!" At this my men begin shouting, "The lion will fall to the mouse."

"In three days on the edge of the world," I say and ride away from the castle. Daniel spurs his horse to catch up with me but I don't slow down and he falls farther behind.

Bull is waiting for me when I ride up to his house. There is a smile on his face; it's the first time I've seen him smile since Martha was killed in battle.

"I've got something for you, Queen Mouse." He holds out a small, elegant sword to me. I take it eagerly and slice the air. It's thinner and lighter than any sword I've ever seen and fits perfectly in my grasp.

"It's made of Damascus steel with a dwarf's eye diamond tip. It can cut through anything even King Richard's stone cold heart I'm betting."

"It's beautiful, Bull, but it's too much. Dwarf's eye diamonds are the rarest in the kingdom and we should use it to help feed my men."

"All the materials were donated by noblemen that didn't have no use for 'em anymore. Besides, what kind of men would we be if we let our queen go into battle with that rusty steak knife you carry around?" I throw my arms around him and simply say, "thank you."

368

Daniel rides up; he's scowling as he dismounts and storms towards us. I smile and ignore his withering look

"Bull has truly outdone himself," I say, proudly displaying my sword. I slice the air between us hoping to dissolve the tension I see there.

"I'm going to call it thorn," I say cheerily.

"It's about the size of one," he says disgustedly.

"It's good you underestimate thorn and I because that means Richard will too."

"I'm nothing like him. I just can't understand this insane risk you're taking. In three days you will face a brutal man who was practically born with a sword in his hand with nothing more than a shiny twig and no armor."

"This shiny twig could slice right through your rock like head. Besides, I already explained to you that the armor is too heavy and that my quickness is my greatest advantage."

"This isn't a game. I know Richard and frost too well. If we lose you I don't know what will become of us, what will become of me? His voice breaks and my eyes fill with tears that I blink back furiously.

"No one knows better than I what the stakes are and the evil I will be facing. I'm not afraid, and do you know why?" He shakes his head and I take his hand, willing him to look at me and understand, "Because no matter what happens it will not be the end but the beginning of a revolution that cannot be stopped."

I turn and head for the square; I seem to be drawn here, to this place where a girl died screaming her defiance in my name. Where I last saw Martha as she sliced through the darkness to cut down my enemies. I think of my village being slaughtered and burned to the ground and my legs give out beneath me. My sword falls among the cinders as I curl up into a little ball beside it. I meant what I said to Daniel, I'm not afraid to die. I'm all too happy to die because this has all been my doing.

The morning of the duel is fresh and brilliant. The sun isn't out yet, but I can already tell that when it shows itself it will be unusually warm. It's arrogant of me to have expected a grim, dramatic backdrop to my battle, but I must admit it's depressing to think I could die while the sun shines and birds twitter about the pleasant break in the chill. Richard looks like a shimmering giant in his gold plated armor. I step forward in my plain brown cloak, all too aware that Richard's sword is as big as I am.

He shakes his massive head in derisive amusement, "This pathetic revolt ends today. Your men should be ashamed of standing behind a mouse of a girl, especially you, Daniel, but what can you expect from bastards and peasants."

Daniel's face turns even more somber, but he simply says, "The lion will fall to the mouse." The rest of my men pick it up until the ground shakes with the promise. Richard's smile falters, and he roars, "The mouse will kneel in pieces before me." He charges at me, I stand perfectly still, watching his wild face barrel towards me. I leap to the left at the last possible moment, using my body to trip him, and his own momentum to send him crashing into the dirt. I roll quickly to my feet, hoping Richard has impaled himself, but he's already getting up and coming at me again. He's more careful this time, his movement's fluid and practiced. I dance and scurry just out of his reach, but he is herding me towards the rocks, trapping me between him and the water. The sea seems to sense my precarious position. It surges, making the rocks slick with its desire, and wrapping around my ankles before retreating. I trip, my feet finding a grip just inches away from the edge. Richard has closed the distance between us in the second I was distracted. His sword whistles towards me; I bring Thorne up to parry the blow. My wrist feels shattered with the impact, but I hold on and when Richard thrusts at me again, Thorne wedges itself between his sword and the fleshy part of his palm. The sword clatters heavily onto the rocks, and I kick it into the waters beyond.

Richard roars like a wounded beast that knows its time is short. With a mighty yank of his hand he pulls Thorne out of my grasp, but it is still firmly lodged in his palm. His eyes are wild as he tries to use his arm, Thorne and all, to knock me down, I duck, but his other arm snakes around me and presses me tight against him. I know we are going to fall before, Richard does. As he slips, he squeezes me even tighter, a deadly embrace that steals my breath as I am dragged off the edge of the world.

Richard is gone, snatched away to some unknown depth. The water is what clutches me now. It gathers around expectant, insistent, as if pleased that we can finally finish what I started. There is a scream in the distance, but I am unsure if it is Daniel or the gull that was with me that first time. I struggle to find my way back, to escape the cold fingers that press upon me, greedy to claim me for its own

Seaweed wraps around my arms and chest, tangling my already clumsy limbs. I try to shake it off, but I am caught as surely as an insect in the grandest web. Another wave slams over me and this time I feel something break. My body goes limp, my tears taking their place among the foam. I'm sorry, I think as I am carried like a jellyfish by the current.

I land like a broken shell on the shore; Daniel drags me completely out of the sea's reach, and pounds me on the back as if in congratulations. I cough out everything that was forced down, and take a shuddering breath. The mermaid is there, bobbing in the water, a bashful smile touching her lips. I motion for Daniel to step back. Once I am alone on the rocky edge she emerges and seats herself a few feet to my right.

"You saved me," I rasp, unable to find the words I really want to say. She beams, and nods at me with fervor.

"Why," I ask, knowing I'm being redundant, but needing to know the answer. She hands me her mirror; I take it and confront my reflection. It is unchanged from the last time I looked, it is just me, scars and all, but this time I also see what she saw all along. I see someone worth saving.

"Thank you," I say simply and she embraces me. I try to return the mirror, but she shakes her head, and leaps silently back into the water. Daniel is by my side again and helps me to stand. We walk away from the edge, our arms around each other for support, there is a long way to go, but somehow that doesn't seem like such a bad thing. Our feet move as one as we make our way back towards the others who are waiting, some cheering, some struck dumb with shock and fear to know that their king is dead and that I am their Queen now. We move steadily forward, my feet never faltering as I approach my people. Traveling is never an easy business, but the journey is always worth making.

Jaguar and the Rising Sun

Robert Santa

On the day Rooster failed to wake up the Sun, Jaguar was on a hunt. He had been waiting for the coming dawn to shake animals from their slumber. But after a long while of darkness, Jaguar took the spear from his atlatl and marched eastward.

Jaguar knew that Rooster roused the Sun from the highest hill of the eastern lands. It was a long journey in full daylight. He called for help, and the stars came down and held their flickering candles cupped against the wind. The light was brighter than before but still weak. Despite eyesight like his namesake, Jaguar jogged unsteadily.

Near the end of a full day of darkness, Jaguar came to a wide river. The water did not rush by, yet it gurgled in places as if it were filled with the voices of hundreds of water nymphs. Jaguar took out his maquahuitl and cut through dozens of thick bamboo growing beside the river. He quickly tired of the sword's bitter complaints about being used for such bloodless work, so he took his obsidian knife from its sheath on his hip to cut the sturdy vines. He lashed a crude raft and poled it into the water. The current took the raft in its arms and carried it slowly downriver.

The surface of the river rippled. A snake swam by, its wedge-shaped head held just above the water. The snake was huge, as big around as Jaguar's massive arm and twice as long as the raft. Jaguar watched it pass and continued to pole.

The raft shook. Jaguar suspected it was a submerged rock until an even larger snake's head rose onto the bamboo. He drew back the pole and jammed it into the snake's open mouth, but it deflected off the hard ridge of its jaw.

The snake pressed more of itself onto the raft. The vines lashing the bamboo together fought the weight as the great beast drove one corner under the water. Jaguar spread his legs for balance and took out his maquahuitl. The obsidian chips sparkled in the starlight, and his sword begged him to drink the snake's blood.

Then Jaguar was in the water, the raft crumbling beneath him. The ungainly snake became a monster of quickness, and Jaguar found himself in its coils. He raised his arms to keep them free, yet the snake crushed his chest and forced out his breath even as it dragged him under the water. The current brushed by Jaguar's ears with its fingertips and told him of his impending death.

He swung the sword. The water deflected the maquahuitl so that the flat of the wood bounced harmlessly off the monster's scales.

Jaguar swung again, and this time the obsidian flakes dug deep. Still the snake crushed him. His vision blackened at the edges, and he swung the sword knowing that it would be his last strike. The maquahuitl added its thirst to his strength as it twisted in Jaguar's hand to guide its edge to the snake's open wound. The sword passed through the beast, and the snake relaxed. Jaguar struggled upward, surrounded by the blood of the bisected snake. His head broke the surface, his lungs filled with sweet air, and his sword shrieked with laughter.

Jaguar climbed the far side of the river and threw himself on the shore. The moon covered him with a blanket of its radiance that was too thin to ward off the night chill. His mantle was soaked and offered no more protection than the cloth around his loins or the chains of tiny shells around both his ankles. He took a moment to regain his breath then put away the maquahuitl over its complaints and continued east.

Jaguar slept when he became tired. He awoke uncertain whether it was night or day in the eternal black. A fat tapir came near his camp, curious of the fire that seemed so much like the dawn. Jaguar slew it and feasted on its meat. He offered the rest of the animal to the bugs and scavengers which accepted the meal on behalf of the earth.

When Jaguar neared the eastern lands, he saw the flat plains were separated from the chain of hills by a gorge that split the world. As far as his eyes could see, the chasm stretched. It seemed he could leap the distance, but Jaguar was smart as well as strong and knew the nearness was only an illusion. He looked down over the edge for handholds; the sides were as smooth as a tortoise's underbelly. A delicate mist covered the floor of the gorge so that Jaguar could not tell whether it was a fog he looked down upon or the tops of clouds.

He walked all morning along the edge of the chasm until he saw a bridge. It spanned straight and wide, large enough for ten warriors to march alongside each other without touching shoulders. It was secured to stone platforms made of rocks that dwarfed Jaguar.

He was about to climb up to the stone platform when a monstrous thing stepped out from behind it. Twice as tall as Jaguar and twice as broad, it looked misshapen, as if a bowl of chaquegue mush had been poured over it. The doughiness of its flesh in no way fooled

Jaguar for the thing carried the solid trunk of a tree, intricately carved with animal designs and ringed with leather strips studded with stone flakes. It was also carried in one hand the way Jaguar would carry his maquahuitl.

The tree suddenly went up. Jaguar dove as the club came crashing down. The ground vibrated with its impact. Jaguar rolled and came to his feet, expecting to be struck. But the giant thing stood there at the foot of the bridge and held its massive club casually.

"I chose to miss you, little man," it said, the words slurred behind offset tusks.

"I understand. My name is Jaguar, and I seek a way to the highest hill in the eastern lands that I might wake the Sun."

"I am Troll. The bridge is mine."

"I seek to cross it, Troll," Jaguar said.

"None may cross that have not defeated me."

Jaguar's maquahuitl asked to taste Troll's blood, but Jaguar quieted it.

"I have no wish to fight you, Troll, for something so trivial as permission to cross a bridge. You and I are not enemies."

"The bridge is mine. None may cross."

"Yet I must to wake the Sun. Have you not noticed the animals languishing in torpor? The trees and plants starving?"

"Troll likes the dark."

Jaguar looked to either side, warily keeping an eye on Troll as he did so.

"How long will it take to go around?" He asked.

"As many as these days," said Troll, holding up all the fingers of one hand. "It is why Troll made the bridge."

"I don't want to fight you, Troll." Jaguar took the atlatl from his back and fitted a spear into it.

"Then answer the riddle."

Jaguar cocked his head to the side, like a dog who had heard a strange noise.

"We do not have to fight?" he asked.

"Maybe. If you are wrong, then Troll and Jaguar still fight, whether you try to cross or not."

"How many have tried the riddle?"

Troll lifted a massive arm and pointed. Jaguar looked and saw a rack of skulls ten strides long and almost as tall as Troll.

"Very well," Jaguar said. "I have not the luxury of time to go around. I apologize now if we must cross weapons."

"Does the little man say he wants to hear the riddle?"

"Yes, Troll. Speak it to me."

Troll's eyes looked towards the darkened sky as if he were searching for the pictographs that would remind him. Then he lowered them and spoke.

"What will bring you all your desires - gold, a kiss, a nation - if only wielded well?"

The maquahuitl begged for attention. It screamed and howled until its handle grew warm in Jaguar's hand.

"If I had any cacao beans," said Jaguar, "I would wager that the men who wore those skulls all said it was a sword, or a spear, or perhaps even war itself." Jaguar nodded in the direction of the skull rack.

Troll said nothing. He did, though, ready his club.

"Yet while gold is easily gained by the slashing of obsidian blades, and nations as well, a sword will never freely bring you the touch of a woman's lips. A blade raised in threat can force the gesture but not the feeling behind it."

"You will not get a clue," Troll said, shifting his weapon into his other hand.

"The riddle itself is a clue, Troll. It is perhaps the greatest of weapons."

"The answer is not 'weapons,' little man." Troll took a step forward, club upraised.

"I did not say it was," Jaguar replied. Even with Troll looming over him, the club head as high as the nearest tree, Jaguar stood motionless, his hand clear of the desperate sword.

"No," said Troll, though he continued to hold the club aloft, "you did not. What is your answer to Troll's riddle?"

"Words." Jaguar smiled. "The answer you seek is 'words.'"

Troll lowered his club.

"It makes Troll happy not to kill the little man and add his skull to the rack."

"As it does me," said Jaguar. He bounded up to the stone platform and crossed the sturdy bridge at a run.

The stars, no longer driven away during the day by the Sun, filled the black void of the sky with their slow march west. They asked

Jaguar if he needed more light, for they could call the moon and tell him to hurry to the horizon. Jaguar declined, seeking stealth over speed.

Jaguar heard the soft language of the ocean long before he saw it. Hidden behind the crest of hills, the water's words blurred into one another as they echoed back to him from dozens of slopes. The highest hill was easy to find, for it dwarfed all others by half again.

Jaguar moved to its northern slope, away from the lights of the stars and moon. He stripped off his jewelry and his headdress. He placed his atlatl and spears and his pack beside them, for he needed both hands to climb. He set foot on the highest hill with only his clothing and maquahuitl.

The moon made its journey across the sky before Jaguar crested the hill, winning the race against the stars as it always did. In the darkness, even with his eyes accustomed to the forever night, the details of the hilltop were lost in shadow. Jaguar could see a second peak, oddly-shaped. It was only after he stood beside it that he knew it was a pyramid.

The stairs were high and sharply-angled; one misstep and Jaguar would tumble to certain injury or death. He padded as quietly as he could, maquahuitl in hand. The sword tingled with anticipation, but it had sense enough to remain quiet.

The pyramid flattened at the top. A square building - probably a temple - occupied the far side. With the darkness of the forest behind him and the empty expanse of the ocean before, Jaguar felt he was standing at the top of the universe. He stretched out his arm, but the cloth of the sky was still beyond his reach.

Jaguar stalked to the temple. Statues - either demons or gods - flanked the entrance. It should have been an open doorway, but it was covered in a thick blanket. He eased it aside only to find another blanket hung behind the first. There were fifteen blankets in all. With the removal of one, a glow brightened on the next until he pushed aside the last curtain and looked upon the Sun.

She was stretched out on her side, clothed only in the shimmering of her jewelry. Her hair languished on the top of the altar stone as if it had been neatly arranged away from her face. Leather straps bound her wrists and ankles, stretching her the full length of the altar. Her radiance was magnificent, and Jaguar paused so that the brightness of it could warm him.

Against one wall of the open temple chamber was Rooster. He was also bound at wrists and ankles, arms and legs splayed. His shaggy hair covered his face, and his naked body bore horrible injuries. His skin was burned almost in its entirety. Scabrous wounds oozed fluids. Rooster's chest rose and fell, each lifting shallow and ragged. He was a giant compared to Jaguar, yet held in his torturous restraints, he seemed a discarded doll. At his feet were his stripped belongings: mantle and breechclout, feathered shield, and war club.

The Sun saw Jaguar and stiffened. Her eyes widened with the slackening of her mouth, yet she relaxed instantly and let her face assume its former drowsiness. Jaguar knew then that whoever his enemy might be, he was around the corner out of sight. The Sun's face and body betrayed no more reaction, so Jaguar couldn't tell whether he had been discovered or not. As stealthy as he was, Jaguar felt he had surely been heard. He squeezed the sword's handle to ready it for battle, and it rejoiced as he pounced.

Jaguar leapt into the singular room of the temple and whirled. He had just enough time to flatten himself on the ground as ugly, black energy vomited over his head. It splashed against the far wall and melted the stone. Jaguar tried to rise but rolled instead as the column of viscous acid chased him across the floor, gouging a channel in the solid rock of the hilltop. The earth rumbled in agony and suppressed a shiver that would have surely loosened the temple from the hilltop.

The magic silenced, and Jaguar jumped to his feet, maquahuitl in both hands.

Bat stood beside the entrance, cloaked in the filthy black robes of his priestly office. They were crusted with the gore of thousands of sacrifices and victims. His long, black hair lay matted against his face and shoulders, plastered there as if by some horrific artist. Both hands were upraised, fingers curled into claws.

"Greetings, Jaguar," he snarled. The menace all oozed from his lips like drool.

"What have you wrought here, Bat?"

"I am tired of the night being so brief. In daylight I am weak and helpless, but here in the dark, I am Master."

"It is not your place," said Jaguar. "You should be happy to rule the night."

"Oh, I am. And with the Sun no more, I will rule until the end of time."

"I cannot allow that."

"You don't have a choice, Jaguar." Bat flung his hands forward. The temple shook with the casting, and Jaguar lost his footing in the moment before he leapt. A column of eldritch fire touched his shoulder. Jaguar clenched his teeth and hissed through the pain.

He swung the sword blindly. Its obsidian teeth whistled a complaint as the blade missed taking Bat's head and sliced only air. Jaguar readied another strike. As he raised the maquahuitl, Bat pushed at the empty space between them. Jaguar flew backwards until he struck the far wall of the temple. The back of his head cracked against the stones. His vision blurred with lightning flashes. When he opened his eyes, he was on his hands and knees, staring down at the disappointed sword.

"Enough of this folly," said Bat. He waved a casual gesture at the temple entrance. "It is the third night of blackness; time for the Sun to be sacrificed."

"Not while I draw breath," Jaguar replied. He regained his feet and shook his head to clear his vision. He held the maquahuitl in one hand.

"I understand. Perhaps this will help."

The blankets over the entrance fell to the ground, ripped from the frame. The two demon statues ducked their heads and entered. They looked at Rooster and the Sun, then at Jaguar, and lastly at Bat. The two statues paused in anticipation.

"Destroy him," said Bat.

The statues moved with surprising quickness. Jaguar ducked as the first swung its fist and took a chunk out of the wall. The second brought both fists down and cracked the floor. Jaguar dodged aside with supple grace, his muscular body rippling. He swung the sword at the second statue's neck and connected.

The maquahuitl's obsidian teeth shattered against the stone, and it screamed in anguish.

The statue swept its arm back and struck Jaguar in the chest. He flew again, but he twisted and landed on his feet. He still held the useless sword.

He moved away from a stone fist and into the path of the second statue. It charged with arms wide. Jaguar waited until it was near then grabbed its wrist and pulled. The statue was heavy, but he forced it down until it tripped. Headfirst, it slammed into the temple wall. Its skull crumbled into gravel, and the statue lay still.

Jaguar saw Bat was oblivious to the melee. Bat stood over the Sun on the altar. He drew out a trowel-like knife that dripped with evil, black energy. Jaguar took out his knife and flipped it at Bat. The blade sailed past Bat's head, missing by a hand's breadth.

The pause allowed the remaining statue to grab Jaguar in its square hands. It lifted him into the air and threw him across the temple. He landed at the base of the altar. The maquahuitl skipped from his hand out of reach.

Bat looked down on him, a broad grin twisting his disgusting features. Then his eyes glanced to the side and saw the approaching demon statue.

"It pleases me," said Bat, "to watch your quest to rescue the Sun end in failure." The statue stepped nearer. "Finish him."

Rooster bounded like a great cat, war club over his head. He brought it crashing down on the statue's chest with such force the stone crumbled. One of the statue's arms loosened and came free, but it continued to attack. It turned its attention to Rooster who drew it away from the fallen Jaguar.

Bat's face showed his surprise, but his recovery was even swifter than Rooster's attack. He pressed one palm against the base of the Sun's throat and moved the knife to the space below her breast.

Jaguar kicked his legs and spun, grabbed up his maquahuitl, and sliced through the leather thongs holding down the Sun's arms.

The Sun brought her hands directly up to Bat's face and spread her fingers. Jaguar threw his forearm over his eyes. Light illuminated the temple with such force that Jaguar could see the bones of his arm through the flesh.

It was a single burst, and Jaguar jumped to his feet. His eyes hurt. Ghostly images danced around the edges of his vision. To his left, Rooster swung his war club and smashed the statue's hip. Its leg came free, and it tumbled to the floor. Rooster raised the club with both hands and brought it down on the statue's head. The statue ceased its wriggling. Jaguar turned his attention back to Bat.

Bat still stood over the Sun, the knife firmly gripped in his hand. Jaguar readied himself to spring at Bat, but he hesitated when the priest stumbled away from the altar. He turned and faced Jaguar with empty sockets oozing the remnants of his melted eyes. The skin of his face was burned completely away, exposing the naked, grinning skull.

Bat sat down heavily in his smoldering robes. Bat's fingers slackened; the knife clattered at his side. Then he leaned over and collapsed atop it.

"That was a well-thrown knife," said Rooster, his chest heaving. His sores had opened during the fight, and they dripped fresh crimson.

"I thought a single throw useless against his black magic," said Jaguar. "But I was certain it could cut a leather strap. Will you live?"

"Most likely. Let us tend to the Sun."

Jaguar and Rooster went to the altar and cut the bonds from the Sun's ankles. Rooster helped her sit up then took his wife in his arms and hugged her. She kissed him freely on the mouth, heedless of Jaguar's presence. She turned from Rooster and faced Jaguar.

"Thank you," she said. "I owe you a debt I don't believe I can ever repay. I would have been forever your friend had you only rescued my husband." The Sun leaned in and kissed Jaguar on the cheek.

"You owe me no debt," said Jaguar. "You shine on the land every day and ask nothing in return. It is I who should owe you."

"Then consider us even. Of all the creatures, from insect to man, that roam the land, only you, Jaguar, will have my blessing. You may stalk these jungles and fear no other for I will be watching over you."

"Darling," said Rooster, "it has been three days without your brilliance. Can you make it into the sky today?"

Before she could answer, Jaguar held up his hand.

"I believe," he said, "we can go one more day without the Sun. Rest, and return to your work tomorrow. I will need the light by then to search for more obsidian so I can silence the complaining of my toothless ward." Jaguar strapped the maquahuitl to his belt, and together the three of them stepped over Bat's broken corpse and walked out into the dark day.

THE END

The Year of the Donkey

Sharon Goodier

THE YEAR OF THE DONKEY

Twelve-year-old Dolores sat in her bedroom doing her Math homework. Whenever she hit a snag, she'd stare out the window at the changing autumn, watching the wind blow the red and gold leaves from the trees, watching as they blew across the front yard of the big ranch house and piled in a heap against the stables.

There were plenty of horses on her father's ranch, but more than anything else in the world, Dolores wanted a horse of her own. And she was angry this evening, angry at her Magic Mother who had always granted her wishes or come up with equally good alternatives to getting what she wanted,

Dolores' father was a successful horse breeder. Shortly after he had bought the ranch, when Dolores was only three, her mother died, leaving Dolores and her father alone in the big ranch house with Antoinette Curry, the housekeeper, with the ranch hands and a stable full of horses. Dolores loved her father and she knew he loved her. But he didn't understand about crying, and so Dolores was six before she cried for her mother's death. Then, one day, she was playing house outside the miniature ranch house her father had built for her in the back yard. She was digging in the red, clay soil to make pretend bread loaves when she thought of the mothers of some of her friends. She began to cry. Her tears fell on the soil she was digging in and slowly it turned into clay. She started to shape the clay, as though she were in a daze. When she was finished, just before Nettie called her for supper, she had made a clay doll. Inside her ranch house she found a doll's apron and a toy wooded spoon, like the one Nettie always seemed to be carrying. Out of the clay and her tears, she had crafted a mother doll which she carefully lay against the side of her playhouse to dry in the next day's sun.

When Dolores came home from school the next day, she ran to get the mother doll. It wasn't there. Nettie must have put it away in the playhouse, she thought. Nettie was always rearranging her things. Inside, rocking in Dolores' rocking chair was a woman who looked just like the clay doll, smiling face, red-checkered dress, apron, even the wooden spoon across her lap. Her doll had turned into a real, live mother.

Dolores talked daily with her Magic Mother, telling her the problems she had and asking for advice. When Dolores needed something special like a new dress for a party, the Magic Mother suggested ways to approach her father for the money. When Dolores went on her first date – a movie with a boy in her grade five class – the Magic Mother was with her in spirit, coaching her on what to say.

And so it was. Dolores and the Magic Mother talked and Dolores grew up.

When Dolores started grade six, she began to want her very own horse. The Magic Mother would not discuss it. Dolores grew angry and stopped going to the playhouse. Besides, she was too grown up now for playhouses – or for Magic Mothers.

That was how it came to be that, at the beginning of her grade seven year, Dolores sat in her room doing her early algebra, ignoring the knock at her bedroom door. Her father was away trading horses and Nettie had gone to bed for the night, so she knew it had to be the Magic Mother.

"Dolores," a voice called from the other side of the door. "If you want your horse, you'd better open the door."

Dolores jumped up and ran to the door crying, "Oh, do you mean it? If I let you in, will you really give me a race horse?"

"Definitely."

Dolores opened the door and gasped in surprise. There, in the hallway, stood a bedraggled donkey, with long, floppy ears and eczema on his back. He brayed at her and looked kindly through his big, brown eyes.

Dolores slammed the door in anger and went back to her algebra, but she had forgotten everything she'd learned in class that day. In addition, the donkey was making quite a racket in the hall.

Afraid that Nettie would hear and discover her secret, Dolores opened the door, grabbed the rope around the donkey's neck and led him outside

"I can't put you in the stable with all our fine horses," she said disgustedly. So, she took the donkey and tied it behind the neglected playhouse where no one would see him, and she left him there. She didn't feed him or protect him from the wind and rain. All she did was pull the cord around his neck so tight that when she finally loosened it, the donkey had lost his bray and could no longer make any noise.

She left him there all winter, unheard, unseen, unfed, and unprotected from the cold. In the spring, her father told her to either paint the playhouse or he would get one of the ranch hands to tear it down. Dolores could not bear to see it destroyed, so she agreed to paint it. When she arrived with her bucket of paint, she discovered the donkey, still tied up behind the playhouse, wedged between it and a side of the barn. What would her father think of her if he saw this? He'd never give her the horse of her dreams if she couldn't even take care of a simple donkey.

Dolores felt overwhelmingly guilty and a little angry, but she acted overwhelmingly angry and a little guilty. Quickly, she put the donkey inside the playhouse and set fire to the whole thing.

Nettie came running when she saw the flames.

"Never mind, Nettie," Dolores said with determination. "It's only my childhood. It's time I grew up anyway. I'll be starting high school in another year. Don't worry. I have everything under control." She had heard her father say that often and wondered what it would feel like for it to be true, but it was disappointingly flat that day.

When the playhouse was reduced to ashes, Dolores remembered the doll. She told herself she was a fool to have burned it; it might have been worth money someday. She took a shovel to the ashes to see if she could find some remnant of the Magic Mother. She didn't find the doll, but there, instead, was a small, glass donkey about three feet long and three feet high. Furiously, she picked it up and hurled it against the barn wall. It broke into two pieces. In between stood the Magic Mother.

Dolores felt her knees turn to water, her stomach to sand. The Magic Mother raised her wooden spoon.

Dolores wailed. "All I wanted was a horse, not a silly old donkey."

"That was no ordinary donkey," Magic Mother said, shaking her head. "That donkey cannot die. People can hurt it, but no one can kill it."

"So what's happened to it, then? Dolores demanded arrogantly. "I don't see it anywhere."

"Look closely," Magic Mother commanded.

Only then did Dolores notice that her own feet were turning into hooves. Her ears were growing longer and a tail was growing behind her. Her arms were becoming legs and her face, too, was becoming a donkey's head.

"No!" She screamed. "No, please. I'm sorry, I'm sorry. I'm sorry."

Magic Mother looked at her severely. "Not sorry enough."

"They'll come looking for me," Dolores bargained desperately.

"My father and Nettie. They'll find out what you've done and arrest you for witchcraft."

Magic Mother pointed with her spoon to Dolores' bedroom window. There, in Dolores' bedroom, was a girl just like her, sitting at her desk, doing her homework.

"You can't do this to me!"

Then Magic Mother took the rope around Dolores' donkey neck and pulled it so tight that Dolores lost her voice. When Magic Mother loosened it, she disappeared, leaving Dolores the Donkey standing forlorn in the backyard of the big ranch house.

Later, when Dolores' father found the little donkey, he called his daughter to come downstairs. Dolores the Donkey looked beseechingly at them both, but all the young girl said was," That's just a dirty, old donkey that's wandered in here. Let's take it in to town and give it to the man who runs the pony rides."

The next day, Dolores the Donkey began her first job, trotting methodically around a ring, carrying on her back the taunting children who thought it hilarious that a donkey should be working with all these cute, little ponies. They dug their heels into her sides and slapped her nose with the willow branches they used for riding crops.

Poor Dolores could not even cry.

She spent seven days a week giving rides, seven days a week listening to the taunts of children who teased her for not being a pony. The owner did not feed her well and she was always hungry. When she tried to steal candy from the children, the owner hit her with a stick. At night, she plotted to kill herself. When her plan was well enough laid, she waited in the shabby, drafty shed where she and the ponies were loosely tied to their troughs until the owner came in to give them their evening meal. In his back pocket, he stuffed the piece of rope used to tie shut the main door to the shed. One night, it dangled from his pocket into her meal. When his back was turned to her while he fed the other ponies, Dolores carefully bit off the knot at the end of the rope. Being a careless man, he did not even notice the shortness of the door rope when he loosely tied the shed door shut, later. It was raining and he was in a hurry.

Dolores was able to force her way out. With determination, she headed for the highway. She stood, depressed, in the middle of one lane waiting for the vehicle to come that would release her from the agony of her life.

The sound of the breaks was deafening. Footsteps followed, then a voice. "Well, little donkey, I saw you giving rides earlier today. Wandered out here and got lost, did you?

The driver tied her tether to the rear fender of his truck and drove slowly back to the pony owner. By then, the owner was quite drunk. He took a big stick and went to beat Dolores, but the truck man stopped him.

"What does the owner of fine ponies such as yours need with such a scraggly donkey, anyway? I can use this donkey up at my studio in the hills. How much do you want for him?"

A deal was struck and Dolores found herself in the back of a truck driving down the highway, then onto a side road, then onto a dirt road, and finally stopping.

"Alright, little donkey," the truck man said kindly, and he coaxed her from the back of the truck until all four feet were on the ground, "From here on, you do the carrying."

He loaded her up with so many parcels and packages that she thought her back would break. He strapped them on with ropes that cut her sides worse than the children's shoes. Then, he led her along a rocky, narrow path to a large barn in the hills where he lived and painted.

Once a week he went to town for food and supplies. The rest of the time, Dolores was free to roam the hills. At night, she slept in a corner of the barn while the truck man slept in another. She had plenty to eat, a warm, dry bed, a kind master, and only one day's work a week...and she was bored. She longed for her father, the ranch, the horses, her algebra, and even Nettie. Dolores hated being a donkey.

Finally, she grew sick with sorrow about her fate. She refused to eat and she couldn't sleep at night. The truck man brought in the vet.

"This donkey is too old," the vet said. "He should have died ages ago. You had better shoot him and put him out of his misery."

Dolores, who formerly had been anxious to die, was now more anxious to live. The improvement in her life after going with the truck man, boring as it was, had convinced her that there was an even better life in store for her if she could only find it. And so, while the truck man was drinking to get up the courage to shoot her, she crept away into the woods nearby.

The trees were tall and thick and the minimal light cast everything in partial shadow. Dolores walked forward with a certain amount of trepidation, wending her way carefully between the trees.

When she reached the first clearing, Dolores saw the strangest creatures. They weren't horses and they weren't donkeys either. They had the bodies of horses and the torsos of people, like in the mythology books she had read. Some had horse's ears and horse's tails. Some had short, stout bodies and others had sleek, racehorse-like physiques. They lived and worked together among the trees. They hired themselves out in teams to pull the loads Dolores had carried alone for the truck man, and when they trotted in circles they had no riders and went in many directions at once. They called themselves Be-ers. Their motto, which they had carved onto every tree, was "I am, therefore, I am."

As time wore on, Dolores grew more and more restless and exhausted. Her body ached from head to hoof. Sometimes, the pain was so bad that she considered leaving the forest.

One day, exhausted from worry, Dolores went to drink from the river that flowed at the edge of the forest. She often wondered if her home, the ranch, was on the other side of this river. She lowered her head to drink again. Reflected in the water, she saw the face of a beautiful horse with a thin white line running the length of its nose. She looked around and realized that the face was hers. The result of all her trials and the physical suffering it caused her was that she was becoming a horse. Slowly, she made her way back to the circle of the Be-ers.

But now Dolores longed for her algebra and for the open spaces of her father's ranch, longed to ride a horse instead of being a donkey with a horse's head. So intense was her longing that Dolores became ill.

Then, she remembered her face. She reasoned that if she had changed into a donkey because she had rejected a donkey, she might change back into herself once she accepted being a horse-donkey. She knew she would never be a Be-er and that if she actually became a horse she would have to leave them.

One sunny day, they all went on a picnic to the river, bringing their musical instruments and dancing and singing as they played. In and out of the water they chased each other, dancing, leaping and laughing. Suddenly, Dolores noticed a force under the water. "What's that pull I feel?" She asked.

An older, woman Be-er replied. "At some time or another, everyone gets caught in that pull."

Dolores was terrified. "Where does it take you?"

"It will pull you along to the end of the river where the water catapults over a waterfall and lands on the gorge below."

Dolores was shocked. "And you die," she concluded.

"Well, of course, you're supposed to land on your feet," she laughed.

"I think I'll just play here in the shallow water where it's safe." Then Dolores remembered that it was in this same water that she had first seen the horse's head. She knew she had changed since then, so she stepped out of the water and looked. This time what she saw was a body that was half donkey, half horse. She gasped in awe.

Several Be-ers laughed. "You have always been half horse, half donkey. It's just that you never saw it before now."

That night she felt the horse's blood stirring in her veins, felt the old desires, the restless longing for what lay beyond the forest, beyond the river. How can I do anything, she asked herself, with a horse's head and a donkey's behind?

The answer came from within: "Let me go. Let me go."

Dolores held on hard while the horse's head and the donkey's ass fought it out together.. "Why couldn't I be half human, like the Be-ers?" She mourned. "Then I could handle this colt."

But she was not. She was Dolores and she knew at last that the Magic Mother had turned her into herself.

The horse's head was straining. The donkey was balking, coming up with excuses, fears, arguments. Dolores found herself one minute holding the horse back with all her strength and the next minute beating the donkey on.

Finally, exhausted, unable to hold, unable to beat, unable to think or feel she gave up. Surrendered. The horse felt her grip loosen, He sniffed the wind. He pawed the ground. The horse snorted at his new freedom. Slowly at first, then faster, he began to pace around between the trees, dragging his donkey behind. Dolores was powerless to halt him now.

He began to run through the trees at top speed, his mane flying.

The donkey's hind legs dragged behind and were soon cut and bleeding. But the horse ran on, on to the edge of the forest, into the river, past the shallow water, out into the midstream. Dolores felt the undercurrent catch her broken hind legs. We're goners now, she judged.

The river was a raging torrent further on. The horse in her swam furiously even though the current was pulling them on. He seemed to hunger for the cliff, the final fall, and the dashing to death on the rocks below. Dolores did not try to resist. She'd had enough. She'd never get back to being human again, never again see her father or the ranch, so what difference did it make?

Dolores did not even try to scream as they went over. She had no voice. Besides, she was glad to be finished being half horse, half donkey. She didn't care about anything but finding rest from it all.

As she hit the rocks, everything went black. She knew she was dead. And yet, she stirred on the rocks as though alive. Looking at herself, she saw feet, legs, hands, arms. She felt her face and nose, two eyes and ears, hair. On either side of her lay the carcass, half horse, half donkey.

"I'm alive," she stammered. "I'm myself."

She looked around. She knew where she was. It was the foot of the hill that led to the bottom edge of the ranch. One glance back at the waterfall, and she started climbing. When she reached the top, she raced across the field to the ranch house. Nettie was there, outside the kitchen. She was angry.

"Don't you know better than to go off roaming on the night of your birthday dinner?" She remonstrated. "Come in and see your father. Supper's ready."

After dinner, Nettie affirmed. "You're growing up now." Thirteen. Time to learn to cook." And she presented Dolores with keys to the pantry.

Dolores' father said, "Come out to the barn, I have something to show you."

There, in one of the stalls, was the mare they had bought together a year ago. "She foaled that colt just today," her father said proudly.

Dolores was ecstatic. "Oh, please, can I have him to raise as my own?"

"Well, now, he's no race horse."

Dolores laughed softly and held out her hand gently toward the colt.

FIRST STEPS

JAMES DAVIS

New Olym – named in honor of the late Divine Majest Olym the Wrathful – squatted like a massive, brooding spider. The entire city was built against the side of a mineral rich cliff face – the excavated sections of the mines having been reshaped and carved into elegant terraces with sprawling gardens and gorgeous pools, on a few of the broader terraces there had even been miniature forests set up and stocked with various wildlife from the farthest corners of the Imperia. Elf-slaves acted as game wardens at the boundaries of the forest, culling when the hunting season was low and caring for the animals that were considered too sporting to let die.

At the height of the Cliff City was the Marble Seat – the palatial sprawl of Governor Delayos Marva. As befitting such a noble station it was sat atop the very cliffs the miners now burrowed through in search of more iron, more gold – but most of all more of the elusive ore thorgrak, the same ore that had been forged by the dwarves in the height of their own imperial power and which had proved so devastating against the human armies until the ancient race had finally succumbed to the brilliance of the engineers and the mystical might of the Templarum. The early discoveries of thorgrak, enough to arm and armor the entire city guard as well as sending off the appropriate tithes back to Ervingard had seen the wealth of New Olym boom.

Of course, such wealth had attracted the attention of the darker elements that existed in the underworld of the Imperia. The warren of tunnels that spread across Mavarra had soon found their way into the workings of the mine system and a new city was carved out beneath New Olym. Where the power of the Marble Seat held dominant sway over all it could see, it was the power of the underlords that caused true fear. The so-called 'Shadow Caste', men and women who had carved out their own illicit holdings beneath the noses of the governors and governesses of the Imperia.

Here was haven and damnation where the only law was the law of the underlord whose territory a person found themselves in. Slaves who thought their lives could be improved struggled to get below the surface where not even the most hardened of veterans would venture without at least four Templarum in tow. This was where Serena found herself running now.

The young elf maid glanced over her shoulder as her bare feet pounded down the smooth steps of the Tiered Straits, guards armored in the natural black-gold thorgraki plate and mail chasing after her and shouting in a confused babble. One cried for civilians to get out of the way, another cried for someone to stop the slave, a third cried for the slave to halt and surrender herself while a fourth shouted for her head. Lords and ladies stood aside, staring in shock at the sight of this lone, slight maid running from nearly a dozen guards.

Glancing over her shoulder once more, eyes wide with fear, Serena stumbled and fell down three steps before quickly scurrying to her feet and starting to pound across the stone steps again – the adrenaline coursing through her allowing her to ignore the stinging pain from the abrasions she had suffered from her fall. Whistles blew behind her, and she prayed fervently to the Raven to quiet the winds and stifle the call of her pursuers – she could not escape from more than one group at a time. She couldn't go back to the Steward's Keep – she couldn't bear to be around that man any longer, nor to see her father acquiescing to the demands of the horrid human.

Serena could only think of making it to the tunnels, of staggering down and hoping her life could be better in the underworld. The Raven had not heard her silent prayers, the shouts of other guards now echoing in her ears. Hitting the last step before the rough cobbles – the girl staggered and ran for anywhere she could – the flatter surface allowing her to quickly leave the pursuing guards behind. She started down an alleyway before pausing, two of the saireen stared at her – the tall lizardmen tilting their heads as they stared at Serena with unreadable faces.

The elf girl turned away, rushing from the creatures and down, sobbing to herself in fear that now she might be on the menu of two cannibals. The confused shouts of the guards eventually died away, Serena stumbling and falling in the muck of an abandoned alleyway, the girl quickly scrunching herself up to hide from any pursuit, arms wrapping around her legs and her wide eyes staring at the rectangular slant of light at the end of the long alley.

The saireens wandered by again, the two pausing to converse with one another in a hissing language. One of the creatures was over seven feet in height and as slender as a rail. Thick pelts adorned it: seal, walrus and bear and a massive spear seemingly carved from bone was gripped in one long hand. This saireen had changed, or at least in the girl's eyes it had, when she had seen it before the creature was an unusual shade of green, now it was almost silver – add to that its eyes had become black and it alone made her shrink further back into the shadows.

The second was shorter, barely reaching five feet in height and stocky. Deer hide covered its squat form, and a vicious looking axe with a long hook draped from the creature's belt. It turned its head, tan scales catching the light, and its yellow eyes stared down the long alleyway before it turned back to its companion, hissing something out as the two saireen started off again.

Serena let out a breath she hadn't known she was holding, burying herself deeper into the rubbish at the back of the alleyway and hunkering down. With the adrenaline gone she felt every cut, every bruise and felt her body beginning to give in to exhaustion. Her green eyes slowly closed and she lost herself into a darkness of sleep.

It was night time when Serena finally opened her eyes, escaping the grasp of her exhausted sleep. She was amazed to find herself still in the same spot, amazed no one had found her or accosted her in her sleep. Standing slowly, Serena stretched and began to limp toward the entrance to the alleyway, wincing with each step – she paid no attention to the bloodied footprints behind her, only the sting of each step she took from the soles of her feet and her bloody knees. The girl tucked her left arm against her body, the entire limb sore and stiff with pain.

She staggered to a halt as a figure started toward her. A wide-brimmed hat and long cloak hiding the person in silhouette against the moons, smoke-like shadows curling around the cloaked shadow as it started down the alley toward her. "You're the escaped slave?" The voice was rough and masculine, the jackboots the man wore striking against the cobbles loudly – as he intended. "You're the slave Baron Veller donated two thousand crowns to be retrieved dead or alive? This is so beneath Templarum as to be laughable."

Serena began to back away, the shadows peeling from the figure and lighting him up. A narrow and cruel face regarded the young girl. An oily, curled mustache hid his mouth from view while a thick goatee of dark hair did the same for his chin. The Templarum reached down, drawing a thorgraki dagger, the blade weeping shadowy tendrils. "Well, he'll have pieces of you, at least..." The

Templarum hissed before taking a few quick steps to grab at the girl, simultaneously bringing his dagger down in a vicious overhand stab.

A hook caught his wrist, jerking his arm upward as a squat, pugnacious face screeched in his face. The Templarum jerked away in shock as the thick form of the squat saireen landed in front of Serena – the same wicked axe held in one hand while a large hooked knife was clutched in its other talon. The Templarum backed away in some surprise, before sneering as he raised a hand, a wall of semi-opaque shadows spawning between himself, the saireen and Serena. "A smarter opponent would strike from behind." The Templarum's words were said through a sneer as he placed his dagger away and raised his hands, beginning to chant.

"A sm… sssmarter opponent would check for multiple threats." A voice rasped behind the Templarum, causing the sorcerous assassin to turn about, watching as a tulwar clove through his chest and out his left hip. The Templarum's eyes were wide in shock as his body split in two, splattering the larger saireen's thick pelts. The creature kicked the body, the shadow wall dying away as it swung its blade up and over its shoulder, returning it to the leather slings across its back, before turning its eyes to Serena and the smaller saireen.

"Elf alright?" It chirruped, striding over the body.

Serena scrunched herself up more, staring as the two saireen now stood above her. "I… I'm fine." She managed in a tiny voice.

The smaller one had tucked axe and knife away and lightly shoved its larger companion back. "Step back Sha'g, the girl's frightened." As the taller saireen, Sha'g, stepped away the smaller turned back to Serena. "Sha'g didn't mean to scare you, girl. He's harmless." The smaller saireen spoke with no trace of irony as its splayed feet were slowly beginning to be overcome by a spreading puddle of blood. "I'm Don'a of the North Islands; he's Sha'g of the Frozen Expanse. We mean you no harm, little elf."

As Don'a spoke, Sha'g had knelt down, beginning to take items from the corpse of the slain Templarum. The dagger, bits of coin and gold, anything of valuable disappeared into the thick furs of the tall saireen, and as it stood it placed the wide-brimmed hat the Templarum had worn onto its head. Serena swallowed, she had heard horror stories about the saireen before, but neither of these creatures was anything like what she had heard tell of. Swallowing, and realizing they had saved her from a Templarum she spoke in a soft, low voice. "S-Serena, servant of House Veller, erm... former servant of House Veller that is."

Sha'g chirruped something to Don'a who hissed in response in the basic language of their people. "What... what'd he say?" Serena asked softly, getting scared again.

"Hrm? Oh... Sha'g asked what you meant. I told him you're a runaway." Don'a offered what approached a smile for his race, holding out a hand for her to take. "C'mon, Serena. Sha'g and Don'a keep you safe."

Serena stared at the thick, taloned hand before asking in that same small voice. "How... How do you know where I'm going?"

Don'a made a series of hissing chirrups; it took her a moment to realize the squat saireen was laughing. "Where all runaways go, the Underworld."